Three royal sheikhs...used to having
everything they want—always!
Three feisty women...about
to be brides?

Royal AFFAIRS:

DESERT PRINCES
& DEFIANT VIRGINS

Fantastic novels from bestsellers:
Sarah Morgan, Susan Mallery
& Kim Lawrence

THE Royal AFFAIRS: COLLECTION

Royal AFFAIRS
DESERT PRINCES
DEFIANT VIRGINS

KIM LAWRENCE · SUSAN MALLERY · SARAH MORGAN

Royal AFFAIRS
PRINCESSES & PROTECTORS

LUCY MONROE · RAYE MORGAN · DAY LECLAIRE

Royal AFFAIRS
MISTRESSES MARRIAGES

DAY LECLAIRE · JENNIE LUCAS · LAURA WRIGHT

Royal AFFAIRS
REVENGE SECRETS SEDUCTION

JENNIE LUCAS · DAY DECLAIRE · ROBYN DONALD

Royal AFFAIRS:

DESERT PRINCES
& DEFIANT VIRGINS

SARAH MORGAN

SUSAN MALLERY

KIM LAWRENCE

Mills & Boon, an imprint of Harlequin (UK) Limited, Eton House, 18-24 Paradise Road, Richmond, Surrey TW9 1SR

ROYAL AFFAIRS: DESERT PRINCES & DEFIANT VIRGINS
© Harlequin Enterprises II B.V./S.`a.r.l. 2011

The Sheikh's Virgin Princess © Sarah Morgan 2007
The Sheikh and the Virgin Secretary © Susan Macias Redmond 2005
Desert Prince, Defiant Virgin © Kim Lawrence 2008

ISBN: 978 0 263 88749 5

026-0611

The Sheikh's Virgin Princess

SARAH MORGAN

USA TODAY bestselling author **Sarah Morgan** writes lively, sexy stories for Modern™ and Medical™ Romance.

As a child Sarah dreamed of being a writer and although she took a few interesting detours on the way, she is now living that dream. With her writing career she has successfully combined business with pleasure and she firmly believes that reading romance is one of the most satisfying and fat-free escapist pleasures available. Her stories are unashamedly optimistic and she is always pleased when she receives letters from readers saying that her books have helped them through hard times.

RT Book Reviews has described her writing as "action packed and sexy" and her books have been nominated for their Reviewer's Choice Awards and their 'Top Pick' slot.

Sarah lives near London with her husband and two children who innocently provide an endless supply of authentic dialogue. When she isn't writing or reading Sarah enjoys music, movies and any activity that takes her outdoors.

Readers can find out more about Sarah and her books from her website www.sarahmorgan.com. She can also be found on Facebook and Twitter.

Don't miss Sarah Morgan's exciting new novel, *Doukakis's Apprentice*, available in July from Mills & Boon® Modern™.

PROLOGUE

'FIND me a way out of this. *And find it fast!*' Simmering with rage and frustration, the Sultan paced across the thick Persian carpet, and then turned and glared at the group of men who sat in frozen silence around the polished, antique table. 'Time is running out, and I tell you now that I *will not marry that woman!*'

His announcement was met by a collective gasp of dismay, and his team of advisors conferred hastily, their communication a series of babbled suggestions and nervous gestures unlikely to produce a satisfactory solution to any problem, let alone one of huge national importance.

They are like stunned rabbits, the Sultan thought grimly as he viewed them with mounting exasperation.

'Your Excellency.' One of the lawyers rose to his feet, his hands shaking. 'We have looked through all the past statutes. There is no way out of this marriage.'

'Then look again.' His voice deadly soft, the Sultan watched as the man paled. 'Look again and find *something* we can use— something that allows us to break this ridiculous contract.'

'That's the problem, Your Excellency.' The lawyer's fingers gripped the edge of the table that provided the only barrier between him and the Sultan. 'There isn't anything. There is no precedent for this. Your father made this agreement with the late Crown

Prince of Rovina sixteen years ago, a few months before his untimely death. They were at school together, and in the army—'

'I don't need a lecture on *why* I find myself in this situation,' the Sultan growled. 'Just advice on how to extricate myself. Fast.'

'There is no way out, Your Excellency. You have to marry the Princess Alexandra of Rovina.' As he delivered the final blow, the lawyer's voice shook. 'Perhaps she will be an asset…' he ventured timidly, his words tailing off as he met the Sultan's hard, cynical stare.

'You think so? "The rebel princess"—isn't that what they call my wife-to-be? Since she was old enough to attend school, this girl has left a trail of chaos behind her. She drives her cars too fast, parties until she is unconscious and treats sex as if it were an Olympic sport. And she's not even twenty-four years old. Please enlighten me as to how such a woman could possibly be an asset to Zangrar.'

A deathly silence followed his question, and the Sultan raised an eyebrow. 'Nothing comes to mind?' Their lack of response frustrated him to the point of explosion, and he turned and walked towards the window, struggling with his temper and *hating* himself for that loss of control. 'Leave me. All of you. Leave!'

There was an undignified scrambling, and the room emptied in a matter of moments in response to his abrupt order.

As the door closed behind them, the Sultan rubbed his long fingers over his forehead, trying to ease the ache and access rational thought. He didn't know which sickened him more: *the thought of marriage generally, or the thought of marriage to a woman like the Princess Alexandra.* By all accounts she was a woman who appeared to possess all those traits that had made him renounce the institution of marriage at a young age. She was shallow, brainless and a princess only by an unfortunate accident of birth. There was nothing royal about her behaviour, and there was no way she was going to become his wife.

She was exactly the sort of woman who would have caught the attention of his father.

A sound came from behind him, and he turned swiftly, his eyes narrowing as he saw his chief advisor standing behind him. 'Omar?'

'Your Excellency.' The man stepped forward. 'If I might be permitted to venture a suggestion...'

'If this suggestion involves marriage, please save your breath.'

'It is understandable that Your Excellency would have strong feelings on the subject, given your late father's somewhat unfortunate history.'

The Sultan felt every muscle in his body tense. 'That is *not* a subject I wish to discuss.'

'Indeed, Your Excellency, and yet it is germane to the current situation. You are right to be concerned. The people of Zangrar will not tolerate another woman like your stepmother.'

The Sultan inhaled slowly. 'You are unusually brave in your choice of conversation topic, Omar. You may have known me since I was two years old, but don't presume too far. I'm experiencing some difficulties with anger management.'

Omar gave a faint smile. 'In the circumstances your anger is understandable. What you have achieved for Zangrar since your father's death is nothing short of amazing. You have given hope to every citizen, and now you are afraid that you will lose what has been gained.'

'And that is what will happen if I marry this woman.'

'Possibly. But Your Excellency *does* need a wife, that fact is not in dispute,' Omar murmured. 'Your people are anxious for you to fall in love and wed.'

The Sultan suppressed an unexpected desire to laugh out loud. 'I am prepared to make many personal sacrifices for the good of my country, but falling in love will not be one of them. In time, I will choose a wife who can give me children. But she will not be some wild, untamed European princess. The people of Zangrar deserve better.'

Omar cleared his throat delicately. 'But the Princess Alexandra *is* of royal blood. In one year from now, on her twenty-fifth birthday, her uncle the regent steps down and she ascends the throne of Rovina.'

'Meaning that she will be in a position to bring even greater chaos to her country?'

Omar allowed himself a smile. 'Meaning that an alliance between our two countries would offer many increased opportunities that would benefit Zangrar. Trade, tourism—'

'Am I supposed to overlook her embarrassing reputation and overall lack of dignity?'

'The Princess Alexandra is said to be quite astonishingly beautiful. Given your own success with women, the simplest approach might be for Your Excellency simply to urge her to moderate her behaviour. It is no secret that you enjoy the company of beautiful women.'

'In a *wife* I place moral stature above any physical attributes,' the Sultan growled, feeling his frustration mount. 'However, my views on the subject are apparently not relevant, since it appears that there is no way I can break this ridiculous contract my father made.' Of the legacy of stupidity and weakness left by his father, this was the issue that angered him most, because it threatened everything he had worked for.

Omar's expression was thoughtful. 'That is true, Your Excellency. There is no way *you* can break the contract.'

Something in his tone made the Sultan narrow his eyes. 'Omar?'

His chief advisor smiled placidly. 'I have studied the contract in minute detail, and it is true that there is no way for you to break the agreement that your father made.' He paused. 'But *she* can.'

The Sultan straightened his powerful shoulders. 'You're saying that the princess has the right to veto this marriage?'

'Absolutely. But, before Your Excellency becomes unduly encouraged by that option, I should tell you that there has been no hint of dissent from the principality of Rovina. It would appear that the princess is eager to marry you.'

'And we both know why.' His mouth set in a grim line, the Sultan contemplated everything he'd read about the Princess Alexandra. 'Rovina's coffers are empty, and her spending powers are as legendary as her rebel behaviour.'

'That could be part of it, but maybe not all. Your Excellency is extremely handsome. You are considered to be something of a matrimonial prize.'

The Sultan gave a humourless laugh and then paced over to the window, his expression bleak. A prize? If the princess knew what she would be taking on, then she wouldn't be so eager to proceed with the wedding. *As cold as the desert at night*—wasn't that how the last female in his life had bitterly described him when he'd abruptly ended the relationship?

He stared down into the courtyard below, wondering why that description didn't bother him more. Possibly because it was true. *He wasn't capable of love*; he knew that. But nor did he see that as a reason for regret. He'd seen what love could do to a person, and he wasn't interested in sacrificing his judgement in exchange for emotional anguish. What *did* interest him was acting responsibly for the good of his country. And marrying the most notorious princess in Europe wasn't going to achieve that objective.

He turned to Omar, his movements swift and decisive. 'You're sure that the princess has the right to break this contract?'

'Absolutely. The only person who can free you from this wedding is the woman herself.'

'Then it will be done.' The Sultan gave a satisfied nod. 'Omar, you have excelled yourself.'

'Your Excellency, I hardly need to remind you that the princess *does* want to marry you, so the details of the contract are somewhat irrelevant.'

'*Not* irrelevant,' the Sultan drawled softly. 'The princess may wish to marry me at the moment, but given time and a little—*persuasion*—I'm confident that she will soon see that this marriage is not for her.'

'You plan to influence her decision, Your Excellency?'

'Absolutely. The problem is solved, Omar. The Princess Alexandra is going to decide that marriage to me would be an *extremely* bad idea. And, given that most women are appallingly indecisive, we are going to offer her every assistance in reaching that conclusion. I intend to see to it personally.' He gave a grim smile.

No matter what she had in mind, she would *not* be marrying the Sultan.

CHAPTER ONE

THE blades of the swords clashed viciously, and the room rang with the sharp sound of metal on metal.

Karim tightened his hand on the hilt of the sabre and lunged, sending his blade towards his opponent's torso with a burst of explosive power that drew a collective gasp from the observers gathered around the room.

Karim ignored them. All his attention was focused on his opponent, whose identity was concealed by the dark mesh of the protective fencing-mask.

Attack, counter attack. Lunge, feint, parry.

They fought with relentless aggression, each trying to out-manoeuvre the other as they fenced for supremacy. The referee stood frozen to the spot, silenced by the sheer ferocity of the duel taking place in front of him.

Even as he fought, Karim was studying his opponent, trying to anticipate his moves. And failing. For the first time in his life, he was equally matched. His nameless, faceless opponent was changing his strategy for each attack, his movements swift and skilled, his footwork immaculate. The man was slight of build, but he moved with the speed and agility of a true athlete.

Karim felt the sweat prickle between his shoulder blades as the pace and intensity of the fight increased.

When he'd been informed that the Princess Alexandra had insisted on watching him fence before agreeing to let him be her bodyguard for the journey to Zangrar, he'd been both amused and irritated. Clearly, she was a real prima donna. It was the first time he'd fought in response to a feminine whim, and he'd strolled into the room prepared to thrash his opponent in a matter of minutes. Instead he was being seriously challenged in a sport at which he'd considered himself unbeatable.

Unaccustomed to meeting anyone who had either the nerve or the skill to take him on, Karim had been pleasantly surprised to discover that his anonymous opponent possessed both qualities in abundance, along with technical and tactical depth. He was even more astonished to discover that he was enjoying himself.

Who was the man in the mask?

Protocol demanded that fencing opponents salute each other at the start of each bout, and his opponent had observed that protocol, but he'd also entered the room fully prepared, his mask already in place.

Accustomed to boredom, Karim felt the adrenaline surge inside him, and vowed to reveal the identity of his partner. Whoever it was would be fencing him again, he vowed as he parried and then thrust, his movements confident and aggressive. The blade struck home in a lightning-fast attack, the force of the blow absorbed by the flex of the blade.

His opponent stepped backwards, his body already poised for the next attack, and Karim gave a low laugh of admiration. Although the man was slightly lacking in height, he was bold and fearless, attacking with an energy and confidence that was unusual.

Briefly distracted by girlish laughter, Karim cast a swift, irritated glance towards the spectators, his attention momentarily drawn to a group of women watching with flirtatious interest.

Which one of those was the Princess Alexandra?

And what indulgent, feminine whim had driven her to demand that he prove himself in this fight before allowing him the honour of becoming her bodyguard? Obviously she was spoiled, bored and entertained by the idea of men fighting for her. *Did she enjoy blood sports?*

He turned his attention back to his adversary, anger giving speed to his attack, but his opponent parried with a renewed burst of energy, grimly determined not to yield a single point.

Karim was as intrigued as he was challenged.

If he hadn't known better, he would have thought that the duel was personal.

And yet how could it be personal when they didn't even know each other?

Deciding that the match had gone on long enough, Karim made the most of his superior strength and speed and executed a perfect lunge that won him the final point.

Breathing heavily, he dragged off his mask.

'My match.' He held out his hand as protocol dictated. 'So, having slain the dragon, I presume I've now won the right to protect the princess. Perhaps you would introduce me so that I can be given my next challenge? Pistols at dawn, perhaps? Remove your mask. I deserve to see the face of the man I just fought.'

His opponent hesitated, and then dragged off the mask. '*Not* a man.' She spoke in a warm, husky voice designed by mother nature to bring the entire opposite sex to its knees, and Karim inhaled sharply as a mass of golden, coppery hair tumbled over narrow shoulders. Even though he knew the dangers that often lurked behind extreme physical beauty, he was blinded.

Observing his reaction with wry amusement, she held out a slender hand and spoke again. This time her voice was soft, as if she were afraid of being overheard. 'I'm Princess Alexandra. And you're supposed to be my bodyguard. The problem is, I don't actually *want* a bodyguard. You weren't supposed to win the match. I'm afraid you've had a wasted journey.'

She'd lost!

Desperately hoping that he couldn't see how much her legs were shaking, Alexa watched incredulity flicker across his handsome face as he acknowledged her identity. And he *was* handsome, she conceded as she brushed her damp hair away from her flushed cheeks. Handsome and strong.

She'd felt the power in his body as he'd fought with what could only be described as restrained masculine aggression. And she sensed that he'd been far from reaching the limits of his capabilities. His broad shoulders and muscular physique suggested that fencing was only one of many activities that he enjoyed in his pursuit of a physical challenge.

She should have picked a different sport.

And now he was watching her intently, his dark gaze arrogant and assured as he slowly loosened the fastening at the neck of his jacket to reveal a tantalizing hint of bronzed skin, shiny with the sweat of physical exertion. His eyes demanded that she look only at him, as if he were determined to read everything about her in one searing glance.

Trapped by the force of his bold gaze, Alexa felt something dangerous and unfamiliar flicker to life, and then a hot, instantaneous explosion of sexual awareness engulfed her. Her body burned and melted, and the feeling was deeply shocking because, although she was accustomed to being on the receiving end of male attention, she was *not* accustomed to responding.

Her knees weakened by the fire in her pelvis, she nevertheless forced herself to hold his gaze, waiting for him to back down and display the deference and respect that she knew was due to her.

He was a bodyguard.

She was a royal princess. Despite her less-than-enviable position in the royal household, she was accustomed to being greeted with the appropriate formality by strangers, but this man clearly wasn't daunted or in any way impressed by her title or position. Instead he held himself tall and proud, his posture one of authority and command, as if he was used to giving orders and being instantly obeyed.

Clearly, he was someone *extremely* senior in the Sultan's security team, Alexa mused as her eyes trailed from his almost-perfect bone structure to the firm, sensual curve of his mouth. *Powerful,* she thought. If she had to find one word to describe the man in front of her, then it would be *powerful,* and she felt her stomach lurch. When the Sultan had promised a bodyguard to escort her on the journey, she'd expected someone who would follow orders.

This man didn't look as though he'd ever followed an order in his life.

Which made the situation extremely awkward. She didn't want him as her bodyguard. She didn't trust him. She didn't trust *anyone.* Whatever happened, she had to be in charge of her own safety; it was the only way she would ever escape from the tangled mess of her life.

She couldn't believe that this moment had arrived—*that she'd actually survived this far.* Her brain fluttered around the edges of panic, as it always did when she considered her impending marriage to the Sultan of Zangrar.

It wasn't that she was afraid of him. She wasn't. Having lived the life she'd lived for the past sixteen years, she no longer cared that he was reputed to be ruthless, controlling and totally devoid of emotion. In a way, it actually helped, knowing that he didn't have a sensitive side, because she didn't have to feel guilty about forcing him into a marriage that was so lacking in romance.

There was no escaping from the fact that, in normal circumstances, this marriage would be the last thing she wanted. But her circumstances weren't normal, and this marriage wasn't about what was best for *her,* it was about what was best for Rovina.

Her hand tightened on the hilt of the sabre. She'd reviewed her options so many times that her brain felt raw with thinking, and no matter how often she circled round the issue she always ended up at the same place.

The future of Rovina depended on her marriage to the Sultan.

And now that goal was *finally* within reach.

Only a journey now stood between her and Zangrar.

But it would be a hazardous journey, and she would need to have her wits about her. Ironic though it seemed, the *last* thing she wanted was a bodyguard. Having him there would simply put her life at greater risk.

A giggle from the women watching reminded her that they were becoming the subject of scrutiny and gossip, and Alexa smiled, reminding herself that she had an image to keep up: *the image of a woman with nothing more serious on her mind except the pursuit of frivolous pleasures.*

'You can go home, bodyguard.' She removed the glove from her fencing hand and spoke softly so that only he could hear. 'I don't need your protection.' Her words provoked a sharp intake of breath from the man standing in front of her.

'My protection is *not* optional.' His dark eyes glinted danger-ously as he studied her face. 'You and I need to speak alone. Now.'

Startled by his autocratic tone, Alexa opened her mouth to refuse, but he closed long, strong fingers around her wrist and propelled her bodily towards the ante-room where the fencing equipment was stored, apparently indifferent to the curious stares of those watching.

He'd been fighting a woman?

Tension erupting inside him, Karim released her and slammed

the door to the ante-room shut with the flat of his hand, his eyes fixed on the cascading mass of soft, silky curls that poured down her back. *Her hair was the colour of a desert sunset.* And that first glance into her eyes had been like throwing himself onto a burning spear. His body had been consumed by the most basic of sexual urges, the chemistry between them so hot and instantaneous that for a moment he'd been able to think only of sex.

'Unlock the door.' Apparently unaware of his response to her, she gave the order sharply, a note of panic in her voice. 'Unlock it now.'

'I take orders only from the Sultan himself.'

'Please…' Her face had lost most of its colour, and he frowned.

'You have just faced my blade without showing the slightest consideration for your personal safety,' he drawled softly. 'And yet you expect me to believe that you're afraid of a locked door?'

'Just open it,' she said in a hoarse voice. 'Please open it.'

Perplexed and exasperated in equal measure, Karim turned the key, watching as she relaxed. The rebel princess was afraid of a locked door? It was so incredibly unlikely that he almost laughed. If she was that easy to frighten then it should take very little to persuade her that life in the harsh climate of Zangrar, in the company of a ruthless Sultan, was definitely *not* for her.

'I don't fight women, Your Highness.'

She stilled and then gave a tiny shrug, some of her defiance returning. 'You do now.' With a single, graceful movement of her shoulders, she removed her jacket. 'And, anyway, you won. Your ego is still intact.'

'My ego requires no protection.' He dragged his eyes away from her hair with difficulty, his brain and body fighting a vicious battle for supremacy. Intellect warred with basic masculine instinct, and the sudden tightening of his body reminded him that the power of basic masculine instinct was never to be underestimated. 'I could have hurt you.'

Only now, when she stood without the thick, protective padding of the fencing jacket, could he see how fine-boned and delicately built she was. Her exquisitely perfect face revealed centuries of breeding, and Karim studied her closely, trying to reconcile the innocence of that face with her debauched reputation. And she studied him back, her gaze fearless and unfaltering.

Then she turned and hung her jacket in the cupboard. 'You're good. But you've had a wasted journey. I don't want a bodyguard.'

'Your wishes in the matter are irrelevant, Your Highness.' Whether she wanted him or not, she was getting him. His mission was to persuade her to change her mind about marrying the Sultan, and he needed to be with her on the journey if he was to achieve that goal.

Her glance was curious. 'Do you guard the Sultan himself?'

It wasn't a question he'd anticipated, and it took him a moment to formulate an acceptable answer. 'I have ultimate responsibility for the Sultan's safety, yes.'

'In that case, I'm sure he's missing you. Go home.' With a swift movement of her fingers, she removed the plastron, the half-jacket that protected her fencing arm. 'Use your talents elsewhere. I don't need them.'

'You are no longer planning to marry the Sultan?'

'Of course I'm marrying the Sultan. But I don't need anyone with me on the journey. I prefer to arrange my own protection.'

'And who have you selected to provide this service?'

'Me.' Her tone suggested that she considered the answer obvious. 'If there's one thing I've learned over the years, it's that, when it comes to safety issues, the only person you can really depend on is yourself.'

'You plan to travel through the desert alone and unaccompanied?'

'Absolutely. And I hope no one threatens me, because I'm lethal when I'm threatened.' As if determined to convince him of that fact, she fixed him with her cool, blue stare, and Karim lifted an eyebrow.

'Clearly you are unaware of the fact that many men find a woman's vulnerability to be one of her greatest charms.'

'Those same men undoubtedly have miniscule egos and need to slay dragons in order to demonstrate their masculinity.' She stooped to put her mask and glove in the cupboard. 'I refuse to put my safety at risk in order to pander to a man's need to flex his muscles in public. I slay my own dragons.'

For the first time in his adult life, Karim found himself speechless. He'd never met a woman like her before. 'You cannot seriously be intending to make the journey to Zangrar alone? You have no knowledge of the route.'

'I can read a map, use satellite navigation and I can talk on the phone. Princesses have a multitude of skills these days. We're a very versatile breed. Haven't you heard?'

What he'd heard was that the Princess Alexandra was a real rebel, and he could see that the rumours had foundation. There was a fire in her eyes and defiance in her stance, and even after five minutes in her company he could see that she was no man's idea of a gentle, compliant wife.

She was a handful.

Even while contemplating the disaster that would ensue if this woman ever arrived in Zangrar, Karim was reflecting on the fact that this next battle between them might be every bit as stimulating as the fencing. Removing his own jacket, he stretched out a hand and dropped it onto the nearest chair. 'Clearly you've never aspired to be like the princesses in the fairy stories.'

'Passive victims, you mean?' A thoughtful frown touched her forehead and then she gave a careless shrug. 'I wouldn't be stupid enough to take a poisoned apple from a stepmother who hates me, and I've always hated sewing, so there's no way I'd prick my finger on a spinning wheel.'

'But you *are* planning to marry a sultan,' Karim pointed out silkily, and she smiled, showing no signs of trepidation at the prospect.

'That's right. I am.'

'And the Sultan insists that you are escorted on the journey, Your Highness.'

The princess turned to face him, and their eyes locked in a battle of wills.

Supremely confident that there was only one possible outcome, Karim crossed his arms and waited.

And waited.

'Fine.' Her gaze slid from his, and she toed off her fencing shoes with a graceful movement. 'If you want to come along then I suppose I can't stop you. I just hope you don't regret it. Who is guarding the Sultan while you are watching over me?'

Surprised by the speed with which success had been achieved, Karim felt a flash of suspicion. *What was she up to?* 'His Excellency is presently on an important and most secret mission that relates to the future stability of Zangrar. His security is being handled—elsewhere.'

She put her shoes in the cupboard. 'You haven't told me your name.'

Distracted by the thrust of her breasts under the simple white tee-shirt, it took him a moment to answer. 'You may call me Karim, Your Highness.'

'And you may call me Alexa. I'm not big on protocol.'

Remembering everything he'd read about her lifestyle, Karim had little trouble believing that statement. 'It would not be appropriate for me to call you by your first name.'

'You weren't worrying about what was appropriate when you dragged me into this room.' Her gaze was speculative.

'Clearly you're a man accustomed to acting on your own initiative.'

'You want a bodyguard who waits for permission before saving you?'

'I don't want a bodyguard at all.' Tucking the last of her clothes into the cupboard, she slammed the door shut. 'If there's any saving to be done, then I prefer to do it myself. Let's get that straight before we leave this room.'

Karim clenched his jaw in order to refrain from pointing out that the only thing she needed saving from was *herself.* Only the month before she'd been removed unconscious from a nightclub, and he knew that she'd had at least two car crashes and a boating accident in the past year, and from all of them she'd narrowly escaped with her life. The Princess Alexandra was clearly as reckless as she was bold.

'The desert is full of dangers, many of which are concealed from all but those who were born and bred there.'

'I have lived with danger all my life. I have a question for you, Karim.' Without glancing in his direction, she slipped on a slim-fitting jumper in a deep shade of green. She still wore her fencing breeches, and he saw that her legs were long and slim.

'Ask your question.'

'How do you feel about the Sultan? Would you die for him?'

Karim reflected on the irony of that question. 'Without a doubt.'

Scooping up her hair, she pinned it haphazardly on top of her head, disregarding the fact that several strands immediately escaped and tumbled down around her face. 'And just how much do you know about *my* country, Karim?'

With perfect recall, Karim summarized the briefing he'd received. 'Rovina is a small principality ruled by your uncle, the Regent, who has been in power since your parents were killed in an accident. You were the only heir, and too young to ascend the throne.' He saw darkness flicker across her beautiful face, and wondered briefly whether that tragic event had been responsible for her wild behaviour. Without the guiding hand of a father, had she gone off the rails? 'Your late father and the Sultan's late father were friends, and made the agreement for you and the present sultan to wed when you reached the age of twenty-four. Your birthday is in four days.' Was it his imagination or was her breathing suddenly more rapid?

'You've done your homework.'

'One year after that, on the day of your twenty-fifth birthday, you will be crowned Queen of Rovina. Knowing that, I am intrigued as to why you would wish to move to a different continent and marry a man you've never even met, and whose culture and beliefs are so different from your own.' If he talked her out of the marriage now, he could save himself an arduous journey with a woman who was undoubtedly going to whine and moan her way across the baking desert, a climate not known for nurturing patience in those who experienced it.

'You don't think I should marry the Sultan?'

'On the contrary.' Karim issued the denial smoothly. 'I'm sure a marriage between you would be a great success. Your Highness is clearly both brave and bold, and you will need both qualities in abundance if you are to tame our sultan.'

'Tame?'

'I once heard a woman remark that the Sultan of Zangrar resembles a tiger who has been taken from the wild and forced to live in captivity.' Satisfied that he had her attention, Karim delivered what he hoped passed for a sympathetic smile. 'The woman who eventually shares his cage would have to be *particularly* courageous.'

Alexa laughed. 'If you're trying to frighten me, Karim, then you've picked the wrong woman.'

'I'm not trying to frighten you,' he lied, concealing his surprise at her laughter. 'On the contrary, the more I see of you, the greater my conviction that you are a match for the Sultan even in one of his most dangerous moods. I just wanted to be sure that you know your own mind. If you wish to back out of the agreement, then you may do so.'

'I *don't* wish that.'

As he stared into her wide, blue eyes he felt another powerful tug of chemistry followed by a vicious tightening in his groin as white-hot lust shot through him. He wondered whether it was too soon to inform her that there was only one way the Sultan would ever want her—and that was flat on her back, naked and *without* the wedding ring. 'Clearly, there is no place for love or romance in your life.'

Her beautiful blue eyes shone with genuine amusement. 'Are you telling me that you believe in love, Karim? Are you a romantic man?'

'This conversation is not about me.'

'Judging from your tone, I've touched on a sensitive subject.' She studied him in silence for a moment and then paced over to the window, her eyes flickering to the palace grounds. 'I'm not pretending this marriage has anything to do with love, because we both know that it doesn't…' Her words tailed off and she frowned, as if surprised at herself. 'Why am I telling you this? My reasons for wishing to marry the Sultan are not your concern. Your brief is simply to escort me safely to Zangrar.'

Karim wondered what she would say if she knew that his brief was a great deal more complex than that. The Princess Alexandra was the only one who could break this ridiculous agreement, and it was his personal responsibility to ensure that she did exactly that.

She was *not* a suitable wife for a sultan.

Her motive for the wedding was clearly greed, and the fact that greed alone was sufficient to compel her to marry a man of whom she knew nothing, sickened him. A woman like her would do untold damage to Zangrar, and threaten the enormous progress they had already made.

Clearly unaware that Karim's own objective was in direct conflict with hers, Alexa paced back and forth across the room, her eyes on the door as if she expected to be disturbed at any moment. 'So, if you insist on traveling with me, then you'd better tell me your plans for the journey.'

'We leave at dawn. The Sultan's private jet is waiting at the airport.'

Had he not been watching closely, he might have missed the way that her slender fingers suddenly locked and unlocked in a manifestly agitated gesture. *The princess was nervous about something.* The question was, *what?*

'My uncle is aware of those plans?'

As she turned to face him, he could almost feel her anxiety sharpening the atmosphere of the tiny room.

'He requested a full itinerary.'

'And you gave it to him. Excellent.' She was silent for a moment, apparently thinking. 'Then we leave at dawn. My uncle wishes you to join us for dinner. As the Sultan's envoy, you are the guest of honour. But I have one more question before we leave this room.'

'Ask it.'

'Are you truly good at your job, Karim? Are you really the best?'

'Your wellbeing is my highest priority, Your Highness. You have no reason to worry about your safety.'

Her laugh was hollow. 'You think not?'

Was she afraid of some sort of physical threat? Resolving to question the palace security-team in greater depth, Karim frowned. 'No one would dare lay a finger on the Sultan's future bride.'

The princess watched him for a long moment, her wide blue eyes fixed on his face with disturbing intensity. 'Except, perhaps, those who don't want me to be the Sultan's bride.'

CHAPTER TWO

ALEXA sat at the long table in the banqueting hall, her hands shaking so badly she could barely hold a knife and fork. She was so on edge that it was almost impossible to sit still. If it wasn't for the fact that her uncle would have become suspicious, she would have excused herself from dinner. As it was, she didn't dare. Too much was at stake.

Although she was staring at her plate, she nevertheless saw Karim's hand reach for his wine, and her attention was momentarily drawn to the strength of his long, bronzed fingers. Then his arm brushed against hers and that simple, innocent contact was enough to send heat rushing to her pelvis.

Instantly she shifted away from him, bewildered and alarmed by her inexplicable reaction to him. What was the matter with her? Why was her body selecting this particular moment to notice the finer points of the male physique? Had her mind elevated him to hero status simply because he'd insisted on remaining by her side for the journey? Surely not, when she knew perfectly well that having him there was going to threaten everything that she'd been working towards.

She needed to be the one in charge, and she definitely couldn't risk having some autocratic, commanding bodyguard thinking that he knew what was best for her. And she *certainly* wasn't going to do anything as foolish as trusting anyone with her future.

'You're unusually quiet, Alexa.' Her uncle William's cultured tones cut through the murmur of conversation around the table, and he raised his glass to Karim. 'I hope you have decent shops in Zangrar. Alexa isn't going to be happy somewhere that doesn't have shops. All that glitters has to be gold, that's her motto—isn't that right, my sweet?'

Knowing from experience that her uncle was always at his most deadly when he used his caring voice, Alexa felt a flutter of panic and focused on the subtle flex of muscle in Karim's forearm as he returned his glass to the table.

She hoped he was as tough as he looked. He'd unwittingly landed himself right in the middle of palace crossfire with no flak jacket to protect him, and she knew that if he happened to be standing between her and her uncle when the final moment came then he'd die alongside her.

Her conscience nagged her.

Why hadn't he just gone home as she'd ordered?

She hadn't wanted to drag anyone else into this.

Aware that her uncle was watching her, Alexa faked a yawn and tried to look like a girl incapable of planning anything other than her next shopping trip. 'I've heard that some of the souks sell amazing silks. I'm looking forward to designing myself a whole new wardrobe.'

'I admit that I've probably overindulged her a little since her parents were killed.' William addressed his remark to Karim. 'I just hope that the Sultan will be as generous as he is wealthy.'

'The Sultan's generosity is not in question, but it is hard to spend money in the desert, and that is where much of his time is currently spent.' Karim spoke in a matter-of-fact voice and Alexa turned her head and looked at him, unable to hide her surprise.

'He lives in the desert?'

'Since the death of his father, the Sultan has spent much of his time in the desert with his people. His wife will be expected to support him in that role. If you wish to augment your wardrobe, you might be wise to include robes and sturdy desert-boots.' He reached for his glass. 'The sort that repel the bite of a snake.'

Reflecting on the fact that dealing with snakes would be a piece of cake after living with her uncle for sixteen years, Alexa gave a shrug. 'I'm sure I can live in the desert if I have to. I mean, when all is said and done, it's just a giant beach, really. Sand, sand and more sand.' She kept her tone as light as the subject matter. 'I'm sure the Sultan isn't going to want his wife dressed in rags. With all that money at his disposal, he's hardly going to begrudge me a few pairs of shoes.'

William's eyes narrowed. 'He might, when he finds out how much they cost! Karim, I've been telling my niece that this marriage is ridiculous. Her father arranged it when she was a child, before he had any idea what sort of a woman she would become. And the truth is that she is *not* a woman who is going to be happy incarcerated in a dusty old fortress in the middle of a baking-hot desert.' He softened his words with a smile and reached for his wine. 'No offence.'

Alexa felt Karim's sudden stillness, and wondered whether it was possible to die of embarrassment.

Reminding herself that Karim's thoughts and feelings had to be secondary to William's, she forced the expected response from her mouth. 'I'm sure the Sultan entertains occasionally. As long as there's a party going on, and everyone is having a good time, it doesn't really matter where it is.' Out of the corner of her eyes, she saw Karim's long, strong fingers tighten on the stem of his glass.

'Parties are not high on the Sultan's agenda. When he entertains, the guest list includes foreign dignitaries and other heads of state. The purpose of the gathering is all about diplomacy and international relations.'

He obviously thought she was shallow-minded and frivolous, which didn't surprise her. What did surprise her was the fact that she minded what he thought. Why would she care about the opinions of a bodyguard? His views were irrelevant. They *had* to be. Tonight of all nights it was essential that she maintained her image of a woman who thought about nothing deeper than what to wear at her next social engagement. If William knew what was truly on her mind, he would be turning all of the keys in all of the doors.

'Foreign dignitaries sound pretty dull.' She suppressed a yawn. 'I'm sure I'll be able to help the Sultan liven things up a bit.'

William's gaze flickered from her to Karim. 'Her head is full of romance. She's expecting Arab stallions, a desert and a glamorous Sultan who is going to sweep her off her expensively clad feet.'

Aware that the expression on Karim's face had gone from mild impatience to thunderous disapproval, Alexa wondered if he was about to lose his temper.

Her heart thumping against her chest, she braced herself for a terrifying display of masculine aggression—but when he finally spoke Karim's tone seemed almost bored.

'There is nothing romantic about the desert. It is a harsh, unforgiving landscape that contains any number of threats. A sandstorm is one of the most deadly natural phenomena known to man, and the desert in Zangrar is inhabited by scorpions and snakes so dangerous that one bite produces sufficient venom to kill ten grown men.'

'Scorpions and snakes. You see, Alexa?' William leaned back, and someone hastily stepped forward to remove his plate. 'It is a long way from Rovina.'

'Indeed, it is,' Alexa said quietly. *She was banking on it.* 'Nevertheless, my father arranged this marriage, and I shall do as he wished. I owe it to his memory.'

And she owed it to the people of Rovina. The only way she

was ever going to reach her twenty-fifth birthday was if she married the Sultan.

Karim's dark gaze fixed on her with brooding intensity. 'You are very young, Your Highness. Your uncle is obviously worrying about how you will fare in a country like Zangrar. You would do well to listen to his advice.'

'I'm not afraid of anything I'll find in Zangrar.'

'Then perhaps you are not sufficiently enlightened as to exactly what awaits you.' He spoke softly, his words only audible to her, and she lifted her gaze to his, wondering what he was alluding to.

Their eyes met and held, and Alexa felt a shiver of awareness and a flash of the same sexual chemistry that had singed her earlier in the day. 'You're doing it again—trying to frighten me.'

He lifted a dark eyebrow in sardonic appraisal. '*Are* you frightened, Your Highness?'

'No.' *But that was only because she knew what true fear was.*

Alexa glanced across the table at William and saw him smiling at her. Her pulse-rate doubled. If the Sultan's bodyguard really wanted to know what frightened her, then he need look no further than the man sitting across from them. Over the years she'd learned to read her uncle's moods, and if there was one thing that scared her more than his temper it was his smile.

His smile widened as he looked at her. 'I hear she fenced you earlier, Karim. Hardly a ladylike sport, I'm sure you'll agree. I think you're going to find that the Princess Alexandra is unusual in many ways. Most of the time you wouldn't even know she was a princess, from the way she behaves.'

Alexa noticed the sudden tightening of Karim's mouth, and knew that William's repeated attempts to undermine her were succeeding. Not for the first time in her life, she was seriously tempted to pick up her knife and silence her uncle in the most permanent way possible.

'I have many qualities which the Sultan will appreciate,' she said lightly, and then saw the glimmer of disdain in the bodyguard's eyes and realized that she'd actually made the situation worse, not better.

Not those qualities! she wanted to shout. Why were men so basic? Why did they only *ever* think about one thing—sex? Well, actually, it was two things. Sex and power. Forget everything else—they seemed to be the only two things that motivated the male species.

And normally she didn't even *think* about sex. So why was it that, since the Sultan's bodyguard had removed his fencing mask and revealed his impossibly handsome face, she'd thought about little else?

Or perhaps it was just that this whole situation was turning her slowly loopy. There was so much at stake. *And so many things that could still go wrong.*

She was a nervous wreck.

Marrying the Sultan was the only way that Rovina would have a future, and if anything happened to prevent that…

Reminding herself that this was *not* the time to lose her cool, she allowed herself a small sip of wine.

William gave her a sympathetic smile. 'Talking of qualities, most of yours are displayed over the front page of today's newspapers. I think the headline read something like, "rebel princess hot for the harem?" I mean, really—' he gave a weary shake of his head '—newspapers have no sense of moral restraint. Always digging up the past when it should be forgotten. We just have to hope for your sake that the Sultan isn't expecting a virgin bride. Perhaps his reputation is way off the mark and he's one of those rare men who values experience over innocence. I'm *so* sorry, Alexa.'

So was she.

Under no illusions as to why the papers had chosen to reprint those pictures, anger suddenly burst through her usual cautious restraint. 'When the time comes, I intend to tell the Sultan the truth about my life. *The whole truth,* Uncle William. And he *will* believe me.' She caught Karim's astonished glance and saw the deadly gleam light her uncle's eyes.

The emotion drained out of her, and she started to shake.

Why had she said that?

She'd gained *nothing* by that remark. Nothing at all. And she could have lost everything.

This was *not* the time to antagonize a man as dangerous as her uncle, and she knew that. Since when had she allowed anger to incinerate common sense?

'You're my niece,' William said smoothly. 'I only want what is best for you, and Zangrar is such a terribly long way away. I'm so afraid that something dreadful might happen to you on your journey. You know how accident prone you are.'

Alexa felt her heart stumble and her palms grow damp. *He was threatening her.*

'Karim will ensure my safety,' she said in a clear voice, hoping desperately that Karim wouldn't choose this moment to mention the fact that she'd tried to dispense with his services.

William gently dabbed his mouth with his napkin. 'If anything were to happen to you, I don't know what I'd do.'

He would have achieved his lifelong ambition.

He would finally have destroyed her family.

Suddenly Alexa felt bitterly cold. 'Your care and concern is always touching, Uncle William. My father would have become quite emotional, had he been able to see everything you've done for me since his death.' Unable to share his table a moment longer, she rose to her feet. 'We leave in the morning. I need my passport.' And this was the moment she'd been dreading.

For sixteen years he'd held her passport.

Would he finally return it to her?

William was silent for a long moment, and then he gave a gentle smile. 'You are such a featherbrain. I will give it to Karim for safekeeping.'

No, no, *no!*

Her stomach turned over. She *had* to have her passport. And the fact that William was prepared to give it to Karim was of no use to her at all, because she knew that he had no intention of allowing her to leave in the morning.

Which was why she had no intention of waiting until morning.

Alexa felt a great weight in her chest. So much depended on the next few hours. If she couldn't gain possession of her passport, then she couldn't take the next step and everything would have been for nothing.

Trying to think her way through the dark mists of panic, she tried to look relaxed. 'That's fine. Give my passport to Karim.'

One way or another she would just have to find a way of retrieving it.

She just hoped the bodyguard was a heavy sleeper.

The room was dark but she could see the faint outline of his body lying under the covers. He was asleep, thank goodness. She'd been relying on that fact.

Where was he likely to have put her passport?

Seeing his jacket on the back of a chair, she moved towards it with the stealth of a burglar, her bare feet making no sound on the carpet. She reached out a hand, and then gasped with shock as someone caught her from behind, unbalanced her and pushed her down hard onto the bed. Flattened against the mattress and panicking, Alexa fought like an animal in a trap, using all the skills she'd learned to defend herself. She twisted, bit and punched, but as her fist connected with solid muscle she realized desperately that this was a hopelessly uneven contest, and she was going to lose.

No! This wasn't going to happen to her. Not when she was so

close to her final goal. Driven by desperation, she managed to free one leg and kicked hard.

With a grunt of pain, her assailant shifted his body over hers, caught her wrists in a vice-like grip and muttered something in a foreign language.

She recognized the voice. 'Karim?'

She felt him still, and then he pinned her to the bed with his powerful body and reached out a hand to flick on the light.

Alexa found herself staring into dark pools of anger and went limp with relief. 'I thought—'

'You thought what? You were expecting someone else?' He stared down at her with incredulous disbelief. 'This is *my* bedroom.'

'Yes, I know that.' The weight of his body made it hard for her to breathe. 'But I saw the lump in the bed and assumed you were asleep. Then someone grabbed me from behind so I thought it was—' She broke off, unwilling to betray more than she had to.

'The lump in the bed was the pillow. I heard you outside the door. I wanted to see who was so keen to enter my bedroom un-announced. What is this, Your Highness—you are now testing me in unarmed combat, or did you have an entirely different rea-son for visiting me in my bedroom in the middle of the night?' His meaning was clear enough, and suddenly she was breath-lessly aware of the strength in his bare shoulders, of the intimate pressure of his body against hers.

'I need my passport. *That* is why I was in your bedroom.'

'Why would you need your passport at three in the morning? Are you planning a trip?'

She tried to wriggle free, but his weight held her pinned to the mattress. 'It's none of your business.'

'If it involves your passport, then it's my business.'

Alexa tried a different tack. 'The Sultan would *not* want you lying on top of his bride!'

'Given that I'm apparently just one in a long line of men who have adopted this exact position, I think it's a little late for that argument to be useful.' His soft tone was faintly mocking. 'My job is to escort you safely to him. If you're intending to vanish in the middle of the night, then your travel plans are of considerable interest to me. Start talking, Your Highness.'

The weight of his body was impossibly distracting, and Alexa suddenly found that she couldn't say a word. Trapped by his virile strength and the fire in his eyes, she just gazed at him, her body paralyzed by a shockingly powerful explosion of sexual excitement.

And perhaps he detected her feelings, because he shifted slightly above her, his attitude softening from aggressor to seducer.

Alexa pressed her hand to his chest intending to push him away, but her fingertips registered warm, naked flesh. Male body-hair and hard muscle singed her nerve endings, but instead of pushing or even drawing her hand away, her fingers made their own decision and slid upwards, exploring the latent power of his physique with unconscious feminine fascination.

Karim inhaled sharply and growled something that she didn't understand.

And then they were kissing.

His mouth was demanding and fiercely possessive, and her body ignited like a dry forest in the heat of summer as every single part of her was sucked in by the ferocious heat generated by that kiss.

She felt the hot slide of his tongue against hers, and the erotic intimacy of that connection drained her body of strength and purpose. She forgot what she was doing in his room. She forgot *everything* as her body was filled with a languorous, dangerous warmth, and his kiss transformed her from a thinking woman to someone only capable of feeling.

Dimly, she registered the hardness of his body against hers and the steady thud of his heartbeat under her clinging fingers.

And then suddenly he dragged his mouth from hers and lifted

his head, his breathing uneven and his eyes angry. '*What* do you think you are doing?'

Dizzy and drugged, it took a moment to focus. '*You* kissed *me*.'

'*Your* hands were on *my* body.'

Unable to defend herself from the accusation, Alexa lay there in shock, trying to work out what had happened. Kissing Karim had been like stepping into sexual quicksand—one move in the wrong place and she hadn't been able to free herself. Every subtle movement of his mouth had just drawn her down deeper until she'd drowned, swallowed up by pleasure and sensation.

Why was that?

Had the agonizing loneliness of her situation finally affected her mind? Was she so desperate for human comfort that she was ready to cling to any man who touched her?

'Please, let me go. I just want my passport.' Her voice was shaking. How had she allowed herself to become so distracted from her task? The clock was ticking. Every moment that passed made her task more dangerous. 'Let me leave tonight without you. You will not be blamed.'

Karim studied her face for a moment and then sprang to his feet in a lithe, athletic movement, relieving her of his weight so suddenly that she felt unaccountably bereft.

Ignoring the confusion in her brain and body, Alexa sat up and than gave a gulp of shock she realized that he was completely naked—*gloriously, proudly naked, and unashamedly aroused.*

She knew she should look away but she couldn't move. Confronted by her first ever vision of a naked man, her eyes remained fixed on this impromptu display of rampant masculinity, and only when she heard his sharply indrawn breath did she finally manage to drag her eyes upwards. But, instead of respite, she was offered just another angle on impressive manhood—wide, powerful shoulders, curving muscles honed by hard physical exercise and a broad, strong chest hazed by curling dark hairs. He was aggressively, imposingly masculine, and it took all her willpower to look away from such physical perfection. Her cheeks were burning, and she honestly didn't know what to say or do to move on from here. Her head had emptied itself of all thoughts that weren't related to sex with this man.

No wonder she hadn't been able to resist his kiss.

'The blushing is sweet, but a little over the top given the kiss we just shared.' Karim's tone was icy cold as he reached for the robe that was flung carelessly over the chair. Without any obvious sign of haste, he slid his arms into the sleeves and belted it loosely, as relaxed and cool as she was embarrassed. 'And your display of shyness is a little out of place in a woman who began exploring her sexuality at such a young age—but if you want to play that game then I'm happy to oblige. It's safe to look, Your Highness.'

Safe?

Part of her knew that this man was anything *but* safe, and the knowledge unsettled her more than she cared to admit. She'd lived with the threat of danger all her life, but this was *entirely* different. Normally she was completely in control of her reactions, but with Karim she wasn't in control at all and the thought terrified her. She couldn't afford to be distracted. She didn't *need* this confusion. Her mind needed to be sharp and focused.

Her future depended on it.

The future of Rovina depended on it.

Her cheeks still flaming with embarrassment, Alexa struggled to find some of her old, rational self. Part of her wanted to melt from the room and never see him again, but another part wanted to…

'None of that is important,' she said hoarsely, saying it for her own benefit as much as his. 'I—'

'You what?' He folded his arms and fixed her with his hard, unsympathetic gaze. 'The Sultan would not approve of the conduct of his prospective bride. He's an *extremely* possessive man.'

'We both know that the Sultan is unlikely to care what happens to me.'

Since when had *anyone* cared what happened to her? She'd been surviving on her own for so long that it was impossible to imagine a scenario where she mattered to someone.

'You're wrong.' Karim studied her with grim contemplation. 'If you marry him then you become his possession, and he's ruthlessly protective of anything and *everything* that is his. The ability to share nicely is not a virtue to which he aspires.'

She stood up, because sitting down made him all the more intimidating and she couldn't think straight when she was facing him. 'You've stumbled into a situation that you know nothing about. Believe me, if you'd known the facts, there is no *way* you would have signed up for this job. Just let me go and perhaps we'll meet up in Zangrar one day.' *If she survived the journey.* She turned and caught the narrowing of his eyes.

'So, your uncle kept your passport from you. Presumably for your own good. You're clearly something of a handful to manage, Your Highness. I don't envy him.'

Alexa straightened her shoulders. 'Your role is not to pass judgement on a situation of which you know nothing. It's not your business.'

'If you're planning to sneak away then it becomes my business. If I wake up tomorrow and you have gone then I will have to answer to the Sultan. His Excellency isn't exactly renowned for tolerating the mistakes of others.'

'Coming with me would be a bigger mistake than you can possibly imagine.'

'If you believe that then you clearly know nothing about the Sultan.' He walked towards her, his expression unreadable. 'If you disappear while under my protection then it is entirely my responsibility.'

'The Sultan wouldn't care. He doesn't want this marriage.'

'Nor does he want an international incident,' Karim said dryly. 'Make no mistake, the Sultan is going ahead with this marriage. The plans for the wedding are already underway. You marry him on the day of your twenty-fourth birthday.'

'Yes, but I intend to travel alone. If you refuse to let me go, then you *will* regret it.'

A muscle worked in his lean jaw, and his eyes were faintly amused as he surveyed her with disturbing thoroughness. 'Never before have I been threatened by a woman who barely reaches my shoulder.'

Alexa felt exhaustion wash over her. As if it wasn't enough to constantly be trying to outwit William, she now had another fight on her hands. Utterly defeated by the constant obstacles that faced her, she sank back onto the edge of the bed, and then noticed something glinting under the edge of the pillow.

Puzzled, she reached out a hand, lifted the pillow and gave a soft gasp. 'You sleep with a gun and a knife?'

'I'm a cautious man.' He walked over to the bed and gently prised her fingers from the pillow before dragging her back to her feet. 'And I want to know *why* you feel the need to leave the palace in the middle of the night.'

She tried to ignore the fact that his hand still held hers. 'Because it's imperative that I reach Zangrar safely.'

He watched her for a long moment. 'You're that desperate to marry the Sultan?'

'I prefer *determined* to *desperate*.' *Although desperate was probably much closer to the truth.*

'And you believe that your uncle is going to try and stop you?'

'If I wait until morning—yes.' Alexa hesitated but decided that she had no choice but to tell him at least part of the truth.

'William feels very strongly that this wedding shouldn't go ahead. Strongly enough to use physical means to prevent it.'

Karim was silent for a moment as he digested that piece of information. 'He must love you very much to have such strong concerns for your well-being. And yet you choose to ignore that love?'

Alexa stared at him for a moment and then gave a short laugh. 'He doesn't love me. He hates me. He has always hated me.'

'You're young. Sometimes, when someone else's wishes for you are in contrast to your own, it can be hard to hear what they are saying.'

'There's nothing wrong with my hearing. My uncle isn't interested in what's best for me.' She eyed the door, knowing that she was wasting precious minutes that she didn't have. 'I have to go.'

'If you leave, then I leave. Make no mistake about that. I'm your bodyguard.'

'Haven't you listened to a word I've said? I don't need you.'

'Why not, if you think you're at risk?'

'I don't trust you.'

Karim frowned. 'What possible reason could there be for you not to trust me?'

'I don't trust anyone. And if you insist on coming on this journey then I certainly can't guarantee your safety.'

One dark eyebrow lifted in mockery. 'I rather thought that *I* was supposed to guarantee *your* safety.'

She sighed and rubbed her aching head with the tips of her fingers. 'Karim, I'm *not* a good person to travel with. It is going to be dangerous.'

'Don't you think you're being a little melodramatic?'

He had no idea. Alexa let her hands drop to her sides and gave a resigned shrug. She'd already wasted too much time on this. She'd warned him. If he chose to ignore the warning, then that was up to him. 'I'm leaving now, whether you come or not is up to you,' she said wearily. 'But, if you wait until the morning, then I'll be gone, with or without the passport. And, if *I* wait until morning, I'll be dead. In case you haven't heard, I'm very accident-prone.'

She heard his sharp intake of breath as she walked across the room. At the door she paused and turned to look at him. 'If you're coming with me then bring the gun and the knife—and I just hope you're as good as you say you are, because you're about to need every survival skill you've ever learned.'

CHAPTER THREE

KARIM slid into the tiny car, wondering at precisely which point in the past twenty-four hours he'd relinquished grip on his judgement.

He brushed the tips of his fingers over his lower lip, trying to erase the delicious taste of her mouth and the memory of that searing kiss, but the gesture did nothing to alleviate the nagging ache of lust that now gripped his body.

Intensely irritated by his own response, he let his hand fall to his thigh.

She was the most hotly sexual woman he'd ever met, and her behaviour was every bit as shocking as he'd been led to believe.

The fact that she was prepared to kiss another man days before her wedding confirmed everything he already knew about her, and that kiss had obviously shorted his mental circuits because he was behaving in a way that was entirely uncharacteristic. Instead of being fully in control of the situation, he was now on his way to a mystery destination with a princess who gave new meaning to the term *drama queen*.

Dead. *Dead?*

What did she mean that if she waited until morning she'd be *dead?*

Clearly, she thought a little exaggeration on her part would help urge him into action, or perhaps she'd just been aiming for the sympathy vote. It was a pity for her that he had vast experience of a woman's ability to manipulate a tricky situation to her advantage, especially where money was involved. Obviously the Princess Alexandra was afraid that her uncle might step in and prevent the wedding. And it didn't need a genius to work out why she would go to any lengths to prevent that happening.

Money had an appalling effect on people. He'd seen it firsthand, and her determination to creep away from the palace in the middle of the night in order to protect her prize, had left him with no obvious alternative but to join her. Until she changed her mind about the marriage, his mission was not complete, and his mission stood no chance of being completed if she travelled to Zangrar alone and unaccompanied.

He needed time with her.

Wincing as his shoulders brushed the door and his head banged the roof, Karim tried to shift himself into a more comfortable position, but it proved impossible. 'I'm surprised you didn't opt for a more luxurious mode of transport,' he muttered, but she didn't even glance in his direction.

'I'm not interested in luxury. I'm interested in anonymity.'

Well aware that that both those statements were in direct contrast to everything he knew about the Princess Alexandra's public displays of extravagance, Karim wondered what she was trying to prove by making him journey in the smallest car available to mankind.

A road-sign flashed past and he frowned. 'You took the wrong road. The airport is the other way.'

She didn't respond. Instead her eyes were fixed on the road, and her hands gripped the wheel of the car so tightly that her knuckles whitened under the pressure. 'We're not using that airport.'

'The Sultan's private jet awaits you at Rovina Airport.'

'I know. Which makes it the first place they'll look when they realize that we've gone.' She glanced in her rear-view mirror and then turned left down a road without indicating. Tyres screeched in protest, and Karim's shoulder thudded hard against the window.

Watching his life flash before his eyes, he inhaled sharply. '*Stop* the car! I will drive.'

'No way. For a start, you don't know where we're going.'

'True. But, wherever it is, I would like to reach there alive.' He adjusted his balance as she took sharp right that virtually flung him on top of her.

'You chose to come, Karim.' She changed gears like a racing driver. 'Are you a nervous passenger?'

'That depends on the driver.'

'I'm an *excellent* driver.'

'And yet you have crawled from the wreckage of two car accidents in the past year.'

'Precisely. A less skilled driver than me would have been killed.'

'A more skilled driver than you wouldn't have crashed in the first place. Why do you keep looking in the mirror? It's pitch-dark out there. There is nothing to see.'

'So far. I need to make sure that no one is following us.'

'Who would be following us?' Karim felt a flicker of irritation. 'Some women are incredibly aroused by drama, I know, but you are taking it to new levels. Stop the car.'

'No. There's a chance that my uncle may have discovered that we've left. If I stop, then I risk losing the advantage we have.'

'Has it ever occurred to you that your uncle may have your best interests at heart?'

'Has it ever occurred to you that he hasn't? Don't lecture me, Karim. You're the one who insisted that I needed a bodyguard. I wanted to leave you behind.' She changed gears smoothly and accelerated fast up a dark road. There were no lights at all, but she seemed to know every bend and curve. 'You chose to come with me. That means that you go where I go.'

'And where is that, precisely?'

'I'm going to the Sultan. By my own route.'

'I hope that you will not have cause to regret that decision.' Her determination exasperated him. Why was it that women became so focused when faced with an increase in their fortunes?

'My father wanted me to marry the Sultan.'

'Your father had never met the present Sultan.'

'True. But he knew his father.'

Karim felt something dark and dangerous curl inside him. 'Perhaps I should inform you that you might find that the present Sultan is not such a soft touch when it comes to a pretty face.'

'It doesn't matter. We both know that the Sultan cannot break the contract that exists between us.'

'I'm sure the Sultan will find your eagerness to wed him most flattering.'

'There's no need for sarcasm. We've already established that I'm not pretending to be in love with him, and from what I've read that should be a pleasant change for the man,' she muttered, crunching the gears as she slowed fractionally to take a corner. 'He seems to spend his life fending off over-eager women. It must be very frustrating for him.'

'You needn't waste sympathy on the Sultan,' Karim drawled. 'He has vast experience with women, and is well able to protect himself.'

'Well, he won't need to protect himself from me. I'm honest.' She trod hard on the accelerator. 'And I certainly won't be pretending to be in love with him. We're going to get along just fine.'

'I'm sure the Sultan will be overwhelmed by your romantic nature,' Karim said dryly, wondering whether greed was any less distasteful when it was practised openly.

'From what I've heard, the Sultan doesn't have a romantic bone in his body.'

'You're very sure about that. What if marriage to you is preventing him from marrying someone else?'

'Oh, come on, Karim! You yourself said that the Sultan has avoided marriage all his life. He's thirty-four years old, and he's dated every beautiful woman in the western hemisphere.' She changed gears viciously. 'If there was someone he wanted to marry, he would have done it by now.'

'And you have reached this conclusion on what basis?'

'He's the Sultan. The absolute ruler. He can marry anyone he pleases.'

'Evidently not, since it seems that he will be marrying you. I'm afraid life is nowhere near as simple as you describe, even for the Sultan.'

'We're here.' Ignoring his last remark, she turned the wheel sharply and drove the car through a gap in a fence and into an open field. Then she flashed the headlights three times. From across the field came an answering flash, and she nodded and switched off the engine. 'We need to be quick.'

She was already out of the vehicle, the collar of her black jacket pulled up and a hat pulled low over her eyes. 'Hurry. I don't know how much time we have.'

Seriously questioning his decision to go along with her, Karim followed her, and then reached out a hand and hauled her against him. 'Enough,' he growled. '*Enough*, Your Highness. *No one is following us.*'

'Maybe not yet, but they will be. We need to get on that plane. Now.' Her voice was urgent. 'They're coming, Karim. They're already on their way. I can feel it.'

Karim felt her shiver in his arms, and his own body stirred in response as he stared down into her beautiful face. *Why was she so desperate to go through with this marriage? Was this really all about money?*

And what had happened to his judgement? Was he seriously going to board a strange aircraft with a woman who he didn't trust, like or even admire?

'You're making no sense. Give me one good reason why I should do as you say.'

Her breath was coming in rapid pants, and then she jerked away from him and pointed a gun—*his* gun—straight at his chest. 'Because if you don't then I'm just going to have to shoot you. I will not allow *anyone* to stop this marriage, and that includes you. We've already wasted far too much time. Make your choice, Karim, but make it fast.'

Her hands shaking, Alexa held the gun as she'd seen it held in the movies, hoping that she looked suitably threatening. 'Well?'

Karim stood still, remarkably calm, given that he was staring down the barrel of his own gun. And then he reached out and gently prised the gun from her shaking fingers with a hand that was entirely steady.

'It's dangerous to play with weapons that you know nothing about,' he said softly, and she made a desperate grab for the gun but he slid it back into the holster under his jacket. 'Next time you want to threaten someone, choose a weapon you're familiar with.' He watched her for a moment, his eyes searching. 'Given that our prompt departure is obviously a matter of great importance to you, we'd better leave.'

'Thank you.' She should have felt relief, but instead she found herself wishing that he'd opted to stay behind. He was the most disturbing man she'd ever met, and she didn't want him in her life. Especially not at this particular moment when concentration was crucial to her very survival. Alexa took a phone out of her pocket and made a quick call. Immediately a set of landing lights illuminated a runway, and she saw the small plane waiting. 'They're ready. Quickly.'

Checking over her shoulder for any glimmer of approaching headlights, Alexa pulled away from him and sprinted towards the plane, not really caring whether Karim followed or not.

She didn't understand why he was asking so many questions.

He was a bodyguard. His brief should have been to follow orders, not to give them.

Arriving at the plane, she climbed the few steps and then sank down on the nearest seat, her insides churning so badly that she could barely breath. Karim sat down next to her and she felt the brush of his arm against hers.

Even without turning her head she knew he was watching her. She could *feel* him watching her.

And then he gave an impatient sigh, leaned across and fastened her seat belt in a decisive movement. Wishing he'd selected a seat across the aisle, Alexa's mouth dried.

'Thank you.'

She didn't look at him. She didn't dare.

She had to stay focused, and looking at Karim just blurred her mind.

A man walked out of the cockpit and nodded to her. 'You are ready, Your Highness?'

'Yes. Just go, David. Quickly.' Knowing the risk he was taking, she looked at him doubtfully. 'You're sure you want to do this?'

'How can you doubt it?' The man's expression was fierce. 'We owe it to your father's memory. We owe it to Rovina.'

Karim lounged in the leather seat, studying the woman next to him through half-shuttered eyes.

The moment the plane had taken off, she'd fallen deeply asleep, and now she lay without moving, her thick, dark lashes forming a crescent against her ashen cheeks.

He still hadn't quite recovered from the shock of seeing her standing there, pointing his gun at him. But the incident had taught him two important things.

Firstly, that the Princess Alexandra was determined to marry the Sultan, and, secondly that she was not such a tough, independent soul as she would have liked him to believe. The slender hands holding his gun had been shaking so badly that, had she actually succeeded in firing the thing, the first shot would have hit his head and the second his toes. Clearly she didn't have a clue how to use a gun.

Still, he'd underestimated her, and he wouldn't be doing that again in a hurry.

Her extreme behaviour had surprised even him.

But it shouldn't have done, should it? He gave a cynical laugh. His wealth of experience with her sex had long since taught him that nothing focused a woman's mind more than a serious threat to her spending power, and the princess appeared to be facing that threat in the form of her uncle.

What would she say, he wondered, if she knew that he, too, was determined to prevent the wedding? The only difference between him and her uncle was that *he* intended to succeed.

Transferring his gaze to the front of the plane, he briefly wondered about the identity of the pilot. He'd been surprised by the loyalty and devotion displayed by the young man. Was he one of her many lovers?

Probably, if her reputation was to be believed.

Not that there had been any communication between them since that first brief greeting.

On the contrary, she'd been sleeping since the plane had taken off.

Deciding that it was time to take back control, Karim took advantage of her unconscious state to make some necessary calls. Blessing modern technology, he removed his hand-held computer from his pocket and sent two urgent e-mails that were both immediately answered. He was just pocketing the device when Alexa's head flopped sideways onto his shoulder.

Karim froze in shock as she snuggled into him. The top of her head brushed his neck as she automatically searched for the most comfortable position, and his senses were engulfed by the delicious scent of her amazing red-gold hair.

She smelt like an English garden in the middle of summer.

Seriously discomforted by the unexpected familiarity, he lifted a hand, intending to push her back into her own seat, but somehow his fingers became entwined in a lock of her hair. The curl looped itself around his fingers like a silken coil, and he studied the vibrancy of the colour with fascination.

Whatever else had been said about her, it was certainly true that the Princess Alexandra was astonishingly beautiful. She was a woman that any healthy, red-blooded man would find impossible to ignore. And as for how she tasted...

Irritated by the dangerous direction of his thoughts, Karim allowed her hair to slide through his fingers, reminding himself that this journey was all about helping her to review her decision to marry the Sultan. To stray from that path would complicate things in the extreme.

The weight and warmth of her body remained pressed against his shoulder, and, although sleeping snuggled against him was an intimacy he'd never before allowed a woman, Karim found himself strangely reluctant to wake her. He had no desire to travel with a tired, irritable woman, he reasoned, and anyway sleep not induced by the exhaustion of sex held no significance whatsoever.

He forced himself to relax in his seat, grimly determined to ignore the intrusive and disturbing reaction of his body. Occasionally he glanced at her, wondering when she was going to wake up.

She slept as though she was never going to regain consciousness, and at one point he found himself leaning closer, just to check that she was actually breathing.

It was only when the plane finally landed in Zangrar that she stirred, perhaps sensing the sudden stillness of the plane. Her head was still resting on his shoulder and her gaze met his, her face dangerously close.

Karim felt something stir inside him and curved his hand around her cheek, tempted to help himself to another taste of her luscious mouth before continuing with the job in hand. His body throbbed and ached with the memory of that kiss, and he realized with no small degree of irritation that he had been in an almost permanent state of arousal since he had met the princess only a day earlier. Only the most ruthless self-discipline prevented him from sacrificing his principles in favour of immediate sexual gratification. His hand dropped and he drew back, and she did the same, apparently dismayed to find herself so intimately entwined with him.

'I slept—I'm sorry.' She sounded astonished. 'What time is it?'

'We have just landed in Zangrar.'

'Landed?' Her expression confused, she looked out of the window. 'But that isn't possible.'

'*Why* isn't it possible?'

'Because Zangrar is a ten-hour flight.'

'And you have slept for ten hours.' *And for most of those ten hours she'd been wrapped around him.* Trying to calm the vicious throb in his body by moving his thoughts as far from seduction as possible, Karim flexed his shoulders. 'It was the middle of the night when we left. It is hardly surprising that you were tired.'

She looked shocked. 'I've slept for *ten hours?*'

'Without waking.'

'But I've never—' Without bothering to finish her sentence, she chewed her lip and glanced out of the window. 'So, if this is Zangrar, then how far is it to the Citadel?'

Karim gave a cynical smile. For single-minded focus, you couldn't fault her. She'd barely rubbed the sleep from her eyes, but already she could see the flash of gold across the desert. He only wished that half the people he worked with were even a fraction as driven. 'I'm sure the Sultan will be most flattered by your eagerness to begin married life.'

It was a moment before she replied, and he wondered whether she'd even heard his comment. Then she looked at him, her face blank of expression. 'I need somewhere to change. I can't wear this.'

'This' was the pair of dark trousers and black jumper that she'd worn to leave the palace, presumably chosen to disguise her identity. Clearly she wanted to change into something more glamorous before she met the Sultan.

'The Sultan is going to be far more interested in the person than the clothes. In Zangrar we have a tradition,' he said softly. 'When a woman marries, she dresses in a very simple gown, and that simplicity is of great significance. It means that she is offering herself to her man, all that she is, unadorned and exposed. It is symbolic of the fact that truth can be concealed, and that the marriage of a man and a woman should be about openness and truth.'

'Truth?' Her eyes fixed on his face. 'You're suggesting that I'm not being honest?'

'I'm saying that when a woman gives herself to a man there should be nothing concealed.'

'And what about when a man gives himself to a woman? How much concealing is allowed then? Or is this honesty one-sided?' Disillusionment rang in her voice, and the expression in her eyes was bleak. 'You still haven't answered my question. How far is the Citadel from here?'

'It's a four-day drive through the mountains and the desert.' Omitting to tell her that a helicopter could make the journey in a matter of hours, Karim watched with satisfaction as something close to horror flickered across her beautiful face. 'Zangrar, as a country, is still comparatively underdeveloped. The terrain is a mixture of sand and rock. When it came to building an international airport, the options were somewhat limited. The fortress city is several days' drive away from here, across harsh desert.'

'No!' Clearly horrified by his announcement, she shook her head vigorously and moistened her lips with the tip of her tongue. 'I studied a map. It looked like a short drive.'

'Distances in the desert are deceptive.'

'I can't do a four-day journey—the desert isn't safe.'

No, it certainly wasn't.

More than content with her reaction, Karim relaxed in his seat. As he'd intended, the princess was clearly afraid of the prospect of a journey through the desert. All he needed to do now was ensure that she spent long enough in those surroundings to convince her that life in Zangrar was *not* going to be to her taste. Once she was exposed to those elements of desert life guaranteed to make a delicately brought-up princess run hard and fast in the direction of the nearest shopping mall, his mission would be virtually complete.

Her eyes were still fixed on his face. 'We have to drive? There is no other way?'

'Four-wheel drive is best.' Pausing, he decided that a little elaboration could only help his cause. 'Camels are equally effective, but obviously not so speedy, and I know that you are desperate to reach the Sultan as fast as possible.'

Apparently missing the irony in his tone, she sank back onto the seat, her breathing rapid as she struggled to control her anxiety.

Karim gave a cynical smile. It wasn't hard to guess the direction of her thoughts. For a girl used to dressing in silk and partying until dawn, a prolonged trip through the desert held little in the way of attractions.

And she was right to be afraid.

By the time she arrived at the Citadel she would, with a little outside assistance, have decided that marriage to the Sultan was not for her. 'Why don't you change your clothes?' She would doubtless select something feminine and unsuitable, and the more unsuitable the dress the more uncomfortable the journey.

And, the more uncomfortable the journey, the faster she would decide to rethink her matrimonial intentions.

Convinced that the success of his mission was already assured, Karim gave a faint smile. 'Welcome to Zangrar, Your Highness,' he drawled softly. 'Welcome to the desert.'

CHAPTER FOUR

WITHOUT a word, Alexa picked up the one small bag that she'd carried on board with her, stood up and moved to the back of the plane.

They were going to travel through the desert and it was going to take *four days*? No. That *couldn't* be right. It was just too dangerous. At any other time she would have been wildly excited at the prospect of exploring the desert, but not right now! Not when so much was at stake.

She didn't know which made her feel more uneasy: the thought of being out in the open where William could intercept them at any time, or the thought of being with Karim.

The memory of waking with her head on his shoulder made her want to curl up and hide with embarrassment.

What was happening to her?

First she'd kissed him—or had he kissed *her?*—and then she'd slept snuggled against him as if they were lovers, not strangers. It didn't make sense. At night she only ever dosed fitfully. She *never* slept. In fact, she'd long since decided that her body had actually forgotten how to sleep properly. In the last sixteen years she hadn't *once* slept for a ten-hour stretch. And yet suddenly she'd done exactly that, and, not only had she slept a deep, dreamless sleep, she'd done it *nestled against Karim*.

It was as if in her sleepy state she'd been somehow aware of his strength and had gravitated towards it.

But that couldn't be the case because she didn't rely on others, did she? Not consciously or subconsciously. No matter how desperate she was, she didn't see Karim as her rescuer. She did things on her own, the way she always had.

She didn't want him here.

Like others before him, he didn't believe that she was in danger, which meant that the danger was suddenly increased, because he would be distracting her when she should be alert.

And he was *extremely* distracting.

Warmth curled inside her as she acknowledged the other reason that she was reluctant to travel with him. It wasn't just that she didn't trust him, was it? It was more than that. She didn't want Karim with her because he made her feel like a woman for the first time in her life. He confused her, with his macho decisiveness and raw sexuality. There was something about the way he looked at her that she found profoundly disturbing. He'd made her feel things she didn't want to feel at a time when the only thing on her mind should have been reaching Zangrar safely.

Alexa groaned aloud with frustration.

She didn't want this now.

Not when she was on her way to her wedding. This was *not* the time to discover that there was actually an intensely passionate side to her nature that had never previously been exposed.

Telling herself that her feelings for the arrogant bodyguard weren't relevant, she dressed swiftly. This wasn't about *her;* her feelings didn't matter and they never had.

All that mattered was reaching the Citadel safely and marrying the Sultan.

She was relying on the Sultan's wealth and influence to help restore Rovina to prosperity.

But if the Sultan refused to help her…

He wouldn't, she told herself firmly as she stuffed her old clothes back into the case. Ruthless he might be, but he was also said to be scrupulously fair. Their fathers had been friends. Surely the Sultan would want to honour the bonds of that friendship?

And as for Karim—well, he was just going to have to learn to follow orders.

Having calmed herself, she walked back to the front of the plane, wearing sand-coloured combat trousers tucked into sturdy desert-boots, and felt a flicker of satisfaction as she saw the surprise in Karim's eyes.

'What's the matter?' She put the case down by her seat. 'You were expecting high heels and a tiara? Don't believe everything you've heard about me, Karim. I knew we had to make at least a short journey through the desert. I've dressed accordingly. What I didn't realise was that it was a four-day journey. I need some time to adjust our travel plans.'

'I have already made the necessary arrangements.' His authoritative tone made her pause.

'*I* make the plans.'

'Not when you are travelling with me, Your Highness. I am your bodyguard. You do as I say at all times. You go where I go and you sleep where I sleep.'

He made it sound impossibly intimate, and suddenly a dangerous heat exploded inside her. 'No way. I'd rather travel on my own.'

'A fool crosses the desert of Zangrar without a guide.'

'A bigger fool trusts another with her life.'

He lifted an eyebrow. 'You doubt my ability to protect you? There is no need. You'll be quite safe.'

Safe.

It was a word that hadn't been part of her vocabulary for sixteen years. The whole concept of 'safe' was a distant fantasy for her. 'How can I be safe when you don't even believe I'm in danger? How can you protect me from a threat you refuse to even acknowledge?'

'The desert is in my blood. If anyone is following us then I will know.'

Alexa stared at him helplessly. She wanted to refuse, but she had to face facts—there was no way she could handle a four-day journey through the desert without expert help. She hadn't planned for that. 'You know the desert well?'

Her reluctantly voiced question drew a faint smile. 'You could drop me blindfold in the middle of it and I would be able to find my way back to the Citadel.'

Arrogant.

That was the other word she'd apply to him. Powerful and *arrogant.*

Alexa looked away from his firm, sensual mouth, trying to think clearly. Relying on anyone else for anything was completely alien to her, but what choice did she have?

She hadn't anticipated a journey of four days.

If she was navigating a complex route, she would never be able to protect herself.

'All right. You do the navigation.' She spoke the words reluctantly, comforting herself with the knowledge that she was still responsible for herself. He was merely providing the transport. 'We travel together.'

But she wasn't going to go where he went, and she *certainly* wasn't going to sleep where he slept.

Two hours later she was beginning to feel relieved that she hadn't attempted the journey alone. The desert was vast, and although the road was clear enough, it was also exposed. There was no way she would have been able to drive and keep watch. There was nowhere to hide and nowhere to run to.

'Can we drive any faster?'

'Not if you wish to reach the Sultan alive with all your limbs still attached to your body.' Karim drove with relaxed ease, sunglasses shielding his eyes from the vicious glare of the sun. 'If your uncle is that desperate to prevent this wedding, then I'm surprised you haven't had doubts yourself.'

'It's the right thing for me.' Uncomfortably aware of his hard, powerful body so close to hers, she kept her eyes forward. It felt bizarre to be discussing her forthcoming wedding while feeling the most intense sexual attraction towards another man. 'You talk a lot for a bodyguard.'

'In our country intelligence is as great an attribute as physical strength, and both are equally necessary.' He gave a faint smile. 'The hunter cannot hunt if he cannot first find his prey, Your Highness.'

Alexa shivered. For the past sixteen years of her life she'd been someone's prey. She'd thought she'd finally escaped, but looking at the dangerous gleam in Karim's dark eyes she suddenly felt the fleeting control she'd had of her life slip through her fingers. She had no doubt that he was now the one in charge, and the thought made her desperately uneasy. Did she want to cross the desert with this man for company? No, she didn't. She didn't want or need other people in her life. She was so much safer alone.

Trying to control her fear, Alexa checked the mirror again for signs of another vehicle, and then tried to relax by studying the scenery.

Before they'd landed in Zangrar she'd seen the desert as nothing more than a land feature that they were going to have to cross. But as Karim had accelerated towards the highway that led through the desert she'd been astounded and then captivated.

Now, as she looked, she saw endless dunes stretching into the distance, the colours myriad shades of burnt orange.

'Like my hair,' she murmured, and Karim glanced towards her.

'What is?'

'The desert. It's the same colour.' For a moment she forgot about William as she gazed out of the window. 'It's astonishing. Fabulous. I never knew that there would be so many colours. I mean, it's just sand, but—' She broke off and shaded her eyes as she squinted towards the top of a steep-sided dune. 'I never thought they'd be that high.'

'Clearly you have never been to the desert before.'

'I've never been *anywhere* before.' Alexa steadied herself as the vehicle bumped over uneven ground. 'This is a better road than I expected.'

'Yes, when you can see it. When the wind blows it lies buried under sand.'

'So how do you find your way when that happens?'

'Modern equipment. And if that lets me down then I rely on experience and more traditional forms of navigation.'

'Such as?'

'The position of the sun, the direction of the wind, the smell of the air.' He shrugged. 'The desert tells you much if you are willing to listen. Why are you asking me, when you apparently intended to travel it yourself with no assistance? Presumably you already possess all these skills?'

'I would have been fine.' Something on the horizon caught her eye. 'There's something moving. I can see something.' Her heart-rate doubled, but Karim didn't slow the vehicle.

'It's a camel train. It's how many people still choose to get around in the desert.'

'Camels?' Alexa stared, fascinated now that she knew it wasn't a threat. 'Can we go closer?'

'You wish to take a closer look at a camel?'

'Is that a problem?'

A look of incredulity crossed his bronzed features. 'No, but it's surprising. A close encounter with a camel wouldn't be high on most women's list of coveted life-experiences.'

'Maybe not. But most women haven't been trapped in one place all their lives. Have you any idea what it's like to see the real thing after staring at a picture?'

'You are telling me that you've never left Rovina?'

Unsettled by her impulsive admission, Alexa clamped her mouth shut. *Why had she told him that?* She knew better than to confide details of her life to anyone.

Ignoring her lack of response, Karim frowned. 'Your uncle is clearly *extremely* protective of you. You should be grateful that he cares so much. Do you not feel that you have betrayed him by running away in the night?'

Protective? 'If you always take things at face value then you're not going to be much use as a bodyguard. Let's just say that my uncle and I seriously disagree about the direction of my future.'

'You are to become Queen in a year. I expect he feels that you should be in the palace, learning everything you can about your new role.'

Alexa leaned her head back against the seat and closed her eyes. She could have told him the truth, of course, but she'd long ago learned the dangers of confiding in *anyone,* so she stayed silent.

But the reminder of Rovina and William had extinguished her innocent enjoyment of the desert, and suddenly Alexa felt sick. There was still so much that could go wrong in the few days before her birthday and the wedding.

She glanced sideways at Karim. *If it came to a fight, would he help her?*

He was certainly capable of it. He was dressed in combat trousers and sturdy boots, and would have looked like a soldier were it not for the dark stubble that hazed his strong jaw after a night of travelling. *Part soldier, part bandit,* she thought dizzily. His hair gleamed blue-black in the harsh desert sunshine, and his bronzed skin betrayed his desert heritage.

He was strikingly handsome and more male than any man she'd met before, his face all hard angles and bold arrogance. He regarded the world with something that came close to disdain, and she knew instinctively that there would be few situations in life that this man wouldn't be able to handle.

Alexa wished desperately that they hadn't shared that explosive kiss. Until that moment she hadn't known how a kiss could feel, and she wished she were still living in blissful ignorance. At least then she wouldn't be using all her energy trying *not* to stare at his mouth.

With the hunger of an addict contemplating the next fix, Alexa's eyes lingered on his powerful shoulders, slid down to his flat, muscular stomach and settled on the hard muscle of his strong thighs. He had the hard physique of a soldier and there was no spare flesh on his lean, powerful frame. The deadly blade of the knife glinted in his belt, and she had no doubt that the gun was also around somewhere close.

'Stop staring at me, Your Highness,' he drawled softly. 'Or is the heat of the desert firing your blood? It has that effect on some people. To be in the desert is to return to life at its most basic and primitive.'

Colour flooded into her cheeks and she looked away immediately, hideously embarrassed that he'd been aware of her scrutiny. 'I wasn't staring.'

'Once you are married to the Sultan you will need to hide the fact that you are attracted to other men.' The vehicle lurched suddenly, and he muttered something under his breath and swung the wheel, skilfully compensating for the deficiencies of the terrain.

Clinging to her seat, Alexa felt her face burn, and suddenly the heat in the car seemed increasingly oppressive. 'I'm not attracted to you.'

'You were gazing at me as you would a lover. The same way you looked at me last night, when you came to my bedroom.'

She'd never had this type of conversation with anyone before, and the breath jammed in her throat. 'I came to your bedroom to find my passport. And I certainly wasn't looking at you as I would a lover. Trust me on that one.'

She'd never had a lover, and after one particularly traumatic experience when she was sixteen she hadn't *wanted* a lover. *Until this moment.*

The thought startled and shocked her, and she rubbed her fingers over her damp forehead, trying to return her mind to its previous state of indifference to romance. The experience of her youth had taught her an important lesson. Once—just once—she'd trusted a man and she'd been paying the price ever since. She hadn't been so much burnt as fried to a crisp. But in a way, that experience had made it easier to do what had to be done. Marriage to the Sultan had somehow seemed less daunting, knowing that love and romance were never going to be an option for her.

Trying to ignore the way Karim made her feel, Alexa stared out of the window, feeling the solid ground of her belief system shifting dangerously beneath her feet. She didn't want to feel like this. *She didn't want to think these things.*

'Try and stay in character, Your Highness,' Karim advised. 'You can't be bold and feisty one minute and embarrassed the next.'

Angered by his remark, Alexa turned. 'That depends on the conversation topic.'

He glanced briefly in her direction, a faint smile touching his hard mouth. 'Thinking about sex is a perfectly natural mind-progression between people of a certain age, wouldn't you agree?'

'No, I wouldn't! And I'm *not* thinking about sex.' But now the word was out there in the open she felt her pelvis burn and her stomach flip. And suddenly she could think of nothing *but* sex. And not sex in the abstract or in general—*sex with Karim.*

With a feeling close to desperation, she felt her eyes stray to his bronzed, capable hands. He handled the vehicle with skill, but the lightness of his touch didn't fool her for a moment. She knew that Karim was in control. *The master.* And then her capricious mind imagined those same confident hands moving over her body, and she suddenly felt as though she'd been seared by the flame of a blow torch. 'Is the air-conditioning working?'

'You grow hot, *habibati?*' His mouth tightened, and it was evident that he didn't welcome the chemistry any more than she did. 'You are worried that you are having such explicit thoughts about one man only a few days before your wedding to another? It's inconvenient, I agree.'

The fact that he'd so clearly guessed her most intimate thoughts left her mortified. 'I'm not thinking about you at all.'

'No?'

'No. And if you think that then you're delusional.'

'I'm honest, Your Highness, but I realize that honesty is not a trait that most women possess, especially when they have their eye on the higher prize.'

'I'm marrying the Sultan in four days.'

'Precisely.' He glanced towards her, but the sunglasses made it impossible for her to read the expression in his eyes. 'You should save those hot, longing looks for your wedding night.'

His words tied her in knots. She didn't want to think about her wedding night. 'I don't want to talk about this any more.'

'Why? It's the future you've chosen. Why wouldn't you want to talk about it?' He turned his attention back to the road. 'I would have thought you would be interested in knowing about the Sultan.'

Her heart was pounding and her mouth was dry. Perhaps talking about the Sultan would return her mind to reality. 'All right. Tell me about him.' It didn't actually matter what they talked about as long as it took her mind off the dangerous chemistry that was pulsing between them.

'He is a typical only child.'

'Overindulged?'

Karim gave a faint smile. 'I was thinking more of the fact that he is a high achiever who is perhaps most at home in his own company.'

'People must fall over themselves to obey his every wish. It must be difficult. He's probably surrounded by people who say what he wants to hear, and he can't really trust any of them because they all have their own agenda.' Her words were greeted by a long silence, and when she glanced towards him she saw that his jaw was tense.

'If you have that degree of insight into the complications of royal life then you are clearly interested in more than shoes and clothes.'

'I've lived in a palace all my life so I know what it's like to be constantly under scrutiny. Everything you do is magnified a hundred times and then reviewed by everyone. I don't suppose it's any different for the Sultan. It's all about manoeuvring and politics. Persuading other people to adopt ideas in a subtle way.'

'The word *subtle* definitely doesn't apply to the Sultan. He gives an order and it is done. That's how things work in Zangrar.'

'No one argues with him?'

'No one would dare. It is not his style to rule by consensus.'

'But you like him?'

Karim frowned. 'I have never before been asked that question.'

'It's a yes-or-no answer.'

He inhaled sharply. 'In that case, it's probably no. I don't think I like him, particularly. In fact, there are occasions when I probably dislike him more than anyone I know. He is infuriatingly autocratic, far too controlling and disturbingly possessive.'

Alexa stared at him, surprised. 'You're very frank.'

'I thought you were looking for the truth.'

'I was, but all the same—aren't you worried that I might tell him what you really think of him?'

Karim laughed. 'No, for two reasons. Firstly, when you are with the Sultan he will not be either wanting or expecting conversation from you. And secondly, the Sultan has absolutely no need or particular desire to be liked. Respect—now, that's a different matter entirely.'

Alexa chose to ignore his oblique reference to sex. 'So you respect him?'

'He and I share a similar vision for Zangrar.'

'And you think he's the man to bring that vision to life?'

'Without a doubt. The Sultan is not a man to entertain the possibility of failure.'

'Well, that's good, then. He wants something badly and he's prepared to go for it.'

'He takes that approach to everything in his life. He decides what is important, and then he pursues that goal relentlessly until it is achieved. He never fails. You might want to remember that.'

'I hope I'll be of use to him.'

'You'll definitely be of use.'

Alexa felt a flicker of disquiet, but chose to ignore the implication behind his words. 'I can give him an impartial opinion.' She knew more about palace politics than most people.

Karim laughed with genuine amusement. 'You think the Sultan will be interested in your opinion? This is Zangrar, Alexa. The Sultan's expectations of your role will not extend beyond the bedroom.'

Suddenly the car seemed like a furnace. 'Don't be ridiculous.'

'I'm being honest. Clearly you haven't thought beyond your wedding.'

Alexa tensed in her seat, knowing that it was true. 'As his wife I can be extremely useful in many ways.'

'There will be only one way that interests the Sultan.' Karim glanced at her briefly, his expression thoughtful. 'But you shouldn't worry about it. As I discovered last night, you are clearly an extremely sexual young woman. I'm sure you'll be able to keep him satisfied, as long as you take plenty of rest in the hours that he is working.'

'Now you really *are* being ridiculous.'

'On the contrary, the Sultan is a man who sets himself a punishing work-agenda. He has little time for relaxation and even less time for physical exercise so these days he tends to combine the two. He has an extremely high sex-drive, but you shouldn't find that a problem. You're clearly a woman with energy and drive of your own. The more I see of you, the more convinced I am that this marriage is to be celebrated by all concerned.'

'The Sultan and I will share a great deal more than sex,' Alexa said stiffly, ignoring the sudden churning of her insides. 'My background is not so dissimilar to his. I'm sure that once I understand him, I'll be able to help in all sorts of ways.'

'The Sultan will not require you to understand him. And he seeks the help of no one. As I said, your role will simply be one of—' he paused as he hunted for the word '—recreation.'

'You can't possibly know that.' Alexa sat back in her seat. 'For a start, he has never even met me. He may not find me attractive.'

'The Sultan does take a great interest in the international press,' Karim said gently. 'Like most people, he is already intimately acquainted with your charms.'

The memory of just how those photographs had been taken made her insides churn with misery. 'Those photographs were taken without my knowledge. I was set up.'

'You weren't really with the man?'

'Yes, I was, but—'

'You don't owe me an explanation. And as for the Sultan…' Karim gave an expressive shrug. 'I have no idea how he feels about it, of course, but it probably isn't a good idea to raise the subject. Obviously he isn't expecting a virgin bride, but that needn't necessarily work to your disadvantage. On the contrary, having an experienced woman in his bed means that he won't feel obliged to curb his appetites. Am I driving fast enough for you?'

His question made her wonder whether he had guessed that she was suddenly wishing they were driving in the opposite direction, and Alexa looked away from him. She didn't want to think about the photographs, she didn't want to think about discussing her past with the Sultan, and she *especially* didn't want to think about being in the Sultan's bed! It just wasn't a thought that had even crossed her mind before now. And then she realized *why* she was feeling so uncomfortable—during all the references to sex with the Sultan, her mind had conjured up disturbingly explicit pictures, and all of them had involved Karim.

The chemistry had been alive from the moment they had met, but it seemed to be growing in intensity with each moment they spent in the desert. Perhaps it was because he seemed so comfortable in these surroundings. Comfortable and confident.

And breathtakingly sexy.

The thought shocked her.

This was *not* the time to be noticing a man.

Alexa kept her eyes forward, reminding herself that marriage to the Sultan could only be a step up from the life she'd had up until now. 'Perhaps the Sultan and I will get on extremely well. Have you known him long?' Glancing towards him, she wondered why the question should make him smile.

'All my life.'

'You were playmates?' She guessed that they were about the same age, so it was the only explanation.

'Of a sort.'

By that he presumably meant that the Sultan was of royal blood whereas he wasn't. 'So you know him well?'

'Too well. I am closely acquainted with all his most irritating personality traits.'

'Such as?'

'The list is endless. He is far too intolerant of the deficiencies of others. Impatient and quick to anger. He's arrogant, and rarely, if ever, believes that anyone else can understand and grasp the subtleties of a situation as well as he can.'

'Perhaps he's right.'

Karim frowned. 'I *wasn't* complimenting him.'

'No, I realize that. But if he's as ferociously clever as they say, then it's entirely possible that no one else *does* grasp the situation as well as he does. Which makes that the truth, rather than arrogance.'

'That's a generous assessment.' He studied an instrument on the control panel and flicked a switch.

'Or maybe simply an alternative assessment. Sometimes the facts don't speak for themselves.' *As she well knew.* 'What else? What matters to him?'

'Honesty and loyalty. Does that worry you, Alexa?'

'No. I appreciate the same qualities.'

'Really? How honest is it to marry a man you don't love?'

'Completely honest, because I'm not pretending to love him.' She glanced towards his arrogant profile, her gaze direct. 'It means that the Sultan and I know where we stand. There are no lies. I think that's a good place to start. I'm confident that we can make this work.'

'And yet you have no idea what the Sultan expects from his wife.'

She didn't care. Once she was safely living in the palace within the high walls of the Citadel, the rest would be irrelevant. They could work it all out, she was sure of it. 'I'll be a good wife.'

'So you're basically happy to do anything at all as long as you have access to his wealth, is that right?'

Not his wealth, no. His protection.

The truth hovered on her lips, but she clamped her mouth shut, bewildered as to why she would even contemplate confiding in this man when she knew the dangers of trusting another person. Hadn't she learned from bitter experience that thoughts were best kept private? 'Does the Sultan have a sense of humour?'

Karim concentrated on the road for a moment. 'In the three years since his father died, there have been many problems in Zangrar, none of which have given much cause for laughter.'

'Disputes over oil and problems with an irrigation project.' Sensing his surprise, she shrugged. 'I can read, Karim. There was a report on the Internet. He takes his responsibilities seriously.' And she'd liked that about him. It had given her hope. *Once she had explained the situation, he would help her with Rovina, surely?*

'The fortunes of Zangrar and the people depend on the Sultan.'

The contrast to William cheered her. 'I'm quite confident that the Sultan and I can have a harmonious marriage.'

'The Sultan isn't a man who could be harmoniously married to anyone.' Karim stopped the vehicle without warning and stared up at the sky.

'What's the matter? Where are we? And where's the road?'

'Underneath the sand. The wind is picking up.' He flicked a switch on the dashboard and several instruments flickered to life. 'The weather is not looking as stable as I would have liked.'

'What are you saying? Is this a sandstorm?' Shielding her eyes from the glare of the sun, she looked at the sky but could see nothing but endless blue, broken by a few wisps of white. 'It looks fine to me.'

'At the moment. Conditions change very rapidly in the desert. We will stop here briefly and rest.'

'Don't stop on my account.' Glancing over her shoulder, she checked that there were no other vehicles in sight. 'I'm quite happy to just push on.'

'It is important to take regular breaks, and crucial to drink.' He opened the door and Alexa felt the sudden rush of heat fill the car.

'I hadn't realized how effective the air-conditioning was. It's hot.'

'It's the desert, Your Highness. Out here temperatures can reach fifty degrees. Without water a human being would not last long. Wait there, I'll come round to you.'

'I don't need help getting out of a car, Karim.' What was he thinking—just because she'd been forced to accept the services of a bodyguard, she was happy to relinquish her independence? No way!

Opening her own door, Alexa was about to jump to the ground when Karim caught her, his strong hands hard on her hips as he pulled her roughly into his arms.

'I told you to *wait.*'

'And I ignored you. I don't know what sort of woman you're used to mixing with, but I'm the sort who can climb down from a car without help.' She wished he'd move his hands from her hips. Caught against his hard, powerful frame, she felt her heart jerk and her body melt. 'What are you doing?'

'Preventing you from killing yourself.' His tone was harsh. 'You *never* step down into the desert without first checking for snakes.'

He was all muscle and masculinity, and her heart was bumping so hard against her chest she could hardly concentrate.

'Snakes?' How was she expected to focus her mind on snakes when all she could think about was *him?*

'This is their home, Your Highness, and during the day they're sleepy and often at their most dangerous. They don't always appreciate being disturbed.'

His gaze flickered over the sand beneath his feet, and then he gently lowered her to the ground, her body sliding down his in a slow, deliberate movement that simply increased her internal agony. Her stomach swooped and she knew that the sudden explosion of heat inside her had nothing to do with the strength of the sun's rays beating down on them.

The sudden harsh intake of his breath indicated that he'd felt it, too.

For a moment they stood there, his fingers biting into her hips, and Alexa couldn't breathe or move, her thoughts and senses smothered by the proximity of his body. She was supposed to be thinking of snakes and the dangers of the desert, but all she could think about was *him* and she felt a flash of panic. *What was it about this man that had such a powerful effect on her?* She never had trouble focusing, never, and yet suddenly...

All she could think about was the kiss they'd shared, and she could see from the slow burn of fire in his eyes that he was suffering a similar torment.

'I'm not that familiar with the rules of the desert.' She forced herself to pull away from him and he released her instantly.

'The Sultan would not forgive me if I failed to protect you.'

'So what do they look like, these snakes?' Her body showed no sign of recovering from the searing heat of the contact. There was a maddening ache between her thighs, and her lips were so dry that she tried to moisten them with her tongue. 'Are they well camouflaged?'

'Extremely well camouflaged. The ability to disguise themselves well is the only thing that stands between them and death in this environment.' His voice was tight and angry, and Alexa knew that he was no more absorbed by the conversation about snakes than she was. In fact, if a snake had picked that moment to come and bite them, there was a strong change that neither would have noticed.

'So now what?' She took another step away from him, hoping that distance might succeed where logic was failing.

'We eat and drink.' Reaching into the car, he pulled out a flask and handed it to her. 'Water. It's another essential part of desert survival. In this heat, you must drink.'

Taking the flask, her fingers brushed against his, and she almost dropped the precious water on the ground. 'This so-called road isn't exactly busy, is it?' Trying to disguise the fact that her hands were shaking, Alexa lifted the flask to her lips and drank. Then she glanced over her shoulder again, as she'd done repeatedly since they'd left the airport. 'Obviously there isn't much traffic between the airport and the Citadel.'

'This is only one of several roads. Are you hungry? Do you want to eat?'

'No, thank you.' Her stomach was churning so badly she knew she wouldn't be able to eat a thing. 'It's hot.'

'Indeed, it is. Even within the stone walls of the fortress the temperatures can reach fifty degrees. Many Western women would find the heat and the dust intolerable. You have led a sheltered life in an air-conditioned palace.'

Sheltered?

He had no idea! 'The heat won't worry me.' But she had a feeling that he wanted it to worry her and for a moment she felt puzzled. Why would the Sultan's bodyguard have an opinion on her impending marriage? Why would he even care?

Karim put the water back in the cooler. 'We should get going. We have a long way to go before darkness.'

'Where are we sleeping tonight?'

'Out in the desert, Alexa. Where else?' He opened the car door for her, a faint smile playing around his firm, sensual mouth. 'You can lie back, look at the stars and dream of the Sultan. Take the opportunity to rest while you can.'

CHAPTER FIVE

THEY reached the tents just as dusk was falling and the setting sun was a deep orange ball in the darkening sky.

Karim was suffering agonies of mental and physical tension. He wasn't sure who had been affected most on the journey. It had been long, trying and *extremely* hot, and he had succeeded in making it hotter still by choosing to talk about topics which would have been best avoided given the intimacy of their current situation.

His plan to plant seeds of doubt in her mind by his descriptions of the Sultan had backfired in the most spectacular way. He'd been in an almost permanent state of arousal since she'd lain underneath him in the bedroom, and his poor choice of conversation topic had merely increased the relentless sexual tension that gripped him. The more he'd talked, the more he'd imagined and the more he'd imagined, the harder it had become to drive.

At one point, he'd been sorely tempted to stop the car and douse himself with the remains of their cold water in a brutal attempt to return his brain to sanity.

But he hadn't taken that option, and to make matters worse— *to raise his temperature still further*—his expansive description of the Sultan's sexual appetites hadn't appeared to worry her that much, which presumably indicated that she believed herself more than capable of matching them.

In the end he'd stopped talking, hoping that a period of reflection might be sufficient to induce the degree of doubt in her mind that he'd been hoping for. But instead of brooding she'd simply snuggled down and fallen asleep yet again, leaving him to cope alone with a rampant attack of unrelieved sexual hunger.

He should have woken her, but he'd taken one look at the blue-black shadows beneath her eyes and the pallor of her skin and found himself unable to rouse her from a sleep she so obviously needed.

Wondering when he'd become such a soft touch, Karim brought the vehicle to a halt outside the tents and glanced at her in exasperation.

All she seemed to do was sleep.

Clearly her hectic lifestyle was catching up with her.

His mouth tightening, he decided that enough was enough. If this woman became Zangrar's queen it would be disastrous, and his absolute priority had to be to prevent it happening. 'Your Highness.' She didn't stir and his tone hardened. '*Alexa.*'

Her eyelids lifted and Karim tumbled headlong into her soft, blue gaze, and suddenly all he wanted to do was spend the foreseeable future exploring the possibilities of her mouth…

Feeling as though he was losing his grip, he dragged his eyes away from hers and tightened his grip on the wheel. 'We've arrived.'

'Arrived?' Her voice husky, she stretched with feline grace, and then suddenly sat upright sharply. 'Oh my goodness—you should have woken me!'

Wondering whether she was more dangerous awake or asleep, Karim gritted his teeth. 'You were tired. We're spending the night here.'

'You sound cross.' Pushing her hair away from her face, she glanced sleepily out of the window. 'I can't believe I fell asleep again.'

'You've obviously been having too many late nights.'

'I just don't sleep well at home.'

Remembering the picture he'd been shown of her being removed unconscious from a nightclub, Karim was tempted to point out that in order to sleep she had to be in her own bed. Then he remembered that antagonizing her was *not* his objective. 'The heat in the desert can be draining.'

'You should have woken me up and let me drive.'

'There was no need.' Having heard about her accidents, he had no intention of allowing her to drive.

She looked over her shoulder. 'I'm just relieved there's no sign of my uncle.'

'You truly believe that your uncle might follow us?'

'Maybe not in person, but he'll send his men.' Her eyes shifted to his face. 'If he can stop this wedding he will, Karim.'

Suffering from an almost agonizing attack of sexual tension, Karim found himself wishing that her uncle had shown more skill in his persuasion techniques. At least then he wouldn't be facing a night alone in the desert with a female who made him feel uncomfortably out of control.

'We will stay here tonight. It is a regular watering-hole for camel trains. The accommodation will be simple but sufficient for our needs.' And hopefully sufficient to convince her that life in a hot desert-country was not for her. For the sake of his sanity, he hoped she would make the decision sooner rather than later. He could have her back at the airport within a day.

Clearly oblivious to his physical torment, she peered out of the window. 'I didn't think trees grew in the desert.'

'They are date palms. And even in the arid desert, there is water.'

'So, who stays in this place usually?'

'Wandering desert tribes. And tourists wanting to discover the "real" Zangrar.' He opened the door of the vehicle. Immediately a man hurried towards them and fell to his knees. Feeling another surge of tension, Karim spoke softly and watched as the man scrambled to his feet quickly and backed away.

Alexa climbed out of the car and joined him, astonishment on her face as she watched the man. 'Why did he bow? What did you say to him?'

Without missing a beat, Karim slammed the car door shut. 'Unfortunately he guessed that you are the royal princess who is to marry the Sultan. I told him that we don't want your identity revealed.'

'Karim, I look like any other tourist. How could he possibly know who I am?'

'The wedding is an important event of relevance to all the citizens of Zangrar. Everyone in the country is aware of your existence.'

'But if he knows who I am—'

'He will be discreet. Do not worry about him.' Karim pulled her small case out of the back of the vehicle. 'The facilities here are basic, but you should be able to wash in the pool under those trees. Just watch out for the local wildlife.' But if he'd been expecting a show of fear and revulsion at the warning, he was once again disappointed. She simply nodded, apparently more concerned with looking in the direction from which they'd just come.

'By now, my uncle will have realized that we've left. He'll be following us.'

'Such perseverance on his part must make you wonder whether this wedding is wrong for you.' Wondering why she refused to see what was so clear to others, Karim walked towards the tents, gesturing for her to follow him. 'You don't think he has your best interests at heart?'

'No.'

'And yet he has a great deal more life experience than you and knows you well, having cared for you since the death of your parents. It must worry him to see you so set on a marriage that he doesn't believe will make you happy.'

When she didn't answer, Karim sighed. Like most women, she seemed to make a point of rejecting all sensible advice that came her way. It was obvious to him that her uncle understood nothing about the workings of the female mind and had taken entirely the wrong approach. Had he *insisted* on the wedding taking place, there was a strong chance that by now the princess would have decided that marriage to the Sultan was definitely *not* for her.

No matter. If she wasn't willing to accept the decision of others then she'd simply have to make the decision herself.

And he was going to help her.

True, he didn't appear to have made an impact on her yet, but they still had three days of the journey to go through the harshest terrain in Zangrar.

He was confident that by the time they arrived at the Citadel she would have made the decision he wanted her to make.

But, as he urged her inside the simple tent, she turned towards him, her expression suddenly anxious. 'I've got a really bad feeling about this. I think we should just rest for a short time and then carry on with our journey.'

'You are not in charge, Alexa.' He watched as frustration flickered across her beautiful face.

'I could drive while you sleep.'

'That would be beyond foolish. We will both sleep here.'

'And if my uncle is already on our tail?'

Then he could add his persuasion to Karim's. 'I will protect you.' Given that the only threat to her well-being was going to come from him, he wasn't remotely concerned.

'How can you protect me when you don't believe there's a threat? Admit it, you think I'm some sort of hysterical drama queen.'

Karim saw no reason to lie. 'Some women are naturally more nervous than others.'

Alexa hooked her thumbs into the pockets of her trousers. 'Do I strike you as the nervous type? Some women have more *reason* to be nervous than others, Karim. You might want to remember that before you stray too far from your gun.'

'I am prepared to believe that your uncle does not want this marriage to happen, but I am sure he has your best interests at heart. You are the next Queen of Rovina. Clearly he does not think that this is a good time for you to leave the country, but that doesn't mean that he would go to the lengths that you suggest. That would be self-defeating.'

She was silent for a moment, and he sensed that she was on the verge of telling him something important. Then she looked away. 'Fine. If you don't think we should travel at night, then we won't.'

Her sudden compliance filled him with suspicion. 'You are unusually co-operative, Your Highness. If you're thinking of making a dash through the desert on your own, then I ought to warn you that we are sharing a tent tonight. You won't be going anywhere without my knowledge and approval.'

'Sharing a tent? Why would you want to share my tent?'

Karim felt his jaw tense. He didn't want to share her tent, but nor was he so foolish as to let her out of his sight. 'Your safety is my responsibility. My brief is to go wherever you go.'

It was her turn to look suspicious. 'And yet you don't believe that my uncle is a threat.'

No, but it was imperative that he stayed close to her if he was going to ensure that her experience of the desert was not a favourable one. 'I believe that *you* are concerned,' he said smoothly. 'And hopefully my presence should reassure you.'

'Oh.' Her tone suggested that she'd hoped for a different answer. 'Well, that's better than nothing, I suppose. If you insist on sticking to me like glue, then please follow me to the pool. Are you going to swim?'

Karim gritted his teeth. It was hard to say which of the two of them was more tense. 'I will *not* be swimming.' The thought of being semi-naked in the water with this woman sent his body temperature soaring to dangerous levels.

'I thought your brief was to go wherever I go.'

For a moment their eyes held, and awareness pulsed between them like a living force. With ruthless determination, Karim reined in the primitive reaction of his body, struggling to ignore the white-hot flash of lust that engulfed him. 'I will keep watch while you bathe.'

'Fine.'

Angry with himself, Karim paced towards the open flap of the tent and then turned slightly, responding to the tension inside him. *The last thing in the world he wanted to do was watch while she swam naked.* 'You are sure you want to swim? Perhaps you would rather just rest before dinner—sleep again?'

'I just had a sleep. I'm going to bathe. I'm ready when you are.' She flipped open her case and pulled out a small towel. 'I don't have a costume or anything. I'll bathe in my underwear.'

Karim felt beads of sweat sting his brow. He did *not* want to think about her in her underwear.

He didn't want to think of her at all.

Alexa slid under the water, regretting her decision to swim. The pool had seemed to offer an obvious, practical antidote to the heat and dust of the journey. But what she hadn't considered was the impact of being semi-naked with Karim standing so close. She was so hyper-aware of him that, far from feeling cool, she felt feverish and hot.

Not that he was likely to notice. He wasn't even looking at her. Instead he stood with his back to her, his eyes apparently fixed on some far point on the horizon. The late-evening sun shone onto the blade of his knife and it winked and flashed, a deadly reminder that this journey was not a pleasure trip.

But her fear was slightly less acute than usual, and she knew who was responsible for the change in her anxiety levels.

Karim.

Maybe he didn't believe that she was truly in danger, but he was still standing there, wasn't he? He was standing there because of *her,* and for the first time in her life she had a glimpse of what it might be like to not be totally alone.

Alexa studied the width of his shoulders and the power of his body, and wondered for a moment what he would say if she told him the truth about her life.

And then she turned and swam in the opposite direction, horrified that the thought had even entered her head.

That wasn't going to happen.

Confiding in anyone was a mistake, as she'd learned at a pitifully early age when she'd still believed that life was fair and people were good.

And now, *finally,* hope had returned and the only way to give it a chance to blossom into a whole new life was to keep her thoughts to herself and *not* talk. Those skills had been essential to her very survival, and she wasn't about to change that now. It appalled her to think she'd even considered it. Yes, he was watching over her, but only because that was his job. To read sentiment or emotion into his actions would be unforgivably naïve. And she wasn't naïve, was she? Just horribly lonely—but she'd been that way for so long she didn't understand why she would suddenly be reaching out to anyone.

Alexa pulled herself from the water, and then froze as she saw movement out of the corner of her eye. 'Karim—'

'Yes?' The word hissed from his lips, but he didn't turn.

Wondering what possible reason he had to be in such a foul

temper, she kept her eyes fixed on the dust at her feet. 'I think this might be one of those occasions when I need saving. If you're not going to turn around, then I need to borrow your knife. We have a visitor.'

Karim turned swiftly, his hand already closing over the hilt of the dagger. Then he spotted the snake coiled in the shadows of a large boulder and breathed out heavily. 'It's all right. It isn't dangerous.'

'Really? How can you tell?'

'The pattern behind its head.'

Alexa dropped to her knees to take a closer look at the snake, fascinated now that she knew there was no danger. 'I've never seen a real one before. The camouflage is amazing. It's exactly the same colour as the sand. I almost didn't spot it.' She ran a finger over the snake's dry scales and it quickly slithered under the rock, as appalled by the contact as she was intrigued. Rising to her feet, she noticed the incredulity in Karim's eyes. 'What's the matter?'

'It was a snake.'

'Yes.'

'It was a *large* snake.'

Wondering what was responsible for his stunned expression, Alexa shrugged. 'A large snake that wasn't dangerous, according to you.'

'You touched it.'

'Yes—it felt dry. Amazing. Not slimy at all.'

He inhaled sharply. 'Women are not usually overly fond of reptiles.'

'Maybe I've just mixed with more reptiles than most,' Alexa said lightly, glancing towards the rock to see if the snake had reappeared. 'Sorry. Bad joke. If you really want me to have hysterics, then it could probably be arranged.'

'You are unlike any woman I have ever met.'

Unsure whether his observation was a compliment or not, she sighed. 'I'm just not afraid of snakes. Different things frighten different people, I suppose. Do you *want* a hysterical female on your hands? Because if not then I think I'll just get dressed. I feel a bit vulnerable standing here half-naked.'

His burning gaze slid from her face to her breasts, and immediately she wished she hadn't drawn attention to her state of undress. His eyes lingered before moving down over her waist to her skimpy pants. Aware that her flimsy wet underwear provided her with no cover whatsoever, Alexa turned quickly and pulled on her cargo trousers, ignoring the fact that the material clung to her still-damp body.

A shout from the camp disturbed them.

'People are coming.' Karim thrust her shirt towards her. 'Get dressed.'

'I'm doing my best, believe me.' Fumbling with the buttons, her cheeks blazing, Alexa finally secured her shirt. The dip in the water had cooled her, but now she felt uncomfortably hot again and knew that it was nothing to do with the desert heat and everything to do with Karim. He was standing so close that they were almost touching, and she knew that even if they'd been traversing the Arctic Circle she would still have felt hot. All she could think about was her body—*his body*.

What was it about him?

Or was it her? Helpless to understand what was going on, she almost groaned in despair. Had she been locked up in one place for too long? Had her loneliness made her desperate? Had she developed some sort of fixation on her bodyguard because he was offering her protection? Some women did that, she knew. They were attracted to strong, powerful men. But she wasn't that sort of woman. Since the death of her father, she hadn't had a man's protection, and she no longer expected or needed it. And she wasn't interested in any other sort of relationship, either.

Yes, she was marrying the Sultan, but only because that was what she had to do.

She owed it to the people of Rovina, many of whom she knew had abandoned hope when her uncle had become the Regent.

Suddenly Alexa felt a flicker of disquiet as the reality of her situation slammed home. Duty or not, she *was* going to be marrying a man she'd never met, and that had suddenly taken on a new significance.

And she knew why.

Her gaze flickered to Karim. Sex suddenly seemed significant because for the first time in her life she was aware of herself as a woman. Karim had awakened her sexuality, feelings that she hadn't known existed.

Her fingers shook as they fumbled with the last of her buttons. This was *not* the time to discover that she had a whole side to herself that she'd never imagined was there. She needed to focus on getting safely to the Citadel and marrying the Sultan, and it didn't matter if he had four heads and no personality—she would still be marrying him.

She had to.

Her life depended on it.

The future of Rovina depended on it.

'I will escort you back to the tent. There will be time to rest before we eat.' His tone icy-cold and discouraging, Karim led her back along the sandy path that led from the oasis through the trees. 'You should rest now. I'll call you when it's time to eat.'

'I don't need to sleep.' How could she sleep when she was her own bodyguard? She needed to keep watch.

'Then rest, at least.' Karim frowned, as if her response had annoyed him. 'I'll be just outside the tent.'

She made no sense whatsoever.

And his reaction to her made even less sense. At one point

he'd been on the verge of stripping off and joining her in the pool, and as if that hadn't been surprising enough he'd then found himself regretting the fact that he was no longer able to follow such impulses.

Karim frowned. These days his mind rarely strayed from duty and responsibility, and yet there had been moments on the journey when…

He cut the thought off before it could develop and fixed his eyes on the road that stretched into the distance, reminding himself that his objective was to show the princess the horrors of the desert.

But so far he wasn't doing very well, was he?

The unexpected appearance of the snake had been particularly timely, but her reaction had been especially astonishing. Once she'd ascertained that it wasn't poisonous, she'd shown interest rather than either the fear or revulsion that he'd anticipated and hoped for.

Off hand, he couldn't think of a single woman of his acquaintance who would have welcomed the opportunity to take a closer look at a snake, and certainly none who would have chosen to examine it at close quarters.

She'd touched it. She'd bent and stroked it as if it had been a domestic pet, and there had been something about that gentle, almost seductive touch that had sent his pulse-rate soaring into the stratosphere.

Wondering what it was going to take to unnerve her, Karim ran a hand over his face, reflecting on the irony of the situation. For the first time in his life he'd met a woman who seemed perfectly at home in these harsh surroundings. How many times in the past had he dreamed about finding a woman who shared his love of Zangrar?

Staring into the desert, he found himself wondering what it would have been like to meet her under different circumstances, and then he closed his eyes briefly, frustrated by his inability to control his own libido around a woman who possessed virtually no admirable qualities.

Yes, her fascination with the desert was surprising, and might actually have been gratifying in different circumstances—but not *these* circumstances.

The fact that she seemed comfortable with the heat, the dust and the wildlife was not enough to make 'the rebel princess' a suitable wife.

Glancing over his shoulder towards the sealed tent, he wondered what she doing now.

Was she asleep yet again?

Or was she lying on the bed dreaming of the riches that awaited her in Zangrar?

Refreshed after her swim and dressed in a pale blue linen dress that fell to her ankles, Alexa wandered out of the tent and bumped straight into Karim.

Disturbed by how good it felt to know he was there, she just stood there, and eventually he broke the tense silence.

'Food will be served by the fire. It keeps the wildlife at bay.' His harsh tone suggested that he wasn't similarly pleased to see her, and she was appalled by how much that knowledge disappointed her.

'I quite like the wildlife. It's very interesting. What sort are we talking about this time?'

His gaze flickered to her clothes and down to her strappy sandals. 'The sort that would grow excited when faced by a pair of bare feet.'

'Are you trying to frighten me, Karim? All you seem to do is tell me about the dangers of the desert.'

'Clearly you're *not* frightened.'

'I love it.' She looked around her. 'I love everything about it. The colours, the solitude, the sheer enormity of the place, reminding you how small and insignificant you are—' She broke off and gave a tiny shrug, embarrassed by her outburst. 'I have never left Rovina before. I haven't been in possession of my passport since I was eight years old.'

'That was when your parents were killed?'

It was a conversation topic that had never come up, and for a horrifying moment her brain was filled with images that paralyzed her.

'Alexa?'

Hearing Karim's voice, she pushed through the dark, terrifying clouds. 'Yes.' Somehow she persuaded her voice to work. 'My uncle didn't want me going anywhere.'

'As your guardian, he clearly takes his responsibilities very seriously.'

Reminded of the reality of her life, Alexa stood still. 'What time will we set off in the morning?'

'Early.' Karim gestured towards the rug that had been placed next to the fire. 'Sit. You must be hungry'

'Not really. I just want to finish the journey.'

'I guarantee your safety, Alexa. I just hope that marriage to the Sultan is all that you are hoping for.'

In desperate need of distraction, she concentrated instead on the robed man who was placing various dishes on the rug between them. 'Let's forget about the Sultan for five minutes. Tell me about yourself. You grew up in the Citadel? Has your family always worked for the Sultan?'

'We have always been close to the Sultan, yes.' He listened while the man spoke to him in a low voice, and then shook his head and dismissed him with a wave of his hand.

Alexa watched as the man melted away. 'Is there a problem?'

'He wanted to know whether he should fetch you a knife and fork. I told him that you want the full desert-experience. That's right, isn't it, Your Highness? That is what you've signed up for, after all.'

'Obviously I'm eager to learn as much as possible,' she said honestly. 'Would the Sultan stay in a desert camp like this one?'

'Occasionally. Sometimes the accommodation would be

much more basic, usually it would be more luxurious. It really depends on the purpose of the trip.'

'And you go with him?'

'Always.'

'He must be missing you.' Alexa took the cup that was handed to her and drank thirstily. 'It's good. What is it?'

Karim lay sprawled on the rug, his dark eyes lazily amused. 'Camel's milk.'

'Really? It's delicious.' She drank again and saw his surprise. 'What? It's rude to stare, Karim.'

'You are used to drinking fine wines from cut glass. Camel's milk from an earthenware cup must be an entirely new experience.'

'But not all new experiences are bad ones.' She finished her drink and selected some food from the dishes in front of her, following Karim's lead and eating with her fingers. 'Did you spend much time in the desert when you were young?'

'Yes. My family's roots are in the desert, and many of our people still lead nomadic lives. It's essential to understand the particular hardships and problems that they face.'

'So that you can understand the Sultan's work, you mean? Or so that you can protect him more effectively?'

'Both.'

'And now you live in the Citadel itself? In the palace?'

'Of course. I go where the Sultan goes.'

'Then I'll be seeing a lot of you once I'm married.'

Karim stared into the fire, and when he finally lifted his gaze to hers there was a mockery in his eyes that she didn't understand. 'If you marry the Sultan, then you will certainly see a great deal of me.'

Alexa felt her heart stumble. The thought of seeing Karim every day was unsettling to say the least. 'Why do you say *if?*'

The reflection of the fire flickered in his liquid dark eyes. 'The Citadel is a fortress, Alexa, not a shopping mall. If the Sultan so wishes, he can keep you inside his palace and not allow you to see the light of day. Is that truly a life that can make you happy?'

Alexa smiled at the thought. Life in a fortress. *With her uncle on the outside.* 'It's what I want.'

'You *want* to be closeted behind high stone-walls with a man you have never even met? It seems a strange choice.'

'That's because you know nothing about my life.'

'Then tell me.' He leaned towards her, his gaze compelling and his voice surprisingly gentle. 'Tell me about your life, Alexa. What is it that makes this match so appealing? We are alone, now, just the two of us. Talk to me.'

Alexa stared at him. She'd lived her entire life alone, devoid of love and friendship, and the sudden flicker of warmth in his eyes was enough to draw her out in much the same way as a starving animal would tiptoe towards the promise of a morsel of food.

'I've never told anyone.'

'Then it is time to confide in someone,' he urged. 'Because such introverted behaviour is *not* natural for a woman.'

Most women hadn't lived her life.

The past oozed into her brain like a deadly cloud, souring the atmosphere, and she scrambled to her feet quickly. She was doing it again! The urge to confide in him was becoming stronger and stronger despite the fact that she knew the dangers of speaking to the wrong person. 'The meal was lovely. Please thank them for me. If we have an early start, then I think it's best if I go to bed now.'

CHAPTER SIX

SHE'D been on the verge of telling him something. The question was, *what?*

And why was he so interested?

Simmering with frustration at her abrupt departure, Karim stood outside the tent, giving her time to prepare herself for bed before joining her. What confession had been clinging to her lips?

Regret for the life she'd led?

Second thoughts about marrying a man just for status and money?

Wondering if her conscience was keeping her awake, he pushed aside the flap of the tent and strode inside.

One glance told him that she was already asleep, apparently oblivious to the hard, simple bed, the spartan surroundings or the nagging of her conscience.

Her luxurious red-gold hair was spread haphazardly over the pillow like sand blown by the wind, and her mouth was the colour of ripe strawberries. *Strawberries just waiting to be devoured.*

Even in the depth of sleep she looked like every man's hottest fantasy, and Karim experienced a monumental surge of desire as he stood watching her. The ache in his loins grew to agonizing levels, and he uttered a soft curse and strode to the far side of the room, vowing to stay as far away from her as possible.

Why had he imposed this ridiculous rule that she was to stay by his side for the entire journey? Just who was suffering most?

He lay down and waited for sleep to claim him, but it was asking the impossible, and he was still staring grimly upwards when the princess gave a frightened moan.

Karim was on his feet with the speed and grace of a panther, the hilt of the knife in his hand as he prepared to defend her.

'Alexa?' The fading light of the hurricane lamp was enough to show him that no one had entered the tent without his knowledge, which meant that her distress was caused by something different.

Spider? Scorpion?

His senses on alert, Karim prowled silently over to the large bed and stared down at the princess who was now sprawled on her back, one arm flung upwards, her cheeks flushed.

Evidently she was still asleep, which meant that her distress was caused by nothing more than a bad dream. So perhaps her conscience was pricking her, after all.

Slowly he returned the knife to his belt, his attention held by the expanse of creamy bare shoulder revealed by crumpled bedsheet. Forcing his gaze upwards, he noticed the faint sheen of sweat on her brow, and then she cried out again and this time he saw the trickle of tears on her cheeks.

Shocked by the sight of those tears, Karim froze.

Completely out of his comfort zone, he then took an involuntary step backwards, retreating from such a visible display of emotion as he would a wild beast.

In fact, he would have been far more comfortable rescuing her from the jaws of a lethal predator. He *hated* tears. In early childhood he'd been given endless opportunity to observe the many uses of female tears, but even he had never before witnessed a woman cry in her sleep.

Reluctantly, he was forced to acknowledge that these were

real emotions, not those constructed specifically to extract something from a man, and he stood frozen with indecision as those silent tears ripped holes through his iron-clad defences in a way that no physical weapon would have done. Suddenly he felt raw and exposed as long-forgotten images settled over his brain like a toxic cloud.

His natural aversion to emotional scenes stifled his ability to think clearly, and he stood paralyzed. What was he supposed to do? He knew *nothing* about dealing with a woman whose tears were genuine.

And then he realised that he didn't have to do anything.

She was asleep, wasn't she?

No action was required on his part.

Relieved to have reached that conclusion, Karim was about to return to his bed when she gave another cry, and this time the sound was so tortured that he sat down next to her.

What was he doing?

What did he know about comforting anyone? It was far more usual for him to be the cause of female tears.

Deciding that by far the simplest and safest solution would be to wake her up so that she could solve the problem herself, he reached out a hand and gave her shoulder a firm shake.

She awoke instantly with a horrified gasp, her eyes wide and terrified.

'Go away!' She sat bolt upright, her expression stricken. 'Don't *touch* me!' Her fist powered into his stomach with surprising force, and the breath hissed through his teeth as pain radiated across his abdomen.

'It's me,' he grunted, closing his fingers over her fist before she could do any more damage, 'Karim. You were dreaming.'

As he waited for the blankness in her eyes to fade and the pain in his muscles to settle, he reflected on the fact that the princess hadn't been exaggerating her claim that she could manage perfectly well without a bodyguard. No one could have described her as defenceless.

So how could a woman who could deliver a punch like that appear vulnerable?

Her breathing was rapid and she gave a little shake of her head, her cheeks still wet with tears. 'Sorry. I—I had a dream.'

'Yes.' Relieved that the problem appeared to be solved, Karim released her hand and started to stand up, but she grabbed his arm.

'Wait a minute. Don't go. Please don't leave me.'

Her request was so unexpected that he simply stared at her. *What did she expect him to do?* 'You're awake now.'

'It's all still in my head. It was so clear…' Her fingers tightened on his arm and he had little choice but to sit down again.

'Think about something else,' he advised swiftly, and she made a sound that was somewhere between a sob and a laugh, fully awake now.

'Sorry. This isn't what you signed up for, is it? Go back to bed, I'll be fine.' With obvious reluctance, she released her desperate grip on his arm and bent her knees up to her chest, cuddling them like a child. 'I'm sorry if I disturbed you.' She was shaking so badly that Karim could feel the movement on the mattress, and he gave an impatient sigh.

'It was just a dream, Alexa.'

'Yes.' Her teeth were chattering and she buried her head in her arms. 'Go back to bed.'

He should have done exactly that, but somehow he couldn't bring himself to leave her, and that impulse puzzled and exasperated him. 'What was the dream about?'

Her head lifted and she looked at him, tears spilling out of her eyes and onto her cheeks. She made no sound, but simply blinked a few times and then brushed her tears away impatiently. 'It doesn't matter.'

'You need to go back to sleep,' he said roughly. 'Whatever it was all about, the memory will have gone in the morning.'

'Not all memories are so easily erased.' She spoke softly, as if afraid that to raise her voice might make those memories still more vivid. 'I thought this would be a fresh start. I thought that I could finally leave it all behind. But it comes with you, doesn't it? It follows you everywhere, because it's been there for so long, it's part of who you are.'

Was she talking to herself or to him?

Was she seriously expecting some sort of response?

Karim had no idea what she was talking about, but it sounded disturbingly like the sort of touchy-feely conversation that a woman ought to have with another woman. '*What* follows you?

'The past. It's always there. You can never shake it off.'

Confronted with a more clearly defined problem to deal with, Karim relaxed slightly. It was obvious that she regretted the things she'd done in her past, and that was hardly surprising, given just how wild her behaviour had been. Evidently her impending marriage to the Sultan had made her wish that she'd behaved with a little more restraint in her youth, which meant that it *was* her conscience that was disturbing her sleep.

'The past is the past.' Wishing that she'd stop shaking, he kept his words blunt. 'There is never any point in looking back. It's over and done with.'

'That isn't true. Don't *you* ever look back?'

'No,' Karim said shortly. 'The past is over. The future is the only thing that matters. And your future requires us to leave at dawn. If you don't get some sleep soon you'll be too tired to travel.'

'I don't want to go back to sleep. Can we leave now? I'm scared, Karim.'

'We're not leaving. Lie down.'

For once, she didn't argue. Like a child obeying a parent, she lay down, and Karim stared at her shivering, half-naked form with exasperation. Wasn't she going to pull the covers up?

After a moment's hesitation he reached out and tugged the sheet up over her shoulders, covering her body and at the same time pondering on the entirely new experience of tucking a beautiful woman into a bed that he wasn't sleeping in. As he rose to his feet her hand shot out and her slim fingers gripped his arm again.

'Will you stay? Just for a moment.'

Her fingers tightened on his arm and he covered them with his own. Her slender fingers were freezing cold, and he rubbed his hand over hers and then realized what he was doing and released her instantly. 'You'll be fine now.'

What was he doing?

What instinct had driven him to offer comfort when he was so inexperienced in that particular skill?

'*Please* stay with me. Just for a minute.'

For what purpose? What did she want from him? His eyes raked over her shivering body, but there was nothing in the least seductive about the way she lay. She looked fragile and vulnerable as she huddled under the sheets, as if she were trying to make herself as small and insignificant as possible.

'*What* are you afraid of?' Irritated with himself for responding to her, his voice was rougher than he'd intended. 'Tell me.'

'Why—so that you can take out your gun and shoot it?' She gave a shaky laugh, released his arm and curled up into a ball. 'There are some things that even a bodyguard can't protect you from, and this is one of them. You're right. You can't help me, Karim. Go back to bed. I'm sorry I disturbed you.'

He had her permission to leave.

So why was he still standing there?

Something about her weary dismissal made it impossible for him to walk away, and the urge to help and protect her was so shockingly powerful that he almost laughed at himself. *So he wasn't entirely immune, then.* Just like his father before him, he was a man capable of being manipulated by a woman's tears.

'There is nothing to be afraid of.' He was impatient with himself, not her, but he saw her withdraw.

'I'm fine, Karim. Go to bed.'

Frustrated by his inability to do exactly that, Karim frowned down at her, studying the dark shadows under her eyes and the almost translucent skin over delicate bones. *She didn't look fine.* She looked like a woman who was hunted by demons. And she was a woman of contrasts—strong and feisty one minute, vulnerable the next. *How had a woman who looked as though a gust of wind could snap her in two, shown such resilience in the desert?* 'Was your dream to do with your uncle?'

'Can we talk about something else? Anything.' Sounding more like a nervous child than a grown woman, she huddled under the covers. 'It would help a lot if you could just talk about something normal for a moment. Tell me about your family.'

'My family is *not* normal,' Karim said dryly. 'I suggest you pick a different topic.'

'*You* pick a topic.'

'I'm not good at small talk.'

'Then it will be useful to practice. Come on, Karim. Talk to me.'

Talk? Telling himself that the sooner she settled down the sooner they'd both get some sleep, Karim sighed and rubbed his fingers over his temple. 'Have you ever heard of dune driving? Because the next stretch of our journey has some of the best dune driving in Zangrar. Steep dunes, spectacular views, exciting drops. It's the best adrenaline rush in this part of the world—' he broke off, surprised at himself. Why had he picked that particular topic? What was it about Alexa that made him remember the heady days when pleasure had come before responsibility?

'Don't stop,' she murmured. 'I want to hear more. You did it when you were young?'

'As soon as I could drive.'

'And did the Sultan go with you?'

Karim stilled. '*Always* you ask about the Sultan.'

'I'm trying to build up a picture.'

'Yes,' Karim said finally. 'Before life became too serious to allow such frivolities, the Sultan had a passion for dune driving.'

'What does it involve?'

'Driving up the side of a dune and plunging over the top. A bit like a roller coaster, only less predictable and more hair-raising. And a great deal more uncomfortable if you topple the vehicle.'

'Did you?'

'A few times.' Karim started to smile and then stopped himself, remembering that this was supposed to be distraction therapy, not a trip down memory lane.

'It sounds dangerous.' Her voice was sleepy. 'I'm surprised the Sultan was allowed to do that if he was the heir to the throne. Wasn't he surrounded by people telling him what to do?'

'He was sent to boarding school at the age of seven, and from there went straight into the army. The time he spent in Zangrar was very precious because no one really bothered with him.'

It was a long time before she spoke. 'That's a very young age to leave your parents.'

'It is the custom.'

'I wouldn't do that with my children. I'd keep them close. Didn't the Sultan's mother object to him being sent away? Or wasn't she given any choice?'

Increasingly discomforted by the direction of the conversation, Karim made a mental note *never* to wake a distressed woman from sleep again. Suddenly the atmosphere in the tent seemed dangerously intimate and filled with shadows of the past that her words had inadvertently released. 'The Sultan's mother died when he was little more than a toddler. He was sent away by his stepmother.'

'Oh. That's terrible,' she breathed softly. 'Then it's no wonder that he isn't interested in emotional relationships, is it? He's probably had no experience of love.'

'I thought you didn't believe in love.'

'I didn't say that.' She smothered a yawn and her eyes drifted shut, her thick, dark lashes forming two perfect crescents on her pale cheeks. 'I said that *this* marriage isn't about love. That doesn't mean I don't think love exists. Actually, I do believe that love exists. For the lucky few. It's finding it that's the problem.'

Deciding that the conversation had progressed far beyond his comfort zone, Karim rose to his feet. 'You should rest.'

She didn't even answer and he realized that she was already asleep, her breathing even and peaceful, the tears on her cheeks now dry.

Karim stared down at her with exasperation and then strode back to his corner of the tent, aware that, while she'd drifted back into the welcome oblivion of sleep, he now had to deal with all the uncomfortable and unfamiliar emotions that their conversation had aroused.

And one thing he knew for sure—sleep would be a long time in coming.

Alexa woke to find herself alone in the tent.

Then she heard Karim's voice just outside and knew that he hadn't gone far. Not that she would have blamed him if he had. After being subjected to the torrent of her emotions the night before, a man like Karim must be stifling the urge to sprint fast in the opposite direction.

She closed her eyes, feeling washed out and weedy. It was a recurring nightmare and it always had the same effect on her.

But it was the first time that she'd shared the experience with anyone. And not just anyone, but a man who epitomized everything it meant to be tough and strong. *A man, to whom the mere concept of being frightened by something so intangible as a dream, must have been unfathomable.*

Alexa covered her face with her hands and gave a groan of embarrassment.

What must he have thought? Even in the depths of her distress, she'd sensed his discomfort. The only reason he'd remained seated on the bed was because she'd gripped his arm and begged him not to leave her.

But he hadn't left her, had he?

Despite being dramatically out of his comfort zone, he'd stayed by her side until she'd fallen asleep. And, because she knew that it hadn't been an easy thing for him to do, it somehow made the gesture all the more touching. He'd stayed, and that was what mattered. Clearly an upset woman wasn't his favourite challenge, but he'd remained by her side until she'd fallen asleep.

No one had ever done that for her before. Not one person.

Pondering on that thought, Alexa slid out of bed, dressed swiftly in her trousers and combat boots, twisted her long hair into a coil and secured it on top of her head. Dressed, she felt more in control. Or did she feel more in control because she'd shared her darkest moment with Karim?

For the first time in her life, she hadn't felt alone.

Feeling pathetically grateful towards him, Alexa left the tent and was immediately confronted by his powerful shoulders and lean, long legs. He was in conversation with several men from the camp, but he turned as he heard her emerge from the tent. Their eyes met and held.

He said nothing, and yet the moment felt intensely personal—a silent acknowledgement of a secret shared. Then he gave a brief nod and Alexa felt her insides tumble. Suddenly she felt ridiculously nervous and had absolutely no idea why.

'Good morning.'

He dismissed the man he was talking to with an abrupt wave of his hand. 'You are feeling all right?'

She dug her hands in her pockets. How was she supposed to reply to that? No, she wasn't feeling all right. Suddenly she felt as vulnerable as she'd felt when she was eight years old, clinging to the desperate hope that someone, somewhere would care for her and take the pain away if only she could find them.

But at least at the age of eight, she'd had childhood on her side as a decent excuse for such foolish fantasies.

What excuse was she using now?

Her eyes slid to Karim.

What was it about the dark and the dreams that had turned her into a child again? Why was she longing to trust him, when she'd long since discovered that the only person she could trust was herself?

Was it because, for the first time in sixteen years, she'd shared her past? She hadn't had to cope with it alone, and that had felt good. And, now that she'd experienced the warmth of human comfort, it no longer seemed easy to shut her emotions away. She wanted more, and the power of that need terrified her more than the nightmare itself.

She wanted to feel his touch again. She wanted to reach out and touch *him.*

But that wasn't allowed, was it? Although his gaze held hers, he held himself slightly apart—distant and unapproachable, as if warning her that the intimacy that they'd shared during the hours of darkness could not be extended into the daylight.

She was alone again.

A little masculine comfort in the darkness of the night had changed nothing, except perhaps to make everything seem just that little bit worse. Because that taste of human comfort had left her thirsty for so much more.

'I'm fine, Karim.' Too confused about her own feelings to hold his gaze a moment longer, she glanced away. 'I'm sorry about last night. Not your favourite scenario, I'm sure.'

He didn't reply, and she wished she'd had the sense not to raise the subject. Even though they weren't touching she could feel the tension in his powerful frame, and sensed that he had every intention of avoiding any reference to the conversation that they'd had in the dark recesses of the night. She sucked in a breath. 'Anyway, I just wanted to say thank you. You were— kind.' It seemed a completely inappropriate word for this man, who was the complete antithesis of the word *kind,* and perhaps he thought so, too, because his dark eyes narrowed slightly as he studied her face in brooding silence.

Finally he spoke. 'No apology is needed. You had a long and tiring day. Enough to trigger bad dreams in the most robust personality.'

'Yes.' There was no need to tell him that the dreams had nothing to do with the day they'd had and everything to do with her dark and tangled past. He didn't need to hear that. *He didn't want to hear it.* The loneliness of her situation rose up inside her and threatened to swallow her whole.

Karim took a step backwards, his tone cool and lacking in encouragement. 'We should leave. Eat something.' He waved a hand towards a rug that had been spread out in front of the tent. 'I'll meet you by the car when you're ready.'

Alexa watched him stride off and dropped onto her knees on the rug, not at all feeling like eating. She nibbled a few dates and some pita bread and took a few sips of water, before returning to the tent to pack her things. *Keep moving forward. Never look back.*

Karim was already loading the four-wheel drive. 'Are you ready?'

'Yes.' She handed him her small case and he stowed it in the back. 'How far are we going today?'

'We should reach the next oasis. It's much bigger than this place. More of a tourist resort. From there it is less than two days' drive to the Citadel. You should be in plenty of time for your wedding.'

'Wedding.' Alexa stared at him and he lifted an eyebrow.

'You'd forgotten your wedding?'

'Don't be ridiculous. Of course not.' But she had. Just briefly, her life had condensed itself down to this one single moment, and the only man in her mind was him. But now she was duly reminded that there was so much at stake. As if remembering that fact, she glanced once over her shoulder and then slid into the car, trying to ignore Karim in the seat next to her.

Strong, she thought wistfully. During the night it had been his strength that had comforted her. And she had to remind herself that there had been nothing personal in the gesture.

'So—tell me about this dune driving.' Trying to distract herself, she covered her eyes with her dark glasses and stared out of the window at the towering dunes that surrounded them. 'They look pretty high. You drive right to the top?'

'And down the other side and then back up to the top again.'

'Sounds fun. Can we do it?'

He glanced towards her, dark eyes incredulous. 'You want to drive to the top of a dune?'

'I thought we could both do with a little light relief.'

'I haven't done it since I was in the army.'

'So what's that supposed to mean—are you too old to have fun?' A devil inside her made her tease him. Or perhaps she was just overcompensating for the misery she felt. 'Or have you lost your nerve since then, Karim?'

'It is *your* nerve that concerns me. You may be a rebel, but I don't think you're brave.'

Aware that he was referring to the tears she'd shed the night before, she drew in a deep breath. 'My nerve is intact. I thought you wanted to show me the desert. So take me to the top of a dune and show me your desert, Karim.'

For a moment she thought he was going to refuse. Then he turned towards her, his dark eyes gleaming with challenge. 'Do you like roller coasters?'

Alexa sensed a change in him. Suddenly he seemed lighter—*less intimidating*—and the tantalizing glimpse of this hidden part of him intrigued her. 'I've never been on a roller coaster. Try me.'

'You promise not to scream like a girl?' A faint smile tugged at the corners of his normally serious mouth, and that smile was so surprising that she felt her stomach flip.

'I promise not to scream like a girl. Go for it. Rediscover your reckless youth.'

'All right. Hold on.' Without giving her a chance to change her mind, he turned the wheel, flattened the accelerator and the vehicle shot straight to the top of the dune.

The sudden rush of speed made her wish she hadn't been quite so rash, and if she could have changed her mind in that split second then she would have done.

Why, oh, why, had she encouraged him to behave like an irresponsible teenager?

As they roared up the side of the steep dune she clutched her seat and cast a look at his profile—and saw not a teenager, but a man.

His eyes were fixed ahead in total concentration, his hands moving instinctively over the controls as he demanded the utmost from the vehicle. And his cool confidence soothed her anxiety and she found herself relaxing, and then gasping with amazement as they crested the dune and she saw more dunes stretching out ahead of them like an exotic, fiery labyrinth.

'Oh, it's beautiful,' she breathed. 'So beautiful. Like another world.'

For a moment they were poised on the top of that world, and

then Karim threw her a slow, wicked smile and hit the accelerator with his foot. The vehicle plunged nose-first down the vertiginous drop on the other side, forcing Alexa to throw out a hand and steady herself against the dashboard.

It was so thrillingly terrifying that at first she couldn't catch her breath. Resisting the temptation to cover her eyes, she braced herself for the moment when the vehicle would topple over and land upside down at the foot of the dune, but it didn't happen. Instead they descended the dune in a smooth rush, Karim handling the wheel so skilfully that Alexa laughed with exhilaration.

They reached the bottom and he jerked on the handbrake.

She gulped in some much-needed air and then turned to look at him, unsure as to exactly what was responsible for her churning stomach: terror or the impact of the devastating smile he'd given her. 'Is this what they teach you in the army?'

'Desert survival.' Still smiling, he released the handbrake and drove back towards the road. 'You're a very surprising woman, do you know that?'

'Because I didn't scream like a girl? I didn't have the breath to scream.'

'Because you're not afraid of any of the things I would expect you to be afraid of. You shrug off the heat, you stroke a snake and you laugh at dune driving—but you hate locked doors, cry in your sleep and you run from a man who has no reason to chase you.'

Her smile faltered. 'Well, fear is a funny thing, isn't it? It's different things for different people.' Dark clouds swirled around her brain like a malevolent stalker ready to snuff out her brief flirtation with happiness. 'Can I have a go behind the wheel?'

'You *have* to be joking.'

His reaction made her laugh. 'So is this *your* fear, Karim? A woman behind the wheel?'

'Driving in the desert is very different to driving on tarmac. The sand is constantly shifting. It isn't as easy as it looks.'

'It doesn't look easy at all. But it looks fun. That's why I want to try it.' Alexa couldn't remember a time when she'd laughed like that, and suddenly she was desperate to recapture the moment. 'Can I?'

'You forget that I've already experienced your driving once. Even without the presence of a sand dune, it was scary.'

'That's not fair. I was afraid we were being followed.'

'You drove like a madwoman,' Karim muttered, adjusting several controls on the dashboard and steering the vehicle back onto the sandy road that cut between the undulating dunes. 'If that is how you drive, then it is no wonder that you have had accidents.'

The feeling of happiness left her as abruptly as it had arrived. 'My accidents had absolutely nothing to do with my driving.'

'You are saying that the tree jumped out and banged into your car?'

'No. I—' *Oh what was the point?* His job was simply to escort her safely to the Citadel, not provide her with emotional support. She didn't need emotional support. 'Accidents happen, Karim.'

He watched her for a moment, his gaze disturbingly acute. '*Not* when I am your bodyguard.' He sounded so confident that for a moment she wanted to believe him. It would have been so tempting to just relax and let someone else take the pressure for a change.

But she knew she couldn't do that.

An unexpected moment of lighthearted fun didn't change the facts. Her life was in danger, and she wouldn't be safe until they were inside the high stone-walls of the Citadel.

CHAPTER SEVEN

THEY arrived at the oasis as dusk was falling.

Alexa watched as Karim avoided the busy tourist hub and drove the vehicle to an elaborately tented area slightly set apart. 'They call this the Royal Suite. It has been set aside for our use. It's more private than the other accommodation.'

'I wish we didn't have to stop.'

'Even I cannot drive for days without rest,' he said dryly. 'You need to relax and leave the worrying to me.'

'But you're not worrying.'

'A worry is merely a problem which hasn't been solved.' He undid her seat belt, and there was a sardonic gleam in his eyes. 'If I see a problem, I solve it.'

Her heart banged against her chest. 'What if you don't see the problem before it hits you?'

'Then the reaction must be all the quicker.'

Leaning her head back against the seat of the car, she closed her eyes. Despite the sleep she'd managed to snatch, she felt mentally and physically exhausted, the strain of the past few weeks building to a crescendo. 'I'm so tired.'

'Hopefully you will sleep better tonight.'

'Yes.' Alexa turned to look at him. 'Thank you. I know I said I didn't want a bodyguard, but I never would have managed this journey without you. I can see that now.' She sensed his immediate withdrawal.

'You are my responsibility.'

In other words he was just doing the job he was being paid to do, and he didn't want her to forget that. Unreasonably disappointed by his reaction, she climbed down from the vehicle and followed him into the tent.

'Well, I envy your stamina. I don't think I have the energy to eat. I'll just go straight to bed, and—' She broke off with a gasp of shock as she walked into the tent and saw the bed. 'Oh my goodness! It's like something out of an Arabian fantasy.'

'Indeed.' Karim opened a bottle of water and handed her a drink. 'The tourists like it. It is the honeymoon suite, I believe.'

Alexa stared at the huge bed draped in jewel-coloured silk and velvet cushions, and felt the colour heat her cheeks. Arabian antiques and elaborate rugs gave the tent a warm, intimate feel. It was clearly a place for lovers. 'Won't we be conspicuous staying here?'

'No one will be looking for you in the honeymoon suite. You're not married yet.'

The *yet* hung between them, and she gazed at him for a moment, noting the sudden tension in his broad shoulders.

It was ridiculous, she thought frantically, to be so sexually aware of a man when she was about to marry another. She had to stop thinking about Karim in that way. Just because he'd been kind, didn't mean that he was thinking…

'We should eat.' His voice sounded unnaturally harsh, and the fact that he turned away from her made her wonder if he'd somehow sensed the way she was feeling.

Was he shocked? Embarrassed? Probably, because she certainly was.

'I'm not really hungry.'

'Sit down, Alexa.' He sounded tired, and he rubbed the tips

of his bronzed fingers over his forehead as if to relieve the tension. 'You must eat. We have almost two days of travel ahead of us, and you ate virtually nothing today.'

'All right. Just something small.'

She wasn't aware that he'd communicated with anyone, and yet moments later several staff entered the tent, bearing a selection of dishes which they placed on the rug. Once they were alone again, Alexa knelt down. 'So this place is actually a hotel?'

'Zangrar is proving a surprisingly popular tourist destination.' Karim picked up a dish and transferred several delicacies to her plate. 'These desert encampments appeal to the romantic nature of tourists. They have a chance to swim, go dune driving, ride a camel and spend a night in the desert under the stars.'

'Tourism was the Sultan's idea?'

'He has driven much of the commercial development, yes. It is important to look forward to the time when our natural resources run out.'

'It's wonderful that he cares so much about the future of Zangrar.' Alexa stared at the food on her plate without touching it. 'My father was the same. He was passionate about Rovina—' She stopped suddenly, horrified with herself. Why was she talking about her father?

'His death must have been a great loss to the country.'

'I miss him every day.' Her hand shook, and Karim reached out and gently removed the plate that she was holding.

'Much of the security of childhood comes from parental love. You were deprived of that.' His astute observation surprised her.

'Yes, it was hard.'

'At least you had your uncle to care for you.'

Alexa felt herself hovering on the brink of unfamiliar territory. This was the point where she should tell him the truth. She *wanted* to tell him the truth. But trusting anyone was so alien that she just couldn't persuade her mouth to form the words. She just couldn't take that final plunge. So she stayed silent, and was just about to change the subject altogether when she heard the sound of a vehicle outside.

She turned her head swiftly towards the doorway of the tent. 'Did you hear something?'

'A car. Probably late arrivals.'

But her sense of danger was so finely tuned that she just *knew*, and she stood up so quickly that she tipped several of the dishes onto the floor. 'They've found us.'

Karim's eyes narrowed, but he rose to his feet. 'They will simply be tourists. Wait here. I will investigate.'

'No!' Forcing herself to think clearly, she grabbed his arm. 'Don't do that. Is there another exit? We need to get out of here before they find us.'

'Calm down.' Clearly believing that her reaction was wildly exaggerated, he gently removed his arm from her grip and strolled out of the tent.

Alexa didn't waste a moment in contemplation.

Her hands and knees shaking, she stuffed her hair under a hat and grabbed her knife. Hoping that the Sultan would agree to pay for the damage, she cut a hole in the back of the opulent tent and slipped out into the night.

She wasn't waiting to see who the visitors were. She already knew.

And she ran. As quickly as she could in unfamiliar terrain she ran, past a swimming pool, between the sloping palm-trees and out towards the desert. She didn't know where she was going, but she hoped she'd be able to find somewhere to hide. Her heart was pounding, her mouth was dry and she stumbled twice as she ran in the darkness.

There were shouts from beyond the tents and then an explosion of gunfire behind her, and Alexa froze. She'd left Karim to handle them alone.

She looked over her shoulder, torn by indecision. He hadn't believed her and that wasn't all his fault. She hadn't told him everything, had she? And now, because of her, he was in danger.

Cursing herself for not forcing him to leave with her, she turned back towards the tents, but then she heard the roar of a car engine and headlights came towards her.

Her heart pounded and a feeling of helpless despair swamped her.

They'd found her. And out here, trapped in unfamiliar terrain, she could do little to defend herself.

It was all over.

Unable to run, she stood staring at those headlights—*stood waiting to die.*

'Alexa! Move!' Karim's harsh tone penetrated her haze of fear, but she was shaking so much she couldn't do anything. He opened the door, jumped down from the vehicle and swung her bodily into his arms. 'Now is *not* the time to stand still.' Behaving as if she weighed nothing, he virtually threw her into the passenger seat, and was back behind the wheel and stamping hard on the accelerator before she'd even had time to catch her breath.

'Do your seat belt up,' he bit out sharply. 'In the dark I can't be sure I'll avoid the holes in the ground.'

Her hands shaking, she did as she instructed and then gasped as she saw the stain spreading on his sleeve. 'You're hurt.'

'It's just a scratch.'

'It's *all* my fault. I shouldn't have let you come with me—'

'Are they behind us?'

Alexa glanced over her shoulder and saw lights. 'Yes. They're following.'

'Then we go where they won't be able to follow.' His tone grim, Karim spun the wheel and took the vehicle off-road.

Realising his intention, she clutched at her seat and looked at him in disbelief. 'You're planning to go dune driving in the dark?'

'It will make it harder for them to follow. There is an old Bedouin camel-trail not far from here. If we can make it to there, then we will be safe.' He took the vehicle up the side of the dune in much the same way as he had done that morning, only this time there was no laughter, and she was horribly aware of the stain darkening the fabric of his shirt.

'I need to stop the bleeding. Does this car have a first-aid kit?'

'Under the seat. Leave it. They're still behind us.' As they reached the top of the dune, he glanced in the mirror and gave a faint smile of triumph. 'But not any more. They didn't tackle it at the right angle and they have rolled to the bottom. Let's move.'

'Your arm—'

'Hold on.' He took the vehicle down the other side, driving with more care than he had during daylight hours. 'Tell me who they are. *Who are those people?*'

'I don't know. Someone working for my uncle. It's always someone different. To be on the safe side, I just suspect everyone.'

Karim muttered something in his own language, and then switched back to English. 'Are you telling me that he employs different people to kill you?'

'I *did* tell you that my life was under threat, but you didn't believe me.'

'Reasons might have helped.'

'Never mind that now. Oh, God, there's blood everywhere.' She dug around under the seat, found the first-aid kit and flipped it open. 'You're going to have to stop so that I can look at your arm, Karim.'

He ignored her. 'Talk to me, Alexa! *Why* would your uncle want you dead?'

'It's complicated, and you need to concentrate on driving.'

Rummaging through the first-aid kit, she pulled out a bandage. 'Is the bullet in the wound?'

'No. I've already told you, it's just a scratch. *Answer my question.* What are we dealing with here?'

'Cain and Abel,' she muttered, and he glanced at her sharply.

'Jealousy between brothers? That is what this is about?'

Alexa ripped the packaging from the bandage. 'His brother—my father—is dead. I'm the last remaining obstacle between him and the throne of Rovina.'

'He already rules Rovina.'

'As Regent. He wants to rule in his own right. He's always wanted that. If I reach my twenty-fifth birthday, then I take over as ruler. He isn't going to let that happen.' She steadied herself as the vehicle plunged and bounced on the uneven ground. 'You need to stop so that I can see what I'm doing.'

'We're not stopping until I decide that it's safe.'

'Then I'll just have to bandage it over your clothes. I'm sorry you were hurt because of me.'

He glanced towards her, his eyes gleaming dark and dangerous in the dim light of the car. 'I'm sorry I didn't believe you when you said that you were in danger. When it is safe, we will stop and you will start talking. And this time I'll be listening hard.'

Her hands shook as she bandaged his arm. 'We won't be safe until we reach the Citadel.'

'We will. The desert is a very unforgiving place for those without knowledge. This is an old Bedouin route. If we drive along here, we will reach the caves and we can rest there.' Karim reached out a hand, punched a number into a satellite phone and then proceeded to speak rapidly in a language that she didn't understand. When he finally broke the connection, she looked at him expectantly.

'What was that about?'

'I have asked for a security team to pick up those men and

question them.' His expression was grim as he gripped the wheel with his hand and drove hard and fast through the desert. 'There may be others.'

The caves formed a dark, forbidding labyrinth at the base of the huge sandstone-cliffs. Alexa leaned forward, peering through the darkness. 'We're going in there?'

'Yes.' Karim parked the vehicle out of sight of the road and winced as he reached for a torch and some blankets. 'No one will look for us here.'

Alexa felt her stomach lurch at the thought of all that dark, confined space, but said nothing. She knew that they needed to get out of sight, and she was worried about Karim's arm. 'Let's go, then.'

She followed him into the entrance of the caves. 'Shall we just stop here?' Her voice echoed and he flashed the torch towards the back of the cave where the rocks narrowed.

'Through there is a smaller chamber. We'll spend the night there. It will be warmer.'

And darker and more closed in. Alexa stood for a moment, finding it impossible to make her feet move. Then she remembered that they were in this situation because of her, and forced herself to follow him through the narrow gap, reminding herself that she wasn't locked in.

There was a way out.

Karim checked that the ground was dry and then dropped the blankets. 'Sit down.'

'*You* sit down. I need to look at your arm.' She undid the emergency dressing she'd applied and waited while he pulled off his shirt. Blood oozed from the wound, and she cursed softly and pressed down hard, staunching the flow. 'It's bleeding a lot. I'll clean it and dress it, but I suspect that it could have done with some stitches.'

'So blood is yet another thing that doesn't frighten you?'

'Don't be ridiculous. Can you shine the torch on this so that I can see what I'm doing?' Removing what she needed from the first-aid kit, Alexa swabbed the wound and took a closer look. 'You're right. The bullet just grazed the skin. I'll clean it, but you probably need some antibiotics.'

'And how can a princess, who supposedly isn't interested in anything more than fast cars and high heels, be so adept at first aid?' He watched as she carefully applied a sterile dressing to his arm and bound it firmly.

'I've spent a lot of time working at the local hospital. William hasn't invested any money in healthcare since he became Regent. The hospitals are struggling—no money, no staff. Morale is rock bottom. I help out when I can.'

'You work in the hospital?'

'As a volunteer.' Alexa closed the first-aid kit. 'I'm not trained, or anything. I would have loved to have been a doctor, but there was never any chance of that.'

He studied her for a moment, his expression forbidding. 'Sit down, Alexandra. It's time we talked about your uncle.'

Alexa sat down on the rug and tried not to think about the darkness. *They weren't closed in,* she reminded herself. 'I'm really sorry I got you into all this. I knew it was a mistake to take you with me.'

'I didn't give you a choice in the matter.' He sat down next to her. 'But clearly, I should have listened to you more carefully. I'm listening now, Alexa. Start talking.' The silence of the cave closed around them like a protective cocoon.

'I wouldn't know where to start.'

'Start with why you're marrying the Sultan.' He shone the torch towards her so that he could see her face. 'It doesn't have anything to do with the money or the status, does it?'

'I'm marrying the Sultan because it's my best chance of staying alive. You keep telling me that he's going to lock me behind the walls of the Citadel, and that's what I'm hoping for,' Alexa said softly. 'I want to reach my twenty-fifth birthday. I want to rule Rovina. Since my uncle took over, I've watched the country slowly crumble. He has diverted money away from the things that matter, like healthcare and education, and instead spends it on things that benefit only him. Like refurbishing the palace, and adding another priceless stallion to his stud farm. My uncle has stripped Rovina bare over the sixteen years since my father died.'

'So you're marrying the Sultan to escape?'

'In the short term, yes. In the longer term…' She hesitated and then gave a shrug. 'The Sultan is a powerful man, and I know he's turned Zangrar around in the past few years. If anyone can help me solve Rovina's problems, then it's him. His father and my father were friends. I just hope that's enough to persuade him to help.'

'Your uncle intends to prevent you from becoming Queen? This is the reason you believe he has tried to have you killed?'

It felt completely alien to confide in someone, and she sat for a moment, trying to find the words.

'I know it, Karim.' It was easier to talk in the semi-darkness. 'It started off as a campaign to discredit me with the public. He thought that if he made me look bad enough then no one would want me as ruler. My wild image was orchestrated by him. Starting with those awful photographs of me topless.'

'The photographs were fake?'

'No.' Alexa curled her legs under her. 'They were real. It was the first and last time in my life that I allowed myself to trust another person. Let's just say that he was an actor, and he was good at his job. I was so lonely, and to have someone pay me attention…' She gave a short laugh. 'Not that that is an excuse for being stupid and gullible, I know.'

'You were manipulated?'

'My uncle paid him to be caught in a compromising situation

with me. They both did very well out of it. The actor's career took off, and the photographs were published again and again all over the world as an example of how I'd gone off the rails. Anyway, although the public was shocked, they still supported me. Perhaps they were tolerant because I'd lost my whole family. I don't know. Maybe they didn't like William. By then they could see that he had no commitment towards Rovina as a country. He just used his position to enhance his own lifestyle. Either way, he obviously decided he had to work a little harder. And that was when I suddenly became so accident prone.'

'Your car accidents—'

'On both occasions, someone tampered with the brakes.'

The breath hissed through his teeth. 'You are *sure?*'

'Yes. I was just angry that I let it happen twice. After that, I stopped driving, or I borrowed cars at short notice.'

'You didn't try to escape? Drive over the border?'

'I was watched all the time. I was lucky if I managed to get beyond the palace walls. When I was little he locked me in.'

Karim muttered something under his breath. 'And that is why you hate locked doors?'

'Yes. Silly, really. It's just a psychological thing. I like to know that I can get out if I want to. He only did it when I was little. As I grew older I was a little harder to contain. He wanted me dead, but if he couldn't have that then he wanted me where he could see me. It became a game of cat and mouse. I'd disguise myself and find different ways of slipping out.'

'He always caught you?'

'He has supporters. Greedy people, like him, who are interested in themselves and not Rovina.'

'The speedboat accident?'

'*Not* an accident.'

With a driven sigh, Karim ran a hand over the back of his neck. 'The time you were removed unconscious from a nightclub?'

'I was drugged. I wasn't even in the nightclub at the time. They staged the photographs, but by then most people just assumed I'd gone off the rails because of my parents' death. "The rebel princess" they called me.' She laughed. 'I sort of grew into the role. I had to, in order to stay alive.'

'You had no one to protect you?'

'You have to remember that most people just thought what you thought—that I was a bit of a wild child. No one really understood what my uncle was capable of.' Alexa felt a lump in her throat. 'Every time I allowed myself to trust someone, it proved to be a mistake, so I stopped trusting. It was safer for everyone if I just lived my life alone.'

'*Why* did you not tell me any of this before now?' He sounded angry and she couldn't blame him for that.

He'd just been shot because of her.

'I did try telling you my uncle was following us.'

'But you didn't give me details, did you?' Karim stretched out a hand and lifted her chin so that she was forced to look at him. 'You omitted all the facts that would have given your story credibility.'

'I *wanted* to tell you,' Alexa murmured, 'and several times I almost did. But you have to understand that in my situation *not* talking is the only thing that keeps you alive. For the past sixteen years, I haven't been able to trust anyone. I disciplined myself to stay silent, and I can't suddenly change that.'

Karim let his hand drop, clearly struggling to absorb the enormity of what she was telling him. 'If William is willing to go to those lengths to keep the throne for himself, then there must have been times when you've wondered whether he could have played a part in your father's death.'

She stared into the semi-darkness. 'He had my parents killed.' Somehow the eerie silence of the cave made her statement all the more dramatic.

Then she heard him draw breath. 'I can see how it would be easy for you to believe that, given the way he has treated you, but—'

'I was there.' She turned her head to look at him and in the dim torchlight his arrogant profile looked hard and forbidding. 'I saw it happen.'

'You *witnessed* the explosion that killed your parents?'

'It was meant to kill me, too. We'd been staying at our country house for the weekend. Just as we were about to leave I remembered that I'd forgotten my doll.' Her heart-rate trebled, and suddenly her palms felt sweaty and her mouth was dry. This wasn't something she talked about. She *never* talked about it. 'I went back to the house and the car exploded.'

Another long silence followed her shaky declaration, and suddenly Alexa found herself just longing for him to comfort her, as he had during her nightmare, but he sat still as if her words had somehow rendered him immobile.

Finally he spoke. 'You are sure your uncle was involved?'

'Well, I had no way of proving it, of course—but, yes, I'm sure. I saw him immediately after the explosion.' She gave a shiver. 'I'll never forget the look on his face, Karim. He wasn't sad or even shocked. The only time he looked shocked was when they found me and brought me to him. And even though I was so young I just *knew* that he'd intended for me to die, too.'

'You were eight years old.'

'He wanted my whole family dead. He hated my father. Hated him for everything he had. And I was terrified,' Alexa confessed. 'To begin with I tried to talk to people, but they just thought I was hysterical. I'd witnessed my parents' death, after all. Then someone I confided in just disappeared. Although I was young, I realized that talking to anyone was dangerous.'

'I can't believe he intended to harm you. You were a child.'

'But a dangerous child.' Alexa's chin lifted. 'My father's child. Rovina is in my blood, and my uncle knew it.'

'You were impossibly young to find yourself so alone.' Karim shook his head in disbelief. 'I'm surprised it didn't break you.'

Alexa was silent for a moment, remembering how terrified and lonely she'd been. 'There were days when I was desperate for someone to just hold me and tell me that everything was going to be all right.'

There was a long silence, and the light flickered as Karim put the torch down on the rug. Then he reached out and lifted her, pulling her onto his lap and curving his arms around her. '*I* am holding you, *habibati*,' he breathed softly, stroking her hair away from her face and guiding her head onto his shoulder with his hand. 'And everything *is* going to be all right, I promise you that. Your uncle will not come near you again. You have my word on it.'

'I—what if the Sultan doesn't believe me?'

Karim was silent for a moment. 'He *will* believe you, I can assure you of that.'

He seemed so convinced that Alexa felt herself slowly relax, and it felt so good to be held that for a moment she just lay there, enjoying the rare indulgence of letting someone else take control. 'It feels funny talking about it. I keep waiting for you to stand up and confess that you're not who you say you are. That you're actually working for my uncle.'

His arms tightened. 'I can understand that you have been extremely traumatized by your experience, but I promise you that you *can* trust me.'

Alexa closed her eyes and snuggled closer and his warm, masculine scent made her stomach quiver. 'Have you any idea how it feels to have someone on your side after a lifetime of being alone?' For the first time in as long as she could remember, she felt safe. 'How is your arm?'

'Barely hurting.'

She smiled in the darkness. 'You're lying.'

'Tell me about your dream, Alexa.'

Her smile faded. 'I don't want to talk about that.'

'Try.' He smoothed a hand gently over her hair, and shifted slightly so that he held her even closer. 'For me, *habibati*.'

'After they were killed, I suppose I was in shock. I just wanted to wind the clock back. I wished I'd made my parents go back for the doll while I stayed in the car. I wished something had happened to stop us leaving at that exact moment.' Alexa paused, hollowed out by sadness. 'That's the dream I have. Time and time again I race towards the car to warn them, but I'm too late. I'm always too late.'

'I cannot *believe* I didn't discover any of this when I was in Rovina.'

'You weren't looking.'

'Why was no one able to protect you?'

'My uncle is very, very clever and he had many supporters. And, don't forget, he didn't exactly present me in a good light. By the time he'd finished, most people were wondering how a princess who couldn't even drive her car straight could possibly run a country. I knew I had to get away if I was ever going to survive. I pinned all my hopes on this marriage to the Sultan. It was my only escape route.'

'And you're taking it.'

'Do you blame me?' She lifted her head and saw Karim's eyes glitter in the torchlight.

'No,' he said harshly. 'After everything you've told me, I do not blame you.'

'You saved my life tonight.' Unable to help herself, she reached out a hand and touched his face, feeling the roughness of his jaw beneath her fingers. 'I just panicked and ran.'

'You have no reason to thank me.' Suddenly he seemed tense. 'It is my job to protect you. And I *will* protect you, Alexa. You can be sure of that.'

His job. Alexa felt despair and disappointment mingle, and let her hand drop. What had she expected? Comfort wasn't part of his job description. 'I don't know what the Sultan told you when he gave you this mission, but I don't suppose the brief included getting yourself shot. It was hard for me to trust you, but I'm glad I did. You're the first person I've met who hasn't betrayed that trust. Thank you.'

'You are safe, and that is what matters.'

She knew she ought to move. He'd taken her in his arms to give her comfort, nothing more. But she couldn't bring herself to move away from his warmth and strength. *In a minute,* she promised herself, her eyes sliding nervously around the shadows of the cave. 'Do you think they'll find us?'

'No. You should get some sleep.'

'I don't want to sleep.'

'Because of the nightmares? I suspect you only have the dream when you are wound up and tense.'

Sensing that he was about to tip her off his lap, she reached up and wound her arms round his neck. 'Can we stay like this? Just for a minute?'

His muscles were rock hard and rigid beneath her quivering body. 'Alexa—'

'Please, Karim?' She whispered the words against the smooth, warm skin of his neck and felt his throat move.

'Alexa, we can't—'

'I just want you to hug me, that's all. Do you know how long it is since anyone hugged me? I was eight years old, and I barely remember it.'

He didn't answer for a moment, and then shifted his body and lay down, taking her with him. 'I will hold you and you will sleep.'

He made it sound like an order, and she gave a contented smile because only Karim would think of ordering a person to sleep.

But at least he was still holding her.

'Do you always try and control everything that goes on around you?'

'Always.'

She felt his muscles flex as he reached for a blanket and covered them both. 'Sleep, Alexa.'

The darkness suddenly seemed intimate and welcoming, and she wondered why she'd ever been afraid of the caves.

But the moment his arms came round her, and she felt his hard, athletic body brushing intimately against hers, she knew that there was no hope of sleep.

Why did she feel like this?

It was just because she'd confided in him, she told herself, because he'd saved her and listened and offered sympathy. These feelings inside her were there simply because, for the first time in her lonely life, she'd dared to share her problems with another person.

It was just gratitude.

But the slow, dangerous curl of warmth low in her pelvis didn't feel anything like gratitude, and she shifted slightly to ease the electric buzz in her body.

'*Stop moving.*' Karim sounded equally tense, and she was just about to pull away from him when he gave a low groan, rolled her on her back and brought his mouth down hard on hers, his kiss hungry and urgent. His hand slid into her hair and cupped the back of her head, holding her firmly while his mouth seduced hers with shocking expertise, demanding a response from her.

And she gave freely. It didn't enter her head to push him away, because why would she want to stop something that felt so completely right?

He kissed in exactly the way she remembered, and her response was as wild and uncontrolled as it had been before. Excitement exploded through her, and she dug her fingers into his hard, strong shoulders, holding on as he drove her wild. She felt helpless and out of control, and when she felt his hand slide over her taut nipple she cried out against his mouth and arched in urgent invitation.

He knew exactly where to touch her—how to touch her—to derive the maximum response from her, and Alexa shifted against the blanket in an attempt to relieve the maddening ache between her legs. And he must have known what he was doing to her, because his hand moved lower still, and she felt the gentle brush of his fingers touching her intimately. And that almost agonizing intimacy jerked her out of her stupor.

She couldn't do this, could she?

No matter how right it felt, it was still wrong.

Karim couldn't be part of her future.

'No.' Never had it felt so hard to say that word, and her fingers closed over the hard muscle of his arm as if she knew that she was never going to have the will-power to do this by words alone. 'No. We have to stop. We have to stop now.' Before she was unable to stop. And she was already so close to that point.

He broke the kiss briefly, but only to look deep into her eyes, and the intensity of that look and the warmth of his breath was as seductive as the touch of his mouth. 'You want to stop?'

No. No, she didn't. *But she had to.* 'I don't want this.'

'That's a lie.' Dismissing her rejection with his usual confidence, his mouth claimed hers again and she felt herself descending into a thick, sensual fog that threatened to consume her.

'No, Karim.' Denying her own sensuality, she dragged her mouth away from his and this time she turned her head. 'You have to stop! It's not right. I'm marrying the Sultan. We shouldn't be doing this.'

'You want me.' His arrogant statement left no room for denial, and she didn't even bother trying.

'Yes. But that doesn't change anything.' Faced with the most impossible decision, she shifted away from him slightly, wishing that she knew how to calm the reaction of her body. 'I— This should never have happened. I can't be with you, Karim. I'm not the sort of woman who can sleep with one man and then marry another. It wouldn't be right.'

She was still a virgin and that, at least, she could give to the Sultan.

He was silent for a moment, his powerful body tense over hers, his breathing harsh and laboured as he struggled to exercise control. Then he rolled away from her and she caught a glimpse of his face. The expression in his eyes was fierce and his jaw was tense. And then he flicked off the torch and they were plunged into darkness.

Now what?

Alexa started miserably into the inky blackness, not knowing what to do or say. She wanted to reach out and touch him, but knew that she had no right to do that, but it was suddenly vitally important that he knew just how much he meant to her.

'You're the first person in sixteen years I've been able to trust,' she said softly, the darkness giving her the courage to say things she never would have been able to say in daylight. 'I didn't dare trust anyone else or let them close, because they always had a reason for being with me and that reason was always something to my disadvantage. It's been so different with you. You insisted on protecting me even though I didn't want your protection. Even though we've only spent a short time together, I feel I really know you. You're the first friend I've ever had. And, if things were different, you would have been my first lover.'

'Enough, Alexa.' His voice was raw, or perhaps the darkness simply exaggerated the emotions. 'Get some rest now.'

The disappointment lay inside her like a heavy weight that couldn't be shifted.

She sat still for a moment, trying to reason with herself. What had she expected—a declaration of love? No, not that. But *something* that indicated that her feelings hadn't been entirely one sided, because she knew that they hadn't been. *He cared for her; she knew he did.* And yet he hadn't once expressed those feelings.

But was that so surprising?

She was about to become the Sultan's wife.

Perhaps he believed that the only way he was going to be able to watch her marry another man was if he denied those feelings.

But she wished, even if it was just for this one night, that he'd told her how he felt. It would have made everything easier, somehow, even though it wouldn't have changed a thing.

She was on her way to marry the Sultan.

But for the first time ever, that marriage felt less like a sanctuary and more like a sacrifice.

Battling with unfulfilled sexual desire, and a *serious* attack of conscience for the first time in his life, Karim lay still until the sound of her breathing indicated that she had fallen asleep.

Her words troubled him more than he would have thought possible.

What was it she had said—that he was the first person that hadn't betrayed her trust?

And yet that wasn't true, was it?

His role as her bodyguard had been secondary to the main purpose of his mission: *to persuade her not to marry the Sultan.*

But now that he had the facts he could see that Alexa's character had been grossly misrepresented. And, knowing the truth about her, he had no doubt that she would make the Sultan a perfectly good wife. She was clearly loyal, resourceful and resilient. And she was remarkably well-adjusted, considering the considerable hardship she'd suffered since the death of her family.

Ironically enough, perhaps the only blot on her copybook was her reaction to *him.* She was about to marry another man, and yet she'd been openly and unashamedly passionate.

But she *had* stopped, he reminded himself, shifting with frustration as he recalled just how much restraint that action had demanded of him. And the fact that she'd stopped had to be a point in her favour.

Knowing how passionate she was, he didn't for a moment believe that she was a virgin, but at least she'd had the decency not to indulge in a little hot desert sex with him, despite the powerful chemistry.

Karim thought for a moment, his eyes sliding to her sleeping form.

What reason was there for him to feel guilty? He had merely done what needed to be done. No blame attached to him for the fact that she'd been so grossly misrepresented by her uncle. It was clear that his mission was no longer necessary, and equally clear what should happen next.

There was really no reason for the Sultan not to marry her.

CHAPTER EIGHT

ALEXA woke to find light seeping into the cave.

She sat up, feeling tired and gritty eyed, having spent most of the night trying not to reach out and touch Karim. Part of her wished she hadn't stopped him. It would have been the first time in her life that she'd actually done something that *she* wanted.

But she couldn't be that selfish.

Her responsibility was to the Sultan and the people of Rovina. Now that a new life was in sight, she couldn't help but dream that a man as powerful as the Sultan might be able to help her transform her beloved homeland.

Shafts of daylight penetrated the cave, and now she could see where they had spent the night. And there was no sign of Karim.

Wondering where he was, she was about to call his name when she heard the unmistakable sound of a helicopter landing outside the cave.

Alexa was on her feet in an instant, her legs shaking and her mouth dry with fear.

They'd found her.

While she'd been lying in Karim's arms, feeling safe and protected for the first time in her life, they'd been tracking her.

And now she and Karim were trapped in the cave.

Shaking with panic, and cursing herself for her stupidity, she sprinted towards the entrance, but strong arms caught her and prevented her from running outside.

'It's all right. There is nothing to frighten you.' Karim's voice was rough. 'I called the helicopter. In the circumstances, I thought it best if we get you away from here as fast as possible before your uncle discovers that he has failed and tries again.'

It took a moment for his words to sink in, and then the breath left her in a sigh of relief. '*You* called the helicopter?'

'That's right.'

'So—I'm leaving? Are you coming, too?'

He hesitated, and for a moment his fingers tightened on her arms. Then he released her and took a step backwards. 'No. They will fly you directly to the Citadel. You will be safe there.'

'I don't want to go without you.' Alexa spoke without thinking and then turned away, embarrassed at having revealed so much. For so long she'd been used to hiding her feelings. She'd trusted no one—*relied on no one but herself*. But all that had changed during her two days in the desert with Karim.

Everything had changed last night.

For the first time in her life since her parents had been killed, someone had been there for her, protecting her and watching over her. For the first time in her life she'd really talked to someone, and someone had held her when she'd had the dream.

And now she had to say goodbye.

So why couldn't she move?

This was the moment she'd been dreaming of for so long. So why was it so impossibly hard to step into the helicopter?

Gratitude?

Alexa glanced at Karim's strong, handsome face. *No, it wasn't gratitude.*

Now that they were due to part, she knew that it was something so much more than that.

She knew that it was love.

The realization shocked her, and she made a little sound, confused and horrified. This was *not* what she wanted.

'Alexa—' He seemed tense, too, and when one of the soldiers approached them he lifted a hand in a silent command that made them stop in their tracks. 'It will be all right.'

How could it possibly be all right?

And then she realized that he was talking about her safety.

He didn't know that she was in love with him. Or maybe he did, and he was embarrassed. He guarded the Sultan, didn't he? Knowing that the Sultan's wife had feelings for him wasn't going to make his job easy.

She *had* to pull herself together. But she'd been deprived of these feelings for so long that it was almost impossible to give them up.

'Yes.' Allowing herself the luxury of one last look, her eyes lingered on the dark stubble that shadowed his hard jaw, and then lifted to his mouth—that same mouth that had kissed her senseless in the night. Would she be able to forget? *When the Sultan kissed her, would she think of Karim?*

Afraid that if she stood there a moment longer she'd make an even bigger fool of herself, Alexa turned and walked quickly towards the waiting helicopter, trying to ignore the pull that made her want to turn her head one more time.

Don't look back, she told herself. *Don't look back. You're not going to be that weak.*

She would marry the Sultan as she'd planned. She'd do it for Rovina and for her beloved father's memory, and she would hide her feelings for Karim because that was what had to be done.

What choice did she have?

Hands urged her aboard the helicopter and Alexa responded

passively, numbed by the strange feeling of loss that consumed her.

She was strapped into her seat, given ear protectors, and then the helicopter rose above the sand.

And the pull became impossible to resist.

All her resolutions exploded to nothing, and she turned her head to look, and through the mist of sand she saw him standing there, his legs planted firmly apart in a typically arrogant stance as he watched her departure.

He'd protected her, given her hope, taught her that love was possible, even for her.

She should be feeling happy and grateful.

So why did she feel as though she'd lost everything a second time?

Had Alexa not been so distracted by thoughts of Karim, she would have been excited by her first view of the Citadel of Zangrar. From the air it spread beneath them in majestic splendour, the walls of buff-coloured stone high and imposing. And inside the walls of the Citadel was the Sultan's palace with its high domes and graceful lines.

Her stomach churned, and suddenly she remembered all the things that Karim had told her about the Sultan.

He gave an order and it was done.

No one would dare argue with him.

The Sultan's expectations of her role would not extend beyond the bedroom.

As those words filled her head, Alexa was suddenly swamped with a feeling of cold dread.

It was all very well talking of duty and responsibility, but with reality this close she was suddenly terrified. What if the Sultan refused to help her?

What if she'd simply swapped one set of problems for another?

What if her new life was worse than the old?

And then she thought of what her uncle had done to her and to Rovina, and realized that nothing could be worse.

All the same, she was so subdued that she barely noticed that they'd landed until eight armed-guards surrounded her and then escorted her swiftly to the Sultan's private quarters within the palace.

Jittery with nerves, she glanced around her, waiting anxiously for the moment when the Sultan would appear. 'Will I meet His Excellency soon?'

'Not before the wedding, Your Highness.' An army of women had been assigned to look after her, and they bustled around her now, clucking over the dusty clothes that she'd worn in the desert and adding rose petals to steaming bath-water.

'I can take a bath by myself.' She wasn't used to being waited on, but no one took any notice of her wishes and soon she was lying in the luxuriously scented water, the warmth and fragrance driving the memories of the sand and the heat from her mind. But no amount of washing or massage removed the memory of Karim. It was as if he'd somehow left a mark of ownership on her. When she closed her eyes, she immediately felt his hands on her skin and his mouth on hers.

The memory triggered a stab of panic, and she sat up in the bath. She couldn't do it.

It wasn't the wedding, it was—the rest of it.

What had Karim said? *The Sultan had an extremely high sex-drive.*

Somehow, when he'd first said it, the words hadn't really registered in her brain. They just hadn't meant anything.

But now, after what she'd shared with Karim…

What if, when the time came, she just couldn't let another man touch her in that way?

Perhaps, if she could just meet him, she thought miserably,

and discover what sort of man he was. Would that make the whole situation less awful—or more awful?

Her brain magnifying the horrors of her position with each passing second, Alexa turned on impulse to the women who were preparing various massage oils. 'I'd like to talk to the Sultan.'

The women gasped with shock, as if she'd made an outrageous request.

'Unfortunately that will not be possible, Your Highness,' one of them muttered. 'It is bad luck for the Sultan to lay eyes on his bride before the wedding.'

Even more bad luck to lay eyes on her after it, Alexa thought gloomily, staring at the rose petals that floated on the surface of the water. What if he took one look at her and ran?

If it hadn't been for the duty she owed her country, she would have run herself.

'The wedding will take place tomorrow, Your Highness. After that you will have the Sultan's full attention.' The women exchanged knowing looks, and Alexa sighed with frustration.

So she wasn't even going to be given the chance to meet the Sultan before she married him.

Sinking back under the scented bath-water, she stared at the rose petals floating in the water and wondered whether there had ever been a more miserable bride.

This should have been a moment of triumph and relief.

She'd reached the Citadel safely. Nothing could stand between her and marriage to the Sultan.

But somewhere on the journey she'd given away her heart, and there seemed no hope of getting it back. Now she knew how love felt, marrying another man felt completely wrong.

The bath was followed by a long, luxurious massage with aromatic oils, and eventually Alexa was tucked up in a large, comfortable bed in a room with the floor area of a small house.

It was so different from the starkness and fear that had surrounded her life in Rovina that, had she not met Karim, she would have felt extremely relaxed and content with her situation.

But she *had* met Karim.

She'd fallen in love with him.

And that had changed the way she felt about everything.

She woke early.

The hot desert sun poured through the arched windows, illuminating the richness of the fabrics that draped the bed, and Alexa just lay for a moment, thinking.

Where was he and what was he doing right now?

Filled with an almost agonizing longing to see Karim, she turned her head and stared towards the window.

Was he somewhere close?

Was he back guarding the Sultan?

Was he thinking of her?

Alexa sat up in bed, realizing that it was her birthday.

Her twenty-fourth birthday.

And today she was going to marry the Sultan.

As if to remind her of that fact, there was a soft tap on the door and the room was suddenly filled with people eager to help her prepare for the wedding.

After that there was no more opportunity for quiet reflection, and the next few hours flashed by as women attended to her hair and make-up and made final adjustments to the fitting of her wedding dress.

Alexa stared down at herself, looking at the simplicity of the silk dress. What was it Karim had said—that a woman came to her husband in a simple dress, denoting honesty?

At the beginning of the journey she'd had no problem with that. She'd had every intention of being honest with him.

But now? How truthful was it to marry a man while loving another?

The nerves in her stomach stirred, and she hoped desperately that Karim would not be present at the wedding. What if he was? And what if she couldn't hide her feelings for him? Hadn't Karim told her that the Sultan was fiercely possessive? Just what would such a man do if he discovered that she was in love with someone else?

'Your Highness is very pale.' The girl in charge of her make-up snapped her fingers, and a woman stepped forward with a selection of jars and pots. She selected one and rubbed the colour vigorously into Alexa's ashen cheeks. 'You should not be nervous. You are incredibly beautiful. The Sultan will be pleased.'

The Sultan will be pleased.

That information didn't cheer Alexa in the least. In fact, she felt sicker than ever. Now that the moment of her marriage was approaching, she was beginning to wonder whether she'd be able to go through with it.

She'd waited for this moment for so long, and yet now it had finally arrived everything had changed. And she knew who was responsible for that change.

Karim.

Her feelings for him had exploded out of nowhere, but they were so powerful that the thought of being with another man seemed unnatural.

But a life with Karim wasn't an option, was it?

Her father had wanted her to marry the Sultan, and it was the right thing to do.

Alexa stood, silent and unresisting, as the team of women finished adjusting her make-up to their satisfaction, and then covered her head and shoulders with several sheer veils.

'The Sultan cannot look upon his bride until the vows have been exchanged,' one of them explained, and then she curtsied low. 'You are ready for His Excellency. If Your Highness would follow me.'

The floor had been liberally sprinkled with scented rose petals, and Alexa forced herself to put one foot in front of the other, her shoes moving silently over the flowery carpet.

She was led into a brightly lit courtyard, and realized with a start of surprise that the wedding was going to be held outside. A small group of people had gathered, waiting, and her eyes searched nervously for the Sultan.

One man stood out from the others. He wore robes and a traditional head covering and had his back to her, but she knew, even without an introduction, that he was the Sultan. It wasn't just the way that those around were deferring to him that revealed his identity, but the way he held himself, with authority and command.

Breathless with nerves, Alexa waited for him to turn and face her, but he stood still, and the women urged her forward.

'The Sultan cannot look upon his bride until the ceremony has taken place,' one of them muttered, guessing at the reason for her hesitancy.

Alexa's despair grew.

So not only was she going to marry a man she hadn't met, she wasn't even going to see him before the wedding.

At least there was no sign of Karim, so that was something to be grateful for. She wasn't going to have to make her vows with the man she loved looking on. She'd been spared that agony.

The ceremony began, and because Alexa didn't understand a word of what was being said they prompted her and she gave the responses that were required of her, in English, barely registering the deep, masculine tones of the man standing by her side. Once, she stole a glance at him, but his profile was hidden from view.

And then everyone in the courtyard fell to their knees and bowed, and she realized that the ceremony had ended.

She was married to the Sultan.

It was done.

Everyone discreetly retreated into the palace, and she was left standing in the sunny courtyard with the tall, broad-shouldered man who was now her husband.

Was he ever going to look at her?

Or was he so angry at being forced into this marriage that they were going to live their lives as enemies?

Unable to bear the tension a moment longer, she closed her eyes in an attempt to calm herself down. And then she heard him move towards her and felt his hands lifting her veils, one by one, exposing her face to his gaze.

Alexa kept her eyes closed, hardly able to breathe.

His father and her father had forced this marriage on him, hadn't they? And, because of her situation, she'd done nothing to prevent it.

This situation was all her fault.

'I presume you are not intending to go through the whole of our marriage with your eyes closed, Alexa?' Now that he spoke in English, his low, masculine drawl was shockingly familiar, and her eyes flew wide-open as she stared in disbelief at the man in front of her.

'Karim?' For a moment she could do nothing more than whisper his name. Happiness bloomed inside her, and then withered instantly as her brain acknowledged the truth of the situation. Despite the intense heat and blazing sun, she suddenly felt deathly cold. 'Oh, God—it was you—'

'That's right.' He made no excuses. There were no denials— no apology—and she shook her head, still trying to digest the enormity of the truth.

He wasn't…

She'd thought…

She'd *trusted* him.

'But you—I—I told you *so* much.' More than she'd ever told another human being. She'd opened her soul to this man, not re-alizing who he was. 'I was honest with you.'

'And that is a good thing, not a matter for either regret or apology.'

'It is to me! What you did wasn't *right*, Karim.' The cold, numb feeling was fading, and in its place was hurt, vulnerability and the beginnings of anger. 'You deceived me! I trusted you, and you deceived me! You pretended to be someone else.'

'The deception was necessary.' He stood in front of her, arrogant and unrepentant, showing not a flicker of the softness he'd occasionally displayed during the journey. 'Being the Sultan's wife is a position of great responsibility. Did you really think I would have given that honour to a woman with the reputation that you possessed?'

His words sank slowly into her stunned brain. 'You never intended me to marry you, did you? That was why you chose to escort me personally. You were trying to make me change my mind.' She stared at him, her breathing shallow as everything fell into place with horrible clarity. 'All those stories you told me about the Sultan…' Her mouth was so dry she was forced to lick her lips in order to speak. 'All those desert experiences—they were just to put me off. You wanted me to back out, didn't you? And, just to be sure that no one else messed it up, you'd do the job yourself, was that right?' *He hadn't had feelings for her.* It had all been a sham.

With a casual lift of his broad shoulders, Karim dismissed the question as irrelevant. 'I am satisfied that most of your reputation was fabricated by your uncle.'

Most? In the back of her mind she registered the word, but she was too busy deciphering the bigger picture to pay attention to detail. 'It wasn't supposed to be a test, Karim.'

'It is behind us.'

'*It isn't behind us!*' There were goosebumps on her arms, and she gave a shiver. 'I can't believe I could have been so foolish. Why didn't I notice anything before? That man in the desert camp that first night—the one who bowed—he didn't recognize *me*, did he? He recognized you. And when we were in the cave and you called for that helicopter—' She broke off and shook her head with disbelief. 'We arrived at the Citadel in a matter of hours. This whole thing about having to journey across the desert...'

Two dark streaks illuminated his incredible bone structure, and for the first time since the conversation had started he actually looked mildly discomforted. 'I admit that communications in Zangrar are not quite as backward as I perhaps led you to believe. But it was necessary for me to spend time with you.'

'To frighten me off marrying the Sultan.'

He inhaled sharply. 'I did *not* frighten you.'

'But you tried, Karim.' Her voice shook with outrage and pain. 'You tried really, really hard. All that talk about snakes and the dangers of the desert. The pictures you painted of the Sultan—yourself—'

'None of that was fabricated. I merely exposed you to the truth of the situation.'

'Except that you omitted to introduce yourself fully.' She couldn't believe she'd actually been so gullible, and suddenly she needed to know everything. 'Tell me the truth. How long would it have taken us to reach the Citadel from the airport?'

'Not long.'

'*How long?*'

'A short helicopter transfer.'

As the deeper implication of his words sank into her numb brain she shook her head in disbelief. 'There was no need for us to be in the desert. We exposed ourselves to unnecessary risk. *You* exposed me to risk!'

'At the time I was not aware that you were in danger. And I would have protected you. I *did* protect you.'

'That does not excuse what you did, Karim! You let me lean on you. I trusted you and you betrayed me.'

'How? When?' His handsome face was all hard lines and un-yielding strength. 'You reached out to me, Alexa. That night in the tent when you had the nightmare, you asked for comfort and I gave it. When you were attacked, you asked for my protection and I gave it. In what way did I betray your trust?'

'By not being honest about who you were.' She felt shattered, vulnerable and horribly exposed.

'If you had known my identity you would doubtless not have been so open, and we would therefore not now be married.'

'Yes, we would. There was never an option for you to stop the marriage.'

He gave a grim smile. 'Believe me, Alexa, I could have stopped it.'

Still bruised, she backed away from him. 'So why didn't you?' She sounded like a sulky child, and he studied her for a moment, his hard gaze lingering on her face.

'Because there was no longer a need. After more than two days in your company it was clear to me that you would make a perfectly reasonable wife. In some areas, more than reasonable.' Thick, dark lashes lowered fractionally and he regarded her with a lazy, slumberous expression in his dark eyes that ignited the dormant flame deep in her pelvis.

'Oh.' Trapped by the raw sexuality in his gaze, she was im-mediately transported back to the night they'd spent in the cave, and she felt her cheeks flush with embarrassment as she remembered the intimacies they'd shared. 'We nearly—we could have—'

'Yes.' His voice was deep and brushed across her sensitive nerve-endings. 'We could have. We almost did. The fact that you held back because of your impending marriage was very much to your credit. It is because of that restraint that you are standing here now.'

Alexa stared at him with horror. 'Was it a *test?* That night in the cave—were you testing me?'

'No. The passion between us was genuine, and I don't blame you for the way you reacted. You have obviously had an extremely difficult life. It was natural that you would turn to someone if support was offered.'

Was that all he thought it was—*hero worship with chemistry thrown in?*

She knew so much better.

Over the years there had been plenty of people who had offered support and she'd trusted none of them. Karim had been different.

Which just showed that, despite her experience, her judgement was still fallible.

How did she feel about him now?

She'd thought that she loved Karim, only to discover that the man she loved didn't exist.

Confused and miserable, she took another step away from him. 'I can't forgive you for what you did.'

'I have not asked for your forgiveness. What is there to forgive? You wanted to marry the Sultan and you have married the Sultan. You have achieved your objective.' His tone was cool and unemotional. 'Be grateful.'

Grateful?

At that precise moment the only thing she felt grateful for was the fact that she hadn't revealed the extent of her feelings for him. At least she'd been spared that humiliation. He seemed to think that what had sizzled to life between them in the hot, barren desert was nothing more than passion. And she had no intention of enlightening him. Why would she, when she'd already exposed far too much? 'What happens now?'

'I succeeded in keeping our wedding a private affair, but tonight there is a banquet in your honour that will be attended by many neighbouring heads of state and dignitaries.'

'I don't want to go.' Alexa stood still, numb with shock. 'The way I feel at the moment, I won't be able to sit next to you and make small talk.'

His handsome face hardened. '*You* wanted this marriage.'

'*You deceived me.*'

His dark eyes flashed with anger. 'I am not in the habit of repeating myself, but I am prepared to make allowances for the fact that you are very upset, so this once I will. As you were presented to me, you were *not* a suitable wife for a sultan. I did what had to be done.'

'So when you kissed me that night in Rovina that was just something that had to be done, too, was it?' Remembering her uninhibited response to him, she burned with humiliation, but he merely shrugged, showing no signs of similar discomfort.

'That night in Rovina it was *you* who kissed *me,* but I no longer blame you for that. The chemistry between us is surprisingly strong and that is a good thing. And, now, enough. I have been away for several days and I have work to do before the banquet tonight.'

'I'm not going to the banquet.'

'You are the Sultan's wife and you are expected to fulfil that role.'

Her eyes slid slowly to his. Just how much of the rest of the role was she expected to fulfil?

She'd wanted Karim with a desperation that had shocked her, but now she knew he was the Sultan...

Everything felt different.

'You chose this marriage because you wanted my protection, *habibati,*' he said softly. 'You now have that protection. In time I will help you tackle the problems facing Rovina. In return I expect your loyalty and respect.'

'Neither of those can be bought,' she said stiffly. 'I'll attend your banquet because it's my job.' She'd expected her words to anger him, but if anything he seemed mildly amused by her small defiance.

'Good. And what about the wedding night? Are you going to regard that as a job also?'

Her face flamed. 'I have no intention of sleeping with you.' Her impulsive declaration was an attempt to regain some control—a flimsy gesture of self-defence—and he obviously realized that, because he smiled.

'Fiery Alexa. Perhaps you are "the rebel princess," after all. Don't pretend that you feel nothing for me, *habibati,* because we both know that that isn't the case.' He reached out a hand and gently fingered a strand of hair that had escaped from the elaborate twist at the back of her head. 'Those hot desert nights didn't lie.'

'But *you* did! I trusted you, Karim, and you *lied.* And that matters. For a woman, sex is about so much more than chemistry. I trusted the man I was in the desert with.'

'And I am that same man. What is the problem?'

'You're not the same man, Karim! You're someone I don't know.'

'Then I will allow you to know me better. The mystery of who I really am will be solved, tonight, when you come to my bed.' His fingers brushed her cheek in a gesture that was unmistakably possessive, and it took all her will-power to jerk her head away from that dangerously seductive caress.

'Don't touch me.'

'I *will* touch you. And you will touch me back,' he predicted, supremely confident in his sexual power. 'You made your choice, Alexa. It was *you* who sought the Sultan's protection. Now you have that protection and everything that it means. I am by your side, day and night, but this time as your Sultan, not as your bodyguard.'

Day and night.

She swallowed, and she saw the dangerous glint in his dark eyes. He was right, of course. She *had* sought his protection. But she was beginning to wonder whether she'd jumped out of the frying pan and straight into the fire.

CHAPTER NINE

THE wedding banquet was a glittering, glamorous affair that involved several-hundred people, all of whom appeared to want time with Karim.

Alexa stood stiffly by his side, accepting the greetings and congratulations that came her way, still furious with Karim, and even more furious with herself for having been so foolish and gullible.

How could she not have known who he was?

Watching him exercise his diplomatic skills, she marvelled at her own stupidity. Why hadn't she realized sooner that he was the Sultan? Now that she knew the truth about his identity, it seemed so obvious. The clues were everywhere—in the way he held himself and in the way he spoke. He was autocratic and confident, utterly sure of himself, as if he'd been making decisions from his cradle. People pressed around him, all eager to capture even a moment of his attention, and suddenly Alexa started to realize the importance and influence wielded by the man she had married.

She stole a glance at his proud, arrogant profile.

In his Sultan's robes, and discussing a broad range of topics from the falling oil price to desert conservation, she found him intimidating.

Listening to the conversations that went on around her, she soon realized that his opinion was being sought on virtually every subject. And his decisions were bold and confident, devoid of doubt, hesitancy or any apparent nerves on his part.

Even when they sat down to eat, the conversation didn't lighten up.

'I am very unsure. It could be a risky investment,' one ambassador ventured when conversation turned to a particular project that was being undertaken in the desert. 'There is no guarantee of success, Your Excellency.'

Clearly undaunted by that gloomy prediction, Karim merely smiled. 'Neither is there a guarantee of failure, Tariq,' he observed mildly. 'Take the risk. Life is no fun without risk.' His gaze flickered to Alexa as he spoke, and she had a feeling that he was including his marriage in that statement.

As his eyes lingered, she felt a tight, tense tingling in her body and almost laughed at herself.

He hadn't wanted her, but she still wanted him.

The fact that she now knew that the Sultan had gone to extreme lengths to personally prevent his marriage to 'the rebel princess' apparently wasn't enough to subdue the curl of awareness in her body.

Did she have no pride?

Why was she still feeling like this when he'd made it perfectly clear that she was the last person in the world that he would have chosen for his bride?

Yes, he'd married her. But only once he'd discovered that her background had been manufactured. Even in her wildest moments she couldn't pretend that this marriage had anything to do with love.

The Sultan needed a wife, and he'd decided that she was good enough to fulfil that role. She ticked the right boxes. There was no more to it than that.

And as for the chemistry that sizzled between them—well, he was obviously an intensely physical man. All that hot passion in the desert had been nothing more than sex. Any gentleness and kindness she'd felt had been no more than wishful thinking on her part.

Seeking distraction, Alexa tried to participate in the conversation that was taking place around her, but as the banquet progressed she could think of nothing but the night ahead. By the time the Sultan finally rose from the table, she was so on edge and her legs were shaking so much that she could barely walk as he led her firmly from the room.

'Is it always like that? You didn't get any peace for the entire banquet.' As the doors to the Sultan's private living quarters closed behind them, Alexa glanced around her, feeling impossibly jumpy.

All evening she'd been aware of him seated next to her. Occasionally she'd felt the brush of his leg against hers, but even that limited physical contact had been sufficient to drive her body to the point where she was ready to explode.

And she'd hated the fact that she could still feel that way, knowing what he'd done.

Apparently oblivious to her inner torment, Karim strolled across the room and poured himself a drink. 'Somewhere back in the mists of time my ancestors decided that the Sultan's wedding feast should be a time for generosity and giving. I believe that the custom had something to do with the sharing of good fortune.' He glanced towards her, a faint smile touching his mouth. 'They apparently believed that the Sultan would be so ecstatic at the prospect of bedding his new wife that he would be willing to say yes to everyone and everything.'

Her heart-rate doubled. 'And did you?'

'Did I say yes to everything?' His smiled widened. 'Not quite, Alexa. But I was quite possibly a little more approachable than usual.'

She didn't find him approachable. She found him intimidating. *And infuriating.* 'You don't have anything to celebrate. This marriage wasn't what you wanted.'

'But it was what you wanted,' he reminded her softly, his dark eyes quizzical. 'You were willing to travel alone and barefoot across the desert to be my bride, Alexa. Have you forgotten that fact? Why are you suddenly looking as though you would like to run out the door?'

Because everything had changed. Since she'd discovered who he was, everything had felt different. 'I was desperate to escape from my uncle,' she said in a stiff voice, and he gave a slow nod.

'Yes, I understand that. And to do so you were prepared to marry a man who you had never met.'

'But now I *have* met you—'

'And the chemistry between us is nothing short of explosive. Were it not for your reluctance to sleep with another man when you were promised to the Sultan, you would be mine already.' His eyes gleamed with sardonic humour. 'Ironic, is it not? Do you want me to dress as a bodyguard and return to the desert with you? Would that help, Alexa?'

The reminder of just how much she'd revealed of herself caused her to retreat both physically and mentally. She'd let her guard down, but she wasn't going to do it again.

No one was going to hurt her again.

She was angry with him—so angry—and she was going to use that anger to protect herself.

'I was afraid. You comforted me.'

'You're suggesting that the fire between us was nothing more than comfort? I don't think so.' He looked thoughtful. 'You were saving yourself for the Sultan, and rightly so. Fortunately for both of us, the wait is finally over.'

His words made the heat explode inside her body. 'You don't want me!'

'It is no secret that this marriage generally would not have been my personal choice.' Karim put the glass down on the table and looked at her thoughtfully. 'But I am fully aware of my duty to Zangrar, and I have now fulfilled at least part of that duty.'

'Part?'

He strolled towards her, his eyes on her face. 'The second part will be fulfilled when you give birth to our first son.'

Her heart was pounding and she took a step backwards. 'It might be a girl.'

'If it is a girl, then she will be much loved. *Stop* running away,' he commanded, the firm movement of his hand around her waist preventing any further thought of retreat. 'You are behaving like a frightened virgin, and it makes no sense. There is no longer any need to deny the passion that we felt in the desert.'

'Karim—'

'*Enough talking.*' He growled the order against her lips, and his kiss felt like a lightning strike, the hot brand of his mouth preventing any further protest on her part. And, whether or not she would have made that protest, she no longer knew because the excitement that exploded inside her body consumed all rational thought.

Alexa forgot that he had deceived her.

She forgot everything except the way this man made her feel, and that feeling was so enormous that it diminished everything she'd ever felt before.

His fingers slid into her hair, and the erotic caress of his tongue in her mouth made her head spin, and she lifted her hands to his chest for support because dimly she knew that her knees weren't going to hold her for much longer. He must have sensed the effect he had on her, because he picked her up and carried her through to the bedroom where he put her down gently.

He slid his hands down her back in a slow, deliberate caress that suggested ownership and possession, and it was only when her dress slithered to her feet that she realized that he'd undone the zip.

At any other time the smooth movement would have shocked

her, but she was shaking and shivering with need, her insides churning with anticipation as she gazed at him helplessly. With a characteristic lack of self-consciousness, he stripped naked, exposing his hard, male body to her shy gaze. But then he noticed the look in her eyes and paused, his gaze suddenly questioning as he lifted a hand and brushed the backs of his fingers against her burning cheek.

'Nervous, *habibati?*'

Oh, yes, she was nervous. But why? Was it because he was so confident and self-assured and she was in unfamiliar territory? Or was it simply that she understood the enormity of the step that she was about to take? He was demanding that she gave herself to him. Demanding that she make herself still more vulnerable. And she knew that once she'd given her body to this man there would be no going back.

But there never had been any going back, she thought dizzily as he bent his arrogant, dark head and claimed her mouth again in a possessive kiss that branded her as his property. She felt his fingers move over her heated skin, removing the scraps of underwear that was all that stood between her and nakedness. Then the tips of her breasts were brushing against the rough hair of his chest, and she tilted her head back and gave a soft gasp as sensation pierced her low down in her pelvis.

He hadn't actually touched her properly, and yet every nerve-ending in her body was humming in anticipation. And he must have felt it, too, because he powered her back onto the bed, coming down on top of her in a smooth, purposeful movement.

And suddenly the gentleness and the caution were gone.

The desire had been building for hours. Days. His touch was urgent and her response equally frantic.

She wanted him to touch her.

And she wanted to touch him.

Her fingers slid over the smooth muscle of his shoulder, her nails scraping over his skin as she enjoyed the hard maleness of his body. And he reciprocated, his mouth seeking and demanding. He captured an erect, pink nipple in his mouth and she whimpered as hot, heady pleasure shot through her body. He drew her deeper into the warm, sensual heat of his mouth and then transferred his attentions to her other breast until the gnawing hunger deep inside her became a madness that had to be satisfied. Her hips squirmed and shifted against the silken sheets until she felt his hand slide down her body and hold her still.

She was so desperate—so *ready*—that when he finally reached between her legs she cried out his name in a frantic plea. A shaft of moonlight lit the bedroom, but she saw nothing except the blinding flash of light that accompanied her first orgasm. The excitement was so powerful that she thought she was going to pass out, and then she felt his mouth claim hers again as he swallowed her desperate cries. Her senses were swamped, overloaded and she was so shaken by the sensations that gripped her body that she just clung to the sleek, smooth muscle of his shoulders, holding on.

'You are incredible. *So* responsive,' he purred, and it was only his voice that returned her back to earth and to the realization that his fingers were still deep inside her.

'Oh…' Acknowledging that intimacy, her cheeks flushed and she tried to wriggle away from him, but he simply smiled and gently nudged her thighs apart, his dark hair brushing against her sensitized breasts as his tongue trailed a path down her body. He savoured her as a gourmet might savour each mouthful of an exquisite meal, and she gave a gasp of shock as she felt him gently remove his fingers and replace them with the warm, moist flick of his tongue. Horribly self-conscious, Alexa tried to protest, but her body was so consumed by delicious, wicked pleasure that she simply responded to his silent demand that she open wider for him. And he used his tongue and fingers so gently and skillfuly that the heat started to build again, and she writhed with impatience, just *desperate* for more.

'Please.' She arched her hips off the bed. 'Please, Karim—'

He shifted his body over hers in a smooth, athletic movement, pressing her legs apart with an unfaltering, confident movement.

She felt his erection, hot and heavy between her thighs. She felt him touching her intimately, and she tried to move, but he positioned her as he wanted her and thrust hard, taking possession of her damp, trembling, thoroughly willing body with purposeful force.

It was hot, wild and momentarily painful.

Alexa gasped and sank her nails into the sleek flesh of his shoulder in an attempt to counteract the sudden pain, but it faded almost instantly and she was left only with agonizing pleasure.

'Alexa?' Suddenly tense, Karim paused and stared down at her, and the flicker of doubt in his voice warmed her insides. 'Am I your first lover?'

She opened her eyes and looked straight into his. 'Yes.' She spoke the word softly and then slid her arms around his neck and arched against him, showing him with that single movement exactly what it was that she wanted.

Something flickered in the depths of his dark eyes. 'No other man has touched you.'

'No.' Why was he choosing this moment to indulge in conversation when their bodies were screaming for an entirely different type of communication?

He let out a long breath and kissed the corner of her mouth in a surprisingly tender gesture. 'You please me greatly.' After the briefest hesitation he drove into her a second time, but this time with slightly more restraint. Watching her face, he altered his position slightly and the movement of his body became indistinguishable from the movement of hers as she was slowly devoured by the most exquisite pleasure. The sensation built and built until she hovered on the edge of ecstasy for a few agonizing seconds, and then finally her body finally convulsed around his and she felt herself tighten around his shaft. She heard him groan something unintelligible, and then felt the sudden increase in masculine thrust as he reached his own completion and ground himself deep inside her.

The explosion left them both spent.

Alexa lay still, shivering with the aftershocks, stunned by the passion that had consumed them, and utterly drained of energy.

Her insides were filled with a delicious feeling of warmth, and not just because of the sex, although that had been amazing. It was because of the physical closeness.

Just as she'd felt that night in the cave, she felt as though he cared. And she cared about him, too, didn't she?

No matter how frightening that thought was, she cared.

She loved him.

Bodyguard or Sultan, she loved Karim.

Softened by that knowledge, she suddenly just wanted to hold him and be held, but at that moment he shifted his weight onto his elbows and rolled off her, leaving her naked and exposed.

Bereft of the contact, Alexa turned towards him, intending to snuggle into him and show him just how much his skilled touch had affected her. And then she caught sight of his hard, unsmiling profile and stopped herself.

What was she thinking?

This man had concealed his identity. He'd deceived her, hadn't he, and then had showed not one flicker of remorse or regret?

He'd been utterly ruthless in achieving his own ends, and trusting him or revealing how she felt about him would be a huge mistake.

That wasn't what this relationship was about, was it? It wasn't about love or caring, and if she started imagining for one moment that he was thinking all sorts of soppy thoughts then she would be setting herself up for a major disappointment, and she'd had enough of those to last her the rest of her lifetime.

Bodyguard or Sultan, this man didn't love her.

Her attention was caught by the blue-black shadow of his jaw and the arrogant set of his features as he lay with his eyes closed, recovering his breath.

Now that their bodies were no longer joined, there was no sign of affection—*not in a glance of the eye or a touch of the hand.*

He'd given her more attention when she'd had the nightmare, and acknowledging that harsh truth killed the tender shoots of happiness that had sprung to life inside her.

He didn't care about her, and it was dangerous to pretend that he did.

He'd married her without even revealing his identity, and that was just *awful.* It meant that he was quite happy to lie when it suited him, which made him no different from all the people who had worked for her uncle over the years. The people who had deceived her and put her life at risk.

Karim wasn't interested in her love. He didn't *want* love. He didn't want to share emotion. Perhaps he didn't even *feel* emotion—he certainly never showed it. He was a loner. A man who didn't need others. And the fact that they'd shared hot, steamy passion in the darkness of the night didn't change that fact.

He'd married her because he needed a wife, and once he'd discovered that her rebel background had been fabricated by her uncle she'd been as good a candidate as the next woman. But she wasn't special to him. It could have just as easily been a different woman lying here now. She couldn't afford to forget that. She wasn't going to make the mistake of confusing sexual intimacy with anything deeper. That would only increase the embarrassment for both of them.

The sleek skin of his bronzed shoulder was within tantalizing reach of her fingers, and she curled her hands into fists in order to resist the almost overwhelming temptation to touch. She lay there wondering how it was possible to experience such intimacy and yet feel so very, very alone.

She'd shared herself with this man, emotionally and physically, but he had no feelings for her and was willing to lie and deceive when it suited him.

Yes, she was finally safe from her uncle.

But she'd fallen in love, and that made her more vulnerable than she'd ever been in her life before. Whether he knew it or not, Karim had the ability to cause greater wounds than anything her uncle had ever inflicted.

Karim lay on his back, struggling to recover from the most explosive climax of his life. The intimate recollection of her willing body wrapped around his was all it took to boost his arousal to almost agonizing levels.

Never before in his life could he remember being so turned on by a woman.

Slightly disconcerted by the power of his feelings, he searched for an explanation.

Amazing sex. Was that what was happening here?

Well, yes, obviously. And he wasn't going to pretend that her sexual innocence hadn't added an extra dimension to their relationship, because clearly it had. The fact that she had been a virgin had satisfied an elemental masculine part of himself, and confirmed that he'd been absolutely right in his choice of wife.

And suddenly he felt remarkably genial towards her.

Normally by now he would have left the bed and distanced himself from the snuggling and demonstrative outpourings that inevitably followed sex, but what was the point of that? He *knew* that Alexa had feelings for him. It would be only fair for her to be allowed to show them. This was not a one-night stand—they were now married.

Karim lay still, waiting for the feeling of panic that had always accompanied the mere thought of the word *relationship,* but nothing happened. He just felt replete and satisfied, and more than ready to haul her underneath him and repeat the entire performance.

Wondering why she was holding back when he was willing to tolerate and possibly welcome her affection, he turned towards her, and it came as a shock to discover that, far from holding herself poised to embrace him, his bride had actually fallen asleep.

Karim stilled, his brooding features locked in an a expression of astounded disbelief as he studied the slumbering woman by his side.

He'd never before known a woman to just fall asleep after sex.

He frowned slightly, his eyes lingering on the softness of her mouth and the gentle flush of her cheeks. The knowledge that *he* was responsible for that flush sent a wave of instantaneous lust tearing through his body, and he was seriously tempted to wake her up just so that he could set about exhausting her one more time.

Their love-making had been exceptionally energetic and passionate, he conceded, stroking a wisp of hair away from her face with a gentle hand. Perhaps it wasn't altogether surprising that she'd fallen asleep immediately, even thought it meant that she hadn't had the chance to express how she felt about him. All the same, it was unusual that she hadn't chosen to drape herself over him before falling asleep. There was something about the female sex that made them need to cling, especially after sex.

But Alexa wasn't clinging. In fact, she wasn't touching him at all.

Studying the fragile, vulnerable woman curled up by his side, Karim felt a sudden burst of explosive anger towards her uncle. She was probably just afraid to trust him. After all, her uncle had made her life hell.

A fierce desire to protect her from any more stress surged through him, and he sucked in a breath, spooked by the intensity of that feeling, and almost immediately reassuring himself that nothing could be more natural than a man wanting to protect his wife. All the same, the irony of the situation didn't escape him. He'd always made it a personal rule not to spend the entire night with a woman, because he'd learned at a young age that they just couldn't separate the physical from the emotional. After sex they just wanted to cling. And here he was, finally willing to allow a woman to cling, and she was too tired to take advantage of his generosity. They could have parked a car in the gap between them in the bed.

Absorbing another possibility for her behaviour—*that she could have been afraid to tell him how she felt*—Karim lay back against the pillows, vowing that once she awoke he was going to encourage her to say all the things that she was clearly holding back.

Alexa opened her eyes to find sunshine lighting the room and Karim watching her. He was just so masculine, she thought dizzily, as her eyes rested on his dark jaw and then lifted to his molten, dark eyes. He acknowledged her scrutiny with lazy, almost sleepy amusement. He was ridiculously, impossibly sexy, and she just wanted to melt against him and beg him to repeat what he'd done to her the night before.

Weakened by the memory, she dragged her eyes away from his, but they merely settled lower on his body and she felt hot colour ooze into her cheeks.

He'd deceived her.

He knew how much it had taken for her to give him her trust, and he'd abused that trust by not telling her the truth. And he'd shown no regret or remorse. In fact, he'd made it clear that the subject was closed.

'How are you feeling?' His tone was soft and encouraging, and connected straight to her insides.

Horribly vulnerable? 'Fine.' As she delivered this minimal response, his eyes narrowed.

'Fine?' Clearly, he'd been expecting to hear something different.

'How are *you* feeling?'

'Generous. You are the most incredible lover, *habibati.*'

The look in his eyes made her forget for a moment that she was angry and hurt. 'Oh.'

'Last night you fell asleep.' His hand rested on her hip and then gently slid down her thigh in a seductive movement that had every nerve-ending in her body tingling.

'I was feeling tired.'

'And I think perhaps you were feeling very shy,' he purred, this time stroking his hand over the soft curve of her bottom. 'I'm sure there were things you wanted to say, and I want you to know that I am prepared to hear whatever it is. You're my wife. I don't want you to hold back. Honesty is important.'

'Really?' That wasn't what his comments the day before had led her to believe, but she was oddly relieved that he was prepared to allow her to talk about how she felt. 'I'm surprised to hear you say that—but if that's the case then you should know that I still think what you did was completely wrong.'

'Wrong?' His body tensed and he repeated the word as if he'd never heard it before, his eyes shimmering with raw incredulity. 'What, precisely, was *wrong?* You were *incredibly* turned on.'

Mortified by that less than subtle reminder of her own feverish response, Alexa drew away from him slightly. 'I was not talking about the sex! I was talking about the fact that you didn't tell me who you were! That was what was *wrong,* Karim. I trusted you, and you took advantage of that trust. I told you everything about myself and you told me *nothing* about you.'

He muttered something that she didn't understand and then

sprang from the bed, apparently indifferent to the fact that he was naked. 'Why do you persist in sulking about something that is now in the past?'

She sat up in bed. 'I'm *not* sulking, and you were the one who said that you wanted me to say whatever I was feeling.' Lacking his confidence, she clutched the sheet against her naked body. 'I've just told you how I'm feeling!'

Karim prowled across the room like a caged beast, and then turned back towards her with something approaching a growl. 'I was not expecting you to use the opportunity to simply rehash an old conflict which should now be in the past!'

'So I'm allowed to speak as long as I say what you want to hear, is that right?' She was trembling with frustration. The fact that he *still* didn't see the need to apologize for his deception somehow made the situation worse. He obviously couldn't see that he'd done anything wrong. 'It isn't in the past for me! You deceived me, Karim. You concealed your identity.'

'And with good reason. My only objective was to find a way out of marrying "the rebel princess."'

'But that wasn't who I was.'

'I know that *now*.' His tone was grim. 'But I did *not* know it until I spent time with you. All I had in front of me was a long list of your extravagances and risk-taking behaviour. The people of Zangrar deserved better after everything they suffered at the hands of my stepmother.'

It was the first time he'd revealed anything remotely personal about his family, and his statement momentarily distracted her from her anger. 'What has your stepmother got to do with this?'

He tensed, and his expression was cold and discouraging. 'Everything. But that is none of your business.'

'I disagree! If I'm being blamed for her misdeeds, then I at least deserve to hear about what she did.'

Karim strode across to the window and paused for a moment.

Then he turned back to face her, his face set in hard, uncompromising lines. 'When my mother died, my father naturally became a target for no end of unscrupulous women.' He gave a cynical smile. 'That's the way the world works, isn't it? Where there is money and power, there will always be women. Unfortunately women, especially beautiful women, were my father's weakness.'

'Oh.'

'Yes, oh.' A muscle worked in his lean jaw. 'My stepmother created havoc. She managed to drag huge sums of money from my father, and spent it all on herself. She thought only of glamour and parties, and had no interest whatsoever in improving life for the people of Zangrar. She was the original rebel princess. Her thoughtless, selfish behaviour caused much unrest.'

'I can imagine.' Hadn't William done much the same to the people of Rovina? 'Didn't you have any influence with your father?'

'She made sure that I didn't. She persuaded my father to send me to boarding school from the age of seven.' He gave a hard smile. 'From there I went to university to study law, and then into the army. At that point I was back in Zangrar for long periods, but often working undercover in the desert. During that time I learned a great deal about what the people thought about my stepmother and also my father.'

'She didn't have children of her own?'

'That would have required caring about someone else other than herself, and she was not the type to share the limelight. As I grew up I saw the effect she was having on Zangrar but was unable to change what was happening. From the army I went to business school, and then I returned to Zangrar, ready to take up a senior post in government and try to curb the behaviour of my stepmother.'

Alexa studied him for a moment, knowing that he would be a formidable adversary. 'You succeeded?'

'He was completely addicted to her, able to see her faults

but unable to resist her. And she was a clever woman. She used every trick in the book to get me on her side.' He caught her glance and gave a wry smile. 'Yes, even that one, but it didn't work, of course. My father's experience had taught me at a young age to be wary of women, especially women like her. Things were fraught, to say the least—' He broke off and Alexa found that she was holding her breath, waiting for the rest of the story.

'And?'

'She was killed in a fall from a horse. My father was devastated, and had a heart attack a few days later. Zangrar was in chaos, but I was optimistic that I would be able to bring things under control and restore the confidence of the people.' He paused and his mouth hardened. 'And then I discovered that my father had, years before, arranged my marriage to another rebel princess, a matter he'd omitted to reveal before his death. I knew that if the marriage went ahead all the good work would be undone. It was the only way of protecting Zangrar.'

Alexa stared at him, her anger fizzling out like a firework doused by a bucket of water. 'I—I didn't know any of that.'

'Well, you know now. Remember it before you fling accusations of deceit in my direction.'

The hardness of his tone sent a chill through her insides. It was hard to believe that this was the same man who had made love to her so passionately the night before. 'I'm not a mind reader, Karim! You should have told me this before.'

'It wasn't relevant.'

'It was to me! It would have helped me understand you!'

'I have never expected or required a woman to understand me.'

Alexa stared at him helplessly. All her preconceived ideas about him had melted away, and now she just felt confused. 'What is it that you want from me? You said that you wanted me to be honest, so I have been honest, and now you're angry. What was it that you expected me to say when I woke up this morning?'

'I *expected* you to show affection!'

His words were so surprising that for a moment she just gaped at him. 'Affection?'

'When we were in the desert, you were happy to show your feelings for me. You clung to me and told me how desperate you were for someone to just hold you and tell you that everything was going to be all right.'

Reminded of her unguarded declaration, Alexa coloured and shook her head. 'I didn't—'

'No!' His tone was hard and he raised a hand to silence her. 'I won't allow you to deny *or* retreat from those feelings, Alexa! Your ability to show your feelings was one of the reasons I decided you would make a suitable wife. I did *not* want to be with a woman like my stepmother, who had no feelings for anyone other than herself. I didn't want that for myself or for our children.'

Their children? Swept along on a tide of a conversation that was entirely unexpected, Alexa froze, suddenly feeling incredibly vulnerable. Had he really guessed how she felt about him? 'I didn't have feelings for *you,* I had feelings for my bodyguard. You made me feel safe—that's all it was.' The need to protect herself was so ingrained that she didn't even think about it. 'And what you saw was gratitude, Karim, and I can't believe that someone as experienced as you would mistake gratitude for something deeper.'

It suddenly seemed desperately important that he didn't know just how much of herself she'd given to him. 'You helped me escape from my uncle. You could have been a flea-bitten camel with three legs and I still would have felt grateful to you.'

He lifted one dark eyebrow. 'You expect me to believe that it was gratitude that made you cling to me when you had a bad dream? Gratitude that made you hold on to me in the cave?'

'Of course.' *What did he want from her?*

Did he really expect her to drop her heart at his feet just so that he could tread on it a second time? No way! As far as she was concerned, she'd already given away far too much about how she felt, and had no intention of exposing any more of herself. 'You might be the Sultan, but you can't just order someone to care for you. Affection has to be earned, Karim. Even by sultans.'

'I rescued you from your uncle. I married you, which is what you wanted. Just how high is the price for your affection, Alexa?'

Extremely high. 'Why would you *want* me to have feelings for you, anyway? You told me that you don't do love.'

'You're my wife.' He spoke with lethal emphasis and there was no missing the possessive note to his voice. 'You have feelings for me, I know you have. I expect you to express them, as you did that night in the cave. I want you to be honest with me, otherwise this marriage won't be a happy one.'

Having delivered that depressing prediction, he turned sharply and strode into the bathroom, slamming the door with such force that she flinched.

Alexa collapsed back against the soft pillows, feeling completely shattered by the confrontation.

He wanted her to be truthful with him, and yet when before this moment had *he* been honest with *her?* He'd allowed her to make her wedding vows before revealing his true identity. *What sort of honesty was that?*

On the other hand, he clearly had no reason at all to trust women, she thought miserably, and everything he'd just told her about his stepmother did explain a great deal about the way he'd behaved.

But it didn't make her any more inclined to reveal her feelings.

She covered her face with her hands, exasperated with herself. *What was there to reveal that he hadn't already guessed?* Clearly he already knew *exactly* how she felt.

And that was the problem, wasn't it?

Love had made her vulnerable in a way that she'd never been

vulnerable before, and she was desperately looking for ways to protect herself.

Yes, they were married, but that didn't mean that she had to give him everything he was asking of her.

Alexa lay there listening to the sounds of the shower, more confused than ever before. The closed bathroom door suddenly seemed symbolic of their marriage.

There was a barrier between them.

The question was, could it be moved?

CHAPTER TEN

KARIM stood under the icy jets of the shower, ignoring the painful throb in his injured arm as he waited for the anger and frustration to fade.

Talk about making a guy jump through hoops.

Did she have any idea how many women had dreamed of lying where she was lying now? And yet, instead of showing the affection that he *knew* she felt, she was obviously still sulking about the fact that he hadn't revealed who he was.

Why was she so reluctant to show her feelings when she was now safe and had no reason to hide?

He allowed the water to stream over his hair and his body as he considered the more disturbing question.

Why did he care?

Since when had he ever demanded affection from a woman before? Never. Usually he was leaping out of bed to avoid any expression of that exact emotion.

'Why are you taking a cold shower?' A faltering female voice cut through his thoughts, and he opened his eyes and dragged a hand over his face to clear his vision.

Alexa stood in front of him. She was wearing his robe, and the fact that it was much too big for her just made her look more fragile than ever. Her amazing bright red-gold hair tumbled over her shoulders, and the expression in her blue eyes was uncertain. She looked like a woman who wasn't at all sure of her welcome.

'I came to apologize.' Her voice was stiff and formal. 'I—I didn't know anything about your stepmother before today. Obviously, I understand now why you wanted to avoid marrying me at all costs.'

Karim reached out and stopped the flow of water with an abrupt thump of his hand. 'Another "rebel princess" was the last thing that Zangrar needed.'

She gave a painful smile. 'Yes, I can see that. I just wish you'd trusted me with the information before, but you didn't, did you? Not even when you knew the truth about me.'

'I'm not accustomed to trusting anyone.'

'And neither am I.' She pulled the robe more firmly around her, as if afraid that it might somehow fall apart, and he noted the gesture with narrowed eyes.

She was always protecting herself. Physically, emotionally.

'You trusted me enough to marry me, Alexa.'

'I had to. You were my last hope.' She hesitated. 'You have to understand something about my life before you judge me too harshly. You're expecting me to reveal everything about myself, but you're forgetting that I've spent the last sixteen years not allowing myself to do that. It's how I stayed alive.'

'I know.' He reached for a towel and knotted it around his waist. 'But you're safe now. Do you believe that?'

'Yes, but I can't change overnight.'

'I expect you to be honest with me.'

'You're expecting me to reveal everything about myself, but you don't do the same thing, do you?'

'I have already delivered what you expected of this marriage. Protection. It was never a part of our deal that I spill my guts.'

She flinched. 'You're right, I *was* the one who insisted on this marriage, and you *did* rescue me from my uncle. I owe you a great deal, I know that. And I'm prepared to be everything a sultan's wife should be—I just didn't expect that to include affection.' She sounded confused and almost humble. 'You took me by surprise. No one has ever wanted that from me before. I didn't know *you* wanted that from me.'

Until last night he hadn't known he wanted it either.

'You're my wife. I want everything from you, Alexa.'

It took her a moment to answer, and she kept her eyes fixed somewhere in the vicinity of his injured arm. 'I'm not used to trusting anyone. I'm not sure that I can do it.' She drew a breath. 'It's scary.'

'Scary?' His own anger and frustration died in the face of that shaky confession. 'From what I can gather, your life has been at risk since you were a child. You've shown astonishing bravery. How can showing affection terrify you?'

'Because I've discovered that trusting someone and then watching them reject you is the most agonizing experience of all.' Looking desperately vulnerable, she took a step backwards, and almost tripped over the trailing hem of his dressing gown.

His hands shot out and prevented her fall. Raw excitement exploded through his body, and he released her as if he'd been burnt. He didn't understand the way he reacted to this woman. When he was close to her he lost all grip on control.

Like his father?

Unsettled by that possibility, it was Karim's turn to take a step backwards. 'You're talking about your uncle?'

'No. I never trusted him. But in the beginning there were others.' She swallowed painfully. 'I was so young, Karim. Just a child. And I was used to being loved. I'd been loved by my parents, and for a while I just turned to everyone, hoping that someone would help me.'

Karim felt something tighten inside him. 'And no one did?'

'They were all too afraid of my uncle. But I was *so* desperate for support that it took me a long time to stop trusting. I suppose part of me just didn't want to believe that this was happening to me. It's been such a long time since I've trusted and showed affection; I'm not sure I can just switch it on again that easily.'

'You can and you will, because you have no need to be afraid now.' His voice harsh, Karim gave in to the impulse and reached for her, pulling her against him. '*No one* will touch you again and, despite what you think, you *can* trust me.'

'Can I?' She looked up at him, her blue eyes wide and vulnerable.

An unfamiliar emotion stirred inside him as he swiftly volunteered the reassurance she was seeking. 'Yes. Everything I said to you that night in the cave still stands. I will not allow anyone or anything to hurt you.'

'Because I'm your wife.' There was a wistful note in her tone that connected straight to his internal alarm-system.

'Of course.' *What did she want from him?*

'Y-you said our marriage might not be happy.'

'I said it wouldn't be if you hold back. Be honest with me, Alexa, and we will do very well together.'

'Will we? But you don't do love, do you, Karim? You've already told me that.'

He could have lied, but he decided that there had already been enough of that between them. 'I've said that you can trust me. I will never let you down as your uncle did. I needed a wife, you need protection. It is a fair exchange.' Deciding that they'd done far too much talking for one day, Karim parted the edges of the robe and allowed it to slide from her shoulders. 'This is much, *much* too big for you.'

'Oh.' Standing in front of him naked, she blushed a shade of hot pink, and he felt a thud of instantaneous arousal at the sight of her smooth, creamy skin.

'You are incredibly beautiful, have I told you that this morning?'

'No.' She sounded oddly insecure, and didn't look at him, her eyes instead focused on some point in the corner of his bathroom. 'Does your arm hurt?'

'Not at all,' he lied, sliding his hand under her chin and forcing her to look at him.

'What is it you want from me, Karim?'

Reminding himself that actions spoke louder than words, he curved her lush, naked body against his. 'Everything,' he muttered against her mouth, and then groaned as he felt her full breasts brush against his chest. 'Everything, Alexa. Remember that.'

She felt so good.

Suddenly kissing wasn't enough, and he caught her up in his arms and carried her back through to the bedroom, where he spread her flat and came down on top of her in a decisive movement designed to prevent any second thoughts on her part.

By the time he'd finished with her she wouldn't be able to prevent herself from showing her feelings, he vowed to himself as he brought his mouth down on hers, and prepared to convert her from shy bride to quivering, adoring female.

The sweetness of her lips sent a vicious punch through his body, and he was about to abandon foreplay and just move straight on to the main event when he remembered just how inexperienced she was.

He did *not* want to hurt her.

So he reined in his natural instincts and instead set about seducing his new wife with every skill he knew. Using hands and mouth, he explored every inch of her trembling, writhing body until it was difficult to know who was the more desperate.

'Karim…' She sobbed his name and pressed her hips against him in blatant invitation but he ignored his own urgent desire and the plea in her voice, and instead continued to drive her wild.

'Karim! Please, please…' She twisted and shifted in an agony of sexual excitement, and he lowered himself over her and slid his hand to the moist juncture of her thighs. She was so hot and wet and ready for him that he had to grit his teeth to prevent himself from taking her hard and fast.

Instead he entered her slowly, his muscles rippling with the effort of holding back, and as her silken warmth closed around him he groaned aloud and buried his face in her neck, breathing in her scent and tasting her skin with his mouth.

And then he felt the first spasms of her orgasm tighten around him like a fist, and he lost all control and drove into her with all the passion and urgency that her body was demanding. Karim slammed headlong into a climax of such explosive proportions that his vision blurred and his mind went totally blank. She felt hot, so *hot*, and he thrust and thrust, drinking in her cries of agonized pleasure, feeling the slick slide of her skin against his as they raised the temperature of the atmosphere from comfortable to steamy.

It was so intense and consuming that a considerable time passed before he was able to regard himself as a human being with a brain.

As the spasms in his body faded and his thought processes gradually reawoke, Karim pressed a lingering kiss on the damp skin at the base of her throat.

So much for restraint, he thought dryly, relieving her of his weight and closing his eyes in an attempt to recover some of his control. And then he felt her roll towards him, and he turned his head to look at her.

Her hair was wildly tangled, her cheeks flushed and her lips softly swollen from his kisses. She looked like a woman who had been well and truly loved, and he was just about to pull her on top of him and teach her an entirely new position when she tentatively placed a hand on his abdomen and snuggled against him.

Karim tensed and then gave a satisfied smile and curled an arm around her, drawing her closer, providing the encouragement she so clearly needed. 'That was amazing, *habibati,*' he said huskily, and gave a satisfied smile as he felt her relax against him.

'Yes.' She spoke so softly that for a moment he wondered if he'd imagined it. Her fingers moved softly, tentatively, across his heated skin as if she was checking that he was real. 'Will it be all right, Karim?'

Knowing just how independent she was, he felt a sudden surge of emotion at this unexpected plea for reassurance. 'Of course.' He tightened his hold on her. 'You're mine now.'

A month later, Alexa couldn't believe how much her life had changed.

For the first time in her life, she felt safe.

There were armed guards everywhere in the palace, and security within the walls of the Citadel was so high that she felt herself gradually relax, soothed by the knowledge that she was finally safe from her uncle. And the ability to walk through sun-filled courtyards without once glancing over her shoulder, and climb into a car without first checking the brakes, felt amazing.

She explored Zangrar, made a concerted effort to learn the language, and then practised it with everyone she met. Sometimes Karim joined her, but the demands on his time were endless and occasionally she had to wait until the evening to spend time with him.

'I feel as though I should make an appointment to see you,' she told him one evening as they ate dinner together in one of the many sunny courtyards that lay within the palace walls.

'You missed me?' Karim leaned back in his chair, his dark eyes teasing. 'That is good to know, *habibati*. I was told that you visited the hospital today. That was generous of you.'

'They showed me round and described all the work they are doing.' Alexa chewed her lip for a moment, and then took a deep breath, unsure as to how her request would be received. 'They need a new MRI scanner, Karim. The head of the radiology department was telling me everything they could do if they had one. Do you think—I mean, I said I'd mention it…' She broke off, and he raised a dark eyebrow, his expression amused.

'You have been spending my money again, Alexa?'

She blushed. 'I promised I'd ask you, that's all.'

With a casual flick of his hand, he dismissed the hovering staff, his eyes never leaving her face. 'The citizens of Zangrar are clearly beginning to learn that the Sultan can deny his wife nothing.' The warmth of his gaze made her blush deepen.

As time passed, she simply wanted him more, not less.

'So—you'll let them have the scanner? I really think they need one.'

He studied her face thoughtfully. 'If you think it, then it will be done. I will direct Omar to deal with it.'

'You will? Really?' Touched that he trusted her judgement, she smiled at him. 'Thank you.'

'What next? Whose life do you want to improve?' He leaned back in his chair, clearly enjoying the conversation. 'Just be careful that you don't become a soft touch, Alexa.'

'It feels good, doesn't it, being able to help?' Alexa's smile faded, and she swallowed back the lump that had suddenly appeared in her throat. 'That's how my father was. It didn't matter how big the request, if he believed that it was right and that it would help Rovina then he would move mountains to make it happen. Everyone loved him. He just cared, you know? He put everyone else first, always.'

'Clearly the spirit of the father lives on in the daughter,' Karim said softly, leaning across the table and taking her hand. 'He would be proud of you, Alexa.'

'No.' She shook her head, feeling despair wash over her. 'What have I ever done for Rovina? I've just watched while William destroyed everything that my father built.'

'You were a child. You had no one, and yet somehow you

managed to stay alive. And you managed to remain brave and honest when people all around you were corrupt.' The Sultan's tone was suddenly hard. 'He will be punished, Alexandra. You can count on it.'

His words startled her. It hadn't occurred to her that he would deal with William. 'You're planning to confront him? You have a plan?'

Karim released her hand and rose to his feet. 'This is not a subject for discussion.'

'But if it involves Rovina—'

'Alexa—' He turned to face her and his expression was forbidding. 'You swore to trust me.'

'I do trust you, but—'

'Then do not question me on this matter. When the time is right I will tell you more. For now, I just require that you stay within the walls of the Citadel. Do you promise me that?'

'Yes, but—'

'Always with you there is a "but".' Clearly torn between exasperation and amusement, he pulled her into his arms. 'And I have learned that when that is the case there is only one effective way to silence you.'

As he swung her up into his arms and kissed her hard, Alexa forgot the point of the conversation. It was always like this. When she was with him, her mind ceased to work.

And during the days that followed she couldn't quite work out why she wasn't completely happy.

This was her dream, wasn't it? Marriage to a powerful sultan who could offer her the protection that she'd never enjoyed before. In fact, it was better than any dream, because never once had it crossed her mind that she might fall in love with the powerful man who was now her husband.

Life was good.

Instead of hiding herself away and being suspicious of everyone, she walked about freely and enjoyed the attentiveness of the Sultan's enormous number of staff.

There was really only one thing missing.

Love.

Karim didn't love her.

In the bedroom he was flatteringly attentive. Every single night without fail, and frequently during the day, as well, he dragged every last bit of response from her shivering, aching body, and she held nothing back because she no longer knew how to.

And it wasn't just in the bedroom that he seemed determined to impress her.

He also made an effort to be thoughtful in other areas, and she was incredibly touched—not by the jewellery or the extravagant gifts that arrived for her on a daily basis, but by the smaller, thoughtful gestures that showed that he'd given real thought to pleasing her. Having discovered her interest in history, he had insisted on taking her on a tour of the medieval Citadel, showing her the narrow passageways, the hidden souks and the ancient temples that had been built by his ancestors.

Karim seemed determined to introduce her to every facet of Zangrar, and Alexa accepted enthusiastically, glad of anything which took her mind off the more personal side of their relationship.

As the Sultan's wife she wanted to fit in.

And, as time passed and she heard more about the reprehensible behaviour of his stepmother, she was more and more determined to make Karim proud of her, and determined to do for Zangrar what she had been denied in her beloved Rovina.

Perhaps in time he might grow to love her, she thought wistfully as she sat in the shade one afternoon, watching a bubbling fountain in one of the many peaceful enclosed gardens that lay within the palace walls.

Hearing someone calling her name, she glanced up and noticed Omar, Karim's chief advisor hurrying towards her across the grass. 'Omar?' Forgetting her discarded shoes, Alexa scrambled to her feet and brushed the grass from her dress. 'Is something the matter?'

'There has been a most terrible accident, Your Highness.'

'The Sultan is injured?' Horrified, Alexa took a step towards him, but he lifted a hand to reassure her and shook his head quickly.

'His Excellency is safe and well,' Omar said hastily. 'But we have received a report of an explosion at one of the oil fields. No one seems to know how serious it is. His Excellency sends his apologies to you. As you know he is presently out of the country, attending a delegation in Kazban, and he was due home this evening. But arrangements are being made to fly him directly to the accident site. He wished me to inform you that he will be in touch as soon as he can.'

'But presumably it will take him ages to reach the site if he's coming from Kazban?'

'That fact is regrettable, but unavoidable.'

'But someone needs to be there to help. To make sure that everything that can be done is being done.' Slipping her feet into her shoes, Alexa made an immediate decision. 'I will go, Omar. I will visit and see how we can help. In that way I can be ready to inform Karim when he arrives.'

Omar stared at her in consternation. 'That would not be fitting, Your Highness.'

'Why not?'

'The last Sultan's wife would not have dreamed of acting in such a way.'

'But I'm not the last Sultan's wife,' Alexa pointed out gently. 'I'm *this* Sultan's wife, and I want to help. I am not some useless wallflower, Omar.'

'But—'

'The Sultan married me because he discovered that I was not like his stepmother, isn't that right?'

Omar inhaled sharply. 'Yes, Your Highness, but—'

'So I would be very grateful if you would arrange a flight for me. How far is this place?'

'Half an hour by helicopter, but His Excellency gave strict instructions that you were not to leave the Citadel.'

'He was being overprotective.' And that knowledge warmed her whole body. 'That danger no longer exists.'

'But—'

'Arrange it, Omar.' Alexa picked up her hat and walked quickly towards the palace. 'I'll just go and change into something more suitable.'

'My wife has flown to the oil field?' Karim's eyes glittered dangerously as he spoke on the phone to his chief advisor. 'And you allowed this?'

The phone crackled. 'She was most insistent, and your wife is *not* an easy woman to dissuade, Your Excellency.'

'Nevertheless, you *should* have dissuaded her. I gave instructions that she should remain within the walls of the Citadel.' Feeling a stab of fear, Karim sucked in a breath. 'Tell me you sent guards with her.'

'Two of them, Your Excellency.'

All the same.

Suddenly a suspicion entered his brain, and that suspicion swiftly changed to cold dread. Could her uncle be behind the explosion? 'Phone through to the helicopter, Omar. I don't want her to land at the oil field. It isn't safe.'

'It's too late. They landed half an hour ago, Your Excellency. Her Royal Highness is already tending the injured.'

And, knowing Alexandra, she wasn't looking over her shoulder. Karim felt a sudden rush of tension.

And that was his fault, wasn't it?

He'd insisted that she trust. He'd encouraged her to open up and give more and more of herself to him. But, in doing so, he had unwittingly put her in danger.

She no longer wore the cloak of suspicion that had kept her alive for so long.

She no longer believed that her uncle was a threat, and he hadn't wanted to disturb her shiny new happiness by telling her the truth: *that the threat against her life was as real as ever.*

Karim stared out of the window, battling with a feeling of helplessness that was entirely new to him. Never had he felt so desperately afraid and out of control of a situation. 'Omar.' Watching as the desert flashed by beneath him, he spoke into the phone again. 'I want you to contact the bodyguards. Anyone. You must get a message through to Alexa. Tell her to leave. Immediately. Tell her to get out of there.' *While she still could…*

'I'll do my best, Your Excellency.'

Karim's jaw tightened as he cut the connection. He would arrive at the oil field in fifteen minutes. The question was, would he be too late?

Alexa worked alongside the paramedics, treating the casualties and helping with the rescue mission. It was hot, filthy work and she had just applied a bandage to another bleeding wound when a man hurried towards her.

'There is someone injured in the control room,' he said breathlessly. 'You are needed.'

'Of course.' Without hesitating, she rose to her feet and followed, wiping her dirty, grimy hands on her trousers.

It could have been worse, she told herself. The drilling equipment was damaged and some of the injuries were severe, but there was no loss of life. Karim wouldn't care about the economic implications, she knew that, but he *would* care about the people.

Hoping that the man in the control room wasn't seriously hurt, Alexa hurried up the steps and pushed open the door. He was lying on the floor, a dark stain slowly spreading across his jacket. 'Call the paramedics…' She turned to the man who had led her there, but he had gone and in his place stood her uncle.

'Well, well.' His eyes slid over her dusty, blood-stained clothes. 'Life as the Sultan's wife is clearly nowhere near as glamorous as you'd anticipated.'

Alexa was so shocked to see him that she just stood staring in horror, unable to speak or think clearly.

Her uncle?

Her uncle was here in Zangrar?

The man on the floor groaned in agony, and Alexa turned, her response to his distress instinctive.

'Don't move, Alexandra.' William's tone was deadly, and her gaze flickered to the injured man and then back to her uncle.

'He needs help.'

William shrugged. 'We don't always get what we deserve.'

Anger mingled with the fear. 'What are you doing here?'

'Claiming what is mine.' He gave a nasty smile. 'And you were always mine, Alexa.'

She felt her heart-rate double and her palms grow damp. 'I have bodyguards outside.'

'Unfortunately for you, they were called away.' William pushed the door shut, turned the key with a deliberate movement and then walked towards her. 'You got lucky so many times, Alexandra. You were the original cat with nine lives. But those lives are all used up now, and there is no one here to save you. It's just you and me. You're not going to be blowing out the candles on your next birthday cake, Alexa.'

The injured man on the floor groaned again, and Alexa bit her lip. 'Please—let me just help him and then I'll go with you, if that is what you want.'

'You're not going anywhere.' William's voice was calm as he withdrew the gun from his pocket. 'You thought the Sultan was going to save you, but you're going to die right here in the desert, along with the snakes and the scorpions. It's long overdue. You should have died with your parents.'

Alexa stared at the gun. 'I never did you harm.'

'You ruined everything I worked for.' The calm left and his tone was vicious. 'I was the Regent, but I was never given the respect I was owed. After your parents' death, all the country cared about was you. The little orphan princess. You really knew how to earn the sympathy vote, didn't you, Alexa?'

Alexa licked dry lips. 'William—'

'Everyone fell in love with you. And that couldn't work, don't you see that? I couldn't allow you to live, knowing that people were all looking towards the day when you would become Queen. You had to have an accident.' William giggled hysterically, and the gun shook in his hand. 'But you were incredibly hard to kill. I had to become more and more inventive.'

Alexa could hardly breathe. She couldn't believe she'd put herself in this situation. 'Killing me will achieve nothing.'

'On the contrary, it will give me great satisfaction. They've taken my throne, do you know that? The Council.' His tone a vicious growl, William pointed the gun at her head. 'They've forced me to step aside. They want you to step into my place. And that isn't going to happen.'

Out of the corner of her eye, Alexa saw movement at the door and the window. Maybe if she could just keep him talking for a moment longer…

'I'm sure it's all just a misunderstanding.'

'Maybe.' His smile was ugly. 'But it will all be cleared up when you are dead. Those guys were meant to finish you off in the desert, but your overzealous bodyguard got in the way.'

Alexa saw his finger move on the gun and flung herself to one side, and at the same time there was a loud crash and the sound of breaking glass as Karim burst through the door along with several bodyguards.

In one smooth, determined movement he disarmed her uncle and punched him so hard that William staggered into the desk behind him and then collapsed to the floor, stunned by the blow.

Without pausing, Karim bent down and yanked him back onto his feet, this time slamming him against the wall with propulsive force, the expression on his face so cold and frightening that for the first time in her life Alexa saw fear in her uncle's eyes.

Karim tightened strong fingers around William's throat, his voice thickened by anger. 'You will never, *ever*, lay a finger on my wife again. Nor will you say a single demeaning word about her in private or in public.' William struggled weakly and started to gasp for air, but Karim didn't release his hold. 'For sixteen years she endured your relentless persecution and she was totally alone. It ends now. *It finishes here!*'

Seeing her uncle's eyes bulge, Alexa struggled to her feet. 'Karim—' But her voice was no more than a whisper, and the Sultan didn't hear her.

He was blind with anger and all his focus was on her uncle. 'She isn't alone any more. She's mine, and she has me to protect her.'

'Karim!' Alexa tried again, her voice louder this time. 'You have to let him go. He isn't worth it.'

'How can you say that?' Karim didn't turn, but his grip relaxed slightly. 'He tried to kill you!'

'But he didn't succeed. And it's over now. It's over. He'll go to jail.'

Karim gave a snarl of contempt, released William and nodded to two of the bodyguards, who immediately responded and took William into custody. 'Yes, he'll go to jail. He has committed a crime in Zangrar, and he will receive his punishment here so that I can personally see that it is just. Get him out of my sight.'

The bodyguards dragged William from the room and Alexa immediately turned back to the injured man. 'Karim, you must call the paramedics.' She dropped onto her knees, swiftly removed the man's jacket, identified where the bleeding was coming from and pressed down on it with the folded jacket. 'I'm so sorry. I'm so sorry I couldn't help you before, but you're going to be fine,' she said soothingly. 'We're going to fly you straight to the hospital.'

Karim barked orders into his telephone, and moments later several paramedics arrived and the man was taken away.

Alexa stood up and wiped her hands on her shirt. Seeing the look of tension and anger on his handsome features, she felt a flash of guilt. 'Thank you. You saved me yet again. It's becoming a habit.' Her hesitant smile faltered under his intimidating glare. 'You're very angry, aren't you?'

'I am so angry with you I could strangle you myself!' His tone was thickened with fury. 'What were you *thinking?* What *possessed* you to fly out to the desert alone?' Ranting and growling like a furious beast, Karim paced the length of the control room and back again. 'You could have been killed. You *would* have been killed if I hadn't arrived when I did.'

Alexa stared at him, stunned that he felt so strongly. 'Yes, that's probably true. I—I was a bit impulsive, but when I heard that there was an explosion and that you wouldn't be able to get here for a while I wanted to come and help.'

He jabbed his fingers through his sleek, dark hair. 'And that was foolish.'

'You wanted a wife who was going to care for the people of Zangrar,' she pointed out softly. 'I care, Karim. Over the past month or so they've welcomed me and made me feel more at home than I've ever felt in my life before. Although it's only been a short time, this feels like my home.'

'You showed the most amazing courage and self sacrifice, as

usual, and I blame myself for the fact that you put yourself at risk today.'

Alexa looked at him in surprise. 'How can you possibly blame yourself?'

'I blame myself on two counts. Firstly, because I am the one who insisted that you show trust and, secondly, because I didn't reveal to you that there was still a risk.'

'You didn't know that he was still going to try and have me killed.'

Karim ran a hand over the back of his neck, unusually hesitant. 'I have had agents working in Zangrar since that night in the cave when you told me your story,' he muttered finally. 'I was aware that he was planning something, but I believed you to be safe because you were within the Citadel. When I learned from Omar that you had flown out to the desert, I almost lost my mind.'

'You guessed that my uncle was behind the explosion?'

'I thought it possible. My agents had started to uncover the beginnings of a conspiracy, but they had no details.'

'But he couldn't have known that I would come myself.'

'It was a reasonable assumption because that's the sort of woman you are. You are strong and compassionate and you care deeply.' Karim reached out and pulled her against him, stroking her hair away from her face. 'It's the reason the people of Rovina love you, the reason that the people of Zangrar love you, and—' He broke off and inhaled deeply. 'And it's the reason that I love you.'

Her heart stumbled. 'You love me?'

'Very much.'

'Y-you never said.'

'I didn't acknowledge it myself until a few hours ago.' Karim stroked her cheek with his fingers. 'When I was told that you had flown out here I suddenly guessed what the conspiracy was, and I knew you were in serious danger. I tried to contact you, but you were already helping the wounded. So I could do nothing except wait, and I thought I was going to go out of my mind. Every minute of the flight through the desert was torture. I had to endure a vivid mental picture of what might have happened to you.'

Alexa placed her hand on his chest, checking that he was real. 'You don't do love.'

'Apparently I do,' Karim drawled softly, lowering his mouth to hers and kissing her gently. 'And it seems that I do it intensely and completely. I love you, *habibati.* You are mine and mine alone, although occasionally I may be prepared to share you with our people.'

His kiss made her dizzy, and when he finally lifted his head it took her a moment to speak. 'I forced you to marry me.'

'And I came to Rovina in person, determined to make you change your mind about marrying the Sultan. But the moment you removed your mask after the fencing match I knew I was in trouble.'

'I was hoping you'd lose so that I could justify firing you. I thought I'd be safer on my own. I didn't trust anyone. I didn't dare.'

'You were feisty and brave and seemed to live up to your title of "rebel princess".'

'I *did* try to tell you that I was in danger.'

'Believe me, I deeply regret the fact that I did not believe you, but you have to understand that all the women in my life up to this point have used drama and hysterics as a means of obtaining what they want.'

'I was being honest.'

Karim gave a driven sigh. 'I know that now. When I discovered everything that you had been through, I just wanted to keep you safe from everyone. That night in the desert—'

'It was so hard for me not to sleep with you,' Alexa admitted softly, faint colour touching her cheeks. 'I wanted you *so* badly.'

'And I wanted you. That was the moment when I decided that the marriage would take place.' He studied her face. 'Perhaps I was already in love with you. I know that you made me feel more alive than I'd felt in years. For a short time, when we were together, I forgot about duty and responsibility.'

'I just wish you'd told me who you were. I was *so* confused. I thought I was marrying the Sultan while in love with another man. It was *horrible.*'

Karim gave a self-satisfied smile. 'Fortunately I am *not* so possessive as to be jealous of myself.'

She placed her hand on his chest and looked up at him. 'You really love me? You're sure?'

He bent his head and kissed her gently. 'My desert princess. I was expecting you to hate everything about my country, and you astonished me. Everything fascinated you. You fell in love with Zangrar, and I—' he murmured the words against her mouth '—I fell in love with you, *habibati.*'

His words brought her emotions rushing to the surface, and Alexa leaned her forehead against his chest to hide her tears. 'Sorry. I'm being stupid. It's just that I'm happy. It's like a dream.'

'But a *good* dream, I hope. Stop crying.' His voice rough, Karim lifted her chin and frowned down at her. 'I forbid you to cry. From now on if anything causes you a moment of unhappiness you have only to tell me and it will be dealt with.'

She gave a shaky smile, still dizzy with the novelty of having someone who cared for her. 'What happens now? My uncle—'

'Will stand trial and will undoubtedly spend the rest of his life behind bars.' Karim gave a faint smile. 'Which leaves you with a problem, *habibati.* The Council are now ruling Rovina, but they are eager to welcome their Queen. I presume you don't wish to abdicate this responsibility?'

'No.' Alexa shook her head firmly. 'I owe it to my father to at least try to sort out the mess that William has made. There are so many problems.'

'And so many solutions,' Karim murmured, lowering his head to claim another kiss. 'I am particularly skilled at sorting out the messes left by previous rulers. I can advise you on many shortcuts.'

The touch of his mouth was making it impossible to think. 'You're suggesting we divide our time between Zangrar and Rovina? Can that happen?'

'We will make it happen. Where there is a will and a fleet of private jets…' His casual shrug dismissed the problem to nothing. 'The distance is nothing, and there is much to be said for spending time in both countries. Our children will grow to love the desert, but they will also experience the forests and fields of Rovina. They will have a privileged childhood, experiencing two different cultures, and they will learn to be tolerant. When he is old enough, our first son will rule Zangrar and our second son will rule Rovina.'

Alexa wound her arms around his neck. 'And if we have a daughter?'

'If she is as brave and resourceful as her mother, then she will be able to rule both countries with her eyes shut, while taking her fencing lessons,' Karim drawled, amusement in his dark eyes as he bent his head and kissed her. 'Whatever we decide, our two countries will now be united for ever, and you will be able to implement those changes that your father would have wanted. You have already had some practice spending my money. Feel free to perfect your talents in that direction.'

Touched by his support, Alexa hugged him. 'You make me *so* happy, and no one has ever done that before.'

'Then get used to it, *habibati*,' he purred in a lazy, masculine voice. 'Because I have discovered that I am incredibly committed when it comes to the issue of my wife's happiness. I am willing to knock down anyone who stands in your way.'

'You already did that.' She glanced around the room, taking in the debris and the broken door, still unable to believe the passion and determination with which he'd defended her. 'You saved me. Again.'

'And I intend to carry on saving you, should it be necessary, but it would be nice if you could give me less cause for concern or my hair will be grey before our children have even been born.'

Alexa touched her fingers to his hair, feeling the silken strands and admiring the deep, bold black. 'You don't seem like a man who worries easily.'

'I'm a man who knows how to defend his own.' He hauled her against him in a possessive gesture. 'Remember that, Alexandra.'

'I'll remember it. And, in return, what do you want from me?'

'You know.' Karim's gaze was arrogant and assured. 'I want everything, Alexa. Everything that you have to give, everything that you are. No holding back.'

Loved and secure for the first time in her life, Alexa smiled. 'Is that all, Your Excellency? Well, I don't think that is going to be too hard...'

The Sheikh and the Virgin Secretary

SUSAN MALLERY

Susan Mallery is the *New York Times* bestselling author of over one hundred romances and she has yet to run out of ideas! Always reader favourites, her books have appeared on the *USA Today* bestseller list and, of course, the *New York Times* list. She recently took home the prestigious National Reader's Choice Award. As her degree in Accounting wasn't very helpful in the writing department, Susan earned a Masters in Writing Popular Fiction.

Susan makes her home in the Pacific Northwest where, rumour has it, all that rain helps with creativity. Susan is married to a fabulous hero-like husband and has a six pound toy poodle... who is possibly the cutest dog on the planet.

Visit her website at www.SusanMallery.com

Don't miss Susan Mallery's charming new novels, *Sweet Talk, Sweet Spot & Sweet Trouble*, out in April, May and June.

Chapter One

"I wondered if you were currently looking for a mistress," Kiley Hendrick said quietly.

Prince Rafiq of Lucia-Serrat stared at the woman sitting across from him. He had thought the biggest surprise of his Monday had been to find Kiley at her desk that morning, instead of on her honeymoon.

He had been wrong.

"You speak of yourself?" he asked.

She nodded, keeping her gaze firmly on the pad of paper she clutched on her lap.

He hadn't seen his secretary in five days. She'd taken off part of the previous week to prepare for her impending marriage. "I take it the wedding on Saturday was not a success," he said.

"There was no wedding." She raised her head and stared directly at him. "Eric and I are no longer together."

"I see."

He allowed his gaze to return to her tightly clenched hands and saw that the modest diamond engagement ring was no longer on her left hand. A thin indentation on her pale skin was the only proof it had existed at all.

"I know that you are currently between, ah, women," she said and blushed. "That is, I sent the final gifts and letter so I thought that you had broken up." She pressed her lips together as if not sure how to continue.

"I am no longer seeing Carmen," he offered helpfully.

Kiley nodded. "Yes. I thought so. And while I know you usually have one or two candidates waiting in the wings, I wondered if you would consider me. Even though I'm not your usual type."

He had a type? "Meaning?"

She released her death grip on her pad of paper and shifted in her seat. "Glamorous. Beautiful. Sophisticated. I'm okay looking, but not in their league. But you've only seen me in work clothes. I clean up pretty well. I'm smart, I have a sense of humor." She paused and bit her lower lip. "I've never had a conversation like this. I don't know what you're looking for when you pick a woman for, um, well, that."

"My bed?"

The blush returned. She swallowed but didn't look away. "Right. Your bed."

Rafiq had not discussed things so openly before, either. He leaned back in his chair and considered what he looked for in a mistress.

"Obviously some physical beauty," he said, more to

himself than her. "But that is less important than one might think. Intelligence and humor are required. Not every waking moment is spent making love. There is plenty of time for conversation."

He thought of Carmen's shrill demands. "An even temper would be desirable."

"You've known me for two years," Kiley reminded him. "I've never gotten angry."

"Agreed." She had not. She was efficient, organized and very much responsible for the ease with which his workday progressed. But his mistress?

While Kiley was attractive and he would admit to finding pleasure in watching her move, he had never considered that more than a bonus. Beautiful, sensual women were easy to find. An excellent assistant was not.

The most sensible course was to politely thank her for the offer, then refuse the invitation. He would—

"There will be advantages," she said, as if trying to convince him. "I understand your work. We can discuss it, if you'd like. Plus I won't mind if you have to stay at the office late."

"Most likely you will be working late with me," he said, wondering why this was so important to her. What had pushed the normally reserved Kiley to make such an outrageous—for her, at least—request?

"Yes, there is that." She cleared her throat. "I don't know what else to say. I just hope you'll consider me."

He had never been approached so openly by a woman intent on joining him in his bed. He would have bet a considerable part of his fortune that she was not the type to be interested in an affair. He still believed that.

"Why do you want to do this?" he asked.

Kiley returned her attention to him. Her dark-blue eyes flashed with pain. "Revenge."

"A noble motive. I assume this revenge is because of your fiancé?"

"Yes. Eric."

She paused, as if considering how much to tell him. Rafiq could guess the basic scenario, but he wanted to hear it from her. He wanted to gauge her emotions and her intent.

While she chose her words, he looked at her. Really looked—not at the ever-present secretary who anticipated his needs and made his life flow pleasantly, but at the woman.

She was of average height—perhaps five foot four or five inches. Her hair, worn short and layered, was the color of gold. Or perhaps the north-shore beaches of Lucia-Serrat at sunset. Her large eyes dominated her face. He'd noticed how the deep blue darkened or lightened with her mood. He had always been able to tell if she was annoyed with him.

She was delicately built, small-boned, with curves that intrigued him. Now he took in the slight swell of her breasts and the shape of her calves below the hem of her knee-length skirt.

She was attractive, he thought. He found her easy to be with. She did not scream or annoy him. Like every other woman of his acquaintance, she wanted something from him. Unlike the others, she had been honest from the first.

But did he want her in his bed?

"He cheated," Kiley said at last, obviously fighting tears. "I'm sure you guessed that. He spared me the cliché of the groom sleeping with the bride's maid-of-honor-slash-best friend, but he more than made up for it in other ways. He had sex with most of the women in his law school class, his neighbors, my neighbor, along with countless others. He propositioned two of my friends. At the time, they tried to tell me, but I wouldn't listen. Talk about stupid."

She spoke lightly, as if the words had no meaning. But he heard the pain in her voice and saw it in her eyes.

"You did not believe them?" he asked.

She shook her head. "I was fooled right up until last Friday morning when I walked in on him and a woman from his study group." She blinked rapidly as if holding in tears. "That wasn't even the worst of it. He c-came after me and told me it didn't mean anything." She paused to swallow, the tears closer to the surface now. "He never was very original. Then he told me that he was doing it *for* me. That he wanted to treat me with reverence and respect. So he kept that side of himself away from me."

She looked at Rafiq. "My idea of loving someone, of feeling reverence, isn't to cheat on her over and over again."

"You canceled the wedding." If Rafiq had planned to attend, he would have known before now. But an out-of-town commitment had caused him to send his regrets.

"Eric was shocked, if you can believe it," Kiley said. "He actually thought I'd still go through with it because it was the next day and we had 250 people coming. Everything was paid for. But I wouldn't do it. I loved him and I thought he loved me and I was wrong. Getting married at that point would only make things worse. So I canceled."

She dropped her head and stared at the pad of paper on her lap. "My mom and I made phone calls. We couldn't get everyone, so I went to the church the next morning and told them as they arrived." She took a deep breath. "It was horrible."

"You? Not Eric?"

She shook her head. "He took the tickets for our honeymoon in Hawaii and left with his flavor of the week. I hope they get rashes. And stung by jellyfish."

Her courage surprised him. She could easily have sent a family member to stand at the church, but she'd done it herself.

"Why me?" he asked.

For the first time since walking into his office, a smile tugged at her lips. "You're a prince, Rafiq. That makes you the best candidate around."

"Ah. I see." He could discern out the rest of it. "Eric has accepted a job with the law firm I use. Therefore he will attend some of the same functions I do. As my mistress, you would go with me."

"Exactly. Eric doesn't like you," she added. "I think he's jealous. He's tried to get me to quit a few times, but I refused. He would talk about the women in your life as if they were sluts or something but I'm starting to believe he was envious. He wants what you have. Or maybe he wants to be you. I don't know and I don't care. But I'm convinced that my being your mistress will destroy him."

Rafiq considered her words. He had only met Kiley's fiancé one or two times. He'd never formed an opinion of the man until now.

"Do you want him destroyed?" he asked.

She nodded. "Then I want to walk away and forget he ever existed." She looked at him. "There's another reason I came to you. You're a good man. You'd never treat a woman the way Eric treated me. You'd simply end things without any of the lies."

Her assessment of his character was interesting. He could name twenty people who would do their best to convince her he was the biggest bastard on the planet. But she was also right—he'd never lied to a woman. He'd never stooped to trickery or deception.

Was he considering her offer? Did he want Kiley as his mistress? He wouldn't mind her in his bed, despite the complications. He liked her. The proposition had possibilities.

"There are logistics to be considered," he said. "If we decide to move forward with this."

They were discussing things so calmly, Kiley thought, more than a little amazed by the turn of events. She was willing to admit she was still emotionally numb from the shock of Eric's betrayal, but even as she'd imagined a thousand ways this conversation could go, she'd never thought it would be so rational. Maybe this sort of thing happened to Rafiq all the time, but it was a definite first for her. Still, she was determined. She could forgive a lot of things, but not betrayal on that level. Not ever.

To think that Eric had tried to make her feel guilty about enjoying her job with Rafiq when Eric had been cheating on *her.* She'd been so careful not to talk about her boss and she'd always gone out of her way to reassure Eric. Just the thought of it made her want to throw something.

He had even complained about Rafiq's generous gift of Baccarat crystal. A gift she currently had boxed up in her office to return to her boss.

"You're the expert," she told him. "You're going to have to come up with the list."

He smiled. "Of course. First there is the matter of what the relationship would entail."

Okay, this might be the first time she'd ever applied to be a mistress, but she was fairly sure the ground rules were simple.

"I thought it would be about sex," she said, then wished she hadn't as his dark eyebrows rose slightly.

"Sexual accessibility is assumed," he told her. "You would be as available as I wished and vice versa."

He would be available to her? Interesting thought. Not that she could imagine herself picking up the phone and telling him to get naked and get ready.

"There is also the matter of fidelity," he continued. "During our time together, there are to be no other men in your life and no other women in mine."

"That one's easy," she said. "I'm not the unfaithful type."

"Consider carefully," Rafiq said. "The human heart is a contrary organ. Your goal is to punish Eric and make him jealous. During the course of our affair, he could try to win you back. By the terms of this agreement, that would not be allowed."

"You don't have to worry about that. There is nothing Eric can ever say or do to make me think of him as anything but a lying worm."

Rafiq didn't look convinced. Kiley knew it didn't matter what he thought. Eric was *her* problem. She could still feel the disbelief that had flooded her when she'd walked into his apartment. He'd given her the key several weeks ago but she'd never used it. Somehow it hadn't felt right. But on the day before their marriage, she'd decided to pay him an unexpected visit and take him breakfast. Only, she had been the one to get the surprise.

She was still in shock. It had been three days, and the truth of what had happened had barely begun to sink in. Part of her was glad. She wasn't looking forward to the moment when the pain hit full force.

"There is also the matter of us working together," Rafiq said. "You are too efficient for me to let go."

"That's fine. I want to keep working. I need to pay my parents back for all the money they spent on the wedding. I have most of it already. You pay me very well and I've been saving so Eric and I could have a down payment for a house. This is Los Angeles and real estate is expensive so I've been putting aside every penny I can. I wanted to give them all of that, but they wouldn't let me. They think I should buy a condo. Maybe they're right. I just…"

She realized she was rambling. "Sorry. The point is, I need the money."

Rafiq stared at her.

"What?" she asked, carefully running her tongue over her teeth to see if she'd gotten a piece of food caught in them.

"You wish to repay your parents for the wedding?" he asked.

"Of course. It was thousands of dollars for nothing. I'm the one who picked Eric. I'm the one who wanted to marry him. So this is my responsibility."

Her parents had disagreed that it was her fault, but it wasn't as if they were rolling in money. Her dad would be retiring in a few years and her mother had only ever worked part-time.

"And while we're on the subject," she said. "If we do this, I don't want work to be weird. We'd need to keep our personal life separate from work. People will probably find out but I'd rather we didn't flaunt things."

"I agree."

"And when it's over, you can't fire me."

"I give you my word. Should working together be too uncomfortable, I would help you find another position that was to your liking. If you stay here, we will never mention the affair again."

Fair enough, she thought. "It won't be uncomfortable for me," she said. Being his mistress was about her wanting revenge, not finding a new boyfriend. Still, this was by far the most surreal experience of her life. "I'll be fine."

"How flattering," Rafiq murmured.

"What?"

"Nothing. In addition to our sexual relationship, I would expect you to accompany me to various social events."

"That's the part I'm most looking forward to," Kiley told him with a smile. "I want to be seen and have word get back to Eric."

Rafiq's expression didn't change, but she had the feeling she'd said something wrong. She ran over her statement. Oh. Yeah. Maybe that wasn't the most flattering thing to say.

"Of course, I'm really excited about sleeping with you," she added, feeling both embarrassed and uncomfortable.

"I can see that."

She wanted to bang her head against the desk. "Have I blown it completely?"

"No. You offer something unique. An honest relationship in which we both get what we want. There is no pretense of more-tender feelings."

"And you're okay with that?"

"Perfectly. I would think a time period of three months would satisfy both of our needs."

"Sounds good to me," she said. In three months Eric was bound to find out about the affair. She could only hope that the news would devastate him as much as learning the truth about him had devastated her.

"Good." He stood. "Then there is only one more detail to be worked out."

"You mean you're seriously considering me?"

She couldn't believe it. Coming to Rafiq had taken all the courage she had and then some. Relief now combined with her sleepless nights and emotional pain and left her light-headed.

"Yes." He walked around the desk and held out his hand to her.

She stared at it, then at him. He obviously wanted her to take his hand.

"Why me?" she asked, not yet ready for actual physical contact. "I'm not your usual type."

His dark gaze settled on her face. "That is part of the appeal. You would present a unique perspective on the male-female relationship. I find you attractive. I believe you will be my mistress with the same efficiency that you use here at the office. Which means there is only one question left unanswered."

She set her pad on his desk and placed her fingers against his palm. She had an impression of warm skin and strength as he gently pulled her to her feet.

He towered over her, and she had on pretty high heels. He smelled clean, just soap and man, and even though it felt strange to have him continue to hold her hand, it was more good-strange than bad-strange.

His dark eyes seemed to see down to the very depths of her being, as if he could read all her secrets. Not a good thing, she thought. She wasn't the secret type and anything he found down there would be pretty pitiful.

She drew in a deep breath. "What's the question?"

"This," he said, and lowered his head.

She hadn't thought he would kiss her. Maybe she should have. After all, she was offering to be his mistress, which meant an impressive level of physical intimacy, and kissing was the first stop on that road. But here? At the office? In the afternoon?

As his mouth gently brushed against hers, he tugged on her hand and drew her closer. She didn't know what to think, what to feel. She'd been numb since discovering Eric with that woman, so she doubted she was going to be able to respond to Rafiq's kiss.

Only, she had to. This was the final test to see if she was mistress material. As she knew deep in her heart she wasn't; she was going to have to fake it. But how?

Frantic thoughts raced through her mind. She felt awkward standing there, not sure what to do with her arms, her hands. Should she embrace him? Should she go for a wildly enthusiastic tongue kiss? Should she grab his free hand and put it on her breast?

Rafiq raised his head. "You have very noisy thoughts," he murmured.

"Can you hear them?"

"Not the specifics, but the general rumble. You are free to change your mind."

Meaning she didn't have to be his mistress. She knew that. "I want to do this."

He stepped back and sat on the edge of his desk. "Chemistry is important in circumstances such as these."

"What with sex being the point," she said, aware that so far they'd yet to create even a spark, let alone a passionate fire.

"Is that what you think?" he asked. "That the whole point is sex?"

"Isn't it?"

He studied her for several seconds. "Perhaps *you* would like to kiss me."

Oh! Wow. Kiley drew in a deep breath. It hadn't actually been her first choice, but she could guess why he would suggest it. If she couldn't kiss him, she certainly couldn't do anything more interesting.

"I would like to," she said as much as to convince herself as him.

He sat without moving, although he watched her. She had the sense of being stalked, which was crazy. Rafiq wasn't dangerous. Not exactly. He was powerful and good-looking. A great body. Eric was a little on the skinny side, but Rafiq had serious muscles.

Rafiq was a man who knew women—he'd had plenty and they'd all been reluctant for the affair to end. Some had called her to beg her to put in a good word for them.

Some had talked about his prowess in bed. Some had accused her of being the other woman.

She'd wondered about him, of course. He was a fabulously wealthy, handsome prince who had been involved with some of the most beautiful women in the world. What, exactly, was he like in his personal life?

But that musing had been curiosity, not the interest Eric had accused her of. Funny how many times she'd defended herself against the very actions she was about to take.

She moved closer, slipping between his parted thighs and placing her hands on his upper arms. She felt the crisp coolness of his cotton shirt and the heat and strength of his body below. He stayed relaxed and didn't try to hurry her. A faint smile drew the corners of his mouth upward. Then, with her eyes fluttering closed, she leaned in and kissed him.

His lips yielded slightly but did not part. She kept the kiss brief and chaste before moving to the left and lightly kissing his cheek. It was early enough in the day that his skin was still smooth, but she felt the hint of stubble that would arrive later.

She rubbed his cheek with hers, then kissed his jaw and the small spot right below his ear. Some tension inside of her uncoiled a little. Breath flowed more easily. She returned to his mouth, and this time she tilted her head and pressed her lips against his with more enthusiasm.

He responded but didn't try to deepen the kiss. Instead he put one hand on the small of her back. The warm pressure gave her the courage to wrap her arms around his neck and lightly brush her tongue against his bottom lip.

He parted for her. She had the brief thought that she hadn't kissed another man in five years. Only Eric. Then curiosity and a wave of pleasure had her slipping her tongue inside to explore what he offered.

He tasted of coffee and something sweet. His heat surprised her, as did his restraint. He let *her* touch *him*. She was the one who discovered the smoothness of the inside of his lower lip. She sought out his tongue and brushed it with her own.

The hand on her back never moved. He neither urged her forward nor suggested retreat. Not sure what to do next, she broke the kiss, dropped her arms to her sides and straightened. He did the same.

Rafiq's dark expression hadn't changed. No one walking in at this moment would guess anything unusual had happened. Yet Kiley felt a deep shift in the rotation of the universe.

She'd liked kissing Rafiq. Okay, maybe she hadn't seen stars, but she was still dealing with a lot of stuff. The fact that she'd felt anything at all was pretty amazing.

"Do you think we will suit?" he asked.

She was more than a little shocked by the fact that she'd been the one kissing him. "Yes."

"As do I. We will begin tonight. I will send my car for you at seven. You will spend the evening with me at my house. We will share dinner and work out the final details." He glanced at his watch. "I have a conference call in fifteen minutes. If you will get me the file?"

Kiley nodded, grabbed her pad and walked out of his office. As she stood by her own much-smaller desk, she had the sudden urge to break into hysterical laughter. Be careful what you wish for, she thought, not sure if she should celebrate or run for the hills.

Now that she had won the handsome Prince Rafiq of Lucia-Serrat, however temporarily…whatever was she going to do with him?

Chapter Two

Kiley wasn't sure what she should wear on her first night as mistress. Honestly, she couldn't even think the question without wanting to giggle like a teenager or throw up from sheer panic. Second thoughts didn't describe her roller coaster of emotion. Fear, excitement, worry and the pressing need to scream. A mistress? Her? She was the most normal woman on the planet. Her idea of wild living was to pay for a pedicure instead of doing it herself. How could she seriously consider being Rafiq's mistress?

And yet she had. She'd offered and he'd accepted and sometime very soon they were going to have sex.

She couldn't imagine it. Not with Rafiq. Not with any man, really. She'd thought about being intimate with Eric, but that was different. She hadn't worried about anything. She'd known he would be gentle and loving and exciting.

"Talk about wrong," she said aloud as she studied the contents of her closet. Eric had turned out to be Toad Boy and was out of her life forever. Now she was the soon-to-be mistress of a fabulously wealthy sheik prince. A thought she couldn't seem to wrap her mind around.

Not that she wasn't grateful he'd agreed to help her out. She intended to enjoy every moment of her revenge. That goal probably made her a bad person, but she was willing to live with it. The condition of her soul was a little less worrying at this moment than what to wear.

She had plenty of work clothes and tons of casual stuff—jeans, shirts, khaki skirts. But no real mistress wear. Not that she could identify mistress wear. It wasn't as if there was a section on it in InStyle magazine. But she had a feeling jeans and a cotton blouse weren't going to cut it and she didn't want to wear an outfit Rafiq had seen at the office.

After flipping through every item on a hanger, she settled on a simple blue short-sleeved dress and high-heeled sandals. She'd fake-tanned the previous week for her wedding, and there was still enough color on her legs that she didn't have to worry about pantyhose. Earrings and a quick application of lip gloss completed the look.

She still had a few minutes until the car was due to arrive. Kiley walked into the living room of her apartment and spent the time packing up what few remaining wedding presents she had yet to return.

Touching items she and Eric had picked out and put on their gift registry made her sad. Where had things gone wrong? What clues had she missed? Okay, her friends telling her Eric had hit on them was a big one. Why hadn't she listened?

"I'll take responsibility for being stupid about that," she murmured as she closed the box and picked up packing tape. "But not for what he did. He was the cheating, lying jerk in all this, not me."

She heard a car pull up and glanced out the window. Sure enough, there was a large, black limo right there in front of her door. As it was unlikely to be for any of her neighbors, Kiley put down the packing tape and picked up her purse.

Five minutes later she'd met Arnold, the very nice driver, and had been escorted to the huge back seat of the vehicle. The only other time she'd been in a limo had been for her high school prom, and she and her date had been one of the three couples sharing it. This was very different.

There was a bar, a TV and enough floor space for a Pilates workout. "This is so not like my world," she murmured as she buckled up.

A voice in her head asked if she knew what on earth she was doing. Kiley was ready to go with no on that one. She didn't. Not really. Being a mistress was an intellectual concept she didn't want to think about. *Actually* being one, in the flesh, so to speak, was a very scary reality she wasn't prepared to deal with. Although she would have to later that evening.

"I went to Rafiq," she reminded herself. "I'm the one who wanted this. Wanted him."

And she still did. Revenge was all she had left.

Traffic was surprisingly light for a workday evening,

and less than forty minutes later the limo drove down a long, narrow driveway that opened up in front of a wood-and-glass single-story house.

Tropical plants lined the walkway and provided a shaded entry. High walls on both sides offered privacy. When Arnold opened the rear door of the car, Kiley could hear the sound of the ocean.

"Have a nice evening," he said as she smiled at him. "I'll be waiting to take you home when you're finished."

Finished with what, she wanted to ask but didn't. Better not to know for sure.

She walked along the flagstone path to the huge double doors. Before she could find the bell and press it, the door opened and Rafiq stood in front of her.

He might have spoken. She wasn't sure. His lips moved, so there was probably sound, but she didn't hear it. She couldn't think, could barely breathe as she stared at him.

He wasn't in a suit. She'd known Rafiq for more than two years, and she'd only ever seen him in a suit. Usually without the jacket. He took that off as soon as he arrived at work and rarely put it on except for certain clients. She'd seen him tired, cranky, mussed, with his sleeves rolled up and his tie pulled off, but she'd never seen him dressed casually.

Tonight he wore tailored slacks and a polo shirt. The latter told her that her first impression about his body had been correct—plenty of lean muscle sculpted into something darned close to male perfection.

She'd known she was out of her league, based on the women he was usually involved with. Now she realized she was out of her league because of the man he was. Talk about a bad idea.

He was rich, royal and dangerous. He was also gorgeous.

She bit back the need to apologize for taking up his time and scurry back to the limo to be taken home. She'd asked, he'd been interested, and the decision had been made. For reasons clear to no one, Rafiq had wanted her as his mistress. As soon as she stopped hyperventilating, she was going to accept that truth and deal with it.

"Are you all right?" he asked.

She managed a smile. "Not even close, but I'll get better."

"What will help?"

"The passage of time or a head injury."

He smiled. "Perhaps some champagne."

"A possible alternative," she said as he led the way from the foyer into a step-down living room.

Seeing a casually dressed Rafiq had been one shock. Seeing the Pacific Ocean spread out before her like a fabulous painting was another. Floor-to-ceiling windows covered the entire west wall of the living room. She could see a deck, then a bit of sand, then moving, swirling beautiful blue ocean.

"Love the view," she said.

"I'm glad. It reminds me a little of Lucia-Serrat. My house on the island there overlooks the Indian Ocean."

"Is there a difference?"

He crossed to a glass-topped sofa table where a bottle of champagne sat in an ice bucket and a tray of appetizers nestled by two white plates.

Rafiq picked up the bottle and opened it. "The smell," he said at last. "The sound of the ocean is the same, but if I close my eyes and breathe deeply, I can always tell where I am. At home, the salt air is more tropical."

"While here it smells like Hollywood," she said, accepting the slender glass he offered.

"Is that the scent?"

"I'm only guessing," she said, staring at the bottle of Dom Perignon. Sure, she'd had champagne before but never anything *this* expensive. "I know in my head that Lucia-Serrat is a beautiful tropical island, but whenever I think of your part of the world, I picture sand and oil."

"There is that, as well," he said, gesturing to the sofa. "You are imagining traditional desert images. You can find the reality of that in El Bahar or Bahania."

She doubted visiting either country was going to be on her near-term to-do list. First she had to get her life back in order.

"You're related to the royal family of Bahania, aren't you?" she asked.

He waited until she'd settled on one end of the sofa and took the other for himself. "The king of Bahania and my father are cousins."

"An interesting extended family."

She tasted the champagne and was pleased by the light, bubbly flavor. "This is nice," she said.

"I'm glad you're enjoying it. Would you like something to eat?"

"No, thanks."

Food? Now? *So* not a good idea. She was already nervous. Eating would only upset her stomach, which could lead to an unfortunate throwing-up incident. Not a memory she wanted for her first visit to Rafiq's house.

Oh, God. She was in his house! She'd agreed to be his

mistress! Soon there would be nudity and sex and possibly bad language. Her life had become an R-rated movie.

She set down the glass and tried to think of something to say. Funny how she and Rafiq had never run out of things to talk about at the office. Of course there they had business to discuss and now they didn't. Somehow it didn't seem right to bring up the latest oil reserves or mention the meeting he would attend in the morning. She needed a slightly more "mistressy" topic. But what?

And how were they going to do it? Did he just make a move on her and she let him? Was there a universal question or signal she was supposed to pick up, because if there was, she was unlikely to get it.

"I can hear you thinking again," he said with a smile. "You are nervous."

"Wouldn't you be?"

"Under the circumstances?" He considered the question, then said, "Yes."

"Okay, then."

"Perhaps if we discussed logistics you would feel more comfortable."

She doubted anything would help but, hey, stranger things had happened. "Okay. Let's talk."

"I have several upcoming social events I would like you to attend. I will get you a list of dates. In return, if there's anything you want me to do with you, I will."

Her sister was about to give birth, and after the baby came, there would be a big family get-together. Somehow she couldn't imagine taking Rafiq to the party.

"I'll keep that in mind," she said.

"Why are you smiling?" he asked.

"Am I?" She shrugged. "Honestly, I can't see you fitting in with my family. Everyone is very normal. We're your basic hearty, peasant stock. Not a drop of royal blood anywhere."

"Why would that matter?"

"I doubt it's what you're used to."

"I adjust very well to different circumstances."

She angled toward him. "I'm one of three girls. The youngest, in fact. My father is a firefighter. My mom works in a gift store. They've been married thirty-one years and have lived in the same house for nearly twenty of them. It's a four-bedroom ranch-style built in the seventies."

"What is wrong with that?" he asked.

She laughed. "Nothing. My point is, you don't have a 'bondy story' to go with mine. What are you going to say? That the smallest family castle only has eleven bedrooms?"

"I believe it has fifteen, but I've never counted." Rafiq stared into Kiley's blue eyes and liked the amusement he saw there. "But I understand your point. We come from different worlds."

"I'm thinking it's more like different planets."

"Yours sounds very nice."

"It is," she said. "But yours has better jewelry."

He chuckled. "That is true."

She reached for her glass of champagne and took a sip. He watched her and knew the exact moment the humor faded and the nervousness returned. Her grip on the glass tightened and she refused to look at him.

"Kiley, we will not be making love tonight."

Her relief was nearly as tangible as the building itself. Tension dropped from her body, as she sagged back against the sofa. "Really?"

"We need to get to know each other first." He was amused by her reaction. Did she really think he intended to take her so quickly? Much of the pleasure lay in the anticipation, in watching her move and imagining her hands on his bare skin. In listening to her voice and knowing how it would sound when she begged him for more.

"Okay. Good point," she said. "It's just I've never done anything like this before. Obviously. In addition to the whole never-been-a-mistress-before thing, there's the fact that I'm not all that good with men." She wrinkled her nose, then took another sip of the champagne. "I didn't date much in high school. I was more the buddy type."

The information didn't surprise him. While Kiley was very attractive, hers was a more-subtle beauty. Still, the flower one must discover was more special than the one simply thrust in one's path.

"You met Eric in college?" he asked.

"My senior year. We were friends for a while, then we started dating. There were a couple of guys before him but no one special."

The women in his life were usually much more experienced. Not that Rafiq minded her relative innocence. "As I said, we will get to know each other," he told her. "Progress leisurely." He paused, then said, "I assume Eric was your only lover?"

He didn't mind the competition, he simply wanted to know how slowly he should move.

Kiley blushed and turned her head. "He, ah…"

"I do not mind if there have been more."

"Yes, well…" She finished her glass of champagne and set it on the coffee table. It was only when she raised her gaze to his that he saw the truth.

Not *more* lovers. *Less.*

She was a virgin.

Rafiq was less startled by the news than by the fierce need to possess her that swept through him. The primitive emotions startled him with their intensity. In his day-to-day life, he rarely felt his desert heritage, but at that moment he was one with his ferocious history.

"I know it's really old-fashioned, especially now," she said, speaking quickly. "Socially, it's not something I really talk about. I don't even know where the idea came from. My mom always talked about the first time being with someone I loved, but never that I should wait. Still, I wanted to. I wanted to give that to the man I married. I wanted to be a virgin on my wedding night."

She stared at the floor. "Eric knew, of course. He was all for it, the bastard. In a way that's what made it worse. I'm not a saint or a sexless creature. We would kiss and touch and I wanted to do more. I thought I was being strong and noble, and sometimes it was really tough. I thought he believed, too. Instead I would go home frustrated and he would head off to sleep with somebody else."

Rafiq had never had an opinion on Kiley's fiancé until she told him what he'd done. Then he'd felt mild annoyance and contempt. Now he wanted to hunt down the other man and horsewhip him into a bloody pulp. How dare he reject such an incredible gift with thoughtless callousness?

"It is better you didn't marry him," he said, careful to keep his anger from his voice.

"Agreed. He was a jerk and I'm lucky I found out before the wedding." She looked into her glass. "I just don't feel very lucky. I feel stupid. Like I did this really big thing and no one noticed or cared."

Her admission of innocence made him want her more. He wanted to be the first to touch her and pleasure her in the unique way a man could please a woman. But to defile a virgin...

"You must reconsider our arrangement," he told her, even as he longed to pull her close and take her. "Someone who was willing to wait so long should not give her gift so easily."

She stared at him. "You've changed your mind? But you can't."

"I have not," he said gently, hating the need to do the right thing. His body told him to take what was offered without question, but his soul demanded Kiley make the choice. "You said yourself you should be in love the first time."

"Were you?"

He smiled. "It is different for a man. We are eager to dispose of our virginity."

"Gee, that's what I'm thinking. I want this, Rafiq. I wouldn't have asked you if I didn't."

Honor demanded he give her an out. Now that he had and she'd refused it, he wouldn't ask again. "Then we will go on as planned," he said. "With one small change."

She frowned. "What's that?"

"I had thought we would wait a few days to become intimate. Now I think we will move even more slowly."

"You don't have to because of me."

"Oh, but I do." He moved closer and touched her cheek. Her skin was smooth and soft.

Based on what he'd heard about Eric, Rafiq would guess the other man hadn't been interested in teaching Kiley the possibilities.

"There are many ways for a man to please a woman," he said, staring into her eyes. "We will explore all of them together. I will show you the way it should be, and when you are ready, we will be lovers."

Kiley felt equal measures of relief and disappointment. On the one hand, she appreciated that she didn't have to get naked right this moment. On the other hand, there was something about Rafiq that intrigued her.

Maybe it was the way he talked—speaking of possibilities and pleasure. Moving slowly toward an ultimate goal. A shiver of anticipation raced up her spine. Maybe this was going to be fun.

"Would you like to see the house?" he asked. "There are some beautiful pieces I brought from Lucia-Serrat."

The change of topic left her blinking. Couldn't they keep talking about how great he was going to make it? Unfortunately there was no way she could ask, and as he stood, she would guess he hadn't read her mind.

"That would be nice," she said.

She accepted the hand he offered and let him pull her to her feet.

"This small chest was built in the sixteenth century," he told her, pointing at a small, carved chest by the end of the sofa. As he spoke, he rested one hand on the small of her back and placed the other on her upper arm.

Both points of contact were warm. Nice, she thought. More than nice. Interesting. Appealing. He moved his fingers back and forth, stroking her like a cat. As he continued to tell her the history of the chest and touch her, she found herself relaxing.

They circled the living room. He pointed out several works of art painted by people even she recognized. They passed through a large, well-appointed kitchen filled with the delicious scent of cooking dinner. Rafiq pointed to the oven.

"Sana, my housekeeper, has left us dinner. Are you hungry?"

As he asked the question, he put his hand back on her hip. She found herself wanting to step closer. How odd. Until this morning they'd never touched, except by accident as she passed a file or they walked together down the hall. Now he had the right to touch her whenever he wanted, and she could place her hand on him.

"Kiley?"

"What? Oh, dinner. Let's wait a bit. If I eat when I'm too nervous, really bad things happen."

He chuckled. "We don't want that."

"No."

She looked at him, at his broad shoulders and the thickness of his chest. Hard muscles under warm skin. What would he be like to touch?

"What are you thinking?" he asked.

She looked at his face. "That these are very unusual circumstances. When two people date, things start out slowly. Hand holding, then kissing and so on. With a few words we've given each other permission to do whatever we'd like, physically."

"What would you like to do?"

She laughed. "I'm not sure. It's just that I can. Does that make sense?"

"Yes. What would you like to do?" he asked again.

What would she?

She turned so she stood directly in front of him, then raised her hand to cup his cheek. The skin was smoother than it had been earlier when she'd kissed him.

"You shaved," she said, more than a little surprised.

"Yes. I grow a heavy beard and didn't want to scratch you."

Because he'd assumed they would kiss. He hadn't wanted her to be uncomfortable. She wasn't sure why she found the thoughtful gesture so intriguing, but she did. Maybe it was because he'd imagined them kissing. Had the idea been fleeting or had he considered it for some period of time? Did he feel anticipation? He did want her?

Her stomach clenched at the thought. Right now a man wanting her seemed very important. If Eric had ever wanted her, he'd managed to keep his feelings to himself. Or perhaps he'd simply burned them up in another woman's bed.

She lowered her hand from his cheek to his chest and splayed her fingers. He was as hard as she'd imagined. Sculpted. She had a sudden vision of touching his bare skin and her breath caught.

"The tour," she said, stepping back. "What's next?"

He stared at her for several seconds before taking her hand. "The bedrooms."

Oh, goody.

As they went down the hall, Rafiq pointed out several pictures. She saw a photo of his father, the crown prince of Lucia-Serrat, and one of Rafiq dressed for riding. He stood next to a beautiful horse. There were more paintings and objets d'art, a few antiques and a tapestry. He pointed out his home office, a very-well-equipped gym, a lavish guest room and then they stepped into what could only be the master bedroom.

A massive bed dominated the large, open space. Dark, carved furniture made the room seem masculine but not unwelcoming. There was a deck that overlooked the ocean, a low dresser, an armoire and a beautifully framed mirror hanging directly across from the door.

She could see herself in it, with Rafiq behind her. He was tall, several inches above her own five foot seven, and dark to her blond. They looked good together, if slightly wicked.

His eyes met hers in the mirror. She found herself caught in his gaze, thinking how handsome he was and how, just twenty-four hours ago, she could never have imagined herself in this exact position. Here. In his bedroom. Watching him watch her.

He put his hands on her shoulders, then bent down and lightly kissed the side of her neck.

Her entire body erupted in goose bumps as she both felt and saw the tender caress. His lips barely grazed her skin, but the warm, soft contact was enough to make her want to turn in his arms and beg for more. When he straightened, she found she'd stopped breathing and she had to consciously force herself to draw in a breath.

"Perhaps we should see about dinner," he said, his voice low and sensual.

Dinner? Oh, yeah. That evening meal she'd been too nervous to eat before. The good news was she wasn't nervous anymore. The bad news was she hadn't just jumped into the deep end of the pool, she'd taken a flying leap into the middle of the ocean.

Chapter Three

"You completed college with two degrees?" Rafiq asked as he poured Kiley more wine. It had taken her most of the meal to drink the first glass. He knew she didn't smoke, it seemed she barely drank and, based on her bright, cheerful, early-morning demeanor, she didn't party.

"Business and early-childhood development." She pushed a slice of chicken around on her plate. "Odd combination, I know."

"Not if one plans to open a day-care facility."

She looked at him and smiled. "You're right. I'd never thought of that. I love kids. Honestly, I never wanted much more than to be a wife and mother. The business degree was so I could get a good job, and the other studies were to help me to be a good mother. Although, my mom didn't study anything and she was the best. I want to be just like her."

Kiley nibbled on a slice of carrot. "You're probably disappointed."

He'd always known she was intelligent, so her multiple degrees didn't surprise him. She'd carried her half of the conversation at dinner and she continued to surprise him.

"What exactly would have disappointed me?" he asked.

"Me being a secretary and wanting to be a mother. Not very big aspirations. A lot of my friends were shocked when I admitted it to them. They think I should be more. Do more. I guess I feel guilty. These days women are supposed to have it all. But I don't want it all. I just want a little house with a garden and a couple of kids and a man who loves us as much as we love him."

He had been born into royalty, so not many of his acquaintances shared his lifestyle, but Kiley was farther removed than most.

He'd never longed for a small house with a garden. While a wife and children were in his future, the assumption that he would one day marry and father children was far more about providing his country with an heir than any personal desire on his part.

She put down her fork and leaned toward him. "I know that I shouldn't care about what other people think, or the expectations of our society in general, but sometimes it bugs me."

Her expression was earnest, her blue eyes wide and intent. The soft light from the chandelier brought out the strands of gold in her hair. She was beautiful and sincere and he could honestly say he'd never had a conversation like this with a woman he intended to seduce.

"Do you spend much of your day worrying about the expectations of society?" he asked.

"No. Just sometimes." She shook her head. "I'm guessing you can't relate to any of this. You knew who and what you were from the time you were born. Is that a good thing?"

"It simply is, for me. I haven't imagined another life. What would be the point?"

"Plus you're really rich and can pretty much do what you want. That has to be a good thing."

"It is."

She smiled. "So you're not married, right? I just realized I never asked about a Mrs. Rafiq sequestered back on the island."

"I wouldn't be here with you tonight if I was."

"Really?" She sounded surprised. "You'll be faithful when you're married?"

"Do you question me specifically or all men in general?"

"I guess the whole fidelity issue is a sore spot for me, but right now I'm asking about you specifically."

"I'm faithful now."

"With very short-term relationships. Marriage is forever. At least it's supposed to be."

"The expectation for me is that my wife and I will only be parted by death."

"And you'll be faithful all that time?" she asked.

"Of course."

"You're going to have to be really sure you love her."

Love? As if that mattered. "My choice will be based

on more practical matters. She will be the mother of my children."

"But if you don't love her…"

Rafiq found it intriguing that, after all she had been through, she was still a romantic. "Respect and shared goals often last longer than love."

Kiley didn't look convinced. "So, is there a place one goes to find a woman fit to be a princess? Like a princess store?"

Her eyes were bright with humor and the corners of her mouth curved up.

"There's an Internet site," he said, pretending to be serious.

"Oh, I'd love to see it. Do you type in specifications? Height, weight, number of sons required."

"Of course. Along with how many languages I want her to speak and what accomplishments she should have."

"You really need to get going on that," she said with a smile. "So you aren't too old when your kids are born. You want to be able to play ball with them."

"I have a few good years left."

"I don't know. You're over thirty."

"By a year."

"Still. You're looking a little creaky."

"How charming," he said dryly. He liked that she was feeling comfortable enough to joke with him.

"How many children do you want?" he asked.

"Three or four. I was one of three and it was great. There was always someone to play with, and with three of us, the blame for whatever bad thing we'd done could get spread around."

He could see her in a small house, raising her children, working in the garden. She would bake cookies and sew Halloween costumes, and ask for almost nothing for herself. He could imagine birthdays and Christmases when the children would receive piles of presents and there would only be one or two for her. But she wouldn't mind, because her world would be defined by her family.

He studied the gold hoop earrings she wore and the delicate chain around her neck. Modest pieces at best. She would look good in jewels, he thought. Sapphires. The traditional blue stones would match her eyes. He would like to see her in pink sapphires as well. And diamonds. Diamonds and nothing else.

The image of a Kiley wearing only diamonds filled his mind. Desire licked through him, heating his blood. He enjoyed the sensation, even knowing he would not have her for some time. In this case, anticipation would sweeten the union.

"I have been invited to a fund-raiser on Friday evening," he said. "The event is formal and I would very much like you to attend with me."

"Sure." She wrinkled her nose. "How formal?"

"Black tie."

"I've never been clear on what that meant, but I get the general idea. The only really fancy dress I have is my wedding dress, and that would probably be tacky to wear, huh?"

As soon as she spoke, she covered her mouth with her hand. "Oh, no. Is it okay that I said that? Are you offended?"

"It was your wedding, Kiley. You may speak of it as you wish."

"Good. Either way, the dress isn't a good idea. I'll come up with something. I need to take off a little early one day this week to get to the post office and ship back the rest of the gifts. I'll go shopping after that."

Dismantling a wedding sounded like as much work as putting it together, he thought. "Where were you and Eric going to live?"

"We rented an apartment together. The lease doesn't start until the end of the month and we'd discussed maybe painting it before moving in, so I haven't given notice at my place, fortunately." She sighed. "I have to break the lease on the new place, which won't be fun."

"I'll take care of it," he said.

She looked at him. "I appreciate the offer, but it's not your responsibility."

"You are right. It's Eric's. But he is not here and I am. Besides, now you are *my* responsibility."

"Is this a mistress perk?"

He smiled. "One of many."

A faint flush darkened her cheeks. "Are you going to get all imperious if I say I want to do it myself."

"Absolutely. I do imperious very well."

She laughed. "Okay, then I'll give in graciously and say thank you. It's really nice of you to offer, and to be honest I wasn't looking forward to making that call."

"Now you don't have to."

Kiley had no idea why Rafiq had taken on the chore. Under other circumstances she would wonder if he was going to pass it on to his staff, but this time she doubted it. After all, she was part of that staff, and as his secretary, she would know.

"Have you finished?" he asked, nodding at her plate.

"Yes. It was delicious." And she'd eaten more than she'd thought. Funny how once they got talking, she forgot to be nervous.

He stood, walked around the table and waited until she stood. Then he put his hand on the small of her back and guided her through the living room, out onto the deck.

The sun had set some time before, so the ocean was barely visible. She could see the faint white of the waves as they crashed into the shore and, in the distance, lights from another house. He moved in close behind her and wrapped his arms around her waist, drawing her against him.

The night was cool; the man, warm. She liked the feel of him pressed against her, liked the way he held her close.

"I enjoyed dinner," she said. "We have a lot to talk about."

"Are you surprised?"

"A little. I thought things might be awkward, but they're not. Why is that?"

"You're intelligent and don't want to talk about clothes and shoes."

She laughed. "Do you get that a lot?"

"You would be surprised how much."

"Then you're in for a treat with me. I promise never to talk about my clothes. They're just not that interesting."

"They would be if you took them off."

The unexpected shift in the chitchat direction made her breath catch. In a single heartbeat she went from enjoying the moment to being hyperaware of the man. His words shocked her, but in a way that made her curious and excited.

"Fear not, Kiley. I meant what I told you earlier. Not tonight. Not for some time. But I will have you."

The low growl of his voice made her shiver. "Will I like it?"

"I will do my best to make sure you do."

As he spoke, he bent down and kissed her neck. He'd done that earlier, in the bedroom. She closed her eyes and remembered how they'd looked standing together, then her mind cleared as her body absorbed the soft brush of his mouth against her sensitive skin.

He kissed her with the slow deliberateness of a man who had all the time in the world. She tilted her head to give him more room and held on to his arms. He worked his way up from the curve where her neck met her shoulder to the sensitive skin just behind her ear.

"What are you thinking?" he asked, his breath tickling her.

"That this is nice. It feels good."

He raised his head and turned her in his arms so that she faced him. Light from the living room spilled out onto the deck and allowed her to see his features. His dark eyes seemed to burn with an intensity she'd never seen before. There was tension in his body but an easy smile on his lips. Funny how she knew so little about him yet she trusted him. She'd asked to be his mistress for the purpose of revenge, but now she found herself anticipating the three months they were to have together.

He touched her face, tracing the shape of her nose, her mouth. He ran his hands down her neck, then across her shoulders to her arms. From there he slipped to her hands, which he took in his.

"You're very beautiful," he murmured.

"Thank you. But not really. The beautiful part, I mean. I appreciate the compliment though."

He studied her face. "I have been with many women. I know of what I speak. Your eyes are large, and the color forever changes. Dark blue, then darker still. Stormy, clear. Your skin is perfection. Your mouth calls to me, begging for kisses."

He raised her right hand and pressed his lips against her palm. She felt *that* tingle all the way down to her toes.

"Every part of you is beautiful."

Okay, maybe this was part of the seduction, but it was working. She felt her knees getting a little weak and her blood zipping along a little faster.

He reached up with one hand and touched her hair.

"Too short?" she asked. "I know most guys prefer long hair, but I like it short. Eric was forever after me to grow it out."

"I like it," he said, sliding his fingers against her scalp and drawing her a little closer.

She went willingly, hoping he would kiss her, because suddenly she needed to be kissing him. She put her hands on his shoulders and shifted that last inch so that her body pressed against his.

His chest was hard and hot against her sensitive breasts. Her thighs lightly brushed his. It was all so…interesting…and she wanted to get moving to the next level. The kissing level.

He smiled. "I sense your impatience."

"Well, there *is* more talking than I'd thought there'd be."

"Are you complaining?"

"A little."

"Just this morning you were uncomfortable with my kiss. I don't want to rush you."

"I'm okay with it now," she said, staring at his mouth. "Completely fine with it. Look how totally fine I am right now."

"Show me."

Kiley hesitated only a second. Her natural shyness battled with the intellectual knowledge that this was a sure thing. Then need overcame reticence as she wrapped her arms around his neck, rose on tiptoe and pressed her mouth to his.

Unlike the kiss from that morning, he didn't wait to respond. He tilted his head and kissed her back, moving with her, teasing, brushing. His hands settled on her hips, holding her against him. The light pressure made her want to shift closer still, although that didn't seem possible. They were already touching from shoulder to knee.

This felt good, she thought as he touched his tongue to her bottom lip and she parted for him. Better than good.

He claimed her with a fiery passion that left her breathless. One moment there'd been gentle, arousing kisses, but the next moment overwhelming desire threatened to consume her.

He swept inside and stroked her tongue with his. Something about the way he touched her, the way he teased and retreated only to take her again and again had her wanting to surrender. Whatever he wanted he could have—as long as he didn't stop kissing her.

She melted against him, wishing she could crawl inside his body. His hands didn't move from her hips even though she silently pleaded with them to touch and discover and knead. Heat flared between her legs; her breasts swelled. She wanted to rub against him. She wanted to suggest they take this inside.

She'd felt wanting before, of course, but never so quickly, and never with someone she barely knew. Except she did know Rafiq—she had for over two years. But not in this way.

Confusion joined with passion to cloud her mind. Not sure what she felt or what she should do, she stepped back.

His dark eyes revealed nothing of his thoughts.

"Rafiq, I—"

"Shh." He pressed his fingers to her mouth. "It's late. I'll have Arnold take you home."

"But…"

He shook his head and kissed her cheek. "I'll see you at the office. I have a business dinner tomorrow night, but I would like to take you out Wednesday evening."

"I'd like that, too."

She would. Not just because of how she felt when he kissed her but because she enjoyed spending time with him. But what had happened tonight?

He escorted her out to the limo before she could figure out how to ask. As she leaned back in the soft leather for the drive home, she closed her eyes and consoled herself with the thought that there would be more. Much more. Three months was a long time and anything could happen.

Kiley wore her favorite silk blouse to work the next day. It was cobalt blue and suited her coloring. She figured she needed all the confidence she could get after the previous night.

What had happened? How could she have reacted so strongly to Rafiq's kisses? She could accept that she'd enjoyed his company, but what about the rest of it? Less than a week ago she'd planned to marry Eric and live with him for the rest of her life.

Maybe it was a post-wedding reaction. She'd been so focused on the path her life was supposed to take. When it hadn't, she'd been set adrift, carried by a current she couldn't control. She was confused, and Rafiq was a familiar and trusted haven.

Okay, that might explain her emotional reaction to him, but what about the sexual one? She'd been so intent on wanting revenge that she hadn't thought past that. She hadn't considered the reality of actually sleeping with him. If she had, she never would have had the courage to talk to him about her being his mistress.

Yesterday she would have assumed she would simply grit her teeth and get through the sex part because it was expected. Now she thought she might be the one hurrying things along in that department.

Which was not like her at all. She'd been comfortable being a virgin for twenty-five years. Why wasn't she more apprehensive about making love with Rafiq?

When no answer popped into her head, she decided to forget the question and concentrate on work. After making coffee and taking a few calls, she settled down to edit a report one of the staff members had put together. She'd barely finished the first page when Rafiq walked in.

"Good morning," he said as he walked by her desk.

"Morning."

It was the same greeting they always exchanged,

only, this time she was hyperaware of him. She could sense the movement of his body, feel his gaze on her. She felt hot and bewildered and shy and not sure what to do with her hands.

"I left the messages on your desk," she murmured as she rose. "I'll bring in coffee."

The familiar routine should have comforted her, but it didn't. Suddenly everything was awkward. Just twelve hours before, she'd been in Rafiq's arms as they kissed. She'd wanted him with a passion that had surprised her. How on earth was she supposed to forget all that and discuss business?

She poured his coffee and carried it into his office, along with her notepad and a pen. She set the cup on the table and took her usual seat across from his desk.

He'd already removed his suit jacket and settled behind his desk. He studied the messages, then returned two to her.

"Schedule meetings for next week," he said. "An hour each. They'll want more. Tell them no."

She made notes. "You have a lunch meeting today."

He glanced at his schedule and nodded. "The reserve report is due this morning."

"I've already told the mail room to send it up to me."

"Very well."

They discussed business for a few more minutes, then Rafiq leaned back in his chair and looked at her. "I would like to take you shopping tomorrow night," he said.

She clutched her notepad. "I don't understand."

"You will need new clothes. There is the fund-raiser Friday night and several other social events coming up."

She'd never shopped with a man before. She didn't

think men ever *liked* to shop with women. Or anyone, for that matter.

"I can shop on my own," she said. "You don't have to—"

"I want to," he said, cutting her off. "Plus, I can explain what will be required for the various events." He smiled. "Believe me, I will enjoy the experience."

"Okay. If you say so."

"I do. Also, I thought we would want to go away for a long weekend in a month or so. Where would you like to go?"

A trip? Just the two of them? Pleasure filled her at the thought. "I'd like that. But I haven't been many places so anywhere would be exciting for me."

"Paris?" he asked.

She blinked. "Wow. Sure. I'd been thinking more on the lines of somewhere within driving distance, but Paris is good."

"Or London."

She grinned. "Hey, maybe you should surprise me."

"I will. You have a passport?"

"Uh-huh. In my sock drawer." It was nearly three years old and every single page was untouched.

"Good."

There was a moment of silence and Kiley realized she should leave. She gathered her pad and pen, stood and walked to the door. When she reached it, she turned back.

"I had a good time last night."

"As did I."

She bit her lower lip, then smiled. "I thought it would be weird, you know? But it was fun. We had a lot to talk about. I didn't expect that. You're great to work for, but honestly, I never really thought of how you'd be outside of the office. You're nice."

"How thrilling."

She held in a laugh. "You don't want me to think of you as nice?"

"Not really."

"Because you're macho and a prince?"

"Something like that."

"Then I won't mention the nice thing to anyone else."

"I would appreciate that."

Chapter Four

After work on Wednesday, Rafiq escorted Kiley to the limo. She hesitated a second before sliding onto the seat.

"What's wrong?" he asked as she shifted several times instead of reaching for her seat belt.

"Nothing serious," she said with a sigh, then grabbed the seat belt. "I'm nervous. It's not a big deal. Right? I mean it's shopping. I've shopped before. Not with you, though."

He smiled. "I assure you the experience will not be that unfamiliar."

"I wish I could believe you," she murmured as she glanced around at the limo. "You have a regular car, don't you? I've seen you in it."

"Yes. I usually drive myself to and from work. However, the trunk is small and there isn't a back seat, so I thought this would be better."

"It certainly made an impression on my neighbors this morning."

He supposed being picked up in a vehicle like this wasn't the normal morning routine for those who lived in her apartment building.

"I thought it would be easier for us to drive together today so we would have one car for this evening," he said.

She nodded. "I agree. It's a great plan." She angled toward him. "It's just that sometimes the difference between your world and my world is pretty startling. You're a prince."

"We have already discussed that."

"I know. It was fine when you were just my boss, but now, it's totally strange. I'm used to seeing princes in movies, mostly as cartoons. Now you're here, in real life." She glanced toward the privacy partition that was in place and lowered her voice. "It's hard to get my mind around. In theory, I could see you naked."

"I hope it is more than in theory."

"You know what I mean."

He did and her concerns amused him. Unlike other women who only wanted him on their arm to show off what they had managed to catch, Kiley wasn't sure she wanted him at all. He was going to have to change her mind about that.

To that end, he reached for her hand and lifted it to his mouth. As she watched, he gently bit the fleshy pad below her thumb, then licked the center of her palm.

"You worry too much," he said as he laced their fingers together. "Think about shopping."

He couldn't be sure, but he thought her breathing might have increased slightly. She shook her head as if to clear it, then faced front.

"Okay," she said. "Shopping. How exactly does that work?"

"I wouldn't have thought this was your first time in a store."

She rolled her eyes. "That's not what I mean. This is my first time shopping with you. I know what you've done with your other women. I've seen the bills."

"Then what questions do you have?"

"Just that I don't really wear a lot of expensive clothes. I'm not sure that I need them."

"The events we will attend require you to dress a certain way. It is my decision to go and therefore the clothes are my responsibility. I know how much I pay you and while the salary is more than generous, it does not cover expenses like these."

She looked at him and narrowed her gaze. "Excuse me? A *more* than generous salary? I earn every penny of that. I work really hard and I'm good at my job and…" She stopped and pressed her lips together.

"Yes?" he promoted.

"You were teasing me."

"That was my original plan."

"Sorry. Okay, so you buy me really expensive clothes. Can we return them in three months so you get your money back?"

"No. You will keep the clothes. Another mistress perk."

She leaned back against the seat. "Except for my father, no man has ever bought me clothes. I'm not in this for the money, Rafiq."

"I'm aware your motives are far more noble."

She considered that. "Is revenge noble?"

"I come from a long line of cruel warriors. It is to me."

"An interesting way of looking at things, but okay. I just want to be sure you understand why I'm doing this."

He leaned toward her and touched her cheek. "I understand completely."

"I don't care about keeping the clothes."

"Perhaps you will change your mind when you see them."

"Unlikely. But I appreciate you doing all this for me."

"A perk," he reminded her

"What are your perks?" she asked.

"You."

"I don't actually consider myself a perk. I'm a sure thing, which may or may not be a plus. I'm not experienced. For all you know, I'll be crappy in bed."

"Unlikely."

"I wish I could be as positive."

"Are you nervous?"

She dropped her gaze. "Of course. When I think about us, you know, doing it."

He smiled. "It will be more than just 'doing it.'"

"Oh." She swallowed and returned her gaze to his. "You have a lot of experience, don't you? I know how many women there have been just since I've been working for you. Doesn't that get old? Don't you ever want more than an endless parade of beautiful, willing women?" She shook her head. "Never mind. I answered my own question."

"The variety is nice."

"Okay. I get that, but what about really knowing

someone? What about feeling connection and a place to belong?"

"That does not come from a relationship. That comes from within." He rubbed his thumb across her mouth. "I say how long. I say when it's over. Then they walk away and I am free."

"So no one gets hurt?"

"I hope they don't," he said. "I make the rules as clear as I can. Sometimes they get too involved and I feel bad about that."

"What about you? Do you ever get hurt?"

"Not so far. I am fairly impervious to most female charms."

"Really?"

He smiled. "Do you take that as a challenge?"

"I can't tell you how much I want to say yes, but I don't think I can. I get nervous just being in your car. But someone, somewhere is going to get to you."

"Do you think so?"

"The law of averages are in my favor."

"Do you want to be there to see it happen?" he asked.

"No. I don't want to see you hurt. Is that what you think of me?"

He studied her blue eyes and the intense honesty he saw there. "No. You worry too much about other people's feelings."

"Not Eric's," she reminded him. "I hope he's feeling horrible, but I doubt it."

He watched the play of emotions as they drifted across her face.

"Are you still sad?" he asked.

"Sometimes. But I thought it would hurt more. I

thought I'd be devastated and I worry that I'm not. I keep telling myself the pain hasn't hit yet."

"Perhaps you were not as in love with him as you thought."

She shook her head. "If that's true, it's not good news. I was going to marry him."

"Love is not required."

"It is in my world. It's bad enough that he treated me like an idiot. If I went through all that and didn't love him, then I'm going to need some serious therapy to get my life on track."

He chuckled, then leaned forward and lightly kissed her. "I always enjoy your perspective on things."

"My sister says I'm twisted."

"Only in a good way."

"I'm not sure that's possible."

She smiled as she spoke. Rafiq realized that he liked Kiley. He'd always thought of her as efficient and attractive, but the more he got to know her as a person, the more he found himself enjoying her company. He could not always say that about the women in his life.

When this was over, he was going to have to do something for her. Perhaps he would buy her a house and pay off the rest of her wedding. Something that would help her future.

But first there was the present—this night and their shopping expedition. He usually found shopping sessions boring, but not this time. Not with her. He had very specific plans to further her seduction.

Kiley had nearly relaxed when the car pulled up in front of a very elegant-looking boutique in the heart of

Beverly Hills. Instantly tension exploded in her stomach, making her midsection ache and her mouth go dry.

She took in the custom awnings, the expensive window displays and the sign for valet parking and knew she was in over her head. Then she saw the Closed sign on the glass front door and nearly giggled with delight.

"Gee, they're not open," she said, trying not to sound delighted.

"To the general public," Rafiq said as Arnold walked around to open the rear door. "I have made special arrangements with the owner."

Bummer. "Do you always come here?" she asked.

"It is one of my favorite stores, but no, there are others I frequent. However, I thought the selection here would suit you best."

"Have you slept with the owner?"

Rafiq looked at her and raised his eyebrows. "Why do you ask?"

She shrugged. "I thought a place like this would be owned by some elegant woman from France or Italy. You know the type—impossibly beautiful with a fabulous accent."

"While Gerald is a delightful gay man, he is not my type, so no. We are merely friends."

Kiley felt the heat on her cheeks and knew she was blushing. Hopefully Rafiq wouldn't notice.

She vowed she would keep her mouth shut at all times and only speak when spoken to. That was the only possible way to get through this. Being Rafiq's mistress had seemed like an easy solution to her problem of how to hurt Eric back, but in reality, it wasn't that simple at all.

He led her into the boutique. The sign might say the store was closed, but the door wasn't locked, and as soon as they stepped inside, they were greeted by a tall, thin, well-dressed man who kissed both her hands and declared her to be completely "precious."

"So much potential," Gerald told Rafiq as he looked Kiley over. "I have the list you sent me and several things already picked out."

Kiley reclaimed her hands and shifted closer to Rafiq. "You sent him a list?"

"Yes. Of events. Via e-mail."

Of course. Otherwise, how would they know what to buy?

"What can I get you?" Gerald asked. "Champagne? Wine?"

Kiley had a feeling that liquor was a bad idea. "I'll have a glass of sparkling water, if you have it."

"Of course."

Rafiq ordered scotch, then leaned close to her. "Sparkling water. You're so wild."

"Hey, I got it with lime."

He smiled at her and in that moment, time stood still. Kiley didn't know what to make of it. Why did one smile matter? But she couldn't help feeling happy and a little floaty as he and Gerald discussed her clothing needs.

She took the glass of sparkling water that one of the sales clerks offered her and nearly choked when she heard the word *lingerie.*

Gerald excused himself to prepare the dressing room. Kiley turned to Rafiq. "Lingerie?"

"Of course."

"But why?" She shook her head. "Never mind. It's

probably a good idea. I buy my stuff on sale. I doubt you'd be impressed."

"It is more about the present than the wrapping, but sometimes the wrapping is nice, too."

She'd never thought of lingerie as wrapping, but she supposed it was. Several minutes later she found herself trying on slacks and blouses, sweaters and boots. There was an entire collection of casual clothes. She put on each outfit and walked out for Rafiq's nod of approval. He often asked her opinion, agreeing when she liked something, telling her not to get it if she didn't.

After a half hour or so of casual wear, she moved into cocktail dresses. There were flirty designs with asymmetrical hems and black silk with beading. These were followed by actual formal gowns.

Kiley found herself zipped into one that was strapless, velvet and flowing. The garment swayed with her movements. The strapless style showed off more than she was used to but she didn't feel exposed. Instead she ran her hands down the velvet clinging to her body and knew this was the one.

"I love it," she said as she burst out of the dressing room and twirled in front of Rafiq. "Isn't it the best? Don't you love the skirt?" She held it out for him, then spun again. "Even the shoes are fabulous." She held out one foot to show the strappy silver sandals Gerald had brought her. "They hurt, but beauty is pain."

Rafiq stood and moved next to her. "So you like it?"

"I love it. But seriously, where exactly am I going to wear something like this?"

"To the fund-raiser on Friday."

"Really? You mean I can get it?"

He smiled. "You are unlike anyone I've known before. So very earnest."

"No. Not earnest. I want to be sexy and exotic and—"

He cut off the rest of her sentence by pulling her close and kissing her. There were no preliminaries this time, no gentle teasing. Instead he claimed her, thrusting into her mouth and taking what he wanted.

Had someone described such a kiss to Kiley, she would have sworn she would hate it, but in reality, she found herself eager to surrender. The act of being taken by a man who knew exactly what he was doing was a short road to pleasure. Blood heated, her thighs trembled, and soon she found herself forgetting about everything but the need to be as close to him as possible.

At last he drew back and rested his hands on her shoulders. "What were you saying?" he asked.

"I haven't got a clue."

"Good. We will take the dress because it was made for you."

He turned her toward the dressing room, kissed her bare shoulder and then gave her a little push.

She moved as if in a dream. Wow, talk about an easy way to cloud her mind and change the subject. He was really good at that whole kissing thing. They should do it more.

But when Kiley walked into the spacious dressing room, she found herself suddenly nervous again. Not because of what Rafiq had done, but because of the lace and silk nightgown hanging directly in front of her.

Oh, my. So, was she expected to, ah, try that on and model it?

She crossed the carpeted floor and stood in front of the lingerie. In theory she could be covered, but the lace didn't leave all that much to the imagination.

Still, this was for Rafiq and he was going to see her naked eventually. She might as well get used to the idea. Besides, so far all their physical contact had been pretty spectacular.

She removed the evening gown and the sandals, then slipped off her strapless bra. As she reached for the nightgown, she would have sworn the lights dimmed just a little.

The silk and lace slid down her body. The cool fabric made her shiver, but not as much as when the door suddenly opened and Rafiq entered the large dressing room.

He seemed taller, bigger and more dangerous. She'd always known he was a man, but at that moment he seemed even more male. Almost predatory.

She had the urge to cover herself, but instead forced herself to stand still, with her chin raised. She wanted this. At least, that was the theory.

His dark gaze swept over her, settling on her face. "You're very beautiful," he said.

"Thank you."

"Do you believe me?"

"I want to."

"You should believe." He took a step closer.

There was something about his eyes, something...

"What are you thinking?" she asked, half afraid of the answer.

"That I want you. I will not take you. Not yet, but I want you."

His words made her tremble, but not with fear. Instead an emotion swept through her—one she couldn't identify right away. And then she knew.

Desire.

She wanted him. While she was nervous and uncertain, she still wanted to know what it would be like to be with him.

He moved close but didn't touch her. Instead he slowly walked around her. "You told me you were a virgin," he said, his voice low. "How far did you and Eric go?"

The question embarrassed her. "Some kissing," she whispered.

He stopped in front of her and touched her cheek. "I only wish to understand how much is familiar and what is new. I want to excite you, Kiley, not frighten you."

Of course. "We, ah, did some touching. You know, he, ah, touched my breasts."

His gaze never left her face. "Anywhere else?"

"A little. Just through clothes."

"Did you touch him?"

"Not, um, there."

"Did you see him naked?"

She swallowed. "No."

"But you do understand what happens between a man and a woman?"

"Yes," she whispered. "I got an A in health class."

He chuckled. "I'm sure you did."

He moved behind her. The dressing room was a circle of mirrors so she could see him as he lowered his head and lightly kissed her shoulder. She saw as well as felt the scrape of his teeth on her skin. Her breasts tightened. The outlines of her nipples were clearly visible.

When he brought his hand around in front of her, she

was sure he was going to touch her there. Instead he rested his palm on her belly and splayed his fingers. She felt the imprint of each one.

Move! She silently screamed at him to shift higher, to touch her breasts. They ached, and she knew that only his touch would make things better. Heat burned her through the silk, but he did not move. Just when she was about to cover his hand with hers and lift him into place herself, he straightened and stepped back.

"We should go now."

"I've never gone through a drive-thru in a limo before," Kiley said as she unlocked her front door and stepped into her ground-floor apartment. "I'm just glad we managed the turn. I'm sure everyone there talked about seeing us."

Rafiq watched as Kiley flipped on lights, then showed Arnold to the bedroom.

"I made room in my closet earlier." She eyed the hanging bags and boxes, then shook her head. "But not enough. We'll be a second," she called to Rafiq. "Make yourself at home."

He did as she requested, moving around the living room, stopping to look at family photographs on a shelf in the corner and above the unit holding the television. There were photos of three girls, obviously sisters, and parents. Pictures from graduations, weddings, and vacations. None that could be Eric, though, he thought.

Arnold and Kiley came out of the bedroom. His chauffeur nodded and left, while Kiley picked up the bags of burgers and fries. "Do you want to eat in here, or in the dining room? Well, it's not a room, really.

More of a nook. But there are chairs and a table. Or we could eat at the sofa. Do you want to watch something on television?"

She still wore the clothes she'd had on at work that day. A narrow skirt and pale-pink blouse, sensible high heels. He preferred her in the nightgown...or perhaps nothing. Yes, that would be his preference. Bare skin.

"Why are you nervous again?" he asked. "I thought you were more comfortable with me now."

"I am. It's not you. It's me and the apartment." She shrugged. "I like it here. The place was built in the 1920s so there are lots of architectural details. I like the high ceilings and arched doorways. But it's still a one-bedroom apartment. You're Prince Rafiq of Lucia-Serrat. Have you even been in an apartment before?"

"Yes. Several times." Although not one like this, he thought. Still, he liked the pretty furniture and the plants that grew in brightly colored pots. "This place suits you."

"Thank you. I like it. No pets, though, and I always wanted a dog. Not that Eric did. Don't you want to eat?"

He shook his head. "I am not hungry, but you go ahead."

"Is it the burger thing? Should we have gone somewhere more upscale?"

"It is not about the food at all."

"Then what's wrong? You seem...restless."

He was. The logical part of him, the civilized man, knew that seduction would be the most pleasurable road for both of them. But the desert warrior wanted to simply take the woman before him. He wanted to know the heat of her embrace, the taste of her skin. He wanted to hear her cries of pleading, then of pleasure, as he coaxed her into surrender.

So he held on, knowing it was too soon and yet still needing that which he could not have.

"I find myself in the unique position of waiting for what I want," he said.

She tilted her head. "I don't understand."

"You."

"Oh." Her eyes widened. "But we have an agreement. I'm a sure thing. You could just…you know. Do it."

He smiled. "As we've discussed. But there is more to being with a woman than the act itself. There is anticipation and then joint pleasure. I'm not interested in getting off, Kiley. I want you to be as ready, as aroused."

Her eyes got bigger and bigger. He moved closer but didn't touch her.

"Besides, there are other pleasures," he told her. "Tonight I enjoyed watching you try on different clothes. I imagined where we would be when you wore them. What we would be doing. Dancing in the ball gown. On the beach with you in shorts."

She stared at him. "The nightgown?" she asked, barely breathing.

"In my bed."

"Is that something you like thinking about?"

"Yes. It makes me want you more."

He reached for her hand and brought it to him. He guided her until her palm pressed against his erection. He kept his touch light, in case she wanted to pull away. Instead she rubbed against the length of him, discovering his hardness.

"All this from thinking about us being together?" she asked.

He nodded.

"What would happen if we kissed?"

Chapter Five

Kiley hadn't meant to kiss Rafiq, but there she was, up on tiptoe, pressing her mouth against his. Something had come over her and she'd given in to the urge. Fortunately, he didn't seem to mind. He kissed her back, moving his mouth against hers.

She put her hands on his shoulders and felt the strength of him. So solid, she thought. So masculine. There was power there, which he kept under careful control. What would happen if he truly let go? Would she be overwhelmed? Swept away? Both thoughts thrilled her.

She wrapped her arms around his neck and leaned into him. He brushed his tongue against her bottom lip as he rested his hands on the small of her back. More, she thought as she parted for him. She wanted more.

Every part of her ached. An unfamiliar wanting made her skin feel too tight. Heat flared within her, moving without purpose, leaving her edgy and impatient.

She circled his tongue with hers, then pressed her lips together and sucked. He tensed in her arms, then nipped at her lower lip.

Was he still hard? she wondered, not exactly sure how to find out. She wanted to press her hips against his, rub with her belly to feel for the thick ridge, but the action seemed too obvious and tacky. Still, touching him had been exciting. To think he could react like that without them doing anything thrilled her. She wanted more. She wanted...

He moved his hands to her waist where he tugged gently on her blouse. The cotton pulled free of the waistband of her skirt. As they continued to kiss, he slid his hands under the fabric until he touched her bare skin.

Excitement filled her. Even as he pulled back enough to kiss his way along her jaw, he slipped his hand around to her waist, then slowly, ever so slowly, up her rib cage.

Yes, she thought, letting her head fall back. He kissed her neck, then nipped her earlobe, and still his hands rose. His fingers moved, his palms brushed. Closer and closer to her breasts. Her body tensed, her nipples tightened so much they ached. He had to touch her. He had to.

And at last he did. He slipped his hands over her bra and cupped her.

It felt good. Better than good. Without thinking, she reached down and began to unbutton her blouse. Her hands brushed against his and she froze as she realized what she was doing. The mood faded and uncertainty set in. She dropped her arms to her sides, opened her eyes and found him watching her.

"I'm sorry," she whispered, not sure what she apologized for.

"Because you were enjoying what I was doing? Because you wanted more?" He reached for her hand and drew her close again. "I would be unhappy if you hadn't liked my caress. It pleases me to touch you. I want it to please you, as well." He put her hand on his chest. "Do you like that?"

She rubbed her fingers against his hard muscles. "Yes."

"Then we are in agreement."

He reached for her blouse and finished unfastening the buttons. Then he bent down. "Want me," he breathed, just before he kissed her.

She surrendered instantly. All doubts faded and she wrapped her arms around him, eager to be closer and feel all of him.

He brought his hands back to her breasts and rubbed her through her bra. He found the front clasp and easily unfastened it. Then he touched her bare skin and it was heaven.

It was all she could do to keep kissing him while he explored her curves. It wasn't that she wanted to stop the kissing, but there was so much to think about and experience. The warmth of his fingers, the way he tickled and teased before finally brushing his thumbs against her tight nipples. The pleasure that shot through her when he rubbed harder there.

More, she thought. More.

He must have heard her because he bent down and pressed his mouth against her breast. Even as his hand continued to touch and stroke and rub, he sucked her nipple, flicked it with his tongue, then sucked again.

She clung to him, barely able to stay standing. Fire shot through her. Need grew until it was all she could think about.

He moved to the other breast and pleasured her there. Her breathing grew ragged. Her panties dampened and her thighs trembled.

"Rafiq," she breathed.

He raised his head and kissed her, then stepped back. His gaze moved to her bare breasts. "So beautiful," he told her, then looked into her eyes. "I will see you in the morning."

"Wh-what? You're leaving?"

He smiled. "It is best. Good night."

Then, before she could grasp what was happening, he walked to the door and let himself out. She was left standing in her living room, half-naked and not quite sure what had just happened. If he was trying to make her want him more, he was doing a really great job.

"The man knows what he's doing," she said as she fastened her blouse. "Thank goodness one of us does."

Friday night Kiley sat in Rafiq's Mercedes SL 600 convertible. The close confines of the car made her very aware of the man next to her. Although, she was starting to think she would be aware of him even if they were at opposite ends of a football field. He'd shown up in a tailored tuxedo, looking elegant and very princely. Just thinking about it made her toes curl.

"You didn't have to let me off work early," she told him as they drove onto the freeway and headed west. "Me being your mistress wasn't supposed to change things between us."

He glanced at her. "Are you complaining because I asked you to work less?"

She smiled. "Is that your way of saying 'shut up and say thank you'?"

"Perhaps."

"Then I will." She looked out the window, then back at him. "This is my first fund-raiser. Is there anything I should know?"

"Not at all. There will be a cocktail hour, dinner, dancing and entertainment. I attend to support the children's hospital and because, as a representative of Lucia-Serrat, it is expected of me. But otherwise it is not how I would choose to spend my evening."

"Me, neither," she confessed. "But being with you is fun."

"Thank you. I enjoy your company as well."

His words made her happy. Funny how she'd been so willing to be his mistress without considering all the intimacies implied in the relationship. Not just that they would be lovers, but also that they would spend time together.

Fortunately, being with Rafiq really was easy and fun. There was also a connection she hadn't expected, which made her wonder how they were going to go back to just working together when the three months were over. Then she reminded herself that it was barely the end of week one of her three-month affair. Perhaps she should not be so quick to anticipate the end.

* * *

They pulled up in front of the large Westside hotel. After the valet helped Kiley out of the low-slung car, she smoothed the front of her dark-blue velvet ball gown.

"Ready?" Rafiq asked as he came around the rear of the car and offered her his arm.

"Absolutely." She felt good. Confident and attractive. It was only after they entered the ballroom that she realized how many people were watching them.

"They're staring," she whispered, trying to keep smiling.

"It's because you're so beautiful," he told her.

"Ha. It's because you're a prince. I'm used to blending in. This is going to take some getting used to."

"Be grateful I didn't bring over any of the really big jewelry."

Even as she laughed, she touched the diamond and sapphire necklace Rafiq had put on her earlier that evening. The sparkling stones had delighted her. Hearing that they were just on loan hadn't diminished her pleasure in wearing something so beautiful.

"The most expensive thing I've ever borrowed before was a pair of shoes from my sister. I guess I'm lucky the jewelry didn't come with security guards."

"The insurance company only requires them when the value is over one million dollars. This is slightly under that."

A million? Dollars? She touched the earrings.

"I'll be really, really careful," she promised.

"Don't worry yourself."

He led her into a massive ballroom decorated in gold, silver and black. Balloons floated overhead, while mirror-covered pillars reflected light. A few hundred well-dressed people filled the space, the sound of their laughter competing with the orchestra.

Rafiq greeted several couples he knew and introduced her. Kiley smiled politely and tried not to wonder what they were thinking. No doubt they were used to seeing him with a different woman every few months. She felt odd, being considered one of his women—not because she minded the association, but because she didn't think she was his regular type.

"Would you like to dance?" he asked. "Or would you prefer to find our table and sit?"

She glanced at the fairly empty dance floor, then back at him. "Can we dance? I took lessons for the wedding so I have some moves." She grinned. "Okay. 'Moves' would be strong, but I think I can follow."

His dark eyes flickered with an emotion she couldn't read. "You and Eric took dance lessons."

"Oh, please. We signed up, and he always had an excuse not to be there. But I was able to practice with other guys there. Am I explaining too much?"

"Not at all."

He guided her to the dance floor and took her in his arms.

"This is nice," she said as he pulled her close and settled his hand on the small of her back. The song was slow enough that she was able to just think about the moment rather than where to put her feet.

"I agree."

His low voice rumbled in his chest.

She closed her eyes and lost herself in the music. Rafiq held her as if she was something precious. She liked how their bodies moved together. The idea of the fund-raiser made her nervous, but being with Rafiq made it worthwhile. Especially the later part. When he took her home.

Anticipation made her breath catch as she thought about them returning to her place. She would invite him in and they would…well, she wasn't exactly sure what they would do, but she was sure it would be exciting. She'd stopped by a gourmet store and had picked up chocolate-covered strawberries to get things going. The price had nearly made her faint, but she'd bought them anyway. Chocolate-covered strawberries sounded exotic and sexy, and Lord knew she needed all the help she could get in both departments.

Although she wasn't sure when they were supposed to eat them. Before they started anything? During? Wouldn't they be sticky in bed?

"You move very well," Rafiq murmured in her ear.

"Thank you. So do you."

"We are well matched."

She liked the sound of that.

"Take a deep breath," he told her.

"What?"

"Take a deep breath. Eric is here."

She heard the words, but they didn't make sense. Eric? "My ex-fiancé?"

"Yes. He just came in. He's alone."

"But he's supposed to be in Hawaii. Our reservation was through Sunday."

Rafiq turned so that she could see the entrance to the ballroom. Sure enough, Eric stood there, looking around.

Everything else faded until she saw only him. Medium height, reddish-brown hair, green eyes. He wore a tuxedo and looked good. She continued to stare, waiting to feel devastated. Surely now her emotions would overwhelm her.

But there was only anger at what he'd done and a strong desire not to have anything to do with him.

"Do you wish to speak with him?" Rafiq asked.

She turned away from Eric and smiled at Rafiq. "No, thanks. I prefer to spend my time with you."

One corner of his mouth turned up. "I must admit, I prefer your company to Eric's, as well."

She laughed. "Gee, that's not much of a compliment."

"How unfortunate, as I meant it as such."

He turned her and they moved back into the growing crowd of dancers.

"Shall I distract you by telling you who else is here?"

"I'd like that."

"There are several television stars. A few from daytime soaps. I shall have to keep you from them so you aren't tempted by their handsome faces."

She looked into *his* handsome face and smiled. "You don't have to worry about that."

"I'm not so sure. These pretty boys can be sly. But if they would challenge me for your affections I would take them all."

"So speaks the desert warrior."

He smiled and joked, but she knew he was only partly kidding. There was a strength to him, a determination. Not that she was interested in anyone else. She'd given her word to be faithful to him for their time together and she would honor that commitment. He made it easy, she thought. Every time he took her in his arms, she couldn't imagine being anywhere else.

Later that evening Kiley excused herself and walked toward the champagne fountain. As she reached for a glass, she felt someone come up behind her.

"Kiley? What are you going here?"

She picked up the glass, then turned and saw Eric next to her.

The last time she'd spoken with him, she'd caught him in bed with another woman. Her first thought was to wonder how she could have been so stupid where he was concerned. Her second was to wish she'd stayed with Rafiq rather than getting something to drink.

"I'm attending the fund-raiser," she said quietly, turning to where Rafiq still stood in conversation with a business associate. "I'm surprised you're not still in Hawaii."

Eric shook his head. "I couldn't stop thinking about you. About us."

"How unfortunate for you."

She started to leave, but he put his hand on her arm. "Wait. You have to listen."

She stared at his hand on her bare skin and waited to feel something. They'd been engaged for three years— there had to be some emotion left.

But there wasn't. Not about Eric, anyway. All she felt was a strong need to return to Rafiq.

Which said what about her? That she hadn't loved Eric? That he'd become a habit? Was it possible? But as much as she searched her heart, she couldn't seem to find anything stronger than bruised pride and anger at being played for a fool.

"I'm talking to you," Eric snapped.

She blinked as she realized he *had* been saying something.

"I guess I'm not interested in listening," she said, and pulled free of his touch.

"Are you with him now?" he asked, pointing at Rafiq.

"Yes."

Eric's eyes narrowed. "I always knew there was something going on between the two of you. Dammit, Kiley, you lied to me."

"I did no such thing. Until Monday morning, he was simply my boss. Of course, all that has changed now."

She had the satisfaction of watching Eric go pale. "You can't be sleeping with him."

"Really? Why not?"

"You're nothing like his other women."

"I suppose that's true, but I'm okay with that."

Eric swore under his breath. "I treated you like a porcelain doll."

"Oh, is that what you call it? From my perspective, you were a lying bastard who cheated on me regularly. It's not my idea of respect or affection."

"We had something great together," he told her.

"That would be my line to you." She took a step back. "You could have had me, Eric, and you blew it completely. Now it's over. Ironically, I'm grateful. A few days away from you have shown me there was a whole lot less to our relationship than I realized." She turned to leave.

He stepped next to her. "Rafiq doesn't give a damn about you. He's just using you for sex."

"Perhaps that has happened in the past, but in this

case, you're wrong. He's not using me for sex. I'm using him."

She thought Eric was going to faint. The color fled his face and his breathing stopped. "You can't be. You were saving yourself for marriage."

"You're right, and look what it got me. Now if you'll excuse me, I must return to my lover."

With that she walked away.

Kiley sipped from her champagne glass and tried not to grin too broadly. But it was hard to act calm when she wanted to race to Rafiq's side and give him a high-five.

She'd faced Eric and had walked away the winner. He hadn't intimidated her or made her feel bad. She'd said what she'd wanted to and then she'd left. It was a huge victory and she felt like celebrating.

But as she approached their table, she saw Rafiq was no longer speaking with an oil executive from Bahania. Instead he was engaged in a very intense conversation with a beautiful woman.

She was petite and perfectly dressed in dark red. A little older than Rafiq, perhaps, but only by a few years.

Kiley stopped and watched them for a few seconds, then headed for the restroom. Her excitement at her victory over Eric faded and in its place was a low pain in her stomach.

She wasn't crazy enough to worry about every conversation Rafiq had with a woman. But there had been something different this time. An intimacy. They knew each other and had for a long time. There was a past between them.

He had demanded fidelity and had promised the same

in return. Had he meant it? Were all men incapable of being faithful, or did she simply bring out that trait in the ones she knew?

Chapter Six

They left the hotel shortly after midnight. Rafiq never liked to stay to the end, and Kiley had seemed pleased when he'd suggested leaving. He wondered at the reasons. Sometime after dinner she'd gotten quiet.

Now, in the silence of the car, he prepared himself to find out what was wrong. In the way of most women, she would at first say nothing. He would be forced to ask again and again until she finally told him. It was a flaw in the female psyche—an inability to state the problem the first time asked.

Often Rafiq simply didn't bother. The pain wasn't worth the reward. But in this case he wanted to know what troubled Kiley and, if possible, fix it.

"You are very quiet," he said. "Did something happen tonight to upset you?"

Was it Eric? She'd told him about her conversation with the other man. At the time he would have sworn she felt nothing for her ex-fiancé, but perhaps she was remembering what could have been.

He didn't like that, but there was little he could do to stop her from missing Eric. Reminding her of what the other man had done to her seemed cruel. He knew Kiley was sensible enough to recover eventually, but selfishly, he wanted her attention now.

"I saw you talking with someone," she said. "A woman. Petite. Beautiful. I told myself it was probably nothing, but the conversation seemed…intimate."

It took him a moment to realize what she was talking about. Had she actually answered his question without prompting? He was so surprised, he nearly missed the point of her words.

"Are you concerned there is a woman from my past who may come between us?" he asked.

"Sort of."

Her honesty surprised him. He recalled the evening and searched for someone who fit her description. There had been no ex-lovers there. No one who could have made Kiley uncomfortable. His conversations had been with business associates and their wives.

Except for one woman.

"Was she a few years older and wearing a red dress?"

Kiley glanced at him. "That would be the one. You know her. You have a past with her. I understand that it's very likely that you'll run into women you've known. I'm not saying you can't be friends with them, but we have an agreement that we'll both be faithful. As you can imagine, I'm a little touchy on the subject. I need to know you'll keep your end of the deal."

Under any other circumstances, he would have laughed, but he was aware of how difficult it had been for her to speak her mind.

"I assure you, I will never be unfaithful to you. I do not give my word capriciously, and once given, it bonds me to the death."

He glanced at her and saw her eyes widen.

"Wow," she murmured. "Okay, then. I guess I have to believe you."

"Even if you did not, I can assure you that the woman I spoke with earlier will never be a threat to you."

"A bad breakup?"

"Not in the way you mean. She is my mother."

He enjoyed the sharp intake of breath, then Kiley's stunned silence. They arrived at her apartment before she could gather her thoughts.

After parking, he escorted her inside and waited while she turned on the lights.

"Would you like something to drink?" she asked. "I have wine in the refrigerator."

"I'll get it," he told her, and made his way into her small kitchen.

Signs of her were everywhere. In the brightly colored curtains at the window, in the stack of books on the kitchen table and the cartoon mug in the sink. He opened the refrigerator and pulled out the bottle of white wine. As he did he noticed a clear plastic container with several chocolate-dipped strawberries and smiled. Did she plan to seduce him later? He must remember to make it easy for her to do so.

When he returned to the living room, she'd kicked off her high heels. He took off his jacket, then settled next to her on the sofa and opened the bottle of wine.

"Tell me about your mother," she said quietly. "If she's here and your father is happily married in Lucia-Serrat, I'm guessing they divorced?"

"They never married." He handed her a glass of wine, touched it with his, then leaned back in the sofa. "Many years ago, she was an actress. She came to the island to film a movie. My father was young, just seventeen and he fell madly in love with her. Or he wanted to sleep with her. At seventeen they can be the same thing. I'm not sure what she felt about him—she never said. I know they had an affair, and I was the result."

Kiley sipped her wine and put the glass on the coffee table. She reached up and unfastened her earrings. "It could have been romantic. Young love, an impetuous relationship that results in a baby."

"It wasn't. My father was too young to marry and *his* father disapproved. My mother pushed hard to be a princess, but when that didn't happen, she agreed to a cash settlement."

Kiley paused in the act of undoing her necklace and looked properly outraged. "Money? She took money for her baby. She let herself be *paid?*"

"On the condition that she leave me behind and not have anything to do with me until I came of age."

"That's horrible." Her blue eyes darkened with compassion. "Rafiq, you must have been crushed."

"I was an infant and unaware of the circumstances." He shrugged. "I was raised by several attentive nurses and nannies. I wanted for very little."

"I don't believe that." She slipped the jewelry into his coat pocket. "Don't forget you have those. I can't believe she left you. Her child. I can't imagine any mother doing that."

Her combination of practicality and compassion delighted him. She was as he had imagined—without pretense. He could gaze into her eyes and see directly into her soul.

She leaned close and touched his face. "What she did was very wrong and I'll never forgive her."

"I'm sure she'll be disappointed."

Kiley smiled. "You know what I mean." Her smile faded. "Are you close now?"

"Not at all. We speak. I have lunch with her once or twice a year. She likes me to come to parties so she can show me off. Sometimes I agree to her request."

He had no opinion of his mother one way or the other. She had made her choice long ago. He had grown up without her and couldn't imagine a world in which she mattered to him.

"What of Eric?" he asked, capturing Kiley's hand in his and kissing the tips of her fingers. "You spoke?"

She nodded. "Not for long. Did you see us?"

"Yes. He was angry."

"I guess." She ducked her head. "When he said you were going to take advantage of me, I informed him that it was the other way around. I was using you for sex."

Rafiq laughed. "Good for you."

She looked at him. "I didn't feel anything. I tried, but there was nothing. A little anger that he was such a jerk and I'm still embarrassed by what I saw when he was doing it with that other woman, but that's it. Shouldn't

I be really upset by now? Shouldn't it all matter? What if I didn't love him?"

"Then not getting married is for the best."

"I know, but what does it say about me that I didn't realize I'd fallen out of love with him?"

"Sometimes we can't see what's right in front of us. You escaped. Be grateful."

"Oh, I am. He's the last man I would ever want to be with. What a loser."

Rafiq had grown tired of speaking of another man. He lightly licked her palm, then asked, "What are you wearing under your dress?"

The question stunned Kiley but didn't embarrass her. She recognized the light of passion flaring in Rafiq's eyes and couldn't wait to get close to the fire.

"A strapless bra and panties."

Nothing about his expression changed, but she felt the tension in his body. Her own answered with a slight quiver. He stood and held out his hand.

"Dance with me," he said.

She allowed him to pull her to her feet. There wasn't any music, but somehow that didn't seem necessary. The evening was perfect—something out of a movie, and she was the star.

He pulled her into his arms. She snuggled close and relaxed into the slow, swaying movements. She was aware of the night, the shadows in the corner, and the quiet. Her senses captured every detail of the moment—the scent of his body, the heat growing between them, the smooth fabric of his shirt, the way his cheek brushed against her temple. She wanted with an intensity that surprised her. He would be her first time, but somehow that thought no longer made her nervous. She welcomed his touch and his instruction.

He kissed her shoulder, then her neck. She turned her head so their mouths could meet. His firm lips pressed against her own. She parted for him, wanting him to take her, to tempt her until she was willing to do anything.

He swept inside and she tasted the wine and the man. As they kissed, she felt his hands on her back. They moved up and down stroking her from shoulder to hip. The rhythmic movement both lulled and aroused. When he tugged at her zipper, she knew he meant to undress her.

Anticipation swept through her. She was eager for the next lesson, eager to discover everything. Rafiq drew back and looked into her eyes.

"When you were with Eric," he said quietly, "did he ever make you climax?"

Talk about a mood breaker, Kiley thought as she blushed, then reached for the front of her dress to keep it from slipping. She cleared her throat, then murmured, "Not really."

Rafiq smiled. "I wanted to be sure."

"Yes, well, now you are."

He cupped her face in his hands. "I want to please you tonight. I want to show you the pleasure locked in your body. Will you allow me that?"

The intensity of his gaze took her breath away. His words made her want to follow him to the ends of the earth. Speaking seemed impossible, so she nodded.

He dropped his hands to hers and slowly drew them down to her sides. Gravity took over and her dress dropped to the floor.

She stood there, practically naked and painfully exposed. Time passed, and he didn't speak, didn't react at all. Just when she was about to duck for cover, he groaned low in his throat, bent down and gathered her in his arms, holding her against him.

"I want you," he said in a low growl. "All of you. I want to touch you and taste you and claim you." He stared at her, his expression possessive. "You will be mine."

The proclamation thrilled her, as much as his physically sweeping her off her feet. No one had ever been interested enough to want to claim her before. She wasn't exactly sure what he meant, but she was willing to go along with whatever he had in mind.

Rafiq made his way into her bedroom and gently placed her on the bed. Before she could worry about what to do next, he pulled her close and began to kiss her.

Long, slow, deep kisses. Kisses that left her breathless and shaken and touched her soul. She clung to him, holding on to hard muscles, straining to get closer, even as he moved his hands over her bare back.

She liked the feel of him touching her skin. He explored the length of her spine, then cupped her hip before moving to the top of her bare thigh. Goose bumps erupted.

He shifted her so that she stretched out on her back, with him looming over her. His lips turned up slightly, as if he were about to smile. She brushed her thumb against his mouth.

"You're very beautiful," he murmured. "Your skin is soft." He rested his hand on her belly. "I want you to relax and enjoy what I do to you. Tonight is just for play, so you can get used to me being close to you."

She wasn't exactly sure what he meant, although she

was fairly certain he meant they weren't going all the way. She had a moment of disappointment, then he began to unbutton his shirt and she found herself distracted by his broad chest.

She put her hands on him and explored the contours, the way flesh molded muscle and how those muscles tensed when she lightly brushed over them. He bent down and kissed her. She parted for him, even as she slid her hands around to stroke his back.

He explored her mouth with his tongue, then slipped away before she'd had all she wanted. But as his destination seemed just as interesting as kissing, she decided not to protest.

Even as her eyes fluttered closed, she felt him move down her neck, then the hollow between her breasts. He licked her there, then nibbled on the sensitive skin by the edge of her bra. He moved his hand from her stomach around to her side. She shifted slightly so he could reach behind her and unfasten the hooks.

Her breath caught in anticipation as he pulled away the bra. A puff of warm air was her only warning, then his mouth claimed her right breast in an openmouthed kiss that made her body clench and her hands reach for him.

She touched his shoulders, his back, then buried her fingers in his dark hair.

"Yes," she breathed.

He licked her nipple, then sucked it into his mouth. After circling the taut tip, he raised his head slightly and blew on it. The combination of damp and cold and heat made her want to beg. Need filled every cell in her body. She ached, she wanted and she had to make sure he understood he could never, ever stop.

He moved to her other breast, and on the first, re-placed his mouth with his hand. She arched her head and savored his caress. Between her legs, her panties grew damp as that most feminine place began to ache.

When he left her breasts, she cried out in protest. "I'm not done," she told him.

She felt him laugh against her stomach.

"Trust me on this."

He moved lower, pausing to lick her belly button. The sensation was both ticklish and erotic. A combination she'd never experienced before. Then he reached the edge of her panties.

Eric had never bothered touching her there more than a couple of times and always through clothes. She remem-bered once when she'd straddled his knee and had rocked against him until he'd pushed her away. Now the aching intensified as she wondered what Rafiq would do there.

But first he tugged on her panties, pulling them down her legs, then tossing them away. She had the sudden thought that she was actually naked before a man—not counting doctors—for the first time in her life. Eek!

She opened her eyes and found him looking at her.

"Lovely," he said with a smile. "Every part of you. I like this spot." He touched her ankle. "And this one." He traced a circle around her knee. "And here." He slid a single finger between her tightly closed thighs.

She planned to be embarrassed and protest and squirm, but that wily finger slipped between her curls, the folds of skin and found an amazing, responsive bun-dle of nerves on the very first try.

Her eyes closed, her legs fell open and she didn't care if he looked at her all day, as long as he kept touching her.

"You like that?" he asked.

"Uh-huh."

"Good."

He continued to rub and circle and explore. She found herself getting lost in the perfect sensations that radiated out from that one spot. Her body burned, her blood seemed to flow faster. She was tense and yet perfectly relaxed.

He moved onto the bed, then nudged her thighs farther apart. She obliged him, even drawing back her knees. She felt his shoulder brush her leg and before she knew what was happening, he claimed her with a kiss.

She knew what he was doing. She'd read about it, seen it in movies, even talked about it. But until that moment, until his tongue brushed over her most sensitive spot with the exact pressure and speed designed to drive her into madness, she hadn't actually understood it.

The sensations were too exquisite, too perfect. She moaned as he licked her, moving a little faster, as if urging her on. Her hips arched in a rhythm she couldn't control. She dug her heels into the bed and pushed toward him, silently begging for more, for all.

Muscles clenched, her body writhed, she tossed her head back and forth as she strained to reach for something she couldn't quite grasp. For some...

He slipped a finger inside and circled it around. The combination was too much, and she felt herself lifted up as her body shattered in a rush of pleasure she'd never experienced before. Hazily she recalled a friend saying that if she had to ask if she'd climaxed, then she hadn't.

Now her release swept through her with the subtlety

of a thunderbolt. It was perfect, her muscles contracting and releasing as Rafiq continued to gently touch her. On and on it went until at last it slowly faded and she found herself back where she'd started, only much more satisfied.

"So that's what all the fuss is about," she sighed when he'd stretched out next to her and pulled her close. "I like it."

He chuckled. "Good."

She snuggled close, liking the feel of his arms around her. "We're going to do that again, right?"

"Yes. As often as you'd like. Although not tonight. I don't want you to get sore."

She was kind of thinking she would endure a little soreness for an experience like that again.

"Is it always that good?" she asked.

"It can be."

"Huh." She raised herself up on her elbow and looked down at him. "So how does anyone get any work done? Why don't people just stay in bed and make love all the time?"

"As pleasurable as that sounds, we have responsibilities."

"I guess. But given the choice…"

He reached between her legs and rubbed her. "I suppose we should consider a second time, just so you have a point of comparison."

She collapsed back on the bed and gave herself over to the pleasure. "If you insist."

Fate conspired to keep them apart. Kiley was determined to be brave about the whole thing. After what had happened Friday night she knew she wasn't in a position to complain that Rafiq had a previous engagement over the weekend and then late meetings the following week. Still, now that she understood the possibilities, she wanted to explore them all.

Wednesday afternoon she sat in his office with a pad of paper, a pen and a list.

"It's your sister's birthday in two weeks," she said. "You need to send a present. I have a list here, if you'd like to choose one."

He raised his eyebrows. "I'm not qualified to decide. You may send what you like."

"You always say that. Don't you want to know what they're going to be thanking you for?"

"I have little contact with my half sisters. I'm sure they're delightful young women who know nothing of their half brother and do not consider themselves injured by the lack of contact."

"You're being cynical."

"It is one of my best features."

"Want to take a vote?"

"An impartial panel would agree with me," he told her.

"Not if it was made up of women."

He leaned back in his chair. "Is this your subtle way of issuing a complaint?"

"Not at all. I think it would be nice if you picked out your sister's present yourself."

"And yet I will not." His dark eyes flickered with something she couldn't read. "Anything else?"

She squirmed in her seat. "I haven't seen you all week."

"I know. My meetings have gone on later than I would like." He smiled. "I have missed you."

Not as much as she'd missed him, she thought. It was like not knowing she'd been starving, then being offered a fabulous meal, only to be told the buffet was now closed.

"Me, too."

"We will have more time this weekend."

Not as much as he thought. Her sister had just had a baby and Kiley wanted to go home for a couple of days. "Actually we—"

The phone in her office rang, cutting her off. She rose to answer it just as his phone rang. Later, she thought. She would tell him that she would be leaving town for the weekend.

"This is Kiley," she said as she picked up the phone.

"Hi, Kiley. My name is Marcy Dumont. We met at the fund-raiser last week. Do you remember?"

Kiley really didn't, but doubted that was the point. "Of course. How can I help you?"

Marcy laughed. "Actually, and this may sound a bit strange, I need you to talk to Rafiq."

"He's right here. You can speak with him yourself."

"I know I *could* but I think it would be better if you did. I work with a children's charity here on the Westside. We would very much like Rafiq to sponsor one of our events. I'd like to send you the information to look over. If you like what we're doing, you can talk to him about it."

It took Kiley a minute to figure out what was going on. "You think there's a better chance he'll say yes if I ask him?"

Marcy laughed again. "Are you kidding? We all saw the way he looked at you. He wouldn't refuse you anything. And it's for sick kids, Kiley. I wouldn't ask otherwise. I'm going to pop the information into the mail. My business card will be there. Check it out, then give me a call."

"But I—"

"Talk to you soon." Marcy hung up.

Kiley did the same, then stared at her phone. It wasn't that she minded helping sick children, she thought grimly. It was that she didn't like being manipulated. Her relationship with Rafiq was private. No one had the right to use that to influence either of them. She felt uncomfortable and unsure of what to do. If the cause had been anything else, she would have simply ignored the material. But sick children? She couldn't just turn her back.

"I need the quarterly reports," Rafiq said from the doorway between their offices.

"I'll get them right away."

He waited until she'd returned with the files, then took her hand. "What's wrong?"

"Nothing."

He stared at her. "Was that Eric on the phone?"

"What? No. He hasn't called."

Rafiq continued to study her. "We have an agreement of fidelity."

She smiled. "Trust me, I'm not about to forget it. Eric didn't call, hasn't called, isn't going to call. If he did, I wouldn't be interested. I swear."

He nodded once, as if satisfied, then returned to his office.

Chapter Seven

"**I'**m glad we're finally spending the evening together," Rafiq said Thursday night as he and Kiley were
shown to a corner table in the small Italian restaurant in
Santa Monica. He'd chosen to give up the view of the
ocean in favor of privacy.

"Me, too," she answered. "You've been busy."

"Unexpected meetings and out-of-town associates.
Fortunately, they are over now. There shouldn't be any
more interruptions."

She smiled at him and put her napkin in her lap. She
was beautiful in her low-cut blue dress. She would have
been more beautiful without it, but he was not about to
share her charms with the other patrons.

The waiter hovered until Rafiq requested the wine

list, then sent him away. But instead of glancing at the pages of available bottles, he stared at Kiley.

"You have something on your mind," he said.

She blinked. "Not really."

"I have felt it for the past day or so."

She shook her head, denying the charge, but he doubted her. Kiley had been forthcoming in the past, but she wasn't now. Did she worry that the topic would distress him? There was only one reason for that—she missed Eric.

He shouldn't be surprised. A few short weeks ago, she'd wanted to marry the man. She had told him she wanted revenge and he had believed her. Perhaps that had been a mistake. Was a woman's heart truly capable of revenge?

"The food here is excellent," he told her, knowing he would come back to the subject of her distraction later. "The chef is very popular. Would you like wine with dinner?"

"Yes, thank you. I'm going to let you pick because what I know about wine wouldn't impress anyone."

"Do you have a preference?"

"Not yucky."

He smiled. "I'll keep that in mind."

She opened her menu and studied the options. He did the same, then picked a wine. When they'd ordered, she leaned forward.

"My sister just had a baby. My mom called the night before last to tell me all about it. This is Heather's first. She's my baby sister. She'd always said she wanted complete natural childbirth. She's into organic everything. So when the time came, she refused to let them give her anything for the pain."

Kiley's mouth twitched slightly. "But Heather isn't very accommodating when she doesn't feel well. Apparently she was screaming so much, the other women in labor came into her room and begged her to take something. She was distracting them. My mom said it was pretty funny. Heather agreed and quieted down, and the baby was born. She had a girl."

Her expression turned wistful.

"You had planned to have children with Eric," he said.

"Three or four. He wanted to wait, but I was willing to get started right away. I always thought a big family like mine would be great. Sure it was messy and loud being one of three, but there was so much love."

"All girls?"

She grinned. "Does that horrify you? No possibility of heirs?"

"It isn't a concern for everyone."

"That's true. I think my dad likes being the only guy in the house. We all treat him very well."

"I think you will be a good mother."

She sighed. "Thank you. I know I'll try. I feel as if I could easily love a couple of dozen kids, but there is the reality of keeping track of everyone." She offered him the bread basket, then took a roll for herself.

"I keep thinking about how it's going to be," she said. "I want to have the house where all the neighborhood kids comes to play. I want to make Halloween costumes and bake and decorate for the holidays. I want a Christmas tree filled with ornaments made out of Popsicle sticks and a couple of dogs making trouble. A suburban fantasy."

"It sounds very nice."

"Oh, right. So speaks the prince."

"Do you think I'm not interested in a domestic situation?"

"I don't know. Are you?"

"I will marry and have children."

"That's right," she said. "We've discussed your need to find the proper woman at the princess store. How's that working out?"

Before he could tease her back, the waiter appeared with the wine. He opened the bottle, then poured them each a glass. When they were alone, Kiley leaned toward him.

"I have a question," she said in a low voice, staring at his shirtfront rather than his face.

"Yes?"

"Is it really just business that's kept us apart? Physically, I mean?"

He reached across the table and took her hand. "Are you concerned?"

"A little. Last weekend we, um, made some progress and since then, well, nothing. Did I do something wrong? I've been thinking about it and I wondered if maybe you thought I was being selfish. The whole thing was about me. I feel really bad about that. I just didn't think…" She bit her lower lip. "Pleasing the man in my life isn't something I'm used to."

Her combination of worry, concern and nervousness charmed him. He squeezed her fingers.

"You are the innocent in the relationship," he told her. "I don't expect you to be aware of my needs or responsible for them. Had I wished things to go differently, I would have told you."

"Okay. But it's been a week. Things were really hot and heavy before." She glanced around, as if making sure no one could hear them. "Are you unhappy with me? Do you want to change your mind about the whole mistress thing?"

If they'd been alone, he would have claimed her right at that moment. He was delighted that she missed their physical contact.

"You are the one I desire," he said, staring into her eyes. "Only you."

Her mouth parted, but she didn't speak. He felt her pulse quicken and heard her breathing increase.

"Wow," she whispered at last. "That's good."

"It's true."

"So you really have been busy? It's just that?"

"Mostly. Also, I thought we were moving a little quickly. I wanted to give you time to get used to our intimacy."

"Now? You take me to the pleasure planet, then pull back? It hardly seems fair."

He smiled. "Then we can change things. You only have to let me know. Or better yet, show me."

Her eyes widened. "As in, seduce you? I'm not sure I know how."

His body clenched at the thought. "You would figure it out." In truth, it wouldn't take much, but she didn't need to know that. Just sitting here with her, talking about making love, was enough to get him hard.

"Really?" She pulled free of his touch, clapped her hands together and shimmied in her seat. "I like that. I like the thought of bringing a big, powerful prince to his knees. Figuratively, of course."

"Of course. Maybe this weekend we can—"

"Hello, Kiley."

Rafiq glanced to his left and saw Eric standing next to their table. Annoyance destroyed his good mood.

Kiley jumped. "Eric! What are you doing here?"

Her surprise seemed genuine. As much as Rafiq wanted to grab the smaller man by the shirt and pummel him, he deliberately decided to wait and see what happened. If Kiley needed his help, he would step in—otherwise it would be better if she took care of Eric herself.

"I have to talk to you," Eric said, ignoring Rafiq. "Come outside."

"I'm not going anywhere with you. Go away."

Not the words of a woman mourning a relationship, Rafiq thought with relief.

"You're making a fool of yourself," Eric said, glaring at her. "Can't you see that?"

"The only fool here is you," she told him. "You didn't realize what you could lose. It's gone now and there's no getting it back. I'm sorry if that hurts, but…" She frowned. "*No.* I'm not sorry. I'm glad it hurts you. I hope it hurts a lot. You treated me terribly. I'm not interested in you or our past or anything you could say to me. My biggest regret is that I wasted three years of my life waiting to marry you. The bright spot is I found out the truth before the wedding."

Eric turned on Rafiq. "This is your fault. You seduced her. How long were you screwing her before all this happened?"

Rafiq started to rise, but Kiley put her hand over his. "I appreciate it," she said, "but I can handle this."

He nodded and sank back in his chair. He would let her be in charge…for now.

"Rafiq has nothing to do with it," she told Eric. "The only one who was unfaithful in our relationship is you. Of course, given how much you cheated, it makes sense that you would assume the worst about everyone else. But I'm not like that. I take my commitments seriously."

"So this just happened?" Eric asked, sounding incredulous. "I find that tough to believe."

She shrugged. "I don't care what you think. Your opinion doesn't matter to me. Not anymore. It's over between us and I'm relieved. I think it's sad I'm not in more pain. It makes me think I haven't loved you for a long time."

Eric pointed at Rafiq. "You replaced me with him? You're an idiot if you think it's going to last. You're caught up in his money and title, but that's not going anywhere. He'll never marry you. You're from different worlds. He thinks this is fun now, but he'll get tired of you and then toss you aside."

"Maybe," Kiley said calmly. "The difference is when Rafiq wants to end the relationship, he'll say it to my face. He'll be honorable. He won't cheat on me behind my back."

Eric reached for her. Rafiq grabbed his arm. "I wouldn't do that if I were you."

Eric jerked free and retreated a step. Rafiq let him.

"I'm not the only one who sneaks around, Kiley," Eric said. "What about you? Do your parents know about him? Do they know what you're doing? It's not as if you're willing to take him home this weekend to see Heather's new baby."

Kiley had been mad before, but now she was furious. She'd seen Rafiq grab Eric. From the look on Rafiq's face, he would be happy to beat up the other man. She was almost tempted to let him do it.

"How dare you?" she breathed. "You called my parents."

"Of course I did. I'm worried about you. They mentioned the baby and that you'd be coming to visit." Eric turned to Rafiq. "Didn't know that, did you? Kiley has a big family. I was always welcome there. They liked *me*. Think they'll say the same about you?"

Kiley wasn't sure what her family would say about Rafiq, and she wasn't planning to find out. In truth, now that Heather had had her first baby, Kiley wanted to go home for the weekend. She'd planned to tell Rafiq over dinner. She still would. She just hated how Eric made it sound as if she were keeping secrets.

Rafiq leaned back in his chair and regarded Eric. "Kiley was telling me about the baby when you interrupted. It is unfortunate you've finally realized what you lost, but the fault is yours. Kiley is gone and you have no one to blame but yourself."

Eric took a step toward him. "I oughta nail you."

Rafiq placed his napkin on the table and stood. He topped Eric by several inches and outweighed him by fifteen or twenty pounds of muscle.

"Do you think that's possible?" Rafiq asked with a casualness that belied his temper.

Kiley didn't know what to do. A part of her wouldn't mind if Rafiq beat the crap out of her ex-fiancé. But this was a public place and she didn't think Rafiq would appreciate the potential publicity.

Just then an older man hurried toward them. Two burly cooks and a big waiter accompanied him. He paused by the table and bowed his head.

"Prince Rafiq, I'm so sorry. I did not realize this man was bothering you. Please allow me to escort him outside." The man snapped his fingers, and the two cooks grabbed Eric.

"Hey, you can't do this," Eric said.

"It seems he can," Rafiq said as he sat down. "Know this. If you bother Kiley again, I will speak with the senior partners at your law firm. She has told you to stay away from her. It would be best for you and your career if you did just that."

Eric was hustled out of the restaurant before he could respond. Kiley felt the interested stares of the other diners.

"I'm sorry," she said, barely able to look at Rafiq. "I don't know how Eric found us or why he even bothered looking."

"Are you all right? Did it trouble you to see him?"

"It's embarrassing to have him make a fuss, and I hate that you had to get involved."

"I would have stepped in sooner, but I thought you would want to handle him."

"I did." She reached for her wine and took a sip. "I don't get it. He was so willing to ignore me for so long. Now that I'm gone, he's acting as if it's a big deal."

"Perhaps it is," Rafiq said. "He realizes what he lost."

"So what? I was an idiot for ever getting involved with him. What a weasel."

Rafiq nodded slowly. "There is a strength about you I didn't recognize at first. I admire that."

His compliment pleased her. "Thank you. I don't feel especially strong. Determined, maybe."

"Was Eric the reason you've been distracted for the past couple of days?"

He'd noticed? And here she thought she'd been keeping her worries to herself. Was she really bad at concealing things or was he more observant than most?

"No. It wasn't Eric. It's actually a couple of things. I didn't want to bring them up at work because I'm trying to keep our personal life out of that."

"Now I'm intrigued."

She drew in a deep breath. "A woman called. Marcy Dumont. I guess I met her at the fund-raiser, although I don't remember her specifically. There were so many introductions. Anyway, she wanted me to talk to you about sponsoring some event. It's for children."

She picked up her fork, then set it down. "It was so strange. I didn't know what to say to her and I felt really awkward. I mean, why come to me for money? She said I could influence you, which is crazy. I couldn't. But even if I could, I think it's wrong to impose on my personal life. She should have talked to you directly."

He was quiet for a long time. She knew he was reasonable enough that he wouldn't blame any of this on her, but she felt awkward about the whole thing.

"None of this is your fault," he said at last. "You're right. If the woman wanted me to sponsor an event, she should have contacted me. What did you tell her?"

"Nothing. She hung up before I could get my thoughts together. I've never had to deal with anything like this before. I didn't know how to handle the situation. Eric's right about that. We *are* from different worlds."

"Next time tell me," he said gently. "I will take care of things."

"I'm not helpless."

"I agree. But you're also not experienced in the nuances of my lifestyle. Your only responsibility is to me."

She couldn't help smiling. "That sounded very sheik-like and demanding. That my only responsibility is to you. As if you're the center of my world."

He raised his eyebrows. "I am Prince Rafiq of Lucia-Serrat. Of course I'm the center of your world."

She laughed, and her worry faded away. "Not on this planet, but it's a nice fantasy."

"You do not respect me."

"I respect you plenty, but I'm not a doormat. I'm an independent woman who chose you to be her lover."

As soon as she spoke the words, she clapped her hand over her mouth. "I did *not* say that aloud."

"You did." He picked up his wine. "I like this independent side of you. Tell me more."

"There's not all that much to say." Except for this one thing. She looked at him. "I have to go away this weekend."

His gaze sharpened slightly. "To visit your family?"

She shouldn't be surprised that he'd figured it out, but she was. "I want to see Heather and the new baby. It will just be for a couple of days. I'll fly out tomorrow and be back Sunday."

"You are welcome to be gone longer."

Not exactly the "I'll miss you" speech she'd been hoping for. "The weekend is plenty."

"Fine. I hope you enjoy yourself."

There was something about the way he said the words. Something that unsettled her.

"You're not mad, are you?" she asked.

"That you wish to visit your family? No. This is a very special time. You will want to be there."

Okay, that all *sounded* right, but it didn't feel right. She studied him, trying to figure out what was wrong. Did he seem to be sitting more stiffly? Was there a flicker of emotion in his eyes.

"I just…" She pressed her lips together. "What's wrong? Are you mad I'm leaving?"

"I assure you, I will survive without your company."

Ouch. "I know you will. Of course you will. You don't need me at all."

She stared at her plate and wondered where the conversation had gone wrong.

The waiter arrived and served their salads. Kiley picked up her fork, then put it down again. Suddenly she wasn't hungry.

"I'm sorry," Rafiq said quietly.

She looked at him and did her best not to show her astonishment. It had never occurred to her a real, live prince would ever apologize. "For what?"

"For hurting you." He shrugged. "I know your assumption is that I would not enjoy meeting your family. Perhaps you are uncomfortable with our relationship and who I am. It is better you go yourself. For my part, it has been a long time since I was reminded I am not like other men."

His words swirled around in her brain. Maybe she was crazy. Maybe she was delusional, but if she understood what he was saying then somehow *he'd* been hurt by her not wanting to take him with her.

"I'm not ashamed of our relationship," she told him.

"It is unconventional."

"I wouldn't exactly tell my mom about the terms of our agreement or that I was your mistress-in-training, but I would be comfortable introducing you. I thought you'd feel weird about going home with me. I thought you'd think it was dumb or boring. We're just regular people. No palaces, no fancy pedigrees. You're a prince."

"I am aware of my title."

She smiled. "I figured you were. Rafiq, you're used to who and what you are, but the rest of us aren't. My folks live in Sacramento in a tract home. We don't even have a second story."

"Are you concerned I'll judge your family and find them wanting?"

Interesting question. "No, I'm not," she said slowly, realizing it was true.

"Then what troubles you?"

When the truth came, it was both funny and sad. "I'm afraid you'll realize I'm not that special. That I'm just like everyone else."

"You are uniquely yourself."

"Does that mean you want to go with me this weekend?"

"I would like it very much."

"Then you should come along." Uh-oh. What exactly was she getting herself into?

Chapter Eight

They left for Sacramento Saturday morning, shortly before nine. The flight would be a little less than an hour, which meant there would be a whole day of family time. Usually the thought would have excited Kiley, but this morning it made her nervous.

Still, if she was going to bring Rafiq to visit her parents and whoever else might be hanging out there, it was very nice to travel in style.

"I've never been in a private plane before," she said as she rubbed her hand over the smooth, soft leather covering the seat. "It's very nice."

Rafiq sat across from her in an equally impressive seat. "There is a larger plane for longer trips."

"That's right. You have two planes."

He shrugged. "It is more convenient."

She had to agree with that. Instead of getting to the airport two hours early and dealing with long lines, they had driven onto a small airfield next to the Los Angeles International Airport. As soon as they had handed over their luggage and gone onboard, the pilot had prepared for takeoff. Who knew this type of travel even existed?

"You're going to make it hard to go back to discount flying," she said as the plane banked, then turned north.

"That was not my intent. I thought you would enjoy this plane."

She looked around at the luxuriously appointed cabin. "It's fabulous. Remind me to be rich in my next life."

"I will."

He unfastened his seat belt, leaned forward and unhooked hers. Then he pulled her across the narrow aisle onto his lap. When she'd settled onto his thighs and had looped an arm around his shoulder, he smiled.

"Much better," he said.

She snuggled closer. "What happened to taking things slowly?"

He put his hand on the back of her head and drew her down for his kiss. "I've been rethinking that plan."

"Good," she managed before he claimed her.

She pressed her hand to his cheek and let herself get lost in the sensual dance of lips and tongues. He explored her, then teased her by retreating. She followed, and he gently sucked on her tongue.

Need grew inside of her. She felt hot and hungry and her breasts ached.

He rested his hand on her thigh. She willed him to move higher, to touch her between her legs. Even through her jeans, the contact would bring her pleasure. But he didn't read her mind and she wasn't capable of asking. Not yet. But soon, she thought, wanting him with a passion that left her breathless.

She raised her head and sighed. "This is nice. I guess I should have seduced you this week, but I was really busy and time got away from me."

"I'm not sure how I feel about coming in second to your work."

"Specifically, it was a report my boss wanted."

He unfastened the buttons at the front of her shirt, then pressed his mouth to the swell of breast just above her bra. "Perhaps next time you should tell him no."

"I'd like to, but he's really demanding. You know the type."

"Regal," he said as he undid the front hook of her bra and pushed the cups aside.

He moved his hands to her hips and helped her straddle him. When she'd braced her hands on the back of the seat, he leaned in and took her nipple in his mouth. At the same time, he slipped his hand between her legs and began to rub her center. Perhaps he could read minds after all.

The combination of sensations was too much, she thought as she gave herself up to the gentle sucking at her breasts and the rhythmic teasing between her legs.

"Tell me the pilot isn't going to walk in on us," she said, her voice thick.

"Don't worry," Rafiq told her. "He won't. Relax."

As he spoke he moved his hands to the waistband of her jeans and unfastened the button there. She swayed back.

"You can't take my pants off," she said, shocked by the suggestion.

He smiled. "Why not? We have plenty of time."

"But we're in an airplane."

"I want to touch you. I want to feel your wetness and bury my fingers inside of you." The smile returned. "You don't have to enjoy it."

She was tempted by what he offered, but nervous about where they were.

"Just for a second," she said.

He chuckled, helped her to stand.

"I can't believe I'm doing this," she said as she slipped off her shoes, then tugged down her jeans. Her panties quickly followed.

Naked from the waist down, she straddled him again and braced herself on the seatback. He immediately went to work on her breasts, even as he made good on his word and slipped his finger inside of her.

She felt herself react instantly. Her muscles clenched around him as he moved in and out of her. At the same time, he used his thumb to rub against her swollen center. His mouth caressed her right breast and with his free hand, he went to work on the other one.

The man was talented, she thought hazily as she tensed in anticipation of her climax. Her eyes popped open. She couldn't! Not here. Not like that.

But everything felt too good. She didn't want him to stop.

"Just another minute," she whispered, her eyes drifting closed. "I'll count to sixty and then you'll have to—"

Her orgasm caught her unaware. One second she'd been determined to stay detached enough to stop, then next she lost herself in shuddering pleasure. She held in a cry of delight and rubbed herself against his hand.

When she was finished, she looked at him. "That was incredible."

"I would agree," he said, then kissed her.

She dropped her gaze to his crotch where she could clearly see his erection. "What about you? Don't you want to…you know?"

"Under other circumstances, I would say yes. But not here. Not your first time."

Soon, she thought as she stood and reached for her clothes.

"Just so you're clear, my family is completely normal," Kiley said as she pointed the way out of the airport.

Rafiq steered the rental car and wondered if she was nervous about him meeting her family or embarrassed about what had just happened on the plane.

He enjoyed giving her pleasure. In time he would take his own, but for now it was enough to please her.

"You have two sisters," he said. "Heather and…?"

"Ann. They're both married. And they'll be there, of course. Along with their husbands, in-laws, Ann's kids, some neighbors and Heather's new baby. A big crowd."

She sounded doubtful.

"It will be fun," he said firmly.

"I hope so. And I told you about the hotels, right? There's no really fancy one. At least, not that I could think of."

"I made us a reservation nearby."

She winced. "Okay, but if you hate it, you can go back to L.A. and I'll fly home on a commercial flight."

"Do you think me incapable of living without royal luxury for two days?"

"Not exactly." She bit her lower lips. "Okay, yes. I do." She hunched in her seat. "Don't hate me."

He laughed. "You're being far too dramatic. I will fit in perfectly, your family will adore me and I will adore them. Relax."

"I'm relaxed."

She looked tense enough to snap. "Yes, I can see that. What have you told them about me?"

"That you're my boss and we're friends. Not that we're dating or anything because this close to the wedding, that would be too weird to explain."

He doubted her family would think of him as just her friend, but he didn't say that to Kiley. She was already worried enough.

"I told you it was just a plain, one-story house, right?" she asked. "Nothing fancy."

He chuckled. "Relax. Everything will be fine."

Rafiq followed her directions and pulled up in front of a ranch-style home on a large lot. There were several cars parked in front. Kiley directly him to pull into the driveway, then sucked in a breath.

"Brace yourself," she said as she unfastened her seat belt.

Just then the front door burst open and several people spilled onto the front lawn.

There was an older couple he took to be her parents, a few small children, a woman in her twenties who looked a lot like Kiley and two men who were probably the husbands. He pushed open his door and got out.

Kiley climbed out of the rental car and hurried to her parents. They both hugged her, then her mother held her at arm's length.

"Are you all right?" the other woman asked. Rafiq assumed she was concerned about Kiley's reaction to the aborted wedding.

"I'm fine," Kiley said and hugged her again. "Great. Really." She squeezed her mother's arm. "Mom, Dad, this is my boss. Rafiq." She grinned. "Actually the official title is Prince Rafiq of Lucia-Serrat."

Her parents stared at him. Long experience had taught him that they weren't sure what was expected of them. He stepped forward and held out his hand to Kiley's father.

"A pleasure to meet you both," he said as they shook hands. He turned to her mother. "Mrs. Hendrick."

"Oh, dear. Just call me Jan. This is Jim. We're pretty informal around here." Jan smiled. "Are you really a prince?"

"I'm afraid so. It's true what they say—you can't pick your relatives. Please call me Rafiq."

They led him into the house where he was introduced to the rest of the family. In a matter of minutes he was in the den with the men, watching college football.

"We're Cal fans up here," Jim said from his place in the black leather recliner, next to the chintz-covered sofa. "Except for Bart there, who likes USC. You have a favorite team?"

"Oklahoma," Rafiq said easily. "This year they're going all the way. Last year's game against Florida showed everyone what they were capable of."

He glanced at Jim, who sat with his mouth open.

"I like football," Rafiq said with a grin.

"I guess you do. Huh. Never would have thought it." He glanced at the clock. "Jan won't let us have beers before noon on game day. Can't say that I blame her. But it's only during the season and it's nearly noon. Bart, you go on and get us some beers. Rafiq? Gonna join us?"

"Absolutely."

By late afternoon Rafiq had learned much more about the Hendrick family in general and Kiley in particular. He'd spent time with each of her sisters and her father. He'd heard about her disastrous appearance in a high school musical where she discovered she really couldn't sing, and had seen pictures of her in her cheer-leading uniform. He'd watched her laugh with her sisters, play with the toddlers and melt over the newborn.

She was very much a part of her world and he could see she'd come by her desire to be a wife and mother honestly. Jan Hendrick clucked over everyone. She'd spent lunch filling plates, passing out sodas and mopping up after the little ones, and she'd done it with an easy grace that had impressed him.

He liked that they'd accepted him and even occasionally forgotten who he was. As he stood on the rear patio and admired the fading colors in the roses, he wondered what he would have been like if he'd been raised in a family like this instead of on Lucia-Serrat.

The back door opened. He turned and saw Jan step out.

"May I join you?" she asked.

"I would be delighted."

She sighed. "You have the nicest manners. I guess you get that, growing up as a prince and all."

"I had nannies and tutors who took etiquette very seriously."

"I can't even imagine." She leaned against the patio railing and looked at him. "I want to thank you for being there for Kiley. These past few weeks have been hard on her."

He studied the older woman's blond hair. There were only a few streaks of gray and, oddly enough, they added to her attractiveness. She had big blue eyes her daughter had inherited and a ready smile. She glowed with life and contentment, as if she'd gotten everything she'd ever wanted.

"Kiley has handled herself well," he said. "You should be proud of her."

"I am, as always. She's a good girl. Or should I say woman. She's all grown-up. And now she's had a big disappointment. I never took to Eric the way I took to the other girls' husbands, but I thought we'd learn to love him. Now, looking back, I can see there were signs, but none of us wanted to pay attention."

"Better she find out now rather than after the wedding."

"I agree." She studied him. "I can't tell you how much I want to ask you your intentions, but I won't. Kiley can handle herself. Still, I can't help worrying about her."

"She's a remarkable woman and I have great respect for her. I don't want to hurt her."

"Sometimes we don't get what we want. I'd like you to be careful with her heart. You're the kind of man a woman dreams about finding."

He grimaced. "Because I'm a prince?"

"I won't say that's not interesting, but it's not the main reason. There's something about you." She touched his arm. "Be kind to my little girl. That's all I can ask."

She walked inside the house. Rafiq watched her go. He almost wished he could have told her the truth. That she didn't have to worry. Kiley had come to him in order to get revenge and she had no interest in making their relationship about much more than that.

As he stood alone on the patio, he found himself wondering what it would be like if he were different. If he was the kind of man who believed in love and happily-ever-after. Then he would have to regret letting her go. But he didn't believe, and when the three months were up, he would walk away without looking back.

"My mother approves," Kiley said as they drove toward the hotel that evening.

Rafiq glanced at her. "I doubt that."

"It's true. She told me. She said you're everything a woman could want in a man." Her mother had also told her to be careful about getting her heart broken, but Kiley already knew that.

"I enjoyed meeting your family," he said. "They are good people."

"Thank you. I'd been afraid things would be awkward, but you fit right in." She glanced at him. "I had no idea you were a college football fan."

"I'm a man with many interests."

"Apparently." Right now she was one of them—but for how long?

Don't go there, she told herself. Don't think about the

future. There was only now. This night, this week, this month. Or three of them, to be precise. And then he would let her go.

When she'd asked about being his mistress, she'd been interested in revenge, nothing more. She hadn't thought about Rafiq as a person. Now she knew more of the man, and she liked him. She also admired him. Being in his company made her happy. She trusted him, laughed with him, wanted him. It was, she acknowledged, a recipe for emotional disaster.

She also knew that if she told him she was afraid of falling for him, he would break things off immediately. So she wouldn't say anything. She would live life to the fullest and deal with the consequences when their time was up. She would also abide by their agreement of an affair—nothing more.

She wanted to believe she mattered to Rafiq, and in some ways she was sure she did. But he was a prince, and the woman he chose to marry had serious implications. He wouldn't choose lightly, and he would never choose a regular woman from a completely normal middle-class American family. It just wasn't done.

There would be pain when the relationship ended, but she would survive. And in the surviving, she would learn and grow. Having been involved with Eric and then with Rafiq, she would know what to look for in a man and what to avoid. She would find the right partner, fall in love and start the family she'd always wanted. And for the rest of her life, she would have the memories of these three magic months.

They drove into the hotel parking lot and stopped by

the valet. As their luggage was unloaded by the bellman, Rafiq took her hand and led her inside.

He checked them in and followed the night manager to their room.

Tonight, she thought as the other man explained about the hotel amenities. They would be together tonight. She was tired of waiting, tired of being the student. She wanted to be his equal—a lover he found fascinating.

"Here is our presidential suite," the manager said as he opened one side of a double door.

Kiley looked at Rafiq. "I didn't book this."

"I know. I had my travel agent take care of it."

The room was lovely, with a view of the city, a spacious living room and two bedrooms. For her it was totally upscale, although she had a feeling that Rafiq normally traveled in more style.

Their luggage was brought up. He tipped the bellman, who left with the manager.

She crossed to the window and he followed. He stood behind her and wrapped his arms around her. She snuggled into his embrace.

"Thank you for staying over," she said.

"We had to. There's brunch tomorrow at your parents' house. I'm looking forward to it."

She smiled, then turned in his arms and touched a stain on his shirt. "I think the baby spit up on you."

"I am sure of it."

"You didn't mind being run over by toddlers or dragged into family arguments about where to go on vacation or the state of the roof."

"I enjoyed myself today. They are good people and they didn't have any expectations of me."

"A pleasant surprise?"

"You don't know how much."

She could imagine, though. The night of the fund-raiser had shown her that she wouldn't have enjoyed growing up in his world, always on display.

She studied his face, the handsome lines and masculine features. She touched his mouth and remembered how he'd touched her on the plane.

He smiled. "There are two bedrooms," he said. "Which would you prefer?"

She pointed to the master, with the large bed and marble bathroom. "That one."

"Then I'll take the other one."

"I don't think so."

His eyebrows rose.

She shrugged. "Unless it's really important to you, of course. I'm not going to force you to sleep with me."

"Kiley?"

"You said to let you know. So I am. I'm ready, Rafiq. I want us to make love tonight."

Chapter Nine

Her words made Rafiq hard in an instant. He ached to claim her right there, to strip off her clothes and bury himself inside of her. Control seemed unimportant in the face of his growing need.

But he held back. As much as he wanted to plunge himself inside of her, he wanted to make this good for her more. There would only ever be one first time for her. He would always be the first man to make her his. He wanted to make sure every moment of their love-making made her tremble with delight.

Without speaking, he took her hand and led her into the bedroom. Once there, he turned to her and pulled her close, then lowered his head so that he could claim her with a kiss.

He felt her instant surrender. She melted into him,

parting her lips and clinging to him. Her breasts pressed into his chest, her thighs brushed his.

He slipped his tongue into her mouth and tasted her sweet heat. She welcomed him, circling, rubbing, dancing. Each stroke, every brush, even the lightest touch of her fingers on his back inflamed him. Need pulsed in time with his heartbeat. He had never been one to simply take what was offered. He prided himself on reducing his bed partners to whimpering puddles of sexual satisfaction, but he had never *wanted* this much before.

It was as if the ancient blood of his heritage, of those long-gone desert warriors, now controlled him. He wanted to tear off her clothes and gaze upon her naked body. He wanted to move inside of her, filling her until they both cried out in ecstasy.

But she was a virgin and patience was required.

He forced the erotic images from his mind and gently stroked her back. He deepened the kiss, but made no other attempt to move things along. There would be plenty of time, he told himself.

She was the one to pull away and kiss his jaw. As she rubbed her body against his, she nibbled on his neck, then sucked his earlobe. His erection pulsed.

"You're going slow," she said, speaking into his ear.

"Yes. It's your first time."

"Don't."

He stiffened. "Don't what?"

"Don't go slow." She looked at him, and he saw the desire in her eyes. "I meant what I said. I'm ready. Touch me."

As she spoke, she unfastened the button on her jeans. He accepted the invitation and slid down the zipper, then eased his hand between her panties and her soft, warm skin.

Then he swore. She was hot, wet and already swollen. He rubbed the engorged center of her pleasure and made her moan. He eased a finger inside of her, and her hips arched toward him. He withdrew and she whimpered.

It was too much, he thought, battling animal urges. He could have held back if she'd been cautious or afraid or hesitant. He could have waited longer if she'd needed more time. But her blatant invitation was more than he could resist. More than he should have to.

He dragged her to him and kissed her again. But this time he claimed her as his. As he entered her mouth, he began unfastening the buttons on her blouse.

She reached for his shirt, but her inexperience slowed her down. He had her blouse off and her bra open before she'd managed two buttons. He broke the kiss and stepped back.

"Perhaps I should undress myself," he said as he finished unfastening his shirt, then tossed it aside.

"I'd like that."

She shrugged out of her bra and toed out of her shoes, then moved back into his embrace. Now her bare breasts rested on his skin. He could feel her tight nipples brushing against him. They groaned together.

He cupped both her breasts and caressed her with his fingers. As she dropped her head back and closed her eyes, he nudged her toward the bed.

Kiley felt the mattress behind her and waited for the flash of fear. There wasn't any. Just a building need that made her want to hurry things along. Her blood raced with an urgency that made it impossible to catch her breath. More. She wanted more. She wanted all of it.

She sank onto the bed, pulling Rafiq down beside her. He wrapped his arms around her and rolled, drawing her across him until they were both stretched out on the sheets. Even as he kissed her, he touched her breasts, rubbing, teasing, making her ache and need.

When his hand moved lower to her already-open jeans, she grabbed for the denim and pushed. Jeans and panties slid down her thighs until she was able to kick them and her socks off. He settled his hand between her legs and began to explore all of her.

She parted for him, knowing what would happen and more than ready to experience pleasure again. But this time was to be for both of them, so as he touched her, she reached for him.

He was hard. She felt the length of him through his slacks. Even as he circled around her and rubbed, she matched the movements on his erection.

After a minute or two he pulled back and looked at her. "You're distracting me."

"Really?" The thought if it made her smile.

"More than you know."

"Then let's do more."

He laughed and sat up. After taking off his shoes and socks, he stood and quickly removed his slacks and briefs. Then he was naked, and she could see all of him.

He was lean and muscled and very much aroused. When he joined her on the bed, she reached for him.

"I want to touch you," she said.

"I have something better in mind."

He knelt between her thighs. As she watched, he

gently parted her, then slowly began to push inside. At the same time, he rubbed that center spot, making it difficult for her to think about anything but the way he made her feel.

Still, even as her body tensed in anticipation of her release, she felt him filling her. The stretching was unfamiliar and a little uncomfortable. She stiffened slightly and he stopped.

"Does that hurt you?" he asked as he lightly caressed her breasts.

"Not really. It's just strange." She fought the need to close her eyes as his fingers worked their magic. "My doctor told me that I'm not going to bleed or anything. There's no physical proof." Ack! Talk about embarrassing. "You know what I mean."

"I do. Does this feel good?"

He lightly squeezed her nipples between thumb and forefinger.

"Oh, yeah. That works."

He moved his right hand between her legs. "And this?"

He began the rubbing again. Instantly she felt herself spiraling toward her release.

"Good," she gasped. "Really good."

"Then let me pleasure you."

He spoke softly, not the least bit commandlike, yet she found herself wanting to obey. He rubbed faster and faster, pressing a tiny bit harder, arousing her until release became inevitable. She felt him moving deeper inside of her but was more caught up in the rising tension and the way his fingers took her to the edge and then pushed her over.

Her climax engulfed her. She got lost in the waves of pleasure. He kept touching her. She rocked her hips, liking the sense of fullness as she came. Rocked a little faster until she realized he was moving, too. Moving inside of her.

Her eyes popped open. He was over her, his arms supporting his weight as he slowly moved in and out of her. She could see the tension in his face, the need in his eyes as he watched her.

"We're making love," she whispered.

"So we are."

"I like it."

"Good."

He moved a little faster. She spread her legs more, inviting him to go deeper. As he did so, she felt a hint of anticipation, a flutter of wanting. This had possibilities, as well.

But that was for next time. Now she simply wanted him to experience what she had.

"Come for me," she whispered.

He smiled. "As you wish."

He closed his eyes and pushed into her twice more before stiffening, then groaning her name.

Rafiq poured more champagne into Kiley's glass. "Are you still hungry?" he asked.

She looked at the demolished plate that had originally held a burger and fries, along with the empty bowl of what had been ice cream.

"Nope. I'm completely full." She sipped the bubbly liquid and grinned. "I've never had champagne with a hamburger before."

"What do you think of the combination?"

"I like it."

They sat next to each other on the comfortable sofa in the suite's living room. She pulled her robe more securely around her and tucked her bare feet under Rafiq's thigh.

It was done. She'd officially changed her status to nonvirgin, and the entire event had been spectacular.

"You look happy," he said as he rubbed her bare calf.

"I am. Thank you for tonight."

"My pleasure, and I mean that most sincerely."

She leaned against the sofa and smiled at him. "This has been a good day. One of my best ever. You made my first time perfect."

"I wanted to."

She believed him. She knew that he'd been concerned about her while they'd made love. She liked that about him, along with other things.

Who was this man who made love with her so wonderfully? How could she have worked for him for two years and never noticed his goodness and humor and how incredibly sexy he was?

"You don't go back to Lucia-Serrat very often," she said.

He looked at her. "An interesting change in subject."

"I was thinking that you've been little more than a boss to me until very recently. I never allowed myself to see the actual man inside the suit. Now I have and it changes things."

He nodded. "I don't go back to the island much. In time it will be important to me to live there permanently. But not yet. My father runs the country well. He is busy with that and with his wife and family."

Kiley tried to remember all she knew about Lucia-Serrat and its ruler. "His wife is American, isn't she?"

"Yes. Phoebe grew up mostly in Florida. They met when she was on vacation. They fell in love very quickly and have been married nearly twelve years. They have two daughters."

"I know. The half sisters you refuse to shop for. You're better about your brothers."

"That's because they're boys and I know what they want."

"Do you stay away to give them a chance to be a family?" she asked.

He shrugged. "In part. I would be expected to move into the prince's residence. While the girls are so young, it is better that they have their father's attention."

She snuggled close and rested her head on his shoulder. "Tell me about the island."

"It's very beautiful. There are beaches and a rain forest. One of the world's largest banyan trees is there. And, of course, the famous Lucia-Serrat meerkats."

"I love meerkats."

"Most women do."

"They look like little bandits. So cute. Do you miss your home?"

"Sometimes."

And yet he stayed away because it was the right thing to do. Talk about a tough act to follow. He was going to make falling in love with someone else a bit of a challenge.

She raised her head and sipped her champagne. "Do you know who you're going to marry?"

He stiffened slightly. "Why do you ask?"

"Don't panic," she said with a grin. "I'm not hinting. I'm asking. You're going to have to marry and have heirs. Do you know who it is? Have you picked out some innocent schoolgirl who will be raised in proper princess fashion?"

"Not yet. I may choose as I like or have my father arrange a match."

"That will never happen," she told him. "You're too stubborn to let someone else pick your wife. You might want to stay away from Carmen, though. She had quite the temper."

"I remember."

The nature of their conversation surprised Rafiq. He braced himself for the not-so-subtle hints indicating that Kiley would make the perfect wife, but they never came. Now that he thought about it, she had never mentioned extending their affair or talked about the future at all.

"You need someone tall," she said. "A lot taller than me."

"Why?"

She sighed. "Because, she'll look better in her clothes and therefore in all the pictures. There's a reason fashion models are so tall. Make sure she's smart and funny. You'd hate it if she was dull. But not too skinny. Look for childbearing hips."

"I find it disconcerting to discuss my future wife with my current mistress."

She looked surprised. "But we've seen each other naked. You deflowered me. I wouldn't have thought there were any topics off-limits. I guess I didn't know you were so sensitive."

"I'm not *sensitive*," he said with a growl.

She patted his arm. "Of course. My prince, a delicate flower. Who would have known?"

He took her glass and set it on the coffee table next to his own. He then grabbed her and pressed her back into the sofa.

"You dare to defy me?" he asked in mock anger.

"Pretty much every chance I get. Is that a problem?"

Her hair was mussed, her eyes the color of midnight velvet. His stubble had rubbed a raw spot on her chin, and the robe she wore was two or three sizes too large. She was possibly the most beautiful woman he'd ever seen.

"You are mine now," he told her. "I have been your first and you will always remember that."

"I know." She smiled and pressed her fingers to his mouth. "I guess neither of us is going to forget, huh?"

He hadn't considered that. Not forgetting. But she was right. Kiley would be with him, always.

"Come live with me," he said, speaking almost before the thought formed.

She blinked. "What? You mean move in with you?"

He understood her surprise. He'd never asked a woman to do that before. He hadn't felt the need to spend that much time with one of them before. But Kiley was different. He wanted her in his bed every night. He wanted to see her in the morning and late in the evening. He wanted her there when he returned home from work.

"Until our time is up," he told her. "Come live with me."

She stared at him, but he had no idea what she was thinking.

"Are you offended?" he asked.

"No. Of course not. A little shocked, maybe. I didn't expect you to ask. What if you get tired of me?"

"I won't." He couldn't imagine it.

She nodded slowly. "I'd need to keep my apartment.

I don't want to have to move my stuff into storage for three months and then move it back. I guess I could temporarily forward my mail. It's not like I have a dog or anything to worry about."

Always practical, he thought with a smile.

"Is that a yes?" he asked.

"It is. If you'd like me to, I'll move in."

"Good."

He bent down and kissed her. As he pressed his mouth to hers, he tugged at the robe until it pulled open, exposing her naked body to his touch.

She reached one arm around him and pushed the other between them.

"Two can play at that game," she whispered as she reached for him.

He was already hard and he relished the feel of her hand on his erection.

"I want to please you," she said.

He heard the hesitation in her voice. "You're sore."

"A little. So I was thinking about all the really interesting stuff you did to me. Could I do that to you?"

His interest quickened. "If you would like to."

Her answer was to push him until he was seated on the sofa. She slid onto the floor and moved between his knees. After taking him in her hands, she licked the tip of his arousal and then smiled.

"Tell me what to do."

Chapter Ten

Kiley walked through her apartment one last time before heading out to Rafiq's place. It was sort of sad to think she'd lived here for three years and had never done anything to make the place her own. Sure, she'd hung pictures and she'd sewn curtains for the eating nook by the kitchen, but she'd never checked with the manager about painting or bought any furniture she really loved. She'd decorated in early hand-me-down because she'd always planned to buy real furniture after she and Eric were married.

How much of her life had been on hold for those three years? How many things had she put off, waiting for the day she would get married and her life would change forever? Since she'd always wanted to be a wife and mother, she'd allowed that desire to reduce the rest of her life to a giant waiting game. In the end, she'd lost her dream and Eric—although that was turning out to be much less of a loss than she'd realized—and the time.

Where would she be if she hadn't expected to marry Eric and become a wife and mother? Although she loved working for Rafiq, in truth she would never have gone looking for a job she considered temporary. She would have looked until she found something that challenged her. Something that made her grow and gave her room for advancement. She would have looked for a career.

Talk about being foolish, she thought sadly as she picked up a picture of her family and tucked it in her tote bag. She'd given up too much for a man who wasn't worth it.

So what was she going to do now? What would she do differently? What changes did she want in her life?

Kiley stood in the center of her living room and turned in a slow circle. When her affair with Rafiq was over, she would start looking for another job. In truth, now that they were lovers, she knew she could never go back to being just his secretary. She couldn't stand to take calls from other women, knowing he was doing to them what he'd done to her. She wouldn't want to make reservations, buy gifts, watching from the fringes.

But expecting him to want to continue things past the three months was just plain crazy. He was a foreign prince and she was just some middle-class American girl. Sure, she was smart and funny and had a lot to offer. But a prince? On what planet?

No, this time she was going to keep her eyes open. This time she wasn't going to be a foolish dreamer. For the next two-plus months she was going to experience a world she knew very little about—everything from drinking champagne while eating a hamburger to living in a stunning home in Malibu. When the time was up, she would return to her regular world and build a life she could be proud of. There wouldn't be any looking back.

That decided, she locked the front door and walked to her car. As she started the engine, she thought about working out a plan with her parents. One in which she paid them back over time so she could buy a condo and have a place of her own. Maybe she would even get a dog.

But in the meantime she needed to get to Malibu. She wanted to see Rafiq, hold him and have him hold her. She wanted to see his smile and make love.

Thirty minutes later she drove down his driveway and stopped in front of the garage. As she stepped out, she looked at her aging but sensible car and started to laugh.

"What's so funny?" Rafiq asked as he walked out of the house toward her.

She grinned. "My car. It's not exactly fitting in with the neighborhood. Quick, get me a remote control for the garage door so I can hide it. Otherwise you'll get complaints from the neighbors."

He crossed to her and pulled her close. "Do you think I care what they think?"

"Not even a little. But it *is* important to build relationships in the community."

"Always the middle child," he said as he brushed his mouth against hers.

She let herself relax against him, enjoying the feel of his hard body so close to her own. She parted her lips and he swept inside. At the first brush of his tongue, tingles raced through her and made her toes curl. Funny how every time he touched her, she only wanted him more.

Trouble, she knew, even as she held on tight. At the end of this, he would walk away and look for his next conquest, and she…well, she wasn't sure what she would do. She had a feeling that getting over Rafiq was going to be more difficult than getting over Eric. Perhaps a smarter woman would have been able to resist Rafiq's considerable charms. Or a more-experienced one. But she didn't know how and now it was too late.

A once-in-a-lifetime event, she reminded herself. That's what this was. If the price was pain at the end, then so be it. She was strong and she would recover.

"Come inside," he said, stepping back and taking her hand in his.

She smiled. "Are you about to use me for sex, because if that's the case, I have to tell you, I won't protest."

He led her to the front door, then waited for her to step inside.

"I had wondered if you being so innocent would make things more difficult," he said.

She stared through to the living room where the ocean stretched out before her. It was as if she could see to the ends of the earth.

She turned back to him. "What was your concern? That I might be shy and afraid of intimacy?"

"It crossed my mind."

"I guess." She shrugged. "To be honest, I have a lot of time to make up for. I guess you'll just get stuck with that."

"I'll do my best to survive."

"How manly of you."

He wrapped his arm around her. "Are you hungry? Would you like something to eat?"

"Are you offering to cook?"

He moved her toward the kitchen. "No, but I have a very efficient housekeeper who keeps my refrigerator filled with items that need only be heated."

They walked into the large, open kitchen. Kiley crossed to the smooth granite countertops and ran her hands against the cool surface. She stared at the six-burner stove, the warming drawer and did her best to hold in a moan.

"Will she mind if I cook in here?" she asked.

"Sana would be happy to share."

Kiley looked at him. "Are you sure? Women can be very possessive about their kitchens."

"Sana would be delighted if I dated someone who knew how to make toast, let alone an entire meal. I assure you, she will not be offended."

Kiley had to admit she couldn't imagine the very beautiful, albeit short-tempered, Carmen knowing her way around much more than an espresso machine or an ice bucket.

"I'll have to come up with a menu," she said. "Then I'll dazzle you."

"You already do."

His words made her whole body sigh.

"Come," he said, holding out his hand. "I know I gave you a tour the first time you were here, but I suspect you were too nervous to remember very much. There is also the matter of where you will be sleeping."

"Didn't we already have this conversation at the hotel?" she asked, walking to him and letting him capture her fingers.

"That was for a single night. This is for more than two months." His dark gaze studied her face. "You have made many changes in the past few weeks. I don't want you to feel you're being pushed into something you're not ready for."

He was sweet. Funny how she'd never realized that before. Sweet and kind and handsome and charming. Talk about a winner.

She stepped close enough for their bodies to touch. With her free hand, she rubbed his chest.

"I'm here for the sex," she said in a low voice. "I want to be perfectly clear about that. Being in different rooms is going to make that difficult. Unless we do it on the phone, and, honestly, I'm not ready for that."

His reply was a kiss that took her breath away. He claimed her passionately, wrapping his arms around her and holding her as if he would never let her go.

"Then we will share a room," he said when they both came up for air.

She had a sudden thought and winced. "Oh, no. Were you trying to tell me that *you* wanted separate rooms?"

He rubbed against her, pushing his erection into her belly and turning her thigh muscles to mush.

"What do you think?" he asked.

She smiled. "I would say you've got yourself a roommate."

Sunlight and the sound of running water woke Rafiq. He'd forgotten to set the alarm and had slept later than usual. Perhaps because he'd gone to sleep so early this morning.

He stretched, then placed his hands behind his head

and stared up at the ceiling. It *had* been a late night. Every time he'd tried to roll over and go to sleep, he would feel Kiley in the bed. She would move or sigh or even just breathe and then he would want her again. Wanting her, he would reach for her. She always welcomed his touch, joining him eagerly in whatever game he wished to play.

While he knew intellectually that she had been a virgin, he would never have guessed how quickly and easily she would discover the pleasures of making love. He barely had to touch her to make her swollen and ready. She raced toward her climax with an eagerness that only made him want to please her more.

The shower turned off. Instantly he pictured her wet and naked. His erection was instant, but he held back. No doubt she was already sore from their previous night. Better to give her a few hours' rest before claiming her again.

He thought about his meetings planned for the day and the weekly teleconference with the parliament leader back on Lucia-Serrat. About twenty minutes later, Kiley opened the bathroom door and stepped into the bedroom.

She was dressed in her usual skirt and blouse. Her short, spiky hair was slightly damp, her makeup fresh. Tiny gold studs decorated her earlobes. She looked prim and proper and it was all he could do not to rip the clothes from her body and take her right there.

"Morning," she said with a shy smile.

Rafiq smiled back. "How are you feeling?"

"God. This is kind of a first for me. A sleep-over. Although, we did at the hotel, so I guess not technically. Maybe it's the whole workday thing. Plus, I'm tired. We didn't get much sleep either night. Not that I'm complaining. So, how are you?"

"Well. Did you want to rethink our living arrangement?"

"What? No. Of course not. I like being here."

"But you are not comfortable."

"I will be. Just give me some time. It's not every day a girl signs up to be the love slave of a prince. Ohh, maybe they'll make a cable movie about my life. What do you think?"

That she charmed him. That he wanted her in more than his bed, he wanted her in his life.

The realization surprised him, and not in a pleasant way. He knew about commitments, what they meant and what happened when people grew tired of them. He knew that love didn't exist, and whatever feelings people claimed in the heat of the moment faded over time.

"Go eat breakfast," he said as he sat up. "I will join you shortly."

She smiled and left the bedroom while he considered why Kiley had the ability to make him wish that things were different, that marriages could be happy and long lasting.

Perhaps it was her family, he thought. They embodied what most people aspired to. But how much of it was real? Did Kiley's sisters' husbands really stay faithful to their wives? Did they love them through childbirth and teething and job losses?

He doubted it. In his world, love was a convenient word used to manipulate. His father had claimed to love him and then had disappeared for months on end. His mother had claimed she hadn't wanted to leave him all those years ago. It wasn't her fault—the money was too good. And the women who moved in and out of his life—how many of them claimed to love him? And when it was over, how quickly did they take up with someone else?

Even Kiley, who was soft-hearted and inherently honest, had forgotten about her fiancé quickly enough. Although, in that case, he was willing to believe she hadn't loved the other man in some time.

No, this was better, he told himself. Taking for the moment. Better to have her leave while he could still think of her fondly than to have things end badly with recriminations on both sides.

He showered and dressed quickly, then found Kiley in the kitchen, eating breakfast and chatting with Sana, his housekeeper.

The tiny, dark-haired woman nodded approvingly as he walked in.

"This one appreciates my cooking," she said, pointing at Kiley's plate of pancakes and fresh fruit. "Not like the others who only want coffee. As if their skinny hips would appeal to any man."

"You've made a friend," he told Kiley, accepting the cup of coffee Sana handed him.

"I love her cooking, and she's telling me all of your secrets. What's not to like?"

He raised his eyebrows, but his housekeeper only shrugged. "I am an old woman. You won't throw me out, so I can do what I like, hey?"

Kiley grinned. "And she likes to talk."

"I have no secrets," he said, refusing to be intimated by a woman older than his mother.

"So you would like to think. What about the one who threw things? You wouldn't want me talking about her, would you? Or the one who sunbathed naked out there on the deck for all the world to see. The teenage boys in the neighborhood would stand on the sand with their binoculars."

Kiley wrinkled her nose. "That's kinda tacky, Rafiq. I'm surprised at you."

He narrowed his gaze. "We should change the subject."

"Oh, look," Kiley said with a grin. "He's getting imperious. I love it when that happens."

"You're not going to be like this at the office, are you?" he asked, already knowing the answer.

"Oh, please. I'll be perfectly professional." She waited until Sana walked to the far end of the kitchen, then looked him in the eye. "No one but you will know I'm not wearing any underwear."

Heat boiled his blood. He glanced down at her skirt. "You're kidding, right?"

She picked up her plate and carried it to the sink. "I guess you're going to have to wait until tonight to find out."

She returned to the island and picked up her handbag. "Thanks, Sana. That was fabulous. And what you suggested for dinner sounds perfect." She turned to Rafiq. "By, honey. See you at the office."

He followed her to the garage. "Not so fast."

She blinked at him. "Are you going to attack me right here in the hallway? I wouldn't want to get on Sana's bad side and have her think *I'm* tacky."

"You're more concerned about my housekeeper's feelings than what I want?"

"Pretty much."

She opened the door to the garage, stepped into the large, four-car structure and came to a complete stop. Rafiq put his hands on her shoulders and squeezed.

"What do you think?" he asked.

Kiley didn't know what *to* think. She'd been having fun, enjoying her morning, her breakfast, the possibility of a new friend and feeling at one with the universe. She liked that she felt confident enough to tease Rafiq about not wearing underwear, even though she was, and that he wanted her. She liked knowing what would happen when they got home that evening. She'd been quiet, shy and uncertain a few weeks ago, and today she was a different woman. Or she had been until five seconds ago.

"Kiley?"

She stared at the shiny red convertible parked next to her old sedan. The big white bow and ribbon gave her an idea it was a present. For her.

"You're giving me a car?" she asked, not sure what to think.

"Yes. Do you like it?"

It was gorgeous. Sporty and sleek, no doubt really fast.

"If you prefer a different color, we can exchange it."

Sure, she thought, not quite able to catch her breath. Just like socks.

"I, ah…"

"You don't like it," he said, sounding disappointed.

"No, I'm just surprised. No one's ever bought me a car before."

"But Eric gave you gifts."

"Not a car."

He turned her until she faced him. "Is it the money?"

"Well, yeah."

He smiled. "I am Prince Rafiq of Lucia-Serrat. Do you think this was any more financially significant to me than a book would be to one of your sisters?"

"No." She could do math. This wasn't even a drop in the bucket for him. It was barely a molecule of water. But... "It's a car."

He took her hand and brought it to his mouth, where he pressed his mouth to her palm. "You delight me in more ways than I can explain. It would give me great pleasure if you would accept this small token of my admiration for you."

She looked at the car, then at him. "What do you give when you want to offer a big token of admiration?"

"A castle."

She smiled. "I understand your point, but this is really strange for me."

"Would you rather have something else?"

Time, she thought. She would rather have more time with him. But to say that would break the rules, and she was determined to abide by them.

"I don't want anything except what I already have," she said. "You."

"But what about what I want? Take the car. When we are finished, you may sell it if you prefer. It is yours."

"I'll drive it while I'm here, but when it's over, I'm leaving it behind," she said.

"I will convince you otherwise."

"Not a chance," she told him. "I have a will of iron. You just haven't seen it yet."

She could tell he didn't believe her, but that wasn't important right now. Instead she focused on the kiss he gave her, then settled into her sassy red convertible and reminded herself this was all about living for the moment.

Chapter Eleven

"No," Kiley said later, her blue eyes wide with something that looked very close to terror.

Rafiq feigned surprised. "You are refusing me?"

"That's generally what no means. Although if used with another word such as 'no kidding,' it sometimes means something else entirely."

"I'm very familiar with the English language." He shook his head. "We are barely a month into our relationship and already you ignore my modest wishes."

She stood in the center of the bedroom, a silk robe clinging to her curves. Her hair was wet, her face scrubbed clean of any makeup. She shouldn't have aroused him, and yet she did. He was very familiar with the rush of desire he experienced whenever she was around.

"I'm not ignoring your wishes," she told him. "I'll take care of all your wishes, just not this one."

"It is a simple matter," he said.

She raised her arms and tightened her hands as if she wished to strangle him.

"It's entertaining. You never said anything about entertaining. I don't entertain. Oh, sure, I can have a few friends over for casual party or a football game or something. But not like this. We're talking about the American ambassador to Lucia-Serrat. That's not casual. That's really formal. I'm living here. I'm your mistress. What will he think? What will his wife think?"

Rafiq held in a smile. "Actually, the new American ambassador to my country *is* a woman."

Kiley made a half-growling, half-laughing noise low in her throat, turned and collapsed facefirst on the bed. "That would be my point. I don't even know who the new ambassador is. I can't be responsible for entertaining. You do it. Have a great time. Save me some leftovers."

"Kiley, it's not so bad."

She rolled to her side and glared at him. "You didn't make Carmen entertain any ambassadors."

"She was not up to the task."

"Neither am I. What are we supposed to talk about? My idea of staying on top of current events is whatever I get on the local news radio station during my drive to work. I don't know social-economic policies or what's happening in Bosnia. I don't even know if I could find Bosnia on a map."

He frowned. "Why would we discuss Bosnia?"

"I don't know. It could come up. Or another country. And then what? I'll stand there with my mouth open, looking really fishlike. It's not a plan for success. You have the party and tell me all about it."

"Social events are part of the deal," he said.

She shifted onto her back and covered her eyes with her forearm. "You never said I had to entertain."

"Would you have refused me if I had?"

"Maybe." There was a pause, then she sighed. "No. I wouldn't have. But this is really, really a mistake." She sat up and looked at him. "I'll do anything if you don't make me give a party."

He walked to the bed and took her hand. After pulling her to her feet, he lightly kissed her. "As appealing as your offer is, I must decline. We have guests coming, and I wish you to be there."

"But I…"

"Have I asked for anything else?"

"Sure. The, ah…" She glared at him, then stomped her foot. "That is incredibly unfair and low. Don't bring up how nice you've been."

"I negotiate to win."

She grumbled something he couldn't hear, then stalked toward the closet. "Fine. I'll be at your party, but I won't like it. And when I mess up, because it's a *when* not a maybe, you will have to suffer with the consequences. Are you clear on that?"

"Perfectly."

Stupid man, Kiley thought as she stared at the clothes in the closet. Not her real ones—they would never do. Instead she flipped through the fabulous designer clothes Rafiq had purchased for her. Okay, what exactly did one wear to a casual-but-elegant, at-home soirée. She'd never been to a soirée. She'd only ever read about them or seen them on nighttime soap operas.

Panic knotted her stomach and made her a little nauseous. An ambassador. Worse, a woman ambassador. What would they talk about? No doubt Madam Ambassador was ambitious and accomplished. What was Kiley supposed to say in the face of that? "Hi, I'm a twit who put my whole life on hold because I thought I was marrying Mr. Right. When that didn't work out, I became the mistress of a sheik. My entire gender must be so proud."

She sank onto the small padded bench in the closet and hung her head. Okay, maybe that was a little harsh. She'd been stupid about Eric, but not about Rafiq. He was a great guy. She'd gotten the revenge she wanted, a chance to discover the magic between a man and a woman in the most thrilling way possible and time to regroup. He'd been nothing but supportive and kind. The only thing he'd ever asked for, aside from this party, was fidelity.

Plus, there was nothing wrong with wanting to be a wife and mother. Those were still her goals. The difference was she would think things through more next time. She would be more clear about the man she wanted to marry. Character was everything and all that.

She stood and reached for a pair of silk slacks and a fitted white silk blouse. When in doubt, keep it simple, she thought.

After hanging them on the hook by the door, she returned to the bathroom where she quickly applied her makeup. When she'd dressed, she returned to the bedroom. Rafiq was gone, no doubt checking on the last-minute details.

"Couldn't we have started with a couple of clerks and maybe an undersecretary?" she muttered to herself as she walked down the hall. "Maybe a gameskeeper or two?"

She found Rafiq in the dining room. Sana stood next to him, explaining what dishes would go where. When he reached for a bowl of nuts, she slapped his hand. Kiley couldn't help laughing.

"Did you see that?" he asked in outrage. "She violated my royal person."

Sana glared at him. "If you snack now, you won't be hungry later," the housekeeper said, and then returned to the kitchen.

Kiley moved close. "I believe the violations are my responsibility," she whispered in his ear.

He chuckled, then stepped back and studied her outfit. "You look very beautiful. Are you feeling better?"

"A little." She shook her head. "No. Not really. I'm intelligent and fully capable of holding my own in a conversation. I know that. It's just…"

He crossed to her and lightly touched her chin. "You wish to make me proud of you."

She let herself get lost in his dark eyes. "Exactly. If I'd known there was going to be a quiz on current events, I would have studied more."

"There isn't a quiz. This is a few friends getting together."

"Right. That's why we've got the good china out."

He leaned close. "This isn't the good china. That has the state seal on it."

She instantly pictured an aquatic mammal before realizing that probably wasn't the kind of seal he meant. "Casual is good," she said. "I can do casual."

He took her hand and led her to the foyer. They stopped in front of a large mirror.

"You enchant me," he told her, meeting her gaze in the mirror. "You are completely yourself at every turn. You worry about me, you fuss, you create a sense of home where none existed."

"I appreciate the compliment, but I don't think I've done all that."

"You have. Simply by your presence. You have become friends with Sana."

He wasn't making sense. "Who wouldn't? She's great. And she's teaching me to make some really cool dishes."

He smiled. "You take time with people. Now, even though you are nervous, you still show up and intend to do your best. I admire you, Kiley. More than I can say."

He reached into his slacks pocket and pulled out a small box. She recognized the trademark, dark-green leather, the edging in silver, and turned to face him.

"No, no. Not required. I'm not here for the money or the jewelry."

"But I want to give you this."

She rolled her eyes. "Yeah, and last week you gave me a car. Rafiq, stop. I'm not like them. I'm here for a nobler purpose." Because she was falling for him, she thought, knowing she could never say that. Oh, sure, this had started out as a way to get revenge, but it was so much more now.

She felt tears forming and willed them away. He could never know how she had fallen for him. She could stand everything but his pity.

Forcing herself to smile, she said, "I'm here for the sex."

As she expected, he laughed, but he didn't put the box away. "You're going to make me beg, aren't you."

"It's something I've never seen, so probably."

He opened the box. Inside was a diamond pendant. The simple design, three stones, each larger than the one above, took her breath away.

He produced matching earrings from his other pocket. "You know I will win this argument," he told her, even as he handed her the earrings. When she would have refused them, he closed her fingers around them.

"I usually prefer much more obvious pieces," he said. "But I knew those would not suit your delicate beauty. You must admit they're modest by my standards."

The pendant gleamed in the vee of her shirt. She winced as the perfectly cut stones caught the light.

"It's beautiful," she said.

"Then put on the earrings."

She looked at him in the mirror. "I'm not here for jewelry."

"I know. But that reality only makes me want to buy you more."

Rather than argue further, she put on the earrings and admired them. One more item on her list of things she was leaving behind when it was time to go. The car, most of the clothes, any jewelry he bought her—and her heart.

"I was substantially younger than I am now," Margaret Redding, Ambassador to Lucia-Serrat, said with a laugh. "It was my first overseas posting. I'd gotten lucky and been assigned to Rome. There was a fabulous party and there he was, Prince Rafiq."

Kiley smiled at the attractive older woman. "He does clean up well."

"I'll say. We danced, he was charming. It was lust at first sight, for me anyway. At the end of the evening, he was gracious and took my number. I waited weeks for him to call. He never did." She laughed again, then tucked her long auburn hair behind her ears. "I was crushed for at least two days. Then I found out the very handsome prince was at least nine years younger than me. It was hard to tell with him in his tux."

Margaret glanced at Rafiq. "He's grown into quite a man. I envy you." She turned her attention to her husband. "In the purely intellectual sense, of course."

Kiley laughed. "Of course." She'd seen the Reddings come in together and didn't doubt that they were very much in love.

"So how, exactly, did you get to be an ambassador?"

Margaret shifted on the sofa. "I rose through the ranks in the State Department. I was very fortunate in my postings, and I managed to make a good impression on the right people. This is my first time as ambassador and I'm delighted. Lucia-Serrat is a wonderful place to live. I enjoy the people so much and Prince Nasri, Rafiq's father, is very determined to maintain a cordial relationship with the United States." She leaned forward and lowered her voice. "Some days I don't actually feel as if I'm working."

"What does your husband do?"

"He's a writer, which allows him to travel with me. He teases me that it's far more interesting for him to be the dependent spouse than it would be for me. He gets to hang out with all the wives. At my previous post, his team won the embassy golf tournament."

"Do you have children?"

Margaret's smile faded. "No. We talked about it, but with my career, it would have been a challenge. Robert was willing, of course. He would have made an excellent stay-at-home father. But the year we were going to try, I was sent to three different posts in nine months. All that moving around isn't conducive to pregnancy. At least it wasn't for me. And then…"

Margaret stopped and shrugged. "Sorry. I'm rambling. I suppose I'm still thinking about what could have been. I always wanted a career more than a family."

Kiley had trouble believing this attractive, incredibly successful woman could ever doubt her choices. Yet it was clear that Margaret was ambivalent about the road she'd chosen.

"If it makes you feel any better," Kiley said in a lower voice, "I've only ever wanted to be a stay-at-home mom. I've always felt guilty about that, as if I should have big career aspirations."

"I think the fact that I want my career and you want to be a stay-at-home mom and both of us can do that is a wonderful thing. As for feeling guilty—" she touched Kiley's hand "—don't. Isn't it a blessing that you know what you want and have the freedom to pursue it? Isn't that the point?"

"You're right."

Kiley thought about her plans for the future—to find another job, to buy a condo, to live her life fully. If a man came along in the next few years, that would be wonderful. If he didn't, she wasn't going to give up her dream of being a mother. She would find another way.

Margaret glanced over her shoulder to where Rafiq spoke with Robert and another couple.

"He adores you," Margaret told her. "I can see it in his eyes."

"Thank you. I adore him."

Margaret waited expectantly.

Kiley laughed. "You're not going to get me to say any more. We're good friends. We have fun together. That's all." Unfortunately, when the time was up, he would let her go, just as he'd let every other woman go.

"Are you sure?" Margaret asked. "He has to settle down sometime."

"I'm sure he has a princess-in-training all picked out. He's not the boy next door. He has to be very careful about who he chooses."

"Agreed. So why not you?"

Kiley knew all the reasons. She didn't have family connections or the right lineage. Loving him wasn't enough of a calling card.

"She's wonderful," Margaret told Rafiq after dinner. "Where did you find her?"

"She works for me."

Margaret smiled. "Your secretary. Then she's not your usual type."

"Meaning?"

The ambassador laughed. "She's a real person with a heart and a brain. You don't always look for that."

"I would have thought that to be in your position, some measure of diplomacy was required."

Margaret shrugged. "I thought we'd known each other long enough for that not to be an issue. But if you'd prefer I can speak more delicately."

"No. I like that you tell me the truth." He offered

Margaret a glass of cognac, then took one for himself. They were the last ones at the dining room table. Everyone else had gone out to admire the sunset.

She took a sip, then set down her glass. "Your father has been speaking with me. You know he's concerned."

Rafiq could imagine the subject of their conversation. "I'm past thirty and not engaged. It's time for me to take a wife."

"A list has been prepared."

"I trust you didn't bring it with you."

"I wasn't privy to it. I only know of its existence, and that I wasn't on it."

Despite his displeasure at the topic, he smiled. "You tell that story of falling for me all those years ago, but in truth you were far more interested in your career than in any one man."

"Perhaps," she admitted. "But it *is* a good story. Now, back to the subject you don't wish to discuss. I am your friend and I tell you this as a friend. You will be recalled by the end of the year. Your father is determined to see you married with an heir."

He shrugged. "Then I will pick a wife."

"You could sound more enthused about it."

"Why? It is a duty, nothing more."

"What about Kiley?"

The idea had crossed his mind. She was all he had ever wanted. But to marry her was to invite disaster. He would start to believe and have expectations. When she let him down, when she proved she was like all the others and that she could not love with any depth, he would be unable to forgive her. There had been too many disappointments in his life for him to be forgiving now.

"No."

"Want to tell me why not?" she asked.

"Not really. I will pick a suitable bride and produce an heir."

"You don't sound very happy about the prospect. I know you're a prince, Rafiq, but you're also a man. Don't you want to fall madly in love?"

He recalled all that had happened to him while he'd been growing up. All the times he'd been left alone because there was no one to bother. He thought of all the women who claimed to love him when what they loved was the promise of title and untold riches.

"I don't believe in love," he said. "I prefer duty. A desire to serve can be trusted."

"I'm sorry," she said, and touched his hand. "I wish I could change your mind."

"I assure you, I won't."

Kiley walked into the restaurant shortly after twelve. The reservation was for twelve-fifteen, but she didn't want to be late. Actually, she didn't want to be here at all, but if her presence was required, then she would prefer not to be tardy.

Why had she agreed to this? What had she been thinking? In truth, the invitation had been such a shock that she hadn't been able to think of a reason to refuse.

She gave her name to the hostess and was shown to a corner table at the rear of the restaurant. Several of the surrounding tables were still unoccupied. Crystal gleamed on white tablecloths as jacketed servers moved quietly among the upscale clientele.

Kiley adjusted the front of her designer dress. It

wasn't anything she would normally have worn to work, but this wasn't a normal day.

At exactly twelve-sixteen, a beautiful, well-dressed woman approached the table. Kiley stood and offered a tentative smile. The woman looked her up and down.

"So, you're the new flavor of the month. You're not exactly his usual type, are you? Well, sit down." The woman took her seat and motioned to the waiter. "A martini. Very dry. Tell David it's me. He knows what I like."

Carnie Rigby, former beauty queen, former actress and Rafiq's mother, glanced at her. "Let me guess. You'll have white wine."

Kiley figured this had to be some kind of test. No one could be that rude on general principle. At least she hoped not. She leaned back in her seat and turned to the waiter.

"I'll have a glass of iced tea, please."

"Yes, ma'am." The man hurried away.

"Afraid you'll be muddled this afternoon?" Carnie asked as she shrugged off her jacket. "I doubt my son will care."

"He might not, but I would."

"That's the secretary in you. A secretary. Whatever were you thinking? I heard you'd been to college. Surely you could have done more with your life."

Kiley was torn. She'd been raised to respect her elders, and she didn't want to insult Rafiq's mother. But she wasn't willing to be a doormat, either.

"I haven't had a chance to look at the menu," she said, picking up one of the leather-bound pages the waiter had left. "What would you recommend?"

"I really don't care what you eat. You're not going to answer me?"

"Was there a question?"

"I suppose not." Carnie glanced toward the bar. "Where *is* that man with my martini?" She sighed heavily, then turned back to Kiley. "You're living with him."

Kiley hadn't known what to make of the invitation to join Rafiq's mother for lunch. She'd thought maybe the other woman had wanted to get involved in her son's life in some way. Obviously not. Either Carnie saw Kiley as a threat, which was flattering but not true, or she resented anyone her son was involved with. Kiley didn't want to add to her distress, but she refused to be walked on.

"Yes," Kiley said calmly. "It's been a couple of weeks now."

"He doesn't usually invite his women to stay at his house. Did yours burn down?"

Kiley laughed. "No. I believe it's still a perfectly sound structure."

"You do realize this isn't going anywhere, don't you? There's been talk. I may not visit Lucia-Serrat on a regular basis, but I still keep up with the news. His father is displeased that he hasn't taken a wife. It's time for him to marry, and you're getting in the way of that."

Kiley didn't know how much of what she said was true. Rafiq was expected to marry and she wasn't going to be considered a likely candidate. The topic made her uncomfortable, but she refused to let this woman know that.

"I am in Rafiq's life because he has asked me to be," she said carefully. Okay, it was a partial truth. She'd asked to be his mistress and he'd said yes. It was almost the same thing. "As for me being in the way, I'm sorry, but that's not possible. He is a man who does as he pleases. If he wanted me gone so that he could go find a wife, he would simply ask me to leave."

"Perhaps he has and you weren't paying attention."

Kiley thought of the previous night, when he had made love with her for hours. She thought of how they had slept, so closely entwined, their hearts had beat in unison.

"Was there anything else?" she asked. "Another topic, perhaps. Because if your sole purpose for asking me to lunch was to try and bully me into leaving your son, then I must leave."

Carnie's eyes narrowed. "You can't just walk out on me," she snapped. "Who do you think you are?"

"Kiley Hendrick," she said as she rose. "I wish I could say it had been nice to meet you."

Chapter Twelve

Kiley returned to the house and phoned Rafiq to tell him she wasn't coming back to the office that afternoon.

"I'm fine," she said when he asked why. "I'm just feeling a little tired. I'll go in early to clear up whatever I missed today."

"Not necessary," he said. "Are you sure I don't need to call a doctor?"

"Positive. I'm fine. I just need a little time."

"I'll be home later. Perhaps you should rest."

Good idea, she thought as she hung up the phone. But after changing out of her designer clothes and into shorts and a T-shirt, she gave in to the call of the ocean and went out onto the beach.

It was midafternoon, midweek. While there were mothers with children, some teenagers and a few surfers scattered on the sand, for the most part, she had the beach to herself. She walked halfway to the water and settled down, digging her toes deep enough to feel the coolness a few inches down.

The sun was high, the afternoon warm, the waves rhythmic. If she closed her eyes she could smell salt and suntan lotion. The cry of seagulls competed with laughter and an oldies rock station on someone's portable radio.

Her brief encounter with Carnie had carried with it one spark of good news. If she, Kiley, wasn't marrying Rafiq, then she didn't have to worry about Carnie as a mother-in-law. Talk about a miserable person. Kiley still wasn't sure of the point of the meeting. To get rid of her? But how could she be a threat to anyone? Maybe Carnie checked out all Rafiq's women. She would have to ask.

As she stretched out her legs and stared at the ocean, she wondered what her life would have been like if she hadn't found out the truth about Eric. How long would it have taken for her to discover he was pretty much a weasel? And then what? She would have left him. No, this way was better. A quick, clean break that turned out to be much less painful than she would have guessed.

And what about when she left Rafiq? How easy would that be?

She found herself not wanting to think about it, which meant she had to force herself to consider the reality. Their affair *would* end. She could either handle that time gracefully, or she could beg and plead.

Graceful sounded mature, but *pleading* had its place. She supposed the real question was whether or not she would tell him she loved him. It wasn't as much about him wanting to know as her not wanting regrets. Years from now would she want to have told him?

"Still time to decide," she thought.

She closed her eyes and listened to the ocean. The tension eased out of her body as she relaxed. Eventually she leaned back in the sand and let the minutes drift by.

Sometime later she felt a slight prickling down her spine. She sat up and turned to see Rafiq walking toward her. He'd changed into jeans and a shirt and, like her, he hadn't bothered with shoes. He carried a towel or something against his chest.

She rose to her knees and waved at him. As she watched him approach, she felt the love filling her heart and knew she would have to say something before she left. Whether or not it mattered it him, the information was important to her.

"How are you feeling?" he asked as he stopped beside her but didn't sit down.

"Better. I've cleared my head."

"Good." He lowered himself beside her. "I have brought you something."

She rolled her eyes. "Not again. Rafiq, no. You have to stop buying me things. I've told you and told you I'm—"

He cut her off with a kiss. "I think you should stop talking now because when you see what I have, you will not be able to resist."

He drew back the towel and leaned toward her. Kiley stared down at a sleeping pile of white, fluffy fur.

"A puppy," she breathed quietly, wanting to pet it but afraid to wake it up.

"Yes. She is a Maltese. Ten weeks old."

She looked at him. "You bought me a puppy? Why?"

"Because you said you wanted one."

Just like that. Would he get her the moon, too? Tears burned in her eyes, but she blinked them back. No crying, not over something this wonderful.

"I did some research. I thought you would want a small dog, but one with a big personality. She seems quiet now, but trust me, when she is awake, she takes over the room."

Kiley laughed and threw her arm around him. The puppy woke up and immediately began to lick her face.

"Look at you!" Kiley said, scooping her up and holding her out at arm's length. "You're so cute!"

She was all white, except for her black eyes and black nose. Her entire fanny swayed from her enthusiastic tail wagging.

"What a pretty girl," Kiley said as she set the puppy in her lap. The dog immediately tumbled into the sand, stood, shook herself and scrambled back into Kiley's lap.

"She seems to have taken to you," Rafiq said.

"Good, because I adore her." She leaned in and kissed him. "Thank you."

He feigned surprise. "What? No protests, no threats to leave her behind when you go?"

"Nope. She's family."

"Good." He put his arm around her and fingered her hair. "Are you feeling better?"

"Yes." She patted the puppy who promptly flopped onto her back, exposing her tender, pink belly for rubbing. "I wasn't sick, just tired, I guess."

"My mother has that affect on people."

She looked at him. "You told me not to meet her. You warned me she would be difficult."

"And was she?"

"Sort of." She sighed. "Okay, yes. She was difficult and rude and I don't know why she wanted to meet with me. What was the point?"

"What did you discuss?"

"Me? Not much of anything. She knew we were living together, although I don't know how. I didn't think you spoke to her very much."

"I do not."

"That's what I thought. She wanted to make it really clear that our relationship wasn't going anywhere, and she said you were supposed to be getting married and I was in the way of that."

She held her breath after she finished, not sure what he would say back. For a long time there was silence. At last he kissed her neck.

"She's a foolish old woman. I hope you didn't let her upset you too much."

Hmm, that was a neutral. "I tried not to. I told her that if you wanted or needed me out of your life, you would simply tell me."

"True enough. But I don't want you to go. I want you right here."

Just where she wanted to be. "You sure know how to turn a girl's head."

He smiled at her. "Do you doubt my affection?" he asked.

"No. I think you like me a lot."

"Is that enough for you?"

Dangerous, dangerous territory. She could see the flashing red lights all around her. The puppy wiggled to get more comfortable, then closed her eyes. And sighed.

"Yes," Kiley said, knowing it was the closest she'd come to lying to Rafiq. Then, to change the subject, she stood and cradled the puppy in her arms.

"Have you thought this through?" she asked. "Puppies can be a challenge. There's the whole house-training bit, and chewing and all kinds of trouble. Oh, and she'll shed. You live in a really nice place."

"I'll survive," he said. "We may have to bribe Sana, if there is extra cleaning for her."

"Oh, don't worry about that. I'll clean up after this little one."

He reached over and stroked the dog's head. "You'll probably want to take her into work with you while she's so small. A workday is a long time for her to be left alone."

"I'd like that. Thank you."

They walked back to the house, his arm around her. Kiley did her best to remember everything about this moment so that she could have it with her always.

Rafiq knocked on the door of his mother's Century City high-rise.

"This is a surprise," she said as she opened the door for him and returned to the living room. "You don't usually just stop by. I assume there is a purpose."

"There is."

He walked into the large, airy condo. The windows faced north, giving him a view of west Los Angeles, Brentwood and Hollywood in the distance.

She sat down and picked up a tumbler filled with clear liquid and ice. "Would you like something to drink?"

"No, thank you."

He crossed the pale carpeting and sat across from the woman who had given birth to him. From the time he could remember until he graduated from university in England, he'd seen her fewer than a half-dozen times. Once he'd grown and, as she had put it on his twenty-third birthday when she'd thrown a party for him, gotten interesting, she wanted to be a part of his life.

By then it had been too late for him. He was willing to treat her with some measure of respect—she *was* his mother—but that was all.

He suspected she used her connection to him when it was convenient, although that came with a price. To claim to be the mother of a prince meant admitting her age—something he knew she hated to do.

She was attractive, he acknowledged. Doctors had worked their magic to keep her skin tight and unlined. She dressed well, could converse on many subjects and knew the value of any antique, piece of jewelry or fine art. In many ways, she reminded him of a snake: cold-blooded, keeping to the shadows and intent only on survival.

"It's about the girl, isn't it?" Carnie said with a sigh. "I knew right away she was going to be tiresome."

"Leave her alone," Rafiq said. "You are to have no further contact with her. I don't know what game you're playing but I won't be a part of it."

His mother sipped her drink. She wore a pale shirt tucked into tailored slacks. Her small feet were bare, her toes painted. She was the epitome of at-home elegance.

"My, my. I don't recall you being so protective about one of your women before," she said with a smile. "How touching." She set down her drink. "But honestly, Rafiq, is she all that different? At night, when you reach for her, couldn't she be one of a hundred different bodies?"

"I meant what I said. Leave her alone."

"Are you threatening me?"

"Yes."

His mother seemed unfazed by the statement, but he suspected it was posturing on her part. They both knew there was damage to be done. Should it come out that she had been snubbed by her own son, invitations would not flow so freely. The rich and famous would be less inclined to frequent her exclusive gallery.

"Interesting." His mother gazed at him. "And this one matters why?"

"I'm not going to discuss that with you."

"Of course not. You wouldn't want to risk me offering advice. What if it made sense? You couldn't possibly take it, because it came from me, and then where would you be?"

"I'm not a child who feels the need to rebel against you," he told her.

"That's true. You're a man. A prince. Your father's heir. Are you aware that Kiley is in love with you?"

The question slammed into him with the subtlety of a California earthquake. He felt the floor shift, shake, then settle back into place.

In love with him? Kiley? It wasn't possible. She could not be.

"Unlikely," he said, keeping his turmoil safely inside.

His mother laughed. "Oh, my dear. You may be all grown-up but you're still a man and blind where women are concerned. Of course she's in love with you. What did you expect? She's your secretary." She paused and nodded slowly. "Yes, I know that. I know more than you think. I know that before you, she was engaged and he was quite the jerk. So she came to you, all sad and broken and you offered to fix her. How kind."

That wasn't what had happened, but he wasn't about to correct her.

"Did you honestly think she was like your other women?" Carnie asked mockingly. "Did you think she would understand the rules and play by them? If so, you were mistaken. She's the kind of woman who leads with her heart, the poor fool. I'm sure she's saying all the right things, but trust me, she is desperately in love with you."

He didn't want to know that. Part of him started to dismiss his mother's words out of hand. Kiley had known him for a long time. She'd seen the other women in his life, was clear on how the process worked. She wouldn't break the rules.

And yet… He couldn't ignore what Carnie said simply because he didn't like the messenger.

"What happens when you walk away?" his mother asked. "For you, she is simply one more conquest, but for her you are her prince. I mean that in the literal sense as well as the figurative. I can't blame her and you shouldn't, either. Look at her life, Rafiq. Look at what you have shown her, done with her. How could she resist? It's not her fault. But it's very sad. Imagine how her life will be when you tire of her. Who will pick up the pieces of her shattered heart then?"

He didn't believe in love, not for himself. He couldn't imagine ever trusting that much. But he knew it existed. He'd seen tiny lights in the darkness, places where people truly gave all they had for another. He'd seen signs of love at Kiley's family's house. In the laughter, the hugs, the memories.

"What is your point?" he asked his mother.

"I just wanted to warn you that you were treading on dangerous territory with Kiley. She's such a sweet girl."

He narrowed his gaze. "And?"

"And I've heard rumors. Your father isn't all that happy with you these days. You're over thirty, Rafiq. It's time you married."

"I see. Let me guess. You have a candidate in mind."

"Yes, as a matter of fact, I do. The daughter of a friend. She's a wonderful young woman. Very beautiful and accomplished. She's extremely well educated and has an advanced degree in music. She plays the violin. I would like to set up a meeting between the two of you. Nothing too stressful. Perhaps a brunch this weekend or next."

He stood. "I'm not interested in the relative of anyone who would call you a friend. If nothing else, I would be forced to question her judgment."

Carnie glared at him. "You're going to have to marry someone, and we both know it's not going to be that fool you're sleeping with. She's a nobody. Who are her parents? What lineage or talent would she bring to that match? Who would your children be?"

She continued to talk, but he wasn't listening. He turned and walked out of her condo, then turned toward the elevator. One word repeated over and over in his head.

Children.

He and Kiley had been lovers for three weeks. In that time he'd taken her several times a day, making love with her until they were both exhausted. Yes, he had used protection…every time but one…the first time.

She'd been a virgin, inexperienced and unprepared. He'd been around her enough to know she wasn't on The Pill.

One time, he told himself. Only one time. Yet she could be pregnant. Condoms weren't foolproof.

He stepped onto the elevator and pushed the button for the parking garage. He was Prince Rafiq of Lucia-Serrat. If there was a child, there was only one thing for him to do.

Kiley sat curled up on the sofa, reading. When she heard the garage door open, followed by the low purr of Rafiq's car, she did her best to continue to concentrate on her book, but she wasn't fooling anyone. Her stomach clenched, her toes curled and everything in her body went on the alert.

She wanted to stand up and shout, "He's home! He's home!" But that seemed silly, what with the entire population of the house currently consisting of herself and the puppy, and the latter had already scampered for the door off the kitchen where she would dance and whine until her pack leader came in and acknowledged her.

Kiley knew she had it bad when she felt a slight flash of jealousy, knowing the puppy would get the first bit of attention. Then she decided to be mature, because that night she would have Rafiq in her bed.

"I'm home," he called as he walked into the house.

"Hi," she said back, and wondered if he made any announcement when he walked into the official residence back on Lucia-Serrat. Or was there some town-crier type who ran ahead telling all that Prince Rafiq had returned?

He came in carrying the puppy. "She gets far too excited about my arrival," he said. "If she spins much harder or faster, she'll injure herself."

"She's happy to see you," Kiley said, willing to do a little spinning herself.

She walked up to him and kissed him. The puppy yipped happily at being caught in the middle and tried to lick them both.

She laughed and took her from Rafiq. "You're a little crazy person, aren't you?" She glanced at him. "I've named her."

He took her free hand and led her to the sofa. "What did you decide?"

"Fariha. It's Arabic. It means—"

"Joyful or happy. I speak Arabic."

She grinned. "Of course you do. I thought the name was appropriate and we can call her Fari for short."

She sank onto the sofa and held Fari up in the air. "Do you like your new name?" she asked the puppy. "Don't you think it's as pretty as you?"

Fari wiggled and yipped her approval. Kiley set her on the floor and watched her scamper to her chew toy by the window.

"How was your meeting?" she asked.

"Interesting." He stared at her. "Are you happy here, Kiley?"

"What?" Silly man. "Of course I am."

He took one of her hands in his and kissed her palm. "I know things have moved quickly between us. Becoming lovers, you moving in."

Was he worried about her? "I'm fine with all that. I like being here. You're a pretty fun date."

"How flattering. Do you love me?"

The question came from nowhere and knocked the air right out of her. She didn't know what to think, what do say. Heat flared on her cheeks as she realized that he must have guessed. Somehow she'd given herself away.

"I, ah…" She pressed her lips together. "Rafiq, I don't understand."

"It's a simple question. Do you love me?"

Panic joined embarrassment. He hated that she'd fallen for him. She'd broken all the rules and he wanted her out of here. Oh, but she wasn't ready to go. Not yet. They still had more time together.

She wanted to protest, to promise to do better. She wanted a lot of things, but wanting something didn't always make it come true. So she drew in a deep breath and looked directly into his dark eyes.

"Yes, Rafiq. I'm in love with you. But before you panic, I want you to know this doesn't change anything. I understood the rules when I first asked to be your mistress and I still understand them."

She couldn't tell what he was thinking. She thought he might be on the verge of smiling, but wasn't sure. He didn't seem angry or upset, so that was good.

"Some rules are made to be broken," he told her, and stunned her by pulling a ring out of his shirt pocket.

Not just any ring, either. This was a huge, sparkling diamond solitaire that looked very much like an engagement ring. The hits kept on coming, then he slid off the sofa onto one knee and smiled at her.

"Kiley, will you marry me?"

She blinked. "Excuse me?"

He laughed. "What is so confusing about the question? I have asked you to be my wife."

Okay, it sounded like English. She was fairly sure she understood all the words, but the sentence itself didn't make any sense.

Yet there he was, on his knees, holding out an engagement ring. What was that old saying? If it looks like a duck and walks like a duck then it's probably a duck.

"You're proposing," she said, just to be completely sure.

"Apparently not very well."

"To me."

"Yes. The only other female in this room is the dog and I assure you I have no interest in her except as a pet."

"You want to marry me."

"Yes."

There was a sliver of doubt, a voice that whispered stuff like this didn't happen to regular people and yet here it was. In the flesh, so to speak.

Happiness bubbled up inside of her until she felt light enough to float away.

"You're not kidding?" she asked, just to be sure.

He leaned forward and kissed her. "On my honor, I very much wish you to marry me."

"Okay, then," she said before she shrieked her excitement, wrapped both arms around him and said, "Yes."

Chapter Thirteen

Rafiq had wondered if he would have second thoughts, but none appeared. Their conversation the next day only reinforced his decision.

"Do you have to tell your parents?" she asked from the large leather chair in his study at the house. "I don't think they'll approve."

She looked so charmingly worried that he found it difficult not to cross to her and kiss away the small frown between her eyebrows.

"You are well educated, articulate, kind and very much in love with their son. Why would they not approve?"

She sighed. "This isn't a time for logic. Besides, that argument isn't going to work with your mother, who, for reasons I can't explain, already hates me."

"She has her own agenda for my future," he said, remembering his conversation with Carnie. "It has nothing to do with who you are."

"A sentiment that isn't as comforting as one might think. As for your father, I'm your basic commoner. Won't he have been hoping for minor European royalty at the very least?"

He smiled. "What do you know of my stepmother?"

"She's very pretty and has two daughters."

"And before she married my father, she was a poor orphan who dreamed of becoming a nurse."

"Really?" Kiley straightened in her chair. "That makes me feel better. You swear she's nice?"

"You will like her very much."

"I just wish you didn't have to tell them."

"They would notice eventually. Besides, what of your parents? They may not approve."

Kiley laughed. "Oh, yeah. Every parent gets totally bummed out to hear his or her daughter is marrying a prince. What a drag."

"They may not appreciate me taking you away. Within a couple of years we will have to move to Lucia-Serrat."

She nodded. "I know, and I'm okay with that." She leaned down and petted Fari who had curled up on the chair's ottoman. "You hear that, sweet face? We're going to Lucia-Serrat where you get to run around in a palace and be a royal dog. Like a puppy princess." Kiley glanced at Rafiq. "Speaking of the whole princess thing, any way I can pass on that?"

"What do you mean?"

"Just that I'm really happy to marry you and all, but the whole being-in-the-public-eye, I'm-the-princess thing really doesn't work for me. I could stay in the background. No one would have to know."

If he hadn't been sure before, her question would have reassured him. He couldn't imagine Carmen or any of the other women he'd been involved with ever wishing *not* to be named a princess. For them, that was the point.

"It is part of the deal," he said. "Does that change your mind?"

She wrinkled her nose. "It's not my favorite part, but I'll survive."

He believed her and in that moment, he found hope. She was the right woman for him, a woman who led with her heart and gave unconditionally. She would be a good mother to their children.

He wanted to be sure she would love them as she had been loved. He knew she would never leave them. There was no temptation he could offer that would cause her to leave them behind. As it was, she barely let Fari out of her sight. How much more would she care when she had a baby?

He glanced at her still-flat stomach. Was she pregnant? Did his child grow there, even now? Time would tell. He doubted the thought had occurred to her and he preferred it that way. Better for them to get much closer to the wedding before she found out she was pregnant. He didn't want her questioning the timing of his proposal.

"I will call my parents later this evening," he said. "I'm sure they will want to fly out and meet you."

She curled back up in the chair. "There goes my good mood."

"You will like them and they will like you."

"Uh-huh." She didn't sound convinced. "Then

they're going to want to meet my parents, and even if they don't, my folks will want to meet them. We're going to have to have some kind of group parental meeting. Let's do that here rather than in Sacramento."

"A brunch," he said, appreciating the irony of borrowing his mother's idea.

"Oh, that would work. It's less formal."

"We'll have to make an announcement to the press, as well. That will come from my father's office, but we must make sure your family knows before they read about it in a magazine."

"Good point."

"There are other considerations," he said. "The wedding will have to be a formal state event."

She practically writhed in her chair. "Yeah, I guessed that was the case. I saw the British royal family's weddings on television. It won't be that big, will it?"

"No. There will be four or five hundred guests, about half of whom are dignitaries."

Kiley wasn't sure how much more of this she could take. The idea of a formal, state wedding made her stomach hurt. She didn't want to be a princess, a figurehead or anything the least bit official. She wanted to marry Rafiq, stay in this house and have babies.

But that wasn't going to be the plan. He wasn't just some guy she'd fallen for—he was Prince Rafiq of Lucia-Serrat—a fact that had been interesting but not especially important until he'd slid the ring on her finger.

She glanced down at the sparkling diamond. She could never have imagined her dreams coming true this way. The most she'd allowed herself to fantasize about was his extending their affair. But marriage? How did she ever get so lucky?

"I haven't the faintest idea how to plan a royal wedding," she said.

"I know. After I tell my parents, I'll have someone trained in such matters flown out. While the wedding itself will be on the island, we can do the planning from here."

Which sounded lovely, but she had a feeling that Rafiq was going to be a typical male. There wouldn't be so much "we" in the wedding planning as there would be "her."

"There are probably a lot of rules we have to follow?" she asked.

"Some. The ceremony will be in the main church on the island, and the reception is held at the crown prince's royal residence."

"At least I don't have to go hunting for locations."

His expression softened. "Did you have somewhere special in mind?"

"No." She hadn't allowed herself to consider it. Not with him. "I'm okay with tradition as long as someone can tell me what's expected."

"I assure you, the wedding planner will be very clear on that. However, you must be willing to stand up to him. There are traditions, but this is also your wedding. I wish you to make it everything you want it to be. Don't give in on what's important. I can't know your mind unless you speak it, Kiley. Tell me if you're having trouble getting through to him and I will intervene."

"Thanks, but I'll be okay." Dealing with the wedding planner could be her initial princess-in-training test. She intended to pass the first time.

"We have to talk about your job."

Kiley started to protest, then pressed her lips together. "You're saying it's not appropriate for your future wife to be your secretary?"

"Something like that."

"But I like working for you."

"And I enjoy having you in the office. To be honest, you're the most efficient assistant I've had in a long time. I don't want to make a change, but your priorities must be elsewhere."

He made sense. Once word of their engagement got out, she would be busy with other things. She wasn't sure what, but no doubt she would find out in time. If nothing else, she would have to learn about Lucia-Serrat. She knew a little of the island by virtue of working for Rafiq, but not enough to represent it as the princess.

Kiley still had trouble getting her mind around that concept. A princess? Her? And yet it came with marrying Rafiq.

While she was on the subject of improbabilities, what about the engagement? As much as she'd fallen in love with him, she'd never dreamed he would return her affection and want to make things permanent. It was as if every dream she'd ever had had come true.

"What are you thinking about?" he asked. "You have the most intriguing smile."

"Do I?" Her smile widened. "I was thinking how lucky I am. I love you so much and I was heartbroken at the thought of having to leave."

He stood and moved toward her. "And now?"

She rose. "Now I get to stay forever."

He reached for her. She went into his arms with a

practiced ease. They had made love so many times in the past few weeks that there was a sense of the familiar. Yet at the same time, everything felt new and delicious.

Even as he began to kiss her, she felt herself needing him. Her body melted, heated, swelled and readied for his sensual assault.

When he tilted his head and claimed her with his tongue, she parted instantly. She danced with him, claiming him herself with a nip on his lower lip.

He chuckled low in his throat, then bent down and pressed his mouth to her neck. She let her head fall back as her stomach clenched and her breasts tightened in anticipation.

"I want you," he breathed against her skin.

"I'm yours."

She was. For always.

As he sucked on the curve where her neck met her shoulder, she unfastened the buttons of his shirt. He nudged her back until she bumped into the desk. Once there, it was a simple matter to straighten, pull off her T-shirt and let him shove down her shorts and panties. She was already barefoot.

He shrugged out of his shirt while she unfastened her bra. Then she was naked before him. He looked at her body, his gaze lingering on her breasts before dropping to the blond curls below her belly.

She could see his erection pressing against his slacks and the rapid rise and fall of his chest. Knowing he wanted her made her want him more. When he put his hands on her waist, she pushed off the floor and landed on the edge of the desk.

The wood was cool on her bare skin, but also erotic.

But she barely noticed. He bent down and took her right nipple in his mouth as he reached between her legs.

She parted for him, pulling her thighs as far apart as she could, wanting him to touch her everywhere. His fingers rubbed her swollen flesh, then settled into a steady rhythm designed to make her his slave.

He rubbed that single point of pleasure with his thumb and pushed two fingers deep inside of her. At the same time, he sucked on her nipple, then licked the tight point and blew on her damp skin.

So much pleasure, she thought, barely able to form coherent thoughts. She clutched at him, never wanting him to stop, needing him, only him. Tension built, as did the promise of her release. She fumbled with his belt and slacks, desperate to have him inside of her.

He straightened and quickly stripped off the rest of his clothes. Then he moved between her legs and pushed into her.

He filled her deeply, moving slowly, letting her stretch to accommodate him. The slow aching gave way to more frantic desire. She needed movement to climax. The deep, thrilling thrusts as he made her his own.

He obliged her by withdrawing, then slipping in again. More quickly this time. She sank back on the desk and gave herself over to the act of love they shared.

He clutched her hips to pull her against him. Need grew. She wrapped her legs around him, holding them more closely together. Tension increased.

She felt her breathing quicken as her body heated. He slipped his hand between them and rubbed that most sensitive place.

It was too much, she thought as she cried out her

pleasure. Her orgasm washed over her, blanking her mind until there was only sensation. She grabbed for him, pulling him in deeper and deeper, taking all of him, riding him until he, too, lost control and they came together in a shuddering climax.

"I've never been to Los Angeles before," Princess Phoebe said from the back of the limo. She touched her husband's arm. "Maybe we'll have time to go to a theme park while we're here."

Rafiq didn't say anything, but he held in a smile. He doubted his father would ever consider going to a place like that on purpose, but he would deny his wife nothing. They'd been together nearly fifteen years and from all accounts seemed happy.

Something to consider, he told himself. Perhaps he and Kiley could be like that, as well, growing in respect and affection over the years. Why was love required?

Prince Nasri patted his wife's hand. "We'll see," he said. "It can be difficult to arrange visits like that on short notice. The park must be closed and—"

Phoebe leaned close and smiled. "We don't have to close the park. Trust me. No one here will have any idea who we are. A few bodyguards will be enough." She turned to Rafiq. "Tell him it's perfectly safe."

Rafiq held up his hands. "That is for my father to decide."

She sighed. "How typical. You haven't seen each other in nearly six months and still you band together to side against me."

Her words were serious, but Rafiq saw the sparkle of amusement in her eyes.

"I'm not willing to make a claim for your safety until I'm sure," he said.

"Very sensible," his father told him. "Speaking of which, who is this girl you want to marry. What do you know about her?"

"Enough," Rafiq said, knowing their few moments of rapport would end now.

Nasri frowned. "There are many well-qualified young women you have yet to meet."

"Yes. I'm sure you have a list."

"We do. If you're interested."

Phoebe took her husband's hand and squeezed. "Now don't get all huffy and regal with Rafiq. I'm sure he's chosen well."

"Yes, but *who* is she?"

"Who was I?" Phoebe asked.

"Someone I adored from the moment I saw you."

"A nobody," she reminded him. "I had no family, no connection to anyone powerful. I hadn't even gone to college."

"That was different," he said, and lightly kissed her.

"This is different, too," she told him. "If Rafiq loves her, then that is enough."

The conversation reaffirmed Rafiq's decision that Kiley should wait to meet his father at the house. Far better for her to be relaxed and for Nasri to voice his concerns out of her earshot. Besides, it didn't matter what his father said. He and Kiley *would* be married.

The prince looked unconvinced. "She is of good character?"

Rafiq nodded. "Intelligent, caring, loyal and very kind. She will be a good mother to my sons."

"And your daughters," Phoebe said with a sigh. "What is it about you men and your sons? It's very annoying. Rafiq, I assure you, your father loves his daughters as much as his sons. You need not fear that they're ignored."

"I am relieved," he said, keeping his thoughts to himself. With Phoebe there to watch over her children, he had no doubt his father participated in their upbringing.

But it had been different for him. Prince Nasri had disappeared from his son's life and had rarely returned. Rafiq could remember months passing without a word. Birthdays and holidays were frequently spent in the company of nannies and tutors. When he'd been old enough to go to boarding school, most of his vacations had been spent there. It wasn't until he'd turned thirteen that his father had decided it was time for Rafiq to learn about his future duties.

They drove up the driveway. Phoebe smiled.

"I love this house. It reminds me a little of Lucia-Serrat, and yet it's completely different. You have the best of both worlds here."

"Is that why my son and heir chooses to stay away for so long?" Nasri asked with a grumble.

Phoebe shook her head. "Be nice. You promised. Part of the reason your son stays away is you're an old grouch most of the time. You're not yet fifty, but you have the temperament of a man close to eighty." She glanced at Rafiq. "Except when he is with the girls. Then he is happy and carefree. I suppose it's the responsibility."

Arnold, the driver, opened the rear door and she slid out.

"You will be a big help when you return," she told Rafiq as she stood on the driveway and smoothed her long, blond hair. "We are both looking forward to that."

"As am I," Rafiq said, speaking the truth. He missed Lucia-Serrat. Now that he would marry Kiley and start a family, he found himself ready to return.

The front door opened. Kiley stepped out and smiled.

"Hello," she said. "It's lovely to have you here."

Rafiq saw the terror in her eyes and knew that she would rather be anywhere but here. Still, he doubted Nasri or Phoebe noticed.

She'd dressed in a pale-blue dress that fell loosely to her calves. Her makeup was light, her jewelry conservative. She hadn't discussed her clothing with him, and he was pleased by her choice. She looked exactly right for the occasion. He could also imagine her brushing close and whispering to him that she wasn't wearing any underwear.

"You must be Kiley," Phoebe said, stepping forward and holding out both her hands. "I'm delighted to meet you. At last someone has captured Rafiq's heart. I'd begun to lose hope."

Kiley laughed as the two women hugged. "He sure has dated a lot. I like to think he got it out of his system."

"Nasri did the same thing," Phoebe said in a mock whisper. "I believe it makes him appreciate me more." She turned to her husband and drew him near. "Here she is. Don't you adore her right away?"

Rafiq moved next to Kiley and put his hand on the small of her back. "Kiley, this is my father, Prince Nasri Majin of Lucia-Serrat."

Kiley offered a very impressive curtsy. "It is very much an honor to meet you, sir."

Rafiq watched as his father looked her over. He wasn't concerned—family opinion mattered little to him—but he wanted the meeting to go well for Kiley's sake.

At last his father smiled. "Welcome to our family, Kiley."

"Thank you."

Rafiq started to say they should all go inside, but before he could speak the words, Fari burst through the open door and began running in circles around everyone. She yapped and spun and shook with delight.

"Oh, no." Kiley reached for her but couldn't catch her. "She's our new puppy. I locked her up in the bedroom. How did she get out?"

Phoebe laughed. "She's a wonder."

"She's just a puppy," Kiley said. "And still a little excitable."

"Here." Prince Nasri reached for her.

"Oh, you don't want to do that," Kiley said, sounding worried. "When she gets excited, she—"

It was too late. Nasri picked up the puppy and brought her to his chest. Fari licked his chin and promptly peed down the front of his shirt.

Chapter Fourteen

Kiley and Phoebe sat out on the deck the following afternoon. Fari stretched out at Kiley's feet and dozed in the sunlight.

"It's beautiful here," Phoebe said. "The first time I saw pictures of Rafiq's house I remember thinking that he'd wanted to keep a piece of Lucia-Serrat with him. While the view is different, the essence of the place is very similar."

"He misses the island," Kiley told her. Not that he talked about it that much, but she had a strong sense of his need to return home.

"And we miss him." Phoebe smiled at her. "I adore my stepchildren. They're all so wonderful. And they seem to like me, which is great. I would have hated to be wicked and live up to that horrible stepmother cliché."

Kiley laughed. "I'm not sure you could be wicked if you tried."

"Probably not, but I do a great crabby. Just ask my husband."

Kiley knew that the princess was in her early thirties, but she looked much younger. Perhaps it was the air of contentment that seemed to surround her, as if she had everything she'd ever wanted.

"Do you miss your girls?" she asked.

Phoebe nodded. "That's the only bad part of traveling. We were going to bring them, but there was a very special sleep-over planned, and that seemed much more interesting to them. Plus, I wanted to have time to get to know you, which wouldn't have happened with my girls around. They're very energetic."

Kiley felt a whisper of envy. She wanted children and soon. Would Rafiq be happy if she got pregnant right away?

"The island is a wonderful place to grow up," Phoebe said. "There's so much for children to do, yet everything is so safe. I couldn't have picked better if I'd tried."

"It sounds lovely. I'm looking forward to seeing it firsthand. Although maybe as a tourist rather than a future princess."

Phoebe's expression turned sympathetic. "A little nervous?"

"More than a little. There's so much to learn. I had to quit my job because it would have been too weird to be engaged and working for Rafiq. I was terrified I wouldn't have anything to do. Instead I'm busy all the time. I'm studying the history of the island so I understand the people. Then there's all the protocol, customs, expectations. It's a lot to take in. I want to be a good wife. I want Rafiq to be proud of me."

"I can see that and I admire your energy. But isn't loving him going to be enough?"

"You'd think," Kiley said, wishing it were. "It's my problem, not his. Rafiq has never asked me to learn anything or change." But she was afraid he would be disappointed if she wasn't the perfect princess.

"You're lucky," Phoebe said. "You won't be the wife of the crown prince for many years. That will give you a certain amount of freedom."

"I know. It must have been difficult for you to step right into that role."

Phoebe shrugged. "I was young and so very much in love. I would have done anything for Nasri. By the time I knew enough to be scared, I knew enough to get by. Then I got pregnant, and once I became a mother, the rest of it didn't seem so important." She touched Kiley's arm. "Don't worry. You'll do well, and Rafiq will be there to guide you."

"Thank you." Kiley did trust that Rafiq would be a help. "You're being very kind."

"I have an ulterior motive."

Kiley couldn't imagine what she could have that the other woman wanted. "Which is?"

"I want to know if Rafiq has said anything about his father." She held up a hand. "I know I'm prying and it's terrible of me, but I do so worry about those two. They've never been close and I know that hurts them both. I kept thinking that as Rafiq got older their differences would fade away, but they haven't. There is a distance between them. I'm sure you've noticed it."

Kiley nodded slowly. She didn't want to be having this conversation. As much as she liked Phoebe, she wasn't going to betray Rafiq by sharing what he'd told her about his father.

"I know Rafiq enjoys his work," Kiley said carefully. "And he looks forward to returning home."

Phoebe smiled. "It's all right. In your position I wouldn't have said anything, either. I just wish…" She stared out at the ocean. "I wish things had been different. Nasri was so young when Rafiq was born. Still only seventeen. He wanted to go off to university in England, to grow up and have a life. He had the means to hire staff to look after Rafiq and so he did. He never saw the importance of being a father. He didn't think about a young child left alone."

Kiley didn't want to think about it, either. It broke her heart to imagine Rafiq as a small boy, abandoned by both his parents.

"As Nasri grew, he fell in love and married. I'm sure his first wife tried with Rafiq, but soon she had children of her own. After she died, Nasri lost himself in grief. By the time he surfaced, Rafiq was away at boarding school. There was never a good time."

"Perhaps the prince should have made time," Kiley said before she could stop herself. "He was the father."

"I agree," Phoebe told her. "As does Nasri. He sees the mistakes he made, but they are in the past and impossible to rectify. I wish I could make you see how much he wants to be close to his son."

Kiley didn't like being put in this position, but before she could protest, Phoebe shook her head.

"Enough of such seriousness. At least the cycle will

be broken. Rafiq will be a better father to his children and you will be there for them as well. I can already feel the love between you."

Kiley smiled. "Does it show?"

"You light up when he walks in the room, but isn't that as it should be?"

She thought about how happy he made her and knew she wouldn't change anything. "Yes, it is."

Kiley did her best not to look at herself in the mirror. Seeing herself in formal clothing would only make her more nervous.

"How did they do it so quickly?" she asked, not really expecting an answer. "It's a formal event. Shouldn't that take weeks?"

"Phoebe is very good at putting parties together."

"Lucky us."

Kiley concentrated on her breathing and did her best not to throw up. Telling herself she shouldn't worry, that this was exactly like the big fund-raiser she'd attended with Rafiq only a month ago, was a big fat lie. It wasn't the same at all. Then she'd been one of a hundred guests. Today she was one of two guests of honor, as the party was to celebrate her official engagement to Rafiq.

There was too much to think about. What she was supposed to say when she greeted people. How could she remember the words to the national anthem of Lucia-Serrat? Or to make sure to keep smiling because everyone would be watching? She also had to worry about what she was going to wear for her official portrait, and the wedding planner, who was arriving in a matter of days, and the fact that they were leaving Fari alone for the whole evening and who knew what trouble she would get into.

"I should stay here with the puppy," she said.

Rafiq stepped out of the bathroom. He wore a tailored tuxedo and looked so handsome, he took her breath away. He crossed to her, took her hands in his and kissed her fingers.

"I'm afraid I can't allow that. People would not understand why my fiancée wasn't at my side. It would cause a scandal."

"I guess."

"You will do well," he told her.

"Do you promise?"

"Yes."

If only she could be as sure. "You're used to this sort of thing. For me it's all very nerve-racking. I think I need to lie down."

He chuckled and pulled her close. "You make me very happy."

"You say that now, but after I say something inappropriate you're going to be giving me a stern talking-to."

"Relax, Kiley. There is nothing to worry about."

She drew in a breath, then released it. Staring up into his dark eyes she said, "You know I'm only doing this for you, right? You believe that I have no interest in the actual princess thing."

"You've made that very clear."

"And you know that I love you."

His smile never wavered. "I know you give with your whole heart and that you mean what you say with all that you are."

Some of her tension eased away. "Okay. Good.

Sometimes I worry that you can't really bring yourself to trust me or anyone." She shrugged. "I talked to Phoebe a little about your father. I think he wants to improve the relationship he has with you."

Rafiq released her instantly. "Did she say that? Did you listen and agree to discuss this with me?"

"No. It wasn't like that. I didn't take her side. Actually, I didn't say much of anything. But I couldn't stop thinking about what she said, and it makes me sad that the two of you aren't close. He's your father, your family. We'll be moving back to Lucia-Serrat in a few years and you're going to be working with him. Wouldn't that be easier if you got along?"

Rafiq turned his back to her. "You don't know what you're talking about."

"I don't know the details, but I understand the circumstances. He was wrong. Very wrong, but he was also young. Just seventeen. How smart were you at that age?"

"Do not involve yourself in things that are not your concern," he said, his voice a low growl.

"This is my concern because I love you. I hate to see you hurt by this."

He spun to face her. "I am not hurt. None of this touches me. You are wrong if you think I mourn a relationship we never had."

"I don't believe you."

"Then you are a fool. We will not speak of this any longer."

He stated the command as if he fully expected her obedience. He had never been angry with her, and while she didn't like it, she wasn't going to let him dictate to her.

"You don't get to decide that," she said softly.

His gaze narrowed. "What did you say?"

"You don't get to say what we will or will not talk about. That's a joint decision and I think this is an important conversation."

"Then it is one you will have with yourself because we will not speak of it again."

He turned to leave, but before he got more than halfway across the room, Sana appeared.

"The car is here," she said, "and your parents are waiting."

Rafiq nodded his thanks, then turned to Kiley. "Are you ready?"

Just like that? They weren't going to finish their conversation?

She collected her purse and followed him through the house. A part of her wanted to insist they continue talking, but she knew this wasn't the time. Not with his parents waiting and an official state party to attend. But it made her uncomfortable to have unfinished business with him.

The drive to the hotel was uncomfortable for her, mostly because she was aware of how much Rafiq *wasn't* speaking. But Phoebe and Prince Nasri chatted and Kiley did her best to relax.

When they arrived, she was unprepared for the number of photographers lined up outside of the hotel. There had to be close to a hundred. Panic seized her, making it impossible to breathe.

"We'll wait for the bodyguards," Prince Nasri said.

Phoebe shook her head. "I don't understand the fascination. On a day-to-day basis, my life is very normal."

Kiley gave a strangled laugh. Normal? Phoebe was

a princess. They were royalty. And she was so not ready to be a part of that.

Rafiq glanced at her. "Are you all right?"

"No," she croaked, barely able to form the word.

"Nerves?"

She nodded.

"I can cure them."

He bent down and pressed his mouth to hers. The kiss was hot, long and very demanding. She felt her anxiety fade away as passion took its place. His tongue claimed her and taunted her until she could only think of her need.

He shifted and pressed his mouth to her ear.

"I want you."

Desire made her shiver. The rear door of the limo opened and the night exploded as dozens of flashes went off, but all she could think about was Rafiq.

The walk into the hotel ballroom passed in a blur. When their party stepped inside, the orchestra immediately began playing the Lucia-Serrat national anthem, followed by the one for the United States. At the end, Prince Nasri stepped up to the microphone and welcomed everyone to the event.

Later, when they were at last free to escape to the dance floor, Kiley smiled at Rafiq. "You rescued me."

"The situation can be intimidating. You'll get used to it."

"I doubt that, but thank you, anyway." She bit her lower lip. "Does this mean we're no longer fighting?"

"We never were."

That surprised her. "What would you call it, then?"

"A conversation of little consequence."

She didn't like the sound of that. They'd had a serious disagreement. Their first. Sure, it was bound to happen and she was okay with that. She just wasn't sure she liked him denying it had ever taken place. Had he not been affected or did he simply not care enough to worry? And did she really want to know which it was?

The evening passed in a blur of dancing, introductions and speeches. Kiley found herself feeling both welcomed by the guests and uncomfortable with being the center of attention. Phoebe assured her she would get used to it, but Kiley couldn't imagine that happening. Still, two months ago she would never have imagined marrying a prince, either, so who was she to say?

She excused herself from a large group and made her way toward the restroom. As she entered a quiet hallway, she felt someone touch her arm. She turned and was stunned to see Eric standing there.

"Why are you here?" she asked, sure this couldn't be good, and uncomfortable to be seen speaking with him.

"I had to talk to you."

Oh, please. Was he really going to make a fuss now? "Eric, go away. There's nothing between us."

"I don't care about that," he told her. "I'm here because I'm worried about you."

"That's a new one."

"You're making a terrible mistake. Everything is happening too fast. You don't love this guy and he doesn't love you. You're reacting to what happened between us."

He took her hand and stared into her eyes. "I can't tell you how sorry I am about that. I was such a jerk."

She pulled free of his touch. "*Jerk* doesn't begin to describe it. I don't know why you're here, Eric, but it's time for you to leave. You're a cheat and a liar and I'm glad to be rid of you."

She walked back toward the ballroom. She had a feeling that if she went into the ladies' room now, Eric would simply follow her, and she didn't need that kind of trouble.

"He doesn't love you," he called after her. "Has he said it? Has he ever actually said the words?"

She shook her head and did her best to ignore him. What a creep. But as she spotted Rafiq at the edge of the crowd and saw him smile, she realized Eric was right about one thing. Rafiq had never actually said he loved her.

Rafiq sat on the deck off the bedroom and listened as Kiley told their dog all about her evening.

"I can see that in addition to learning about the history of Lucia-Serrat and the protocol of being a princess, I'm going to need some dance lessons. I think I stepped on a lot of toes tonight, which can't be good. You want to learn to dance with me?"

Fari yipped in agreement. Rafiq smiled as he thought of the tiny puppy twirling around a ballroom.

Kiley stepped out onto the deck and plopped down next to him. She'd changed out of her ball gown and into a silk robe. Her makeup was gone, as was her jewelry. She looked young and fresh and very beautiful. But her eyes were troubled and he wanted to know why.

"You are still angry with me," he said.

"What?" She picked up Fari and set the dog on her lap. "Of course not. Why would I be mad?"

"Because of our conversation before."

"You mean when you were being unreasonable and stubborn? I'm sure I don't know what you're talking about." She leaned back in her chair. "I think you're wrong. I think it's important for you to let go of the past and meet your father as the man he is today. If you could simply walk away from him and wanted to do that, I would support it, but that's not the plan. You're moving back to the island where the two of you will work in close proximity. I can't imagine that going well if you can't get the past behind you where it belongs."

He liked that she held to her opinion even if he didn't agree with it. "Anything else?" he asked.

She shrugged. "You're not going to listen to me, which I accept but it makes me think you're not as bright as you look."

"So you insult me now?"

"I don't mean to, but it *is* a happy by-product of our conversation. I also know I can't make you do anything about your father. You're a grown-up and much bigger than me, so force is out of the question. I hope you'll deal with it, but if you won't, I'm going to try to let it go."

"Very wise. So what happened to upset you?" he asked. "Was it your conversation with Eric?"

She didn't act surprised that he knew about that. "I figured you saw us. What is it about that guy, always showing up everywhere? It's creepy."

Rafiq was less interested in that than the reason she was unhappy. "What did he say?"

"Nothing important. I just wish…" She looked at him. "Do you love me?"

He'd known they would get to that question eventually. He reached for her hand. "I have chosen you to be my wife, Kiley. I wish to marry you and have children with you. I ask you to join me as we rule over my country. You will be much beloved by my people."

She continued to study his face. "I get all that, but you didn't answer the question. Do you love me?"

"Is that so important to know?"

"It is to me." Tears filled her eyes. "Can't you say the words?" she asked in a whisper.

Her pain burned him, but a lie would burn more. "There is more to a marriage than love. There is respect, passion, caring. I will be true to you. I will treat you with respect and be there for our children. Isn't that enough?"

A single tear rolled down her cheek. Fari whined, as if sensing the tension between them.

"Rafiq, please. You must love me a little."

He rebelled against her attempts to weaken him. "How many times have we been together?" he asked, his voice more harsh than he would have liked. "How many times have I claimed you in the past few weeks?"

"I don't know. What does that have to do with anything? You can't seriously be equating sex with love. They're not the same at all."

"Are you on any birth control?"

There was little light on the deck and yet he saw the color drain from her face. Her eyes widened as she reached down to touch her stomach.

"You think I'm pregnant."

"I believe it is very likely."

She shrank from him. "Is that all this is about? A child? Are you s-saying you don't care about me at all?"

"I'm saying I want to marry you, Kiley. I want to be the father of your children. Isn't that enough?"

She stood, taking the puppy with her and walked toward the bedroom. At the French door, she looked back at him.

"It's not enough. It will never be enough. How could you think I would settle for that?"

Chapter Fifteen

Kiley was up before dawn the next morning. She'd barely been able to sleep at all. Her mind whirled with too many questions and possibilities, but nothing could be answered until she knew the truth.

So shortly after sunrise, she rose and dressed and made her way to the garage. Twenty minutes later she'd driven to the twenty-four-hour drugstore and bought a home pregnancy test. As she drove back to Rafiq's house, she wondered why she hadn't thought it could happen to her.

It's not as if she were an idiot. She knew how babies were made, and she and Rafiq had been doing that a lot lately. Condoms helped, but they also failed. But getting pregnant had never been a reality for her. She'd gone on The Pill six months ago so she wouldn't have to worry after she and Eric got married, but she'd had a bad reaction and had been forced to go off it. She'd discussed other options with her doctor yet hadn't acted on any of them. In truth, she'd wanted to get pregnant quickly and start her family.

But not like this, she thought as she pulled into the garage and sat in the car. Not when she'd just found out that Rafiq didn't love her, that he'd only proposed to her because he thought she was pregnant.

What if she was? She knew enough about the laws of Lucia-Serrat to know that the child of a member of the royal family could not be taken out of the country without permission from both the biological parent and the Crown Prince. As neither Rafiq nor Prince Nasri were likely to agree to that, she was well and truly stuck. Unlike Rafiq's mother, she would never turn her back on her child.

Tears burned in her eyes. She blinked them away. She'd done enough crying in the night, weeping silently as Rafiq had slept beside her. Pain had ripped through her and a sense of betrayal so deep, she knew she would bear the scars forever.

She'd loved him with every fiber of her being, and he hadn't loved her back. The truth couldn't be ignored or wished away.

Nearly as bad, she'd been so *sure* that he was the one. How could she have been wrong twice in a row? Why did she seem destined to fall for men who would lie to her?

She didn't have an answer and she couldn't stay in the car forever. After picking up the small bag from the drugstore, she made her way into the house and quietly walked down the hall to the bedroom.

For the first time since moving in with him, she wished she had her own room. She wanted space and privacy. She supposed she could move back to her own apartment. If she wasn't pregnant, she would. She would take some time and figure out what to do. Unlike her feelings for Eric, which had died over time, she loved Rafiq with an intensity that couldn't be described. She didn't think she could simply walk away from him forever.

He had to care, she told herself as she paused outside the bedroom door. He couldn't have made her so happy if he didn't. There had to be something between them, something he was unwilling to acknowledge. After his past was he unable to admit to any softer feelings?

She didn't have any answers, and right now what she most needed to know was whether or not she was carrying his child.

She walked into the bedroom and was surprised to find the bed empty. The bathroom door opened, and Rafiq stepped out. He'd already showered and dressed.

"You were up early," he said, his dark eyes giving nothing away.

"I couldn't sleep."

He glanced at the bag she held. "A pregnancy test?" he asked.

She nodded. "Then we'll both know."

"I'll wait."

She crossed to the bathroom, then stopped and looked at him.

"Is that why you proposed?" she asked. "Because you thought I might be pregnant? What if I'm not? Do you care about me even a little? Is any of this about me?"

"What do you want to know?" he asked. "You came to me, Kiley. You asked to be my mistress. I did not seek you out."

"I know." She squeezed her eyes shut, then opened them. "This was all my doing. You didn't force me. I thought I was tough. I wanted Eric punished and you were the best way I knew to do that. After a while I figured out I wasn't as interested in revenge as being with you."

She thought about the arguments she'd had with Eric. How he'd pressed her to admit there was something between her and her boss.

"He used to claim I had a thing for you and I always told him I didn't. Looking back at how quickly I fell for you, maybe he was right. Maybe he saw something I couldn't see. I mean, what was I thinking? Asking to be your mistress? It's crazy. You're right, you didn't force me to do anything. Not even to fall in love with you."

She paused, hoping he would say something to comfort her, but he didn't. There was only the quiet sound of her breathing.

She wanted to ask if he could ever come to love her, if she mattered at all, but she was afraid of the answer.

Ten minutes later she stared at the plastic stick and knew that her life had changed forever. There would be no going back to her old world, no moving out of Rafiq's house. She was bound to him as much as if they were chained together.

She washed her hands and dried them, then stepped out of the bathroom and faced him. "I'm pregnant," she whispered.

Rafiq heard the words but didn't believe them at first. He'd known it was possible, but to have it confirmed surprised him. He would have thought fate would give Kiley a chance to escape.

He didn't want her to go, he acknowledged, if only to himself. But without the baby, he had no other means to keep her.

She would be a good mother. She would care for their child, perhaps even love it. He would be there, as well, to make sure his son or daughter knew that there was a safe place to grow up. He knew all the things he had missed in his own childhood. Those mistakes would now be undone.

"I am pleased," he said.

"Really? I wouldn't think you were interested in a child. Will you love it? Will your baby matter?"

"Our children will be my world."

She leaned against the door frame and wiped the single tear that spilled out of one eye. "That's not the same. You have to be willing to give up your heart. You have to love children with all that you have, no matter what."

"As you will do," he said, stepping toward her and touching her chin. "Be happy. You said you always wanted to be a wife and mother. I am offering you that. You will be my princess and you will want for nothing. Our children will have untold opportunities to see the world, to grow strong. I will be there for you, all the days of my life. I will honor you. I will never betray you or be unfaithful or cruel. Is that not enough?"

She looked at him, her blue eyes damp with unshed tears. "There is a particular cruelty in not loving your wife," she said. "The kind that eats away at the soul."

She could be stubborn, but he'd always known that. "We will travel. See things, do things."

"You can't buy me, Rafiq. I'm not like your other women, remember? I'm not interested in pretty things."

"But you carry my child."

"That I do. Already I feel the chains tightening around my wrist."

"You're being overly dramatic. We will be married and you will be happy."

She stared at him. "No."

How like a woman. "Your refusal to accept happiness is your own decision."

"You misunderstand me. I'm not saying I won't be happy, I'm saying I won't marry you."

Disbelief held him in place. Otherwise he would have gone to her. To do what, he couldn't say. "You have no choice."

"Actually, I do. I might not know much about Lucia-Serrat, but I'm pretty sure there isn't a law that allows you to marry a woman against her will. Which means you can't make it happen without my agreement and I won't agree." She swallowed and wiped away tears. "I won't marry someone who doesn't love me."

This wasn't right, he thought. How dare she defy him? "You will not be able to take my child from me."

"I know that. I haven't figured it all out yet, but I do know that I'm not going to marry you. And aside from convincing me you're in love with me, there's nothing you can do to change my mind."

Rafiq battled fury for the next two days. While Kiley didn't labor over the topic, he sensed her determination. And try as he might, he couldn't seem to come up with any words that would convince her to see his side of things.

The prince and Phoebe seemed to sense the disquiet, for they spent much of that time touring the area, as if they wanted to avoid the house.

If Rafiq could have avoided it, he would. He hated that Kiley was so withdrawn. He missed her laughter, her pleasure in his company. In truth, he understood her need to stand firm on this issue. Unfortunately her principles brought her in direct opposition to his wishes. And he would win this battle, one way or the other.

"Aren't you going to the office?"

He looked up from his desk at the house and saw Kiley standing in the doorway. As always, the sight of her brought him gladness, followed by intense anger at her determination to be difficult.

"Eventually. I wish this resolved, first."

She stepped into the room. "You probably shouldn't wait that long. There are things you need to take care of."

"You won't marry me but still you worry about my work?"

She shrugged. "One has nothing to do with the other. Not marrying you doesn't make me care any less. It doesn't make me not love you."

She moved forward until she stood behind the chair in front of his desk. "I've been trying to figure out what's wrong," she said quietly, her voice filled with pain. "I have given my heart to you so completely that it's impossible for me to believe you don't want to do the same. You have all the symptoms of the condition, and yet you claim not to love me. And then I remember your past. What happened with your parents. Is that it,

Rafiq? Were you hurt too many times as a child to believe in love?"

The question made him sound weak and he refused to answer. "My reasons aren't important."

"They are to me. I comfort myself with the fact that this isn't personal. You wouldn't love anyone, would you? What are you afraid of?"

He glared at her. "I have no fear."

"You have something. Is it being hurt? Is it that I'll go away? Because I won't. I don't want to. I'm not your parents. If you don't believe me, look to my family, at what I've been taught. My parents are as much in love today as when they were married. My sisters have wonderful relationships. I made a mistake with Eric, but even there I was loyal. He was the one who betrayed me."

Her words hurt him as much as if she'd attacked him with a knife. "You will marry me."

"No. Not until you can admit you love me. Because that's the irony of the situation. I think you do. I think I matter more than anyone has ever mattered and you're terrified of that. You're afraid of being hurt and abandoned. There's nothing I can say or do to convince you otherwise, so this is all about a step of faith. Are you willing to take it?"

He stood. "Do not presume to know my mind," he told her coldly.

Her shoulders slumped. "Right. Because pride matters the most. Don't you get tired of always being right but always being alone?"

She turned and left the room. Silence surrounded him, pressed down on him, gutted him and he could not say why.

* * *

Rafiq transferred most of his operation to the house. He told himself it was so that he could spend time with his father and Phoebe, but in truth it was so he could keep an eye on Kiley. How long would she stay? When would she bolt for freedom?

That had to be her plan and he couldn't let her escape with his child.

He reviewed the oil reserve reports, stopping only when his father walked into the study and took a seat.

"Good news?" Nasri asked, nodding at the papers.

"Yes. The reserves are much larger than we calculated at first. Unlike other parts of the world, we will have oil into the next century."

"That bodes well for our future economy," the prince said. He leaned back in the leather chair and studied his son. "Do you see much of your mother these days?"

Rafiq shook his head and tried not to show his surprise at the question. "I have spoken with her twice in the past two months, but before that it was nearly a year since our paths crossed."

"So you don't have regular contact with her?"

"No. There is no reason."

The prince shrugged. "She *is* your mother."

"She and I have a biological connection, but little else."

"She was never warm or maternal," Prince Nasri said. "But she was very beautiful. I remember the first time I saw her. She was filming a scene on the beach. I was taken with her beauty. She was older by five years. When I was seventeen, that made her seem a woman of the world." He smiled. "I wanted her to be my first."

Rafiq hadn't known that, and frankly he could have

gone a long time without hearing the information. He and his father weren't very close, but that didn't mean he was comfortable discussing the man's sex life with Rafiq's mother.

"I didn't love her," Nasri continued. "Love wasn't important to me. Fortunately she didn't love me, either, so neither of us was hurt. Although there was an injured party."

He paused significantly. Rafiq knew his father meant him, but refused to say anything.

"It was never my intention to wound you," the prince said.

"I survived and grew up," Rafiq told him. "Unless you have complaints about my work?"

"Not at all. You do your duties extremely well. Somehow you managed to raise yourself with the help of a few nannies and tutors. You should be proud."

Rafiq shifted in his chair. "I find no cause for pride."

"I'm sure that is true, but still I have regrets. I think about what you went through and how I should have been there. I was but a child myself, yet I find that excuse has less and less meaning as I get older."

If Rafiq didn't know it wasn't possible, he would swear that his father had been speaking with Kiley. She had been pushing for a reconciliation. Instead it had come from an unlikely source. At what point should he explain that none of this was necessary?

"The past is just that. Over," Rafiq said. "I appreciate your worry on my behalf, but it doesn't matter now."

"I think it does. I am worried about your relationship with Kiley."

He bristled. "That is not your concern."

"You are my son. That makes it my concern. Phoebe and I noticed that you both seem less happy than when we arrived."

"It is nothing."

Prince Nasri didn't respond. Silence filled the room. At last Rafiq spoke.

"She has refused to marry me, despite the fact that she carries my child. While I offer her the world, she wants only a declaration of love."

"Which you will not give her," the prince said. "Because you do not believe."

Rafiq wanted to hurry from the room. He didn't like this conversation.

Nasri leaned toward him. "My son, I cannot tell you how sorry I am. It is my fault you resist Kiley's precious gift. You haven't seen much love in your life and that is because of me. I wasn't there. I didn't show you what—"

Rafiq rose. "Do you think any of this matters to me?"

"It should."

"No. She will marry me. With the child, she has no choice."

The prince stood and faced him. "Why won't you trust her? Why won't you let her prove herself?"

Because no one had ever loved him enough to stay.

Rafiq didn't speak the words, but they reverberated inside his brain. All his life people had left. He had learned not to care, not to let them close enough so that their disappearance was more than a sting. So it was with Kiley. He would keep her at arm's length, but he *would* keep her.

Without saying anything more, he walked out of the room and left his father. There was a solution, he thought. And he would find it.

Chapter Sixteen

Kiley was thinking that this wasn't the best week she'd ever had. Everything had started out with such promise. How had she ended up sad and afraid? Afraid because she didn't know how to convince Rafiq that caring about her was safe.

"May I join you?"

She looked up and saw Phoebe had strolled onto the deck. "Thank you, yes," Kiley told her. "I'm tired of my own company."

Rafiq's stepmother stretched out on the lounge chair and sighed. "I'm enjoying my time here. At home there are a thousand-and-one things that need my attention. Not to mention how much the girls keep me busy. But here there is only family and a chance to relax."

"I'm glad you're enjoying yourself."

Phoebe turned to look at her. "You are not, I fear. Nasri and I know about your situation with Rafiq."

Kiley winced. "Tell me you didn't hear us fighting."

"Of course not. You've been most discreet. But the mood changed, and then Rafiq spoke with his father."

"On purpose?" Kiley asked before she could stop herself. "Sorry. I just didn't think they talked about anything personal."

"They don't. Nasri never knows what to say, although he would rather slice off his arm than admit it. The fear of saying the wrong thing causes him to be critical. Rafiq expects the worst and jumps on any misstep. I have tried, but they are both stubborn. Still, they spoke. I don't think the wounds are healed, but they are acknowledged."

"I wish Rafiq could get along with his father. He needs that connection." He needed a place to call home, she thought. "He's so good with me, and I know he'll be good with our baby. It's just…" She winced. "You knew about the baby, didn't you?"

Phoebe smiled. "Yes. That's one of the reasons I wanted to talk to you." She glanced back toward the open door, then lowered her voice. "Kiley, I can help you."

"How? No offense, but I have trouble believing you're going to click your fingers and have Rafiq falling at my feet."

"Unfortunately, no. But I can help you get away."

Kiley shifted Fari off her lap and sat up in the lounge chair. "I don't understand. You want me to leave?"

"Of course not. It's just…I know you're unhappy and I'm very clear on the law of the land. Your child will have to be raised on Lucia-Serrat. Your choice is to leave the child or live on the island and deal with Rafiq."

"I figured that part out." It was like being between a rock and a hard place. "I'll be moving to the island."

"You don't have to." Phoebe stared at her intently. "I can take you to a place where Rafiq will never find you. There you can raise your child alone. Without him." Phoebe sighed. "I don't like making this offer, but as a mother, I understand how much you love your baby. You would do anything to keep him or her close. I wanted you to know this was an option."

Kiley wasn't sure she could have been more surprised if Phoebe had sprouted wings. "That's not possible."

"It is. It will take time, but it can be done."

Go away? Leave Rafiq?

"I would have liked your offer a lot better if you'd come to me with a way to make Rafiq fall in love with me." She sighed. "Actually, I don't think I need help with that. I think he does love me, but he won't admit it. Maybe he doesn't know what love feels like and he can't recognize it. A remote possibility but one I hold out hope for. I think it's more likely that he's simply not willing to trust me."

Kiley petted Fari. "I wish I knew how to let him know I'm not going to abandon him. Not ever."

"That requires a step of faith."

"I don't think Rafiq is very interested in faith right now." Kiley looked at Phoebe. "Thanks for the offer, but no."

"Don't you want to think about it?" Phoebe asked.

"I don't need to. I love Rafiq and I love his baby. I'm not turning my back on either one. I have no idea how I'm going to make this all work out, but I'll come up with a plan."

"I would be most interested to hear it," Rafiq said as he stepped onto the balcony.

His timely arrival and Phoebe's look of guilt was all Kiley needed. She grabbed Fari, stood and faced her former fiancé.

"You set me up," she said, her voice shaking with fury. She wanted to scream and hit and punish him for doing this to her. "How dare you?"

"I am Prince Rafiq of—"

"No one here gives a crap," she told him, glaring at him and wishing she was big enough to beat some sense into him. "It's not enough that you tricked me into an engagement you didn't mean, but now you're using people I like and trust to set me up?"

"I'm sorry," Phoebe murmured.

"I know," Kiley said, aware that it would be a while before she could forgive the other woman. "That's not the point." She turned back to Rafiq. "What was the purpose? What were you looking for?"

"The truth."

"What? Did you want to know if I was like your mother? You already have that answer. What other information do you need? Tell me and I'll give it to you." She squared her shoulders. "Which would have made you feel more like a man? Having me choose you or our child? I'm sorry, but you're not going to get that question answered. I refuse to choose and you can't make me."

She started toward him, then pushed past him and walked into the living room. Once there, she faced him again.

"This was a big mistake, Rafiq, because now I think less of you. You hurt me and you have no right to do that."

"I need to know."

"What? What is missing? You can keep trying to trip me up, but it's not going to work. I love you. There are no strings, no games, and only one expectation, which is that you'll love me back. Why is that so hard for you to understand?"

Rafiq watched her walk away. Phoebe came up beside him.

"That was a mistake," she said. "I warned you. I didn't want to do it and I feel horrible for being a part of your ridiculous plan. Don't ask me to do something like that again."

He felt her anger, but it was nothing when compared with Kiley's. He felt uncomfortable and didn't know why. He had the right to do as he pleased.

"I must be sure," he said, as much to himself as to Phoebe.

"Of what? That her love is real? Let me give you a word of advice. Love stretched too far can break. And then what will you have?" Phoebe shook her head. "Is that what this is all about? Are you trying to make her leave so you are once again right? Who wins then?"

She left and he was alone. Below, on the beach, several children played in the surf. There were teenagers and couples, families and an old man reading the newspaper. Life continued and yet he felt trapped in silence. As if he was out of step with all of it.

He wanted to believe. He wanted to trust. But how?

He sank onto the chair Kiley had vacated and closed his eyes. Her sentences replayed in his mind. Her question asking which would make him feel more like a man—her choosing him or their child.

He didn't want to feel more like a man, he told himself. He wanted…

"I wish Rafiq could get along with his father. He needs that connection."

Kiley's words were as real as if she'd just spoken them again. She worried about him. She wanted him to be happy. She wanted him to have a family beyond just her.

He knew why. He knew what her parents meant to her, and she wanted the same thing for him. She wanted him to have more. To be more. He knew in his head that she was all he could want, but in his heart…

Fari walked onto the deck. She trotted to the edge and looked over at two boys playing with a Frisbee. Her entire body quivered with excitement as she silently pleaded to be included.

Rafiq stood and walked toward the puppy. She was enthusiastic and foolish. If she didn't pay attention—

It happened so quickly. The Frisbee sailed too close to the deck and Fari grabbed for it. She slipped easily through the railing and nearly caught the toy, just as gravity caught her. Rafiq lunged for her and barely snagged the scruff of her neck.

Man and dog stared at each other. Fari twisted her head and licked his arm as she waited for him to pull her to safety. It never occurred to her he wouldn't. He could drop her and she would fall nearly twenty feet. She could be injured or killed and it never crossed her tiny puppy mind.

It was because she didn't know better, he told himself, even as he acknowledged her instinctive faith in him. She had never fallen before and he had never rescued her, but it didn't occur to her that he wouldn't.

He pulled her up to safety and set her on his lap.

"Just as well," he muttered to the dog. "Kiley adores you. She wouldn't want anything to happen to you."

He thought about how she fussed over the dog, talking to her, playing with her, caring for her. How much more would she love their child? How much more would she care and fuss and worry?

There were so many people in her life and yet she managed to love them all. How big was her heart? Big enough to hold him?

He set Fari down and she scampered out of the room, yipping for Kiley as she went. He stood and faced the same doorway. A single step of faith. That was all she wanted from him.

In his past were too many people who had let down a child desperately in need of affection. In his future…who could say? But he knew what was offered.

He walked after Fari, following the sound of her barking. But instead of settling in one place, she circled through the rooms, her barks growing more frantic as she was unable to find Kiley.

Rafiq searched, as well. He collected the little dog and did his best to reassure her, but she wasn't comforted. When he couldn't find Kiley anywhere, neither was he.

She was gone along with Phoebe and his father. Had they taken her away? Was she even now being whisked to a location he would never find?

"Kiley!" he yelled as he hurried toward the garage and jerked open the door. Her car was still there, but what did that symbolize? She'd never been overly impressed by what his money could buy.

He raced to their bedroom and threw open the closet doors. All her clothes were still there. He stopped and breathed in the scent of her perfume. If her clothes were still here, then—

The front door slammed. He ran toward the sound, then came to a stop when he saw her walking through the living room.

"Where have you been?" he asked more harshly than he would have liked.

"Watering the plants on the front porch. They were looking a little dry. Your parents have gone out to a movie. Your father said it's been years since he's been in a real movie theater. He's looking forward to the popcorn."

She smiled as she spoke, but her eyes were still sad. He wanted to go to her and offer comfort, but he was the problem.

Fari squirmed. He set her down and she raced over to Kiley who picked her up.

"What have you been getting yourself into?" Kiley asked. "Something bad. I can tell."

"You didn't leave."

Kiley looked at him. "What?"

"I thought you'd left. I couldn't find you and I thought…"

She sighed heavily. "I wish I could crawl into your brain and do a little work there. I'm not leaving. I don't know how many times I have to tell you that. I'm angry. I think you're a clueless jerk, but I'm not going anywhere."

She cuddled the dog as she looked at him. "I think you love me and that's what keeps me hanging on. I think somewhere deep in the cloudy brain of yours is a seed of faith, and I'm going to figure out how to get to it."

"Are you going to marry me?"

"Eventually. When you stop being stupid."

He narrowed his gaze. "You toss your insults around very freely."

She actually smiled. "So what are you going to do about it? Punish me? I'm the mother of your child and the woman you want to marry. You're going to fall all over yourself to treat me with reverence and respect. You're going to cater to my every wish, even the silly ones." Her smile faded. "So I'm not scared of you and I'm not leaving. Somehow we're going to become a family."

"But you won't marry me."

She stared at him. "Earth to Rafiq. Could we get some new material here?"

"So you're willing to give up being my wife and a princess. You'll have my child outside of marriage, return to Lucia-Serrat with me and live in the palace as the mother of my child, but you won't be my wife."

She considered for a moment, then nodded. "That about sums it up."

She spoke the truth. He could feel it in her words and the steadiness of her gaze. Not once in all the time he'd known her had she ever lied. She'd never even stretched the truth. She acted with integrity and honored her commitments. She *loved*.

He moved closer but didn't touch her. "I learned to write very early," he told her. "My tutors marveled at my ability to grasp the concept. What they didn't know is that I had been waiting since I realized what writing was. I knew that if I could get a letter to my mother, if I could explain that I was alone, that I loved and needed her, she would come and be with me."

Kiley felt her heart crumble. As Rafiq spoke, she pictured the lonely little boy, abandoned by his parents, growing up in the company of the palace staff. Somehow this proud, strong man had survived, had *thrived.*

"What happened?" she asked, already suspecting the answer.

"It took her several months to write me back, and when she did, she told me to ask my father for a pony. She said he was plenty rich and would give it to me."

Kiley set Fari on the floor, then rushed toward Rafiq and wrapped her arms around him. "I'm so sorry," she whispered. "I wish I could go back in time and beat up both your parents. Or at the very least, find you and take care of you myself."

He kissed the top of her head, then touched her chin so that she looked at him. "I do not."

"Why?"

"Because I would rather have you as my wife today than as my babysitter twenty-five years ago."

"But the little boy needed so much love."

"So does the man."

She blinked. "Excuse me?"

"This man needs your love with a desperation he cannot describe." He stroked her cheeks with his thumbs, then kissed her mouth. "I need you, Kiley. I need you to love me, to keep loving me. I need you to show me what is possible. What we can have together. What we can be."

"Rafiq."

Her chest tightened until it was difficult to breathe. Was this the first crack in the shell? A way to get through to him? Oh, please, let it be so.

His dark eyes stared into hers. "All my life I've held myself back from the people closest to me. No one was allowed to be in a position to hurt me again."

"I would never do that," she breathed.

"I know."

"I love you."

He gazed at her for a long time, then kissed her again. "I know," he said at last.

Hope burst forth and made her want to laugh with happiness. "You believe me? You believe that love is possible?"

"With you."

Was it wrong to want it all? "Could you love me?"

In a movement that stunned her, in a moment she would treasure for the rest of her life, Kiley watched as Prince Rafiq of Lucia-Serrat fell to his knees. He grasped her around her thighs and buried his face in her stomach. She felt the tension in his body, the battle that raged.

How she ached for him, for *them*. If only he could—

"I love you," he said, his voice cracking with emotion. "Dear God, I love you, Kiley."

She dropped next to him and pulled him close. He held on to her as if he would never let her go.

"I love you, too," she whispered into his ear. "I think longer than I should have. Perhaps since I first met you, which, given my former engagement, is fairly tacky."

He raised his head and smiled at her. The powerful emotions in his eyes, the love there, was so bright it nearly blinded her.

"Imagine if you hadn't caught Eric cheating," he said.

"No. I don't want to do that. I don't want to imagine any future without you."

"Nor do I." He touched his chest. "I feel a release. The walls are crumbling."

Tears filled her eyes, but for the first time in days, they were happy ones. She clung to him and rested her head on his shoulder. He wrapped his arms around her.

"Just hold me," she whispered. "I never want to let go."

"Eventually you will have to. Fari will need to be walked and fed. We will get hungry ourselves."

She straightened and shoved him back. "We're having a moment here. It's not every day the future Crown Prince of Lucia-Serrat tells me he loves me."

He leaned in and brushed his lips against hers. "Yes, it is," he murmured. "So many times a day, you will grow tired of hearing it."

She was so happy, she could have floated. "That's not going to happen." She grinned. "So I guess the wedding's back on."

"No."

"What?"

"Don't marry me," he told her. "Wait until I have proved myself."

"What?" she repeated. "Are you crazy?"

"A little. I want you to be sure. I want you to know that I mean what I say. That this isn't a trick to get you to the altar."

She stood up and put her hands on her hips. "There's going to be a wedding when we planned."

"No, Kiley. My way is better."

She raised her eyes to the heavens. "I'm going to have to kill him. I see that now and I apologize in advance. I'll probably go to prison but it will be worth it."

He stood and picked her up in his arms. "Before you

get out the swords or however it is you plan to do me in, I want to make love with you several thousand times."

She settled an arm around his neck and relaxed against him. "Okay, but just so we're clear, there's going to be a wedding."

"We shall see."

Epilogue

There was a wedding and it was held on the originally scheduled date in the beautiful church on the island of Lucia-Serrat. The fall weather was perfect, warm and sunny during the day and cool and clear at night.

The royal families from both El Bahar and Bahania attended, and there were whispers that the bride of the king of El Bahar, who was also the mother of the Prince of Thieves, was with child. At her age, that was both a miracle and a scandal. King Givon and Queen Cala weren't talking, but their glow of happiness gave them away.

Kiley and Rafiq attended many parties in their honor. She found herself meeting princes and princesses she had only read about in magazines. But all were gracious and accepting. The crown prince of El Bahar bemoaned the beauty of his now-teenage stepdaughter and he was furious to find her flirting with the youngest brother of Princess Billie of Bahania.

The wife of the Prince of Thieves offered an incredible Ming dynasty vase collection as a wedding gift without being clear on where it had come from. Princess Dora of El Bahar exchanged phone numbers with Princess Daphne of Bahania, and Kiley felt as if she'd fallen into the middle of a very exciting, very royal soap opera.

Kiley could have been intimidated by her new friends and relatives, but when she saw the light of love in the men's eyes, the same love she saw in Rafiq's, she knew there was nothing to fear. These strong, powerful kings and princes weren't all that different from other men. They worked, they worried, they loved. The desert blood that flowed through their bodies made them loyal unto death, and she couldn't wait to be a part of all that.

On the morning of her wedding, her sisters and her mother helped her into her beautiful white gown. There were buttons to fasten, shoes to slip into and a tiara to anchor to her short hair. Rafiq had sent sapphires to match her eyes, rubies to represent his heart and a diamond necklace to bind them together always.

At last it was time. Ann and Heather walked down the aisle first, then Kiley linked arms with her father and they moved toward the entrance to the church.

"You sure about this?" her father joked. "We could still make a run for it."

She laughed. "I love you, Daddy. I'll miss you and mom so much, but this is where I belong."

He kissed her cheek. "I always knew you were a princess, honey. I just didn't know you were going to get a crown to go with it."

The tall doors to the church opened, and Kiley and her father stepped inside.

There were nearly five hundred guests in attendance. Music swelled to the high rafters, and sunlight poured through the stained-glass windows. But Kiley didn't see any of it. For her there was only one person there. A man who waited, who loved her.

Rafiq stood at the end of the long aisle, and she had to remind herself to walk slowly. A bride racing to her groom would give the press too much to talk about.

So she took small steps and smiled at the guests, but in her heart she waited to be with her prince. And when she finally stood next to him, he took her hands and gazed at her.

"I'm going to be saying it for all the world to hear," he told her quietly, "but I want to say it to you first. I love you, Kiley."

"I love you, too." She smiled. "I was thinking about how all this started. With that very unusual question."

He grinned. "As it happens, I'm not looking for a mistress. I'm looking for a wife. Interested?"

"Oh, yeah."

The minister cleared his throat. "The wedding?"

Rafiq squeezed her fingers. "Sure. Let's do that."

The old man smiled, then spoke in a solemn voice. "Dearly beloved…"

Desert Prince,
Defiant Virgin

KIM LAWRENCE

Kim Lawrence lives on a farm in rural Anglesey. She runs two miles daily and finds this an excellent opportunity to unwind and seek inspiration for her writing! It also helps her keep up with her husband, two active sons, and the various stray animals which have adopted them. Always a fanatical consumer of fiction, she is now equally enthusiastic about writing. She loves a happy ending!

CHAPTER

CHAPTER ONE

PEOPLE assumed that Tair Al Sharif was a natural diplomat, but they were wrong.

He was so *not* a diplomat—though there had been many occasions when that role had been forced upon him by necessity—that as his cousin's glance once more drifted from him to the young Englishwoman seated on the opposite side of the table he wanted quite badly to drag the other man from his chair, give him a good shake and demand to know what the hell he thought he was playing at.

'How is your father, Tair?'

The soft buzz of conversation around the table stilled as Tair removed his steely stare from the Crown prince of Zarhat's profile and turned his attention to the man who was the hereditary ruler of that country.

'Hassan's death was a shock to him.'

The king sighed and shook his head. 'A man should not outlive his children. It is not the natural order of things. Still he has you, Tair, and that must be a comfort to him.'

If this was the case his father was hiding it well.

There was an ironic glitter in Tair's blue eyes as his thoughts were drawn back to his last verbal exchange with his father.

'I trusted you and what did you do, Tair?' King Malik's face had been suffused with a dark colour as he'd slammed his fist down on the table, causing all the heavy silver to jump.

Years ago when he had been a boy, Tair had struggled to hide his reaction to his father's sometimes violent and unpredictable outbursts, though such displays of unbridled fury had left him sick to the stomach. Now he did not need to struggle, as his father's rages no longer seemed frightening to him, just vaguely distasteful.

'It is a pity it wasn't *you* who walked in front of that car instead of your brother. *He* knew what loyalty and respect is due me. *He* would have supported me in this, not taken advantage of my grief to go behind my back.'

'I tried to contact you in Paris.'

His father's grief had not interfered in any noticeable manner with his social life.

King Malik dismissed this comment with a wave of his short, heavily ringed fingers and a contemptuous snort.

'But I was told you were not to be disturbed.' Tair knew this had been shorthand for his father being in the middle of a very high-stakes poker game.

The king's eyes narrowed further as he glared at his remaining son without a hint of affection.

'Your problem, Tair, is you have no vision. You do not think on the grand scale, but of such things as a water-treatment plant…' His sneer registered utter contempt for such a project. 'You exchanged those mineral rights for a water-treatment plant instead of a new yacht!'

'Not just a water-treatment plant, but an undertaking to recruit locally whenever possible, a training programme for our people and fifty per cent of the profits for them once they have recouped a percentage of their initial outlay.'

The deal he had renegotiated had not made the international firm he was dealing with exactly happy. They had been under the impression he was there to rubber stamp the contract as it stood, but they had at least viewed him with grudging respect as they had walked away looking like men who were not quite sure what had just happened to them.

Of course, Tair conceded, he'd had the element of surprise on his side. Next time—though considering his father's reaction that might not be any time soon—he would not have that advantage.

But Tair was not a man to avoid challenges.

'Profits!' His father had dismissed those intangible projected figures with a snap of his swollen fingers. Over-indulgence had left its mark on his coarsened features and his once athletic body. 'And when will that be? I could have had the yacht next month.'

His suggestion that it would perhaps be no great hardship to make do with last year's yacht had not been received well! And though Tair had not expected, or fortunately needed, praise, the lecture had been hard to take.

It was much easier to accept the censorious finger his uncle waved in his direction because Tair knew that, unlike his own father, King Hakim's remonstrance was well intentioned. His uncle was a man who had always put the welfare of his people above his own comfort and would be able to appreciate what Tair was trying to achieve.

'Remember the next time you feel the urge to fly into a desert storm…*alone*…that you are all your father has left.'

It was hard to tell from his manner which action appalled his uncle the most: the danger of the desert storm or the fact his nephew had not travelled with an entourage of hundreds as befitted his station in life.

'There are responsibilities in being heir.'

Tair inclined his head in courteous acknowledgement of

the royal rebuke. 'I am new to the role, Uncle, so I'm bound to make some errors.'

From the moment Tair had become heir to the throne many had considered his life public property and he accepted this, but there were some freedoms that he was not willing to relinquish. He needed places, moments and people with whom he could be himself in order to preserve his sanity.

'But you are not new to fobbing off old men. Do you think I don't know that you smile, say the right things and then do exactly what you want, Tair? However I know that, despite your action-man antics, you are aware of your duties. More aware than your brother ever was. I know one should not speak ill of the dead, but I say nothing now that I would not have said to his face and nothing I have not in the past said to your father.

'Malik did nobody any favours when he turned a blind eye to your brother's scandals and as for the dubious business dealings…?' Clicking his tongue, King Hakim shook his leonine head in disapproval. 'I have always been of the opinion that your country would have been better off if you had been born the elder.'

It wasn't often that Tair struggled for words, but, more accustomed to defending his actions from criticism, he was stunned to uncomfortable silence by this unexpected tribute from his uncle.

It was Beatrice who came to his rescue.

'I wouldn't mind getting my pilot's licence one day.'

The innocent comment from a heavily pregnant and glowing princess successfully diverted her father-in-law's attention from his nephew—as Tair was sure it was intended to—and began a good-natured joking debate among the younger generation around the table that centred on the hotly disputed superior ability of men to master any skill that required hand-eye co-ordination.

Everyone joined in except the mouselike English girl, who either through shyness or total lack of social skills—Tair suspected the latter—had barely spoken a word throughout the meal unless directly addressed.

The second silent party was Tariq.

Tair's irritation escalated and his suspicion increased as he watched the pair through icy blue eyes.

Tariq was the man who had it all, including a wife who adored him, a wife who was carrying his first child.

Tair's expression softened as his glance flickered to the other end of the table where Beatrice Al Kamal sat looking every inch the regal princess even when she winked at him over the head of her father-in-law the king.

He turned his head, the half-smile that was tugging at his own lips fading as he saw that Tariq was still staring like some pathetic puppy at the English mouse.

Tair's lip curled in disgust. He had always liked and admired the other man, and had always considered his cousin strong not only in the physical but also in the moral sense. Tair had felt it couldn't have happened to a more deserving man when Tariq had met and married the glorious Titian-haired Beatrice after a whirlwind romance.

If two people were ever meant to be together it was Beatrice and Tariq. Their clear devotion had touched even Tair's cynical heart, and made him hope in his less realistic moments that there was such a soul mate waiting for him somewhere, though even if there was it seemed unlikely they were destined to be together.

His future was intrinsically linked with that of the country he would one day rule. What his country needed and deserved after years of neglect by his father and

Hassan, who had both been of the opinion the country was their own personal bank, was political and financial stability. It was Tair's duty to make a marriage that supplied both. Improving transport links and dragging the medical facilities of Zabrania, the neighbouring country to Zarhat, into the twenty-first century were more important things than true love.

He directed another icy glare at his cousin, and considered the other man's stupidity. Tariq didn't seem to have a clue as to how lucky he was!

Didn't the man know he had it all?

And even if he wasn't insane enough to risk his marriage by actually being unfaithful—though in Tair's eyes the distinction between fantasy and physical infidelity was at best blurred—he was obviously stupid enough to risk hurting Beatrice by being so damned obvious.

Even a total imbecile could have picked up on the signals his cousin was being so mystifyingly indiscreet about hiding, and Beatrice was far from stupid.

It was totally inexplicable to Tair that Tariq could have so little respect for his wife that he would insult her this way, and for what…?

He allowed his own scornful gaze to drift in the direction of the English girl, who was clearly not the innocent she seemed because no man acted like Tariq without some encouragement. Tair tried and failed to see something in the mouselike girl that could tempt a man like Tariq…or for that matter any man!

Unlike red-headed, voluptuous Beatrice, this was not a girl who would turn heads. Small and slight, her brown hair secured in a twist at the nape of her neck—a good neck, Tair grudgingly noticed as he allowed his glance to linger momentarily on the slender pale column—she was not the sort of woman who exuded any strong allure for the opposite sex.

Trying to picture the small oval-shaped face without the large heavy-framed spectacles that were perched on the end of a slightly tip-tilted nose, Tair conceded that an investment in contact lenses might make her more than passable.

But such a change would not alter the fact that her body, covered at this moment in a peculiar sacklike dress the shade of mud, totally lacked the feminine curves which, like most men, he found attractive in the opposite sex.

His blue eyes narrowed as he watched the English girl turn her head to meet Tariq's eyes. For a moment the two simply looked at one another as though there were nobody else in the room. The outrage, locked in Tair's chest like a clenched fist, tightened another notch.

Then she smiled, her long curling eyelashes sweeping downwards creating a shadow across her smooth, softly flushed cheeks and the corners of her mouth. How had he missed the blatant sensuality of that full pouting lower lip?

Tair's mild concern and annoyance at his cousin's un-characteristic behaviour morphed abruptly into genuine apprehension. Up until this point he had thought that his cousin had simply needed reminding that he was one of the good guys; now it seemed that more might be required.

This silent exchange suggested to him a worrying degree of intimacy. For the first time he seriously consid-ered the possibility that this situation had progressed beyond mild flirtation.

Tair's long fingers tightened around the glass he was holding. Under the dark shield of his lashes his blue eyes, now turned navy with anger, slid around the table. The other guests at the family party continued to talk and laugh, seemingly oblivious to the silent communication between Tariq and the deceptively demure guest.

His brows twitched into a straight line above his strong masterful nose. Were they all blind?

How was it possible, he wondered incredulously, that he was the only person present who could see what was going on?

Could they not see the connection between these two?

Then his study of his guests revealed that Beatrice was also watching the interchange between her husband and friend. Tair's admiration of the woman his cousin had married went up another level when she responded to a comment made by her brother-in-law, Khalid, with a relaxed smile that hid whatever hurt or anxiety she might be feeling.

Beatrice was a classy lady. Clearly her mouse friend was not; she was a predator in mouse's clothing and his cousin was her prey.

He briefly considered the option of speaking directly to Tariq and telling him point-blank he was playing with fire. Such a discussion would end at best in harsh words and at worst in an exchange of blows—not really ideal from either a personal or political perspective. On reflection he decided it would be better by far to speak to the woman who was pursuing Tariq.

He would warn Miss Mouse that he would not stand by and watch her ruin the marriage of his friends. And if Miss Mouse didn't listen he would have to take direct action. He had no idea what form that direct action would take, but Tair's inspiration had so far not let him down. He had frequently walked into a room full of dignitaries whom his brother had insulted with no idea what he was going to say, but the right words had always come.

Though maybe this situation would require more than words… He gave a mental shrug, as he was capable of that too. Capable, according to some, of great ruthlessness, but Tair did not think of it in such emotive terms, he just did what was necessary and he never asked anyone else to perform an unpleasant task that he himself was not willing to do.

He looked at the sexy curve of the Mouse's mouth and wondered if that unpleasantness would take the form of sampling those lips…? Perhaps at a chosen moment when his actions could be observed by his cousin. The plan, unlike the lady, had some virtue as he was sure Tariq was not a man who would enjoy sharing any more than he would.

She was, he mused, staring at that mouth, nothing like any woman he had ever kissed. She had nothing to recommend her beyond neatness, a conniving nature and a sexy—actually very sexy—mouth, and he had done worse to help a friend.

The Mouse, perhaps sensing his study, suddenly stopped gazing at Tariq and turned her head, the action briefly causing her gaze to collide with his cold, hostile stare.

He watched with clinical detachment, the guilty colour rise up her slender neck until her small face was suffused with heat.

His lip curled in contempt as he smiled and watched her literally recoil before she looked away. At least she now knew that there was someone who was not fooled by her meek and mild act.

Tariq was still wearing the dark formal suit that he had been wearing at dinner, but his tie now hung loose around his neck.

Molly closed the door and motioned him to a chair. She perched on the edge of the big canopied bed suspecting her cotton pyjamas looked totally incongruous against the silken opulence, much the same way as she looked totally incongruous and out of place in the palace.

Some of the awkwardness and wariness she felt in Tariq's presence had dissipated over the past couple of weeks but she still couldn't totally relax around him.

She got the impression that he too was still feeling his way. Which wasn't that surprising given this relationship was still very new for them both. Fortunately Khalid, with his naturally outgoing nature, had not been similarly stilted and Molly felt much more at ease in his company.

Tariq, tall and lean, took the chair, turned it round, then straddled it, resting his hands on the back as he looked across at her. Molly realised that Beatrice had not been exaggerating when she had told her that her husband was not a man who felt any need to fill silences. Molly, impatient to know the reason for his visit, stifled her impulse to demand an explanation.

'I have not disturbed you? You were not asleep?'

She shook her head and there was another lengthy silence while she wondered some more why he had come.

'Khalid is concerned he might have offended you.'

Molly's bewilderment was genuine. 'Why would he think that?'

'He introduced you to Tair as Beatrice's friend.' For once Tariq had not been pleased to see his cousin and he had been hard put not to show his lack of enthusiasm for the extra dinner guest. 'He is afraid,' he explained, 'that you might mistake his reasons for not revealing your true identity.'

Tariq's voice receded into the distance as an image rose in Molly's head of the tall man with the electric blue eyes who had arrived at dinner looking dusty but remarkably good considering he had apparently just made an emergency landing at the airport after flying through an unexpected dust storm.

'The families are connected, loads of intermarriage. He's a cousin and heir to the throne of Zabrania.' Beatrice had explained the stranger's presence in a quiet aside to Molly while the men spoke together in a bewildering mixture of rapid Arabic, French and English.

'He has blue eyes!' Deep cerulean blue, the most intense shade that Molly had ever seen.

'You noticed?'

Hard not to!

'Apparently blue eyes crop up every so often in the Al Sharif family. There's a nice story about that, according to family legend. How true it is, I don't know, but they say a Viking got lost way back when. Rumour has it he got a bit too friendly with a royal princess and since then the blue eyes pop up every few generations. Tair is quite a looker, isn't he?'

Vaguely aware of Beatrice's amusement but totally unable to control her own expression, Molly closed her mouth with an audible snap and lowered her gaze, wondering if it was the incredible level of testosterone circulating in the room that was responsible for her erratic heartbeat.

'Really...?' she said, adopting a look of wide-eyed, exaggerated innocence. 'I hadn't noticed.'

Her humour was a little shaky, though Beatrice seemed not to notice, responding to the husky irony with an appreciative chuckle.

Molly's gaze was drawn back to their dinner guest.

Not notice! There was no way women hadn't been noticing this man from the moment he began shaving, a task that the shadow on his firm angular jaw suggested he had not performed since at least that morning.

Casting a covert look at the newcomer through her lashes, she noted the rest of his skin was the shade of vibrant gold and blemish-free if you discounted a fine white scar that began just beneath one razor-sharp cheek-bone and terminated at the corner of his wide, mobile and almost indecently sensual mouth.

Actually there was no almost about it—his mouth was indecent. The maverick thoughts that popped into her head when she looked at it certainly were!

His strongly delineated brows were the same raven shade as his hair, which looked like black satin and touched the collar of the open-necked shirt he wore. Under the layer of red dust the shirt might be the same colour as his eyes, though she doubted it—that unique shade of blue was not one that would be easy to duplicate.

Fortunately nobody seemed to notice her compulsion to look at him as her eyes roamed across the angles and strong planes of his face. She was staring, but how could she not? Beauty was a term that people flung around casually but here was someone who actually merited the description, although not in a Hollywood type of way. The newcomer had looks that affected the onlooker on a much earthier and more primal level.

Or maybe it's just me, she thought.

It was a worrying thought, but she doubted her reaction was unique. She doubted any woman would not be inclined to stare open-mouthed when they saw the six feet four inches of lean muscle and hard sinew that was Tair Al Sharif. He really was the most extraordinary-looking man Molly had ever seen.

But the prim voice in her head reminded her that looks were not everything.

It was something her father, thinking he was being kind, had told her frequently as she grew up beside two stepsisters who were as beautiful as they were lovely-natured. Sometimes, Molly reflected, it would have been easier if

Rosie and Sue had been mean and nasty. At least then she could have been jealous without feeling guilty. And there was something much more romantic about being oppressed and exploited by mean stepsisters than spoilt and indulged and told you were lovely inside.

Only last month Rosie had offered her a makeover when she had wailed in frustration that she'd prefer to be lovely on the outside and happily exchange ten points of her impressive IQ for another inch on her flat chest.

She snapped out of her reverie and drew herself back to the present to respond to Tariq. 'I completely understand why Khalid said what he did. Please tell him not to worry. However, I don't think the prince…' She stopped, realising this did not narrow the field much in the circles she was currently moving in, where princes were pretty thick on the ground! She gave a rueful grin as she added, 'Your cousin—I don't think he likes me much.'

The grin died as she recalled sensing, *feeling*, his extraordinary and unbelievably eloquent eyes upon her.

'Tair?' Tariq said, shaking his head. 'You must be mistaken. He does not know you. Why should he dislike you?'

Good question, but Molly knew there had been no ambiguity about the message she had seen in those glittering azure depths.

Having never in her life inspired any strong feelings in gorgeous-looking men—obviously they remained oblivious to the fact she was lovely inside—to have someone looking at her with that level of hostility and contempt had been quite disturbing.

His face floated into her mind gain; she tried to expel the image but it lingered. It was a face with a 'once seen never forgotten' quality. Even if you wanted to forget the golden skin stretched over hard angles and intriguing hollows, the sensual mouth and searing blue stare.

'You must have been mistaken, Molly.'

'I expect so,' she said, already wishing she had not introduced the subject. But no matter what Tariq said she knew she was not mistaken—Tair Al Sharif could not stand the sight of her.

Not that she was going to lose any sleep over his opinion of her. As first impressions went she hadn't taken to him either.

'If it will make you feel better I will explain our relationship to him straight away.'

'There's really no need.' She wondered if the flicker she saw in her brother's eyes was relief. The possibility shouldn't have hurt, but it did. 'And I'd actually prefer if you didn't.'

On a practical level she knew the searing dislike she had read in the Arab prince's face was not going to alter just because he knew she was Tariq and Khalid's English half-sister.

No, it had been loathing at first sight.

Besides, there were some people you didn't want to like you, and he was one of them, she decided. She mentally ticked off the qualities that made him undesirable—off-the-scale arrogance, no sense of humour, and he was in love with himself. The last seemed a reasonable assumption to Molly, who reasoned a person who looked at that face in the mirror every day would have to be just a little fond of himself.

'It is up to you, Molly, but what I came to say to you is that it is not a relationship that we are ashamed to acknowledge, quite the contrary...though,' Tariq conceded with a grimace, 'obviously it would be difficult to go public because…'

'This isn't easy for your father.'

Tariq looked grateful for her understanding of the situation. 'It was hard for him when our mother left… He is a proud man and the scandal of a divorce in our society, the gossip and stories, left its mark.'

It had been hard for Tariq too, but this was something Molly had not appreciated until very recently.

'Your father has been very kind to me and I wouldn't do anything to embarrass him. I'm not about to go public. I promise you I won't breathe a word to a soul. If anyone asks I'm Bea's friend.'

It was not a hard promise to make, as the level of hospitality she had received from the king had touched her deeply. However, she realised it could not be easy for him to have his ex-wife's child as a guest.

Molly knew enough about Zarhat culture to recognise that when Tariq had touched on the subject of the royal divorce he had, if anything, been downplaying the situation, yet the king had welcomed her into his home when many in his position might not have even wanted reminding of her existence.

Her solemnity as she made her vow of silence brought an affectionate smile to Tariq's face 'I appreciate that, Molly. But you do know that Khalid and I would both have been proud to have introduced you as our sister tonight.'

Warm moisture filled Molly's amber eyes as emotion clogged her throat. 'Really…?'

'You can doubt this?' he asked, before a spasm of self-condemnation twisted his dark features. 'Of course you can. Why would you not after I have ignored you for the past twenty-four years? If you had told me to go to hell it would have been what I deserved.'

A grin spread across Molly's face as she flicked away a strand of waist-length hair that had drifted across her face. It was still slightly damp from the shower. 'The way I recall it I pretty much did just that.'

The reminder of that meeting brought a rueful grin to his face.

'If it wasn't for Beatrice coming to see me I wouldn't be here now,' she said frankly.

It was true. When the half-brother who had ignored her since birth had suggested they should get to know one another, her response had been to angrily reject his overtures. What did she need with a brother who she knew had caused their mother so much heartache by refusing any contact with her after her second marriage to Molly's father?

They were strangers and Molly had been happy for it to stay that way; she'd wanted nothing to do with him.

Why would she?

She owed Tariq nothing. He hadn't just ignored the fact she existed, he had pressured Khalid, whom she had seen and adored as a small child before their mother's premature death, to reject her too.

It had been a visit in person from Beatrice pleading her husband's case that had persuaded her to accept the invitation.

Molly had come prepared, almost wanting, to despise this brother, but to her amazement after a slightly rocky start she had found herself liking Tariq.

'And you are glad you did come?'

Molly uncurled her legs from underneath her as she lifted her chin and scanned the lean dark face of the brother she still barely knew. 'Very glad,' she admitted huskily.

Tariq smiled and got to his feet. 'And you will think about what I have said?'

'I will,' she promised, walking with him to the door.

'Tariq!'

Standing framed in the doorway, he turned back.

'I do understand, you know…why you wouldn't come and visit Mum when she was alive.'

She hadn't always. As a small child the only thing she had understood was the desperate hurt in her mother's eyes when the eldest son she had been forced to leave behind when she'd divorced the King of Zarhat had not accompanied his brother for the arranged visit.

It had not crossed her mind at the time that Tariq had been hurting too and perhaps feeling betrayed that the mother he had loved had chosen her freedom over her sons.

'Dad told me, when he knew I was coming here, how she never stopped feeling guilty about leaving you and Khalid, but she knew you would be safe and loved. She always knew that your place was here.'

'And hers was not.'

There was no trace of criticism in Tariq's manner but Molly felt impelled to defend the choice their mother had made.

'She must have been very desperate.'

Molly could only imagine the sort of unhappiness that would make a woman make that choice. She knew nothing about the strength of maternal bonds, but something deep inside her told her that to leave a child would be like ripping away part of yourself and you'd walk around with that awful emptiness the rest of your life.

Without being judgemental, Molly really couldn't imagine a situation where she would make the same decision.

'But she knew you and Khalid would be well cared for and I think me being here would have made her very happy.'

Without a word Molly stepped into arms that opened for her and the years of rejection and anger melted away.

'God, look at me, I'm crying,' she said as she emerged from a crushing brotherly hug. She wiped the moisture from her face with one hand and pushed back her hair with the other.

'Go on,' she sniffed. 'Or Beatrice will be sending out the search party.'

CHAPTER TWO

FROM where he was standing, Tair witnessed the embrace and heard Molly's parting warning. He could feel the anger burning inside him like a solid physical presence.

He stayed where he stood concealed in the shadows until the echoes of Tariq's footsteps on the marble floor died away. Then he began to walk towards the door that had just closed, his long stride filled with purpose.

A muscle clenched in his firm jaw as he imagined her in the room feeling pleased with herself because nobody suspected her game. Her mask was good, he conceded, but he had seen through her disguise.

There was no effort involved in recreating in his head the image of her standing in the doorway.

He had barely recognised the mouse minus the glasses and with her hair hanging loose to her narrow waist like a silken screen. The light streaming from the bedroom had acted like a spotlight shining through the fine fabric of her demure nightclothes, revealing every dip and curve of a slender but undeniably female form. Female enough to cause a lustful surge of his own undiscriminating hormones.

Who would have guessed, other than Tariq, that under the baggy top there was that body?

He stopped a few feet from the door and forced himself to think past both the memory of those small plump breasts and his anger—the two seemed inextricably linked in his head—and took a deep breath, forcing the fury boiling in his veins to a gentle simmer.

To confront her would give him pleasure of a sort, but what would it achieve? Other than to watch her struggle as she tried to explain away what he had seen. She would have her work cut out, Tair thought. He was not a man to jump to conclusions, but in this instance he felt he was fully justified to assume the worst.

However, what he had witnessed showed how deeply she had her unvarnished claws into Tariq, and threats from him were not going to make her back off. Him barging in might even have the opposite effect and actually make the situation worse. Right now the situation was retrievable, but if the affair became public knowledge…?

He needed to think. He needed to think about this like any other problem. He needed to analyse the problem, decide what he wanted to happen and then choose how he was going to make it happen.

Tair inhaled deeply, then released the breath slowly. With one last look at the door he turned and strode away in the opposite direction to the one his cousin had taken.

Tariq, who had been walking across the courtyard, stopped when he saw his cousin. 'Tair!'

Tair stepped towards him thinking, You idiot, as he smiled. Tariq looked exhausted. Perhaps guilt made him lie awake at night?

He too had lain awake the previous night, but he was not feeling any effects from the lack of sleep; he was actually feeling quite pleased with himself.

Some might consider his plan reckless, but Tair preferred to think of it as inspired.

'I'm glad I bumped into you.'

The relief he saw on the other man's face struck Tair as darkly ironic.

'Actually—' Tariq, his brow furrowed, glanced down at the watch on his wrist '—you could do me a favour. I don't suppose you would take a message to Molly for me?'

Tair inclined his head to indicate his willingness to help out and thought that this was working out much better than he'd anticipated.

It wasn't very often the victim of a scam actively helped facilitate the scheme. Not that he had a lot of personal experience with scams, and this was one being perpetuated with the most altruistic of motives. He didn't expect that Tariq would immediately he able to make the differentiation, though obviously when he had come to his senses he would appreciate his good fortune.

'You'll find her in the glasshouses,' he explained, glancing down at his watch in a manner that seemed uncharacteristically distracted to Tair. 'She's interested in that sort of thing. Well, she would be, wouldn't she?'

'She would?' Tair, who was mentally bringing forward his plan by an hour, pretended an interest he did not feel.

'Well, yes, she's head of the science department but her first degree was in botany. When I told her about the glasshouses built by great-grandfather and his collection she was fascinated. I was looking for Khalid to do the honours for me, but I can't track him down.'

'She is a teacher?' he said, unable to hide his doubt. Surely in order to command the respect of pupils a teacher needed to project an air of authority?

Tariq looked amused. 'Have you spoken to her at all?

She teaches at a girls' school.' He named a prestigious establishment that even Tair had heard of and added, 'Molly is really very bright.' He said this with an obvious pride that set Tair's teeth on edge.

'I know she seems quiet, but once you start talking to her…she's actually got a great sense of humour and—'

'She seems to have a most articulate advocate in you,' Tair cut in before his cousin waxed even more lyrical and was unable to keep a guard on his tongue. 'I will,' he promised, 'certainly make the effort to know her better.' He knew all he needed to know about Miss Mouse.

'So we have you for a few more days?'

'My travel plans are not certain yet,' Tair lied, thinking of his refuelled plane and freshly charted flightplan.

'Tell Molly I'm sorry, but I'll have to take a rain check. Bea had a bad night. They think it's a good idea if she checks into the hospital.' He glanced down at his watch again. 'I've been banished while she packs a bag. She says I'm driving her mad fussing.' Despite his joking tone the lines of strain around his mouth made it clear that Tariq was worried.

'You should have said something!' Tair exclaimed. 'Is she—?'

'It's just a precaution,' Tariq cut in quickly. 'Her blood pressure is up a little and, well, the fact is she's been doing too much. It's my fault—I shouldn't have left her alone.'

Tair thought it was a little late for the other man to realise this, but given his obvious agitation it seemed unnecessarily cruel to labour the point so he contented himself with an abrupt, 'Your place is with your wife.'

'So you'll explain the situation to Molly?'

Could he not forget the woman even now? 'I will make sure she understands.'

Tariq laid a hand on his arm. 'Thanks, Tair, and try not

to scare her. Poor Molly has the impression you can't stand the sight of her.'

The girl was highly perceptive, Tair thought, while lifting his brows in an attitude of amazement.

'I know, crazy,' Tariq remarked with an indulgent smile that made Tair's teeth grate, 'but I think you make her nervous... I know you can be charming, Tair, and I'd be grateful if you'd make the effort for me. This is her first visit here and I want her to come back.'

Not if I have anything to say about it. 'For you, yes, cousin, I will make the effort.'

'Thanks for this, Tair.'

'It is my pleasure.' And if not his pleasure, it was certainly his duty to remove temptation from Tariq's way.

The perfectly preserved glasshouses built in the Victorian era covered acres of ground and they contained not only historical and rare fruit and vegetable varieties, but a unique and priceless collection of orchids.

Tair was familiar with the glasshouses as when he was a boy visiting his cousins they had played there. It took him a short time to locate Molly, though he almost walked past her, only catching sight of the shiny top of her head at the last minute.

He backtracked and saw she was sitting on the floor with her knees drawn up, her attention divided between the sketch-book balanced on her knee and an orchid in full fragrant bloom. Its heady scent filled the air around them.

She was so intent on her task that she didn't hear his approach and as she continued to remain unaware of his presence Tair had the opportunity to study her unobserved.

Her body was hidden once more behind another unattractive outfit—an oversized shirt and shapeless skirt that reached mid-calf. But his attention remained on her face. Like last night, she was not wearing the librarian glasses, but unlike last night he was close enough to appreciate the delicacy of her bone structure and the smooth creaminess of her skin. Still oblivious to his presence, she turned her head as she laid down the pencil in her hand to pick up another from the tin that lay open beside her and he was able to see that her face was a perfect oval.

Her delicate winged brows drew together in a frown of concentration as she turned her attention back to the drawing, her slim fingers flying over the paper.

When she finished the frown deepened into a grimace of dissatisfaction as she compared what was on the paper to the waxy petalled bloom she was studying.

'Hopeless!' she muttered in apparent disgust at her inability to do her subject justice.

'A lack of talent can be frustrating.'

She started as though shot and turned her head jerkily, causing several strands of hair to break loose from the knot tied at the base of her slender neck. Their eyes connected and Tair was struck by two thoughts simultaneously. Her eyes were pure gold and she was looking at him as though he were, if not the devil himself, then certainly a very close relation. She appeared not to notice as the pencil slipped from her nerveless fingers and slid into the decorative grating of an air vent.

He raised one brow and she astonished him by blushing to the roots of her hair. Hair that turned out not to be boring mousy brown, but a subtle combination of shades ranging from soft gold to warm conker.

The knot on the nape of her neck appeared to be secured by a single barrette; presumably if it was removed her hair would spill like silk down her back.

Had Tariq done this?

He pushed the thought away, baring his teeth in a smile. Tariq wouldn't be doing that or anything else that involved Miss Mouse any more.

Even before she turned Molly had known who was standing there. Tair Al Sharif's voice had to be just about the most distinctive on the planet! He could have made the ingredients on a cereal packet sound like an indecent proposition. The velvet smoothness had an almost tactile quality that sent tiny secret shivers up and down her spine.

Even when he stopped speaking she could hear it in her head.

Molly kept her head down and got to her feet slowly to allow the heat in her cheeks time to dissipate.

Even when she was standing straight he remained a full foot, probably more, taller than her. Molly would have liked to believe it was simply the extra inches alone that made her feel at such a disadvantage. But even without looking directly at him she could feel the effect of the leashed power and blatantly sexual aura he radiated lying like a stone fist in her chest. It made her conscious of each breath she took.

He was dressed smart-casual, or in his case sexy-casual, in jeans, secured across his lean snaky hips with a leather belt, and a blue open-necked shirt.

Molly had never thought before that the words denim and disturbing could be in the same sentence as she glanced at the way the material clung to his long muscular thighs.

Last night Molly had tossed and turned in bed unable to get this man's voice or face from her mind although she had tried to blame her inability to sleep on the second cup of coffee she'd had at dinner.

At about two a.m. she had decided that she had imagined the hypnotic quality of his searing blue eyes and the inexplicable hostility she saw in them when they were turned in her direction.

Now a caffeine-free zone, she had to admit she had been fooling herself.

Even after having adjusted her stare to a point over his shoulder she could feel his eyes on her. The sort of eyes that layers of skin and bone seemed a poor defence against—it felt as if he could see inside her skull.

When she was this close to him she felt as though every protective layer she had built up over the years had been peeled away. Chastising herself crossly at the whimsical illusion, she kept staring into the safety zone over his shoulder, deciding it was preferable to have him assume she was cross-eyed than maintain direct eye contact and do something stupid like trip over her own feet, drool or forget her name.

This is stupid—you look ridiculous, Molly thought. Look at the man—you can't talk to the wall! Surely nothing should scare a person who had stood in at the last minute for an absent colleague and delivered a sex-education lecture to a hall of sixteen-year-old girls?

It had turned out the girls knew a lot more than she did!

'You startled me,' she said, brushing the dust off the seat of her skirt before tucking a stray strand of hair behind her ear. 'I didn't hear you.' And if I had I would have run in the opposite direction.

It was still an option, she thought, staring at his shiny boots.

'Sorry,' he said, not looking it, but not actually sounding as openly antagonistic as he had the previous evening.

It was possible she'd been wrong about the hostility, not that he had the sort of face that was easy to read if he didn't want you to. And right now it would seem he didn't want her to.

Her gaze flickered across the hard contours and angles of his lean face and a sigh snagged in her throat. He might not be easy to read, but he was damned easy to look at! A lot more than easy!

Her glance dropped to his feet shod in leather boots and then, as though drawn by an invisible magnet, worked its way upwards, lingering over some areas more than others, until she reached his face. Everything about him was worth looking at.

She applied the tip of her tongue to the moisture that broke out along her upper lip and struggled to disguise the fact that her feet were nailed to the ground with lust.

No man had ever elicited this type of raw response from Molly in her life and she found it both utterly mortifying and deeply scary.

As he reached across to take the sketch-book from her she opened her mouth to protest but nothing came out. With fingers clenched almost as tight as her teeth, she injected amusement into her voice as she held out her hand.

'I doubt my scribbling will interest you, Mr al... Prince...'

His eyes lifted, meeting hers momentarily. He ignored the hand. 'Or my opinion interest you?'

'I'm holding my breath.' Actually the entire breathing thing was currently something of a chore. She was twenty-four and had never been in a situation where sexual awareness caused her brain to malfunction before.

The acid sweetness of her retort caused his eyes to narrow before they dropped. Biting her lip, Molly watched in dismay as Tair Al Sharif, his dark head tilted a little to one side, continued to study the sketch.

So far he hadn't been overly impressed by anything about her, so why, she asked herself dourly, should now be any different?

She stopped and blinked... Will you just listen to yourself, Molly? Have you any idea how pathetic and needy you sound?

She took a deep breath, lifted her chin and advised herself sternly to grow up. For goodness' sake, he was not an art critic. Why should she give a damn what he thought?

She didn't!

So why was she standing here shuffling her feet like a kid called to the headmaster's study?

This was ridiculous. She was acting like some needy loser who wanted everyone to love her... Someone might be nice, but that someone was not going to bear any resemblance to Tair Al Sharif.

The internal dialogue came to an abrupt end as he lifted his raven head.

He was surprised that she actually did have the talent he accused her of lacking, a fact that was obvious even to his uneducated eye. The drawing leapt off the paper. It was detailed and delicate and if it did not meet with her approval the artist was an extremely harsh critic of her own skills.

He removed his eyes from the sketch-book and turned his attention to her, his dark gaze drifting over the outfit that was not what most women would have selected for a meeting with a lover, but clearly Tariq was able to see past the dowdy disguise. The thought of his smitten cousin brought a dark scowl of disapproval to his face and it was still in place when their eyes connected.

Molly went to push up the glasses on her nose only to discover they weren't there. She experienced a moment of total panic, the sort she felt in nightmares.

She didn't need his approval, she told herself sternly, and she didn't need a safety blanket either. The glasses had been useful once, but she was no longer a precociously bright but gauche kid plunged into the university environment among people who were older.

Tair had seen the gesture. 'You have mislaid your spectacles... Can you not see without them?' It amused him that the teacher was looking at him as though she were a pupil expecting a reprimand from a headmaster.

She gave a shrug. 'They'll turn up.'

'The picture is very good.' He handed back the sketchbook, which she took and slowly closed.

A gratified smile lifted the corners of her sensual lips, and her eyes looked like polished amber as they shone with pleasure. The permanent groove above his hawklike nose deepened. Her reaction struck him as a wildly over-the-top response to what had been a grudging observation.

As if the same thought had suddenly occurred to her, the smile vanished and she lowered her eyes. 'Thank you.'

CHAPTER THREE

'I CANNOT be the first person to tell you that you have…talent.'

The harsh emphasis Tair placed on the last word confused Molly. 'It's a hobby…it's just for my own amusement.'

And did it amuse her to steal another woman's husband? The muscles of his brown throat worked as he regarded her with distaste.

His rigid disapproving stance made her shift uncomfortably, and she dropped her gaze. Seeing her glasses lying on the floor, she bent to pick them up with a grunt of relief. Unfortunately Tair did too, his brown fingertips brushing the skin of her wrist as he reached them just before her.

The brief contact sent a surge of tingling sensation through her body. She stepped back, almost stumbled, then, breathing hard, she straightened up.

Tair watched as she nursed one hand against her chest, his eyes drawn to the visibly throbbing blue-veined pulse spot at the base of her throat.

The air was dense with a sexual tension you could have reached out and grabbed with both hands. It hung in the hot, humid air like a crackling field of electricity.

Tair viewed this unexpected development with as much objectivity as he was able—which wasn't very much when he was seeing life through a hot hormonal haze.

It hadn't been slow burn, it had just exploded out of nowhere and it still held him in its grip.

Tair's jaw clenched as he struggled to reassert control; he was not a man who let his appetites rule him. Of course he had experienced his share of lustful moments but he'd never been drawn to anyone in such an elemental way before.

This personal insight into what this woman could do to a man ought to have made him feel sympathy for his cousin, but it was not empathy he felt when he thought of Tariq following up on the sort of impulse he had just resisted.

Resisted, even though he was free to follow his urges, unlike his cousin.

His hooded gaze slid to her mouth.

'It's just for my own amusement,' she repeated hoarsely.

His own amusement was very much in Tair's thoughts as his eyes stayed on the soft full outline of her lips. If he followed up on his impulses it would be because he chose to and not because he couldn't help himself.

He had control.

So why had he been staring at her mouth for the last two minutes as if it were an oasis and he were a man who needed water?

Hands clenched at his sides, he removed his eyes from her lips. If he did kiss her it would be at a time and place of his choosing.

Pushing back strands of loose hair from her brow, Molly extended her hand towards him. 'Thank you…'

As he looked at her fingertips Tair thought about them trailing over his damp bare skin. A spasm of irritation drew

his lean features into a frown. His problem was that there had
been too much work in his life recently and not enough sex.

His problem, he acknowledged, was her mouth.

To Molly's utter dismay, instead of handing her the spectacles Tair held them up to his own eyes.

She watched his dark brows lift towards his hairline
and thought how it was typical that the only person who
had ever seen past her harmless charade had to be him.

'Clear glass…?'

He struggled to hide his extreme distaste at his discovery. Presumably the clothes and unmade face were all part
of the same illusion. The one that made other women
dismiss her as no threat, but every man she came into
contact with knew different.

He knew different.

Molly, feeling an irrational level of guilt as though she
had been caught out in some shameful crime, shook her
head mutely.

She was not about to explain that when arriving at university via an educational hothouse scheme for gifted
children, aged sixteen and looking fourteen, she had come
up with the inspired idea of looking older by adopting a
pair of heavy spectacles. She realised now that they hadn't
made her look older but over the years they had become a
safety blanket.

'A fashion accessory.'

'I think you should change your fashion guru.'

The suggestion drew a forced laugh from Molly.
'Fashion isn't really my thing.'

'But wearing clothes two sizes too big is?'

He didn't come right out and say that she looked like a
dowdy bag lady, but that was clearly the message in his

comment. The voltage of Molly's smile went up and her muscles ached from the fixed and slightly inane grin her facial muscles had frozen into.

She was comfortable in her own skin, and if this man with his perfect face and better than perfect body couldn't see past superficial things like make-up and clothes that was his problem. She only had a problem if she started caring what men she met casually thought about her.

It could be she had a problem.

She looked at his fingers holding her glasses. They were rather incredible; long, tapering and the lightest contact with them had sent her nervous system into meltdown. She was sure there was a perfectly logical explanation for what happened—a build-up of static electricity and a freakish set of circumstances that couldn't be repeated if she tried.

But Molly wasn't about to put her theory to the test. As far as Prince Tair was concerned she had a strict no-touch policy—her body was still shaken by intermittent after-shocks from his light touch. Anything more intimate and she might well end up hospitalised.

Just as well him getting more intimate with her was about as likely as snow in the desert.

With the fixed smile still painted in place, she reached out to carefully take her glasses from his fingers.

He gave a sardonic smile that Molly didn't choose to respond to, her cheeks pink as she slid the spectacles onto her nose while expelling a shaky sigh of relief. Of course he knew he was gorgeous. Of course he knew women fainted away when he deigned to throw them a smile, but, God, she didn't want to be one of them.

It was all so shallow and silly. It seemed a good moment to remind herself that she was neither.

'I'm meeting Tariq,' she explained, hoping he would

take the hint and go away. There were only so many times a girl could make a fool of herself. 'He should be here any minute now.'

'I know.'

'You do?' Then why hadn't he just said so straight off instead of giving her the opportunity to act like a total imbecile?

'He asked me to deliver a message.'

She gave an encouraging nod. Dragging a sentence out of this man was like dragging blood from the proverbial stone.

'He is not coming.'

Molly's face fell. 'Right, well…thank you.' She urged him to go—her system couldn't take all this undiluted testosterone.

'Beatrice is not well.'

Molly's mask fell away. 'Beatrice…' She pressed one hand to her mouth and, all hint of self-preservation gone, she caught his arm with the other. 'What happened?' she asked, her mind turning over the events of two days earlier when she had come across Beatrice sitting with her head between her knees recovering from a slight dizzy spell.

Molly's first inclination had been to get help, but Bea had begged her not to, saying that Tariq was already wildly overprotective and he would worry himself silly over a moment of light-headedness.

She shouldn't have let Bea dissuade her, she thought. She should have told Tariq.

Tair felt the fingers curled over his forearm tighten.

'Apparently she had a…troubled night.'

'Troubled? What do you mean troubled?'

Anyone who hadn't seen Tariq come out of her room the previous night might have believed that wide-eyed concern. The mouse was clearly a very good actress,

although earlier she had not been good enough to hide her
response to his touch. The shocked expression in her
widely dilated eyes had been a total give-away.

'The doctor came this morning.'

'Doctor…oh, God!'

Tair watched the rest of the colour leave her face. Her
fainting on him hadn't been any part of his plan.

'And he advised she be transferred to hospital.'
Presumably her reaction had more to do with guilt than
genuine concern, or if it was it was a very selective form
of that sentiment.

'Is she…is the baby…? She hasn't gone into labour
yet?' She quickly reminded herself that lots of babies were
born perfectly healthily at thirty-five weeks.

'As far as I know it is just a precaution…?' He deliberately injected a questioning note into his voice.

Molly let go of his arm and lifted a hand to her head.
Closing her eyes, she leaned back against a tier of elabo-
rately carved cast-iron shelves spilling with lush greenery.
'This is my fault.'

Tair saw no reason to let her off the hook. If she was beginning to realise that her selfish actions had consequences
it was long overdue, he thought grimly.

'What makes you say that?'

She inhaled deeply and opened her eyes. 'A few days
ago Bea sort of fainted—well, she said not, but I think she
did. She asked me not to say anything to Tariq… I knew I
should have told him…' She shook her head and gave a
self-recriminatory grimace as she slapped the heel of her
hand hard against her forehead. 'If she's ill, if anything
happens to the baby, it's my fault.'

She was either a brilliant actress—and no one was that
brilliant—or this woman had a seriously skewed take on

morality. How could she care about the wife and cheat with the husband?

'Do you know what's wrong? Is there something you're hiding? Is Bea in danger?'

He shrugged. 'I'm not hiding anything. Tariq wasn't that forthcoming.'

'He must be frantic!' If anything happened to Bea or the baby she knew he would be utterly devastated. Her half-brother's obvious adoration of his wife had been one of the first things that had made her warm towards him.

'I'm going out to the hospital so I could take you if you like? I'm sure you will be a great comfort to Tariq.'

Molly, deaf to the ironic inflection in his steely addition, turned to him with a beam of gratitude.

'Really?'

'I'm sure Beatrice would like to have such an old friend around.'

She smiled and reached out impulsively to touch his arm again as she said, 'It really is kind of you.' Then Molly saw he was looking at her hand and with a self-conscious grimace she let it fall away.

'Not kind.'

The strange way he said it made her throw him a frowning look of enquiry, but his expression told her nothing.

'Come.'

Molly responded to the command, falling into step beside him as he went through a door that linked the glass-houses with the main building. 'I was thinking, perhaps I should ring the hospital? They must have left in a hurry. Maybe,' she mused, quickening her pace to keep up with Tair's longer stride, 'there is something Bea would like me to bring for her…'

Molly knew if the positions were reversed she would

like to have a few personal things around her to make her hospital room seem more homely.

'There is no shortage of people to bring the princess what she needs.'

Molly gave a rueful grimace and felt foolish. 'Of course there is. I just can't get used to that.'

'To what?'

'The fact that there are people to tie her shoelaces if she wants.' And Beatrice seemed so normal.

'I forget that you knew Beatrice before she was married. Have you been friends long?'

Molly, never comfortable with the lie, shrugged and mumbled, 'It feels like for ever.' Which was true; her rapport with Beatrice had been instant. She doubted she could have felt closer if Bea had been one of her own sisters.

When they reached the courtyard a four-wheel drive was waiting there for them. Tair spoke to the man behind the wheel, who got out and, with a courteous nod in her direction, retreated.

'I prefer to drive myself.'

Molly dragged her eyes from the vehicle to the man she was going to share it with and felt her stomach muscles tighten nervously. Suddenly this didn't seem like such a brilliant idea.

'Should I change?' she asked, lifting a hand to her head. 'I should probably tidy up and get something to cover my hair. Look, you don't have to wait for me—you go. I'll make my own way to the hospital.'

'You look fine as you are.'

Tair slid into the driving seat but still Molly hung back. She recognised the reason for her reluctance and knew it was ridiculous, but the thought of being in an enclosed confine with this man and his sexual magnetism scared her witless.

Though wasn't magnetism meant to work both ways? If so this must be something else because he wasn't drawn in her direction, reluctantly or any other way!

He glanced across at her, with one dark brow elevated, looking more like a dark fallen angel than ever. 'Are you coming?'

'I was just…' She stopped, her eyes sliding from his as she realised she could hardly tell him his aggressive masculinity made her feel raw and uncomfortably vulnerable.

A spasm of irritation crossed his dark features as she continued to hesitate. 'Do you want this lift or not?'

Molly told herself to calm down. This was just a lift; she wasn't signing away her life. All she had to do for Tariq and Bea was to survive for twenty minutes in this man's company.

'Well, if it's no bother.'

CHAPTER FOUR

MOLLY had assumed that Tair was taking a short cut to the airport when he turned off onto a dirt track, but after they had been travelling for forty minutes it occurred to her that short cuts were meant to be…well…shorter.

Were they lost?

They hit another bump in the road and Molly let out an involuntary little cry as she was jolted.

He flicked her a brief sideways glance. 'Are you all right?'

'Fine.'

Tair turned his attention back to the road and she slid a covert look at his patrician profile. He didn't look like someone who didn't have a clue where he was. He looked like someone who always knew exactly where he was going. On the other hand, she supposed, men were notoriously reluctant to admit when they were lost.

Her lips curved into a secret smile as she looked at him and thought how he was definitely *all* man. The gusty sigh that lifted her chest caused his eyes to find her face once more.

'Are you sure you're all right?'

'I bit my tongue, that's all.'

Feeling the guilty heat rise to her cheeks, she fixed her gaze on her hands clasped primly in her lap. Adjusting her regard onto the arid scenery they were driving through, she thought how there wasn't a single landmark in the miles and miles of featureless desert. It had to be very easy to miss a turning out here. It wasn't as if there were signposts or, for that matter, anything else.

She averted her gaze from the bleak landscape with a shudder, unable to see the beauty in this empty land that Beatrice spoke of. Presumably her mother had seen no appeal in it either.

'I suppose satellite navigation must be essential out here,' she remarked casually. The vehicle they were in was equipped with it, but Tair had not switched it on.

His broad shoulders lifted in a shrug. 'Useful, I suppose, if you are not accustomed to negotiating the desert terrain.'

'Which you are?'

'Which I am,' he agreed. 'It is in my blood.'

Molly could have listed the constituents of blood and to her knowledge the items would not include a sense of direction. She kept a discreet silence on the subject but possibly her scepticism showed because he volunteered further information to back up his claim.

'My mother came from a Bedouin tribe, and my grandfather is the sheikh of his tribe.'

Her eyes widened. As she glanced at him it was impossible not to see him as a romantic figure in flowing desert robes. 'People still live that way?'

'The tribal way of life is dying out,' he admitted.

It was hard to tell from his expression if he considered this a bad thing or not.

'But there are some like my grandfather who keep tradition alive.'

'Your grandfather is alive?'

He flashed her a grin and for a brief moment looked less

austere and stern. 'My grandfather is very much alive, but Mother died when I was a child.'

'Mine too.' Which was about the only thing they could possibly have in common.

'You have no family?'

Her eyes dropped as she shook her head. 'Dad is alive and I have two stepsisters, and two half-brothers.'

His brows lifted. 'A large family.'

Families were a place Molly did not want to go! She was beginning to wish she had stuck to a safer subject like the weather.

'Big queues for the bathroom,' she said, trying to close down the subject, though she couldn't help but wonder what his reaction would be if she said, Actually I'm Tariq and Khalid's half-sister—my mother divorced the king.

His blue eyes looked over at her face. 'But you could not have been lonely growing up.'

Did that mean he had been? Did lonely little boys turn into men as self-reliant as this one? Despite the extreme unlikelihood of this, an image of a dark-haired little boy with lonely blue eyes flashed into her head. The sort of little boy you'd want to pull into your arms.

Only, little boys you wanted to hug grew up into men around whom it would be wise to keep such impulses under control!

Besides, she thought, her glance drifting towards his powerful shoulders, relaxed despite the rough terrain he was negotiating, it was obvious that there wouldn't be many people who could pull him any place he didn't want to go these days!

He was far more likely to be the one doing the pulling and very few women she could think of would do any resisting!

Her lashes brushed her cheeks as, eyes half closed, she

wondered what it would feel like to have those arms close around her. Her eyes darted, as though drawn by an invisible force, to his mouth, her pupil dilating dramatically as she stared at the sculpted outline. It was a fascinating combination of passion and control. A fractured gasp locked in her throat and she pressed a hand against the pounding pulse at the base of her neck.

How would it feel to be claimed by that mouth? She ran a finger across the upper curve of her lips and thought it would surely be pretty mind-blindingly sensational.

God, what was she doing?

She was weaving a sexual fantasy about someone she didn't even like doing something he was never going to do. Men like Tair Al Sharif did not kiss women like her.

But if he did?

The question popped unbidden into her head and once it was there it wouldn't go away, even when she tore her eyes from his mouth.

They hit another pothole and Molly, teeth gritted and eyes trained on the dusty track ahead, barely noticed—even though her seat belt cut painfully into her shoulder. She picked up the thread of their conversation.

'I wasn't lonely.'

Molly winced to hear the note of defiance in her voice. Tair had struck a sensitive nerve she hadn't known she had because she hadn't been lonely. Not as such.

How could a person be lonely with a great dad and stepsisters who never excluded her? Sue and Rosie had always gone out of their way to involve their studious, less popular little sister. The fact that she had always been conscious of a sense of being different was down to something in herself, Molly suspected.

'And I really would be a lot happier if you kept your

eyes on the road—if you can call it that.' Now that she said it Molly realised that she wasn't sure there was even a track anymore. It had deteriorated over the past couple of miles to the point where it was hard to tell where it ended and the desert began.

'If I was a more suspicious man I might think you were trying to change the subject.'

The man was far too perceptive. 'No, I simply don't want to arrive at the hospital in need of medical attention,' she retorted tartly while thinking psychiatric analysis might not be such a bad idea.

She lasted thirty seconds before she responded to the overpowering compulsion to look at him. She was studying the strong, aggressively male curve of his jaw from beneath the concealing sweep of her lashes when he turned his head. Caught staring like a child in a sweet shop, Molly fought the impulse not to look away guiltily.

He smiled the sort of smile that suggested it wasn't anything new for him to have women stare in lustful longing at him, which it no doubt wasn't, but that in her eyes did not excuse the arrogance. In fact it made it worse!

She cringed inwardly imagining him thinking she was a pushover—another one unable to resist his alpha-male magnetism.

Insufferable egotist!

'I was just wondering...' if you're as good at kissing as you look? '...if your male ego...' she choked as her colour heightened '...would take a bashing if I asked you if we're lost?'

He grinned again and Molly thought he really should do that more often.

'My ego is pretty robust, but thank you for caring.'

She'd never seriously thought any different—he hardly

looked as if he had a self-esteem issue. 'I don't,' she muttered under her breath.

She was relieved when Tair showed no sign of hearing her childish retort. She wasn't childish, or inarticulate, and she definitely wasn't sex-starved—well, only out of choice and it had never felt like a problem before—so why was it she displayed all these embarrassing characteristics around this man?

'So I'll risk it. Are we?'

He probably wouldn't look on getting lost in a desert as a crisis—he'd more likely relish the challenge of being forced to rely on his ingenuity to survive in a hostile environment.

A frown of dismay twitched her brows as it occurred to Molly that the thought of being lost in the desert didn't alarm her as much as it should have. A circumstance that might have something to do with whom she'd be stranded with.

'No.' He flashed her a quick sideways look.

Was she meant to find the monosyllabic response comforting? 'Then where are we?'

'We are almost there,' he said in the manner of an adult humouring an impatient child. 'In fact,' he added a moment later, 'we are there.'

She shook her head, repeated, 'There?' and looked out of the window. 'Here! This isn't an airport.'

This wasn't anything! Apart from a couple of large corrugated metal buildings that had seen better days, there seemed very little to differentiate where they were from the previous dusty miles of empty red sand they had just driven across.

The entire place seemed totally deserted—it looked like a ghost town minus the town.

'It was twenty years ago.'

She looked at his profile and the nebulous feeling of something not being quite right crystallised into fear. 'Why have you taken me here?'

As she spoke they rounded the side of the largest building and she saw a solitary plane sitting on what she supposed would once have been a runway, but which now had several visible and large potholes.

'It's all part of my devious plan to abduct you.' One dark brow elevated.

The embarrassed heat flew to Molly's cheeks. 'Sorry!' she mumbled, feeling utterly mortified that she'd questioned him.

'It's just when you said plane I assumed...' She broke off and gave an awkward shrug. 'And it did feel as if we've been driving for miles and...'

'You suspect my motives?' he suggested, not looking offended by the possibility as he brought the big vehicle to a halt a few hundred yards from the plane.

'Of course not. I'm a bit tense. The desert makes me nervous.' You make me nervous, she thought, her glance drifting to his mouth, and you make me feel other things too.

Things that brought into question Molly's deeply held belief that she could only ever be sexually attracted to someone she liked, and respected. Someone suitable. Molly simply didn't accept the idea that you had no control over the person you fell for. It was the equivalent of saying she saw a hole in the ground and she had to step into it— she didn't have to and she was never going to!

It was all about walking around the obstacle. So far her life had been obstacle-free—depressingly so, it seemed at times, but when she saw one heading her way she was going to get out of the way!

Molly could see how the rule might be bent a little if

both parties were just after casual sex, but she had more or less ruled that out a long time ago as not really being her.

As she slid a sideways look at her companion she doubted he shared her view of casual sex—he probably had a very high libido...

He turned his head and gave her a look of enquiry.

For a moment her brain refused to function, and the silence stretched uncomfortably.

'Where's the runway?' she finally blurted, hoping to give the impression she had been thinking hard about navigational problems and not his appetite for sex.

If he wondered why she was blushing, to her intense relief he didn't ask for enlightenment. 'Just there.'

Glad to be able to look at something that wasn't him, Molly followed the direction of his gaze to the same bumpy piece of ground she'd noticed before.

'You landed here?' she asked as she thought back to how he'd arrived at dinner last night. Her voice rose to an incredulous squeak as she added, 'In the dark?'

'Visibility was not good.'

A laugh was drawn from her throat—she had not appreciated until this moment what a master of understatement he was or how much he had played down the incident the previous evening.

She looked at the potholes in the optimistically named runway, holes that on closer inspection were more like craters, and gave a small shudder as she thought of him landing that small plane in the middle of a dust storm. He was either a very good pilot or very lucky.

Molly was sure that if she had been forced to endure similar circumstances she would be a gibbering wreck, but there had been nothing about him last night to suggest he had done anything out of the ordinary.

'There was very little option,' he told her wryly.

'For a man with nerves of steel maybe,' she said sarcastically. 'Hysterics would have worked a treat for me.'

'You don't strike me as the hysterical type.' He angled a narrow considering glance at her face. 'Hysterics require a loss of emotional control. A degree of spontaneity.'

Her firmly rounded jaw tightened in response to the cold disdain in his voice.

'And I think you're a teacher who likes to be in charge and call the shots.'

He said it without a trace of irony…it was staggering!

Her frown died as a gurgle of incredulous laughter escaped her.

'You find something amusing?'

She had seen a flash of wary caution in his eyes and was puzzled by it, but there was so much about this man that confused her that if she tried to work out what made him tick she could be here until the next century.

'You,' she admitted frankly.

The look of blank amazement her response elicited drew another gurgle of laughter from her and the dry suggestion from him she might like to elaborate.

She gave a shrug and thought it wasn't her problem if he didn't like what he heard. She had no doubt he wouldn't because, although he might be a bit unorthodox as Arab princes went, the bottom line was that he *was* an Arab prince and he took a certain amount of respect for granted.

'Me like control? This from someone who is probably the most domineering man on the planet!' And she'd only seen his royal persona. Goodness knew what he was like behind closed doors…closed bedroom doors…

She lowered her eyes to shut out the sight of his dark sardonic features and clicked her tongue pretending an amusement she was no longer feeling. 'As if you go with the flow?'

She lifted her eyes and was irrationally annoyed to see that he *was* looking amused. It goaded her on to add unwisely, 'I always think men like you are threatened by women who know their own minds.'

Looking at him through the mesh of her lashes, she saw he didn't appear very threatened, but neither was he looking pleased. She closed her mouth but almost immediately opened it again…the buzz, the adrenaline rush she got challenging him was exciting and addictive. Had she lost her mind?

'That's why they pick the ones who act as if everything they say is a pearl of wisdom.'

This went some way to explaining his hostility towards her—but she realised this theory only worked if she had come across as a woman who had a mind. The previous night she had barely said more than a few words and they were please and thank you.

She had actually acted pretty much like his perfect woman…minus the obligatory beauty. Now if she had looked like Bea…?

Well, she didn't, so she'd have to get used to it. 'At least I have a sense of humour.'

She wasn't aware that she had voiced this wistful observation out loud until Tair said, 'Tariq appears to find it one of your most attractive qualities.'

'Do you?' she blurted.

There was a long enough pause to allow Molly time to squirm and despairingly wonder why she kept saying cringing things like that.

When he finally responded there was no discernible expression on his dark, devastating features. 'No.'

It wasn't what he said or the way he said it—his voice was flat and devoid of emotion—it was where he was looking when he said it, her mouth, that made the pit of her stomach disintegrate and her temperature rise by several uncomfortable degrees.

After he delivered his flat, monosyllabic response he carried on staring. Trapped by the heat in his shimmering eyes, she stared back.

A pulse of hot liquid longing and then another and another thudded through her. She struggled with the reckless impulse to reach out and touch his lean face, to press her fingertip to the nerve that clenched spasmodically along the side of his chiselled jaw.

She lifted a hand, then, fingers clenched tight, she pressed it to her own throat. Growing dizzy, she struggled to draw adequate air into her lungs—they felt scorched by the heat that engulfed her.

Molly had no idea how long they stayed that way, but when he did speak she blinked like someone waking up. The question was what was she waking from—a nightmare or an erotic dream?

'Do you want to wait here or would you like to look around the plane?'

With a sigh she released her seat belt. 'I wouldn't mind stretching my legs.' A cold shower would have been better but she eagerly seized on the opportunity to not think about what had just happened. 'I suppose we should crack on.'

He looked at the nape of her neck and wondered how he had ever *not* seen past her disguise. He agreed in a colourless tone, 'By all means let us…*crack on.*'

It was predictably hot outside, but Tair appeared not to feel the heat as he led the way to his plane. Molly, trotting a few feet behind him, was uncomfortably conscious of the sweat breaking on her skin and by the time they got inside the plane everything was sticking in an unpleasant way.

Without a word Tair left her in the passenger section while he went towards the cockpit area, to retrieve whatever it was he had presumably taken the detour for.

'I'll just take a look around, shall I?' she called out. He ignored her. 'Rude rat,' she muttered, mentally conceding that he was a very sexy rude rat! She had never got the dark, smouldering, bad-boy thing before, but she was starting to see the appeal. Her eyes widened with horror at this realisation and she pressed her fist into her mouth to stop herself groaning out loud.

What was she doing?

Nothing, she hadn't done anything. *Yet*, said the voice in her head and she groaned again, pressing her arms to her stomach and rocking forward.

At the sound of the engine roaring into life she pulled upright and walked quickly towards the cockpit that was partitioned off from the rest of the plane by a curtain.

She pulled it back to reveal Tair sitting in the pilot's chair, clicking switches.

'I don't know if you've noticed,' she said, trying to sound casual, because she didn't want to come across as some sort of neurotic female, 'but we're moving.'

Not looking at her, he carried on clicking and consulting dials. 'Yes.'

'So is that normal?'

'When you're about to take off it is.'

'I thought for a second you said take off.'

He turned his head and flashed her a smile that sent a chill of apprehension through her. 'I did.'

She gave a shaky laugh. 'If you're trying to scare me, it worked.'

'Then I'm not trying, I'm succeeding.'

Molly gritted her teeth… Don't lose it, she told herself. 'Will you look at me?'

He did, but only for a split second. 'That might not be such a good idea just now.'

His sardonic tone brought a flush of anger to her pale face. 'What are you doing, Tair?'

'I could tell you but I think the technical detail might pass over your head.'

Molly felt as if her head were going to explode. 'It's insane, if you're doing what it looks like. Are you really…?'

'You should belt yourself in.'

Molly paled, her shaking hands reaching for the back of a seat as her mind started to spin. 'But surely you can stop it?' She felt stupid for asking, but she needed some reassurance and if he was coping with an emergency she probably ought not to ask such questions.

'I could,' he agreed. Molly barely had time to start relaxing when he flashed her a flat look and added after a pause. 'But I'm not going to.'

Presumably this was his idea of a joke. The alternative was not one she wanted to think about. She gave a laugh to show him he hadn't spooked her.

'And this is the moment I'm supposed to panic?' Pursing her lips, she shook her head slowly from side to side. 'Sorry, but I'm not falling for that one.'

He turned his head and looked at her just for a second, an arctic coldness in his azure eyes that appeared far too realistic to be part of any joke. His dark brows arched.

'Suit yourself.'

Molly's temper flared at the dismissal in his manner. 'Will you look at me when we're talking?' she yelled shrilly.

'You can talk, and you no doubt will—I've yet to meet a woman who understood the value of silence—but I'm busy flying a plane.'

She glared at the back of his neck in frustration. 'Will you stop saying that? You're *not* flying a plane!' The fear she was struggling to control sent her voice up a quivering octave.

'Well, if I'm not, who is? Sit down and belt yourself in. We're taking off. We can discuss this later.'

Molly abandoned reason. 'We can't…' She heard the throbbing note of rising panic in her voice and stopped to take a deep breath. 'Tair,' she said hoarsely. 'Please think for a moment about what you're doing.'

She had tried shrill demands and now she was resorting to husky seductiveness, Tair thought. He wondered if the husky little catch in her voice normally worked and decided if the damage it was doing to his concentration was any indicator it probably did.

'You're insane!'

Not that he looked it—in fact he was emanating a statuesque calm as he sat behind the control panel.

'I don't know why you're doing this. Maybe you have your reasons.' Most lunatics did. 'But it's nothing to do with me so why don't you stop the plane and let me off?' Preferably now before they were several thousand feet above the ground. The way the plane was picking up speed suggested that this moment was not far off.

He flashed her a contemptuous look. 'It has everything to do with you.'

'I don't know what you're talking about,' she said miserably. She shook her head slowly from side to side, baffled confusion in her pale face as she tensely grabbed hold of the back of his seat to steady herself and looked around the enclosed space like a hunted animal seeking an escape route.

'Look, nobody's going to hurt you.' While Tair was totally furious with her and felt nothing but utter contempt for her lack of morals and selfishness, he didn't get anything but an uneasy feeling from making a woman look petrified. 'Sit down, buckle up and shut up.'

Molly would have loved to tell him what he could do with his orders, but as the aircraft put on a final spurt of speed self-preservation seemed more of a priority.

Like an automaton she did what he had curtly ordered with the addition of closing her eyes.

'You can unfasten your seat belt now.'

Molly opened her eyes, but her white-knuckled fingers stayed tight around the metal clasp. They really were in the air!

'What are you doing?'

'Switching to autopilot.'

'No, I mean *what are you doing*?' Her voice rose to a shrill shriek.

'I would have thought that was obvious.'

Her mind still shied away from putting words to her situation. 'You're kidnapping me?' she said, hoping he'd laugh and say something cutting about how he could have any woman so why would he want to kidnap her.

He didn't laugh, he just said calmly, 'An emotive way of putting it, but I suppose essentially accurate. Though, like I said, you are not in danger. Nobody is going to harm you.'

'Are you mad?' A stupid question because if he was he would deny it. The mad people in films always thought they were sane.

'You can't go around kidnapping people.'

'I don't. This is a first.'

'I feel so special,' she inserted weakly. His mental health was no longer in question. 'Did you plan this or did you wake up this morning and think you might try abducting someone today?'

'As I said, you're not in any danger, so why not just sit back and enjoy the ride?'

Molly's chest swelled with indignation. 'Enjoy?' She took a deep breath and forced herself to smile, though the effect was slightly spoiled by the gold glow of fury in her eyes. 'Look, take me back and I won't say anything. I won't tell anyone,' she promised.

He looked at her with a chilling lack of emotion, and it was that that scared Molly more than anything yet.

'Do you dislike me so much?'

'This is not personal.' At least, it shouldn't be, thought Tair. But as an inherently honest person, he recognised the moment he spoke that this was not so—he had a personal reaction to everything this woman did, including when she stared at him with big reproachful eyes. 'I have no feelings one way or the other about you,' he added with a contemptuous sneer that said otherwise.

Molly lifted a hand to her head. 'This is surreal. It can't be happening.'

'As I said, you might as well relax and enjoy the ride.'

'I'm not going to enjoy anything. I hate you—you're…' She stopped, sucking in a steadying breath while forcing her stiff features into a smile of appeal. 'Look, just turn this thing around. You can't do this! What about Beatrice? What will she think when we don't turn up at the hospital?'

If they taught duplicity she would be a straight-A student. Tair considered himself a pretty good judge of character, but even when he looked in her eyes all he saw was genuine anxiety for a friend.

He saw different things when he looked at her mouth, so it was probably better not to go there, he thought. It was a pity his cousin had not displayed a similar amount of self-control where the Mouse's mouth was concerned, he reflected, his jaw hardening.

'I imagine that Beatrice will feel relief if she's got the faintest idea about what you're up to.'

'What are you talking about? Beatrice will be worried sick.'

He turned in his seat, his eyes like ice chips. 'Enough!'

Molly flinched at the staccato command and drew back in her own seat. His blazing blue eyes raked her face.

'You should know, Miss Mouse, that I have zero tolerance with liars and cheats, so no more of this nauseating pretence of concern.'

Molly shook her head in utter confusion.

Tair watched as she gave a brilliant performance of being scared and even though he knew it was fake he still felt like a total brute.

'Stop acting!'

'I'm not.'

His lips curled expressively. 'I doubt that a woman like you knows the meaning of the word care. How could you when you pretend to be Beatrice's friend and all the time you're seducing her husband?'

Her jaw dropped. 'I've never seduced anyone in my life. I wouldn't know where to begin.'

She forced her next words past the wild hysterical laugh that was locked in her throat. 'You think I'm having an affair with Tariq…?'

'There are others? You are a serial seductress?'

She ignored the acid insert and carried on staring at him blankly. She wiped the moisture from her eyes, the tears having been an emotional release of a sort—at last she finally knew what this was about. 'You have no idea.'

She had no idea how badly he wanted to cover her mouth with his, Tair thought, or she might not look so relaxed.

'Is anything about you the real thing?' His lip curled in disgust. 'There's nothing about you to alarm a wife, is there, with your meek mouse look and the ridiculous glasses you don't need?'

Molly wiped away the tears from her cheeks and hastened to set the record straight. 'I can't help my face and there's nothing sinister about my glasses. They're just…I wanted to look older and it got to be a habit…'

Her voice trailed away as she recognised that even to her ears this explanation sounded weak. So much for honesty being the best policy!

Her present predicament was a perfect example of how in the real world a lie frequently sounded more credible than the truth. Laughter would be the most likely response she'd get if she went around telling her family and friends an Arab prince had kidnapped her because he thought she was some sort of… How on earth *had* he decided she was some sort of *femme fatale*?

'I'm flattered you think I'm so irresistible, but—'

'I am not such an easy mark as my cousin, Miss Mouse.' His voice dropped to a nerve-tingling purr as he added softly, 'I prefer to be the hunter and not the hunted.'

Looking at his dark, proud, predatory features, Molly did not find this statement hard to believe. 'That was a joke,' she said hoarsely. 'This isn't what you think…'

A look of bored irritation, slightly marred by the nerve that clenched and unclenched in his lean cheek, settled on his handsome face. 'Before you launch into an impassioned and lengthy speech of denial, let me explain that I saw Tariq coming out of your room last night.'

'Last night…' Her eyes widened. 'Oh, last night, but that was…' She stopped, her soft features stretching into a grimace as she recalled her promise to Tariq.

'Perfectly innocent?'

The sarcasm brought an angry tide of colour to her cheeks. 'As a matter of fact it was.'

'The sad thing is that Beatrice is probably trying to tell herself the same thing.'

Molly's eyes locked with his contemptuous gaze as she struggled to follow. 'Should I understand what you're trying to say?' It seemed safe to assume there was an insult in there somewhere.

If she had shown a flicker of remorse and not maintained this ridiculous denial he might have felt more inclined to show some tolerance. Weakness was forgivable, but her calculated selfish attitude was not.

'If you had an ounce of empathy you might. But you are clearly incapable of putting yourself in anyone's skin but your own.' As his scornful gaze drifted down the pale column of her throat he was forced to concede that it was pretty perfect skin, pale and flawless with a glow he might have imagined was an outward sign of inner radiance had he not known what a selfish little cheat she actually was.

'Whereas you are totally able to identify with a wronged wife? Or is it just Bea that has a special place in your heart?'

He sucked in an angry breath through flared nostrils. 'Be very careful what you say, Miss Mouse.'

Molly tossed her head, but beneath her defiance she was actually nervous. Tair Al Sharif was a dangerous man and she was making him very angry. The problem was she couldn't seem to stop herself.

After a lifetime of caution and prudence she was suddenly acting with a reckless lack of restraint and a part of her was actually enjoying it! It was almost liberating, she thought, before also thinking that she must be deeply twisted to feel that way.

'Well, you do seem very concerned about Beatrice.' She hoped that he couldn't hear the undercurrent of unattractive jealousy that made her inwardly wince. 'Maybe,' she speculated, 'you're projecting your guilt onto me because you think I'm doing what you'd secretly like to. Or maybe you're a hypocrite and have already done it?'

She knew she'd gone too far the moment the provocative jibe left her lips, but, unable to back down, she lifted her chin and watched the dull colour run up under his golden skin.

If someone had offered her a million pounds to take her eyes off his face it wouldn't have made any difference—there was something totally compelling about the fury etched in the powerful lines and sharp angles of his overwhelmingly masculine features.

Her defiant façade wobbled as his anger hit her like a solid wall. She swallowed as she lifted a shaking hand to her throat, where a pulse ticked like a time bomb.

'Is someone flying this plane?' she asked, hoping to divert him. 'I suppose,' she added nervously, 'that you can multitask.' As in throttle her while flying a small plane across the desert.

'I would *never* creep around and have some sordid affair!' He didn't raise his voice but Tair managed to pack enough menace in his soft words to scare the life out of anyone with an ounce of self-preservation. 'Do not judge others by your own gutter standards.'

His contempt caught Molly on the raw. How dared he take the high moral ground? She was pretty sure he had more skeletons in his cupboard than she did—she didn't have any, which made her incredibly boring.

In some ways, she mused, it was almost better to be thought a bitch than boring.

'Have I got this right?' she said, adopting an expression of exaggerated bemusement. 'It's not that you wouldn't like to have an affair, it's just that you're too pure, too good to have an affair?'

'I do not pretend to be a saint—'

With a mouth like his—a mouth that invited sinful thoughts—it would have been pretty pointless, she thought, her eyes lingering on the firm sensual curve.

'I would never have an affair,' he repeated in a goaded voice. 'Because I saw firsthand what my father's affairs did to my mother. He never tried to hide them, he actually seemed to take a malicious pleasure in humiliating her, parading his women in front of her. She was a proud woman but he wore away her spirit and her pride.'

Tair thought how his mother would be little more than a memory to him had it not been for the diaries her maid had given him when he was sixteen. Those diaries had provided some insight into how a woman who was humiliated by her husband's repeated infidelities might feel.

Tair Al Sharif was the last man on the planet Molly had ever expected to feel any empathy for, but as she watched him close his eyes and drag a hand through his dark hair her heart ached for him.

To watch one parent do that to another and be unable to do a thing but stand and watch must be terrible for any

child. The king sounded like a vile man. He might not
have actually raised his hand to his wife, but his actions
were another equally damaging form of abuse.

Molly voiced her next thought without realising. 'He
must have loved her once.' Although she couldn't understand how anyone could do that to another person, let alone
someone they had ever cared for.

At the sound of her voice Tair's head lifted and he
looked straight into amber eyes glowing with the compassion he'd accused her of not possessing.

He bit back a curse. He had broken the habit of a
lifetime by allowing her to goad him into justifying
himself and as a direct result he had got sucked into a
conversation that touched on deeply personal issues.
Issues he would not have chosen to discuss with his
closest friends.

'It was my father's second marriage, a political arrangement not a love match.'

He spoke in a manner designed to close the subject and
make it quite clear he didn't require her understanding.

Any more than he required Molly James's good opinion.

'To force someone into a loveless marriage is so callous
and cruel!' she exclaimed.

Clearly she had not received the message.

'Possibly,' he conceded in his most chilling voice. 'But,
please, no more of the slushy sentimentality. I have a
weak stomach.'

And, it would seem, an allergy to sympathy. She had
never seen him look so uncomfortable. He obviously didn't
want anyone to suspect he had any weak spots.

'Relax,' she drawled.

He shook his head in irritated incomprehension. 'I beg
your pardon?'

'I'm not going to feel sorry for you—if it makes you feel any better I still can't stand the sight of you!'

It might have been her imagination but the glimmer in his eyes might have been humour. 'Or I you.'

'And I'm allowed an opinion.'

His brows lifted. 'One?'

'I still think arranged marriages are totally wrong.'

'Not all arranged marriages are unhappy and there is no force involved in such arrangements. Many arranged marriages are successful. Sometimes they are necessary. A person cannot always put their happiness ahead of their duty.'

She not only didn't look convinced, she looked appalled. Her eyes suddenly widened. 'Would you…?'

'I am the heir, and political alliances are important.' He consulted the dials, made a quick mental calculation and nodded before turning back to her.

'But surely seeing how unhappy a marriage like that made your mother…'

'Many love matches do not end in undiluted joy… Tariq professed to love Beatrice.'

A flash of anger lit Molly's eyes. 'You're not comparing Tariq with someone like your father?'

'No, I'm not, but you're a lot more dangerous, Miss Mouse, than my father's mistresses.'

The novelty of being called dangerous momentarily robbed her of speech.

'With them what you saw was what you got. They were not exactly subtle.' His lips thinned with contempt. 'You're insidious, you creep up on a man and because you seem so benign and harmless there are no alarm bells, a man doesn't realise you've crept under his skin and your voice has seeped into his bloodstream until it's happened.' He reached out and touched a strand of the shiny hair that had escaped its confinement. 'There's something about you that takes a man over the edge.'

Her insides trembled as his fingertips grazed her cheek before his hand fell away. His shoulders lifted in a fluid shrug while his eyes drifted across her flushed features. 'With temptation out of the way—' his eyes slid to her mouth and he thought how that sort of temptation did not come more appealingly packaged '—I don't think it will take Tariq long to remember where his loyalties lie. For him to realise that Beatrice is worth ten of a woman like you!'

CHAPTER FIVE

It was so mind-bogglingly weird to have a man who looked like Tair talking as though she were some sort of sexy siren that if Molly hadn't been so furious she might have been flattered.

'Temptresses don't wear B-cup bras.'

His blue gaze fell to her chest and stayed there.

Painfully conscious of her tingling nipples, she clenched her fists to stop herself covering them. 'And if,' she continued hoarsely, 'I *was* having an affair…'

This brought his eyes upwards and she saw there was a cynical gleam in his sky-blue beautiful gaze. 'So you admit it.'

She ground her teeth. 'I've never been a swearing sort of person but I'm starting to feel I could learn fast. How can I spell it out so that even you can understand? I am not having an affair with anyone.

'But,' she added, miming a zipping motion across her lips to forestall the inevitable sarcastic intervention from him. She was guessing from the look of sheer stunned incredulity on his hatefully perfect face that he didn't get told to shut up even in sign language very often.

'Even if I was, what gives you the right to interfere in

other people's lives?' Given the fact she was going to have to break her promise to Tariq, because nothing but the truth was going to stop this man going through with his crazy plan, she felt she had the right to demand a few explanations from Tair Al Sharif first!

She gritted her teeth, resenting the fact that she was left with little choice but to expose her connection with the Al Kamal Royal household. She watched as he fixed her with a contemptuous stare.

It was so unfair, she thought, eying him with simmering resentment. The man couldn't look anything less than incredible even if he tried. His hair probably looked sexily rumpled when he woke in the morning. Her eyes narrowed as the mental picture of him in bed first thing grew in her head. The dark shadow on his jaw…the sleepy sex look in his heavy-lidded eyes…?

She stopped and moved her hand in a sweeping motion in front of her face in an effort to make the image disappear. It could not be healthy or wise to spend time wondering about how a man who had just kidnapped her would look after a night of passion. This was something someone who had just been kidnapped should definitely not want to know. Though this didn't seem to stop her eyes from being drawn to the firm contours of his sculpted lips and a little shiver shimmying up her spine as she considered how he would hardly be a low-maintenance lover.

As if she knew much about lovers.

She ignored the voice in her head and the little bubble of excitement that exploded in her belly like a hot star-burst as Tair answered her question.

'You mean I should cross to the metaphorical other side of the street and watch my friends' marriage destroyed?

Which wouldn't, if last night was anything to go by, be very long. How long do you think it would have been before people caught on? I mean, you were hardly very discreet—all those yearning looks and meaningful glances across the table.'

'Not everyone has a mind like a sewer. This is so stupid!' she wailed. 'Why couldn't you just have minded your own business? But I forgot—everything *is* your business,' she added bitterly.

Her insults slid off him like water off a duck's back.

Molly sucked in an angry breath through flared nostrils and glared at the back of his neck. 'Will you look at me when I'm talking to you? Not only are you a control freak, you're a control freak with no manners.'

'You can have manners or you can arrive alive—take your pick. There is some turbulence ahead that requires my attention.' As if to back up this point the small plane took a sudden unscheduled drop. 'Fasten your seat belt.'

Molly was already buckling up.

The pocket of turbulence lasted another few minutes, but it seemed longer to Molly, who was not a good flyer at the best of times.

She expelled a long shaky sigh when Tair removed his brown fingers from the controls and struggled to match his nonchalant attitude to the white-knuckle ride they had just endured.

'You were saying?' He did not pause to allow her to respond but added, 'Let me help you—you were explaining that I am a control freak with no manners. You might incidentally like to keep such opinions to yourself when we are not alone as it is not exactly customary to speak to me this way.'

'You think you're so clever, don't you? If you were half

as omnipotent as you like to think…' She squeezed her eyes tight shut and *just* managed to stop herself blurting out the truth. She wanted to choose her moment and watch this man's ego deflate when he realised his mistake.

'Your arrogance really is off the scale, you know. How would you like it if Tariq interfered in your love affairs?'

He wouldn't like it all, but to Tair's way of thinking that was not the point.

'I interfere because I can and because seeing them together gives hope to the rest of us…' He stopped, perturbed that he had allowed her to goad him into the admission, an admission he had not previously acknowledged even to himself.

The utterly unexpected response made Molly, who was mentally rehearsing her speech about how Tariq and Khalid were her half-brothers, lose her thread. 'You envy what they have?'

Envy implied he wanted what they had, and he was the last person in the world who she would have thought craved love and babies.

'There is very little point envying what you cannot have.'

She struggled to hide her curiosity and failed. 'Why can't you have it?'

His eyes narrowed. 'Why can't you stop talking?' he cut back sharply. He did not care for Miss Mouse applying her amateur psychology to him.

'Possibly it is a reaction to being kidnapped. You haven't thought this through. What do you think's going to happen? I can't just vanish off the face of the earth?'

He gave a scornful snort. 'You are so important?'

'Not like you maybe,' she snapped sarcastically. 'People don't bow to my every wish, but I hope you realise they do that out of fear, not respect.'

'Actually it is tradition.' It was a tradition he would happily have consigned to history, but such changes were not brought about overnight.

Her expression showed what she thought of tradition, but, in case he didn't get the message, she added with a sneer, 'I'd *die* before I bow to you!'

He threw back his head and laughed. The deep, uninhibited sound was attractive. Unlike his personality, she muttered under her breath.

'Bowing is not essential to my plan. You really do have a turn for the dramatic. That is something I had not anticipated,' he admitted, his glance moving from her sparkling eyes and flushed cheeks to her heaving bosom. Neither had he anticipated feeling attracted to her this way.

Her cheeks flamed. 'You think *that's* dramatic,' she said, tossing her head and waving her finger at him.

He pursed his lips and let out a silent whistle. 'My, you do have a temper.'

'It's not the only thing I have. I have people who care about me,' she told him in a voice that shook. 'My half-brothers…actually, you know—' She stopped abruptly mid-tirade and gasped. 'Oh, my God!'

Tair watched as the colour drained from her skin, leaving her paper-pale.

'Dad,' she whispered in a stricken voice, her eyes widening in horror.

'Your father?'

She nodded. 'My dad has a heart condition. He's waiting for bypass surgery—if he finds out I've gone missing it will kill him.'

'Of course it will.'

She looked at him in total disgust. 'You callous bastard!'

He gave a fluid shrug. 'Possibly, but not a gullible one,

though I have to admit you are good. Have you thought about writing fiction?'

'But it's true!' she protested, tears of frustration standing out in her eyes as she struggled to convince him of her sincerity.

'Dad had his first heart attack when he was forty! Then last week—' She stopped and gulped as the memory of that phone conversation the previous week came rushing back.

A conversation that had begun with the words 'Don't panic but' had never been one she was going to enjoy.

She hadn't.

Molly had listened with a knot of apprehension like a boulder lodged behind her breastbone as her dad had explained that he'd had a few twinges recently.

'Define twinges or, better still, get the doctor to define them. You have to promise me to make an appointment right now.'

'No need. Actually I was out cycling the tow-path the other day and I had a slightly bigger twinge and a chap passing by called an ambulance.'

'You mean you had a heart attack.' By this point Molly was already mentally booking her flight home.

'Not a heart attack, just angina.'

'Just angina?' she echoed, wanting to scream with sheer frustration. 'Oh, well, that's all right, then.'

His sigh vibrated gently down the line. 'I told your sisters you'd react this way but they made me ring you.'

'I'm coming home right now.'

'Look, Molly, there is absolutely no point you coming home now. They won't be doing the bypass until next month or most probably the month after—the waiting list is huge.'

Molly, who had been pacing the room, sat down with a bump. 'You need a bypass?'

'Didn't I say?'

'Well, heart surgery is something that could slip a person's mind, isn't it, Dad?' she said bitterly. 'You're impossible!' And the possibility of not having her impossible parent around to drive her crazy filled her with gut-churning terror. 'I'm coming home.'

'The doctors have told me to avoid stress and if you come home now because of me I'm going to feel stressed.'

Molly hadn't been convinced by this argument, but after she had spoken to her sisters she had realised there was a grain of truth in it. Now she knew it was the biggest mistake of her life. If she had gone home when she should have she wouldn't now be in a plane with a certifiable lunatic.

She took a deep breath and reached out, her fingers curling around Tair's forearm as she levelled her gaze with his. 'Look,' she said, pointing at her face. 'Do I look as though I'm lying?'

He looked bored and said, 'This is old ground.'

'You don't understand. If my father hears about this…' She clamped her quivering lips tight as she added in a fearful whisper, 'It will kill him. He needs heart surgery, you see—he's not supposed to be stressed.'

'That is very inventive.'

Her fists balled in frustration. 'It's not an invention, it's the truth.'

His lip curled. 'Do I look like a gullible idiot?'

'Look…I'm wasting my breath, aren't I?' She fixed him with a glare of sheer loathing as she added, 'If anything happens to my father you'll be responsible and I'll make you pay if it's the last thing I do.'

She turned her head sharply so that he couldn't see the tears that welled up in her eyes, and she missed the flash of uncertainty in his face.

'There are not going to be any alarm bells ringing to alert your father. You haven't vanished. Being a considerate friend you have decided not to impose on Beatrice's hospitality at a moment that is essentially a family time. You left a note.'

Molly closed her eyes. She could only imagine Tariq's face when he read that note. A laugh escaped her dry lips.

'You're not going to have hysterics again, are you?'

Molly just stared. 'Won't they think it odd that I didn't write personally?'

'You're avoiding an embarrassing scene.'

'But why in this alternative universe am I embarrassed?'

'You have accepted an invitation from a man you have just met…' He stopped as the gulping sound of a strangled sob escaped her throat.

He looked at the tears sliding down her cheeks and was irritated to feel an irrational stab of guilt. This woman is a born manipulator, he reminded himself.

'Do you actually have a father?' he wondered harshly.

'I do and I also have brothers…Tariq…'

'Is your brother, I suppose?' he drawled.

Molly's shoulders relaxed. 'Yes…but it isn't public knowledge and I'd prefer it stayed that way.'

'I imagine you would.' He smirked as he scanned her face. 'I'm disappointed,' he admitted.

'Disappointed?' she echoed, wishing she'd come clean straight off and avoided this journey. 'Don't worry, I won't start some sort of diplomatic incident by telling everyone about this.'

'Disappointed,' he corrected, 'because I had thought your powers of invention were limitless, but apparently not. Let me offer you a word of advice. The thing about lies is that one needs to keep them this side of reality. The "seriously ill father" story was far more convincing.'

Her horrified eyes flew to his face. He thought she was lying.

'*He is!*' Even as she spoke she knew that there was not a chance in hell of convincing him. It was all about timing and hers stunk!

She shook her head and narrowed her eyes. 'Tariq is my brother and he will come looking for me…and then you'll be sorry,' she promised, sheer will-power holding back the tears that threatened to fall from her glistening eyes.

His lip curled. 'I think you overestimate your value to Tariq. As far as he is concerned you got a better offer and are with me.'

'He will come,' she said, fixing him a glare of complete loathing.

'I can't decide if you actually imagine you're in love with Tariq or if it was a harmless flirtation that went too far, and quite frankly your motivation doesn't interest me.'

Despite this declaration of disinterest he immediately began to speculate. 'Is this pay-back time for all the years you must have stood in Beatrice's shadow? It must have been frustrating—with Beatrice around nobody was going to look at you, were they?' His burning blue eyes slid with dismissive contempt over her slender body.

'Who could blame you,' he continued, 'for being tempted when the opportunity arose? Someone was looking at you, not Beatrice.'

'You seem to be managing it.'

The observation brought a flash of anger to his lean face. 'Did it not even occur to you that you were hurting people?'

'Did it occur to you that you're wrong?'

CHAPTER SIX

'SILLY question, of course it didn't. But you are wrong about everything. Tariq will come and when he does you won't look so smug and self-satisfied.'

It was hard to tell how long the uneasy, hostile silence had lasted before Tair finally raised his voice and called out.

'Fasten your belt—we're going to land.'

Molly, who had taken a seat in the rear of the plane as far away from him as possible, did as he requested. Rebellion for rebellion's sake was not going to achieve anything. She had to plan her strategy and in the meantime she could only hope that her brothers would have the sense to shelter her dad from the truth for as long as possible.

'It might be a little rough.'

Molly considered this an understatement, but when she looked out of the window and saw where they had landed she was amazed that they were still in one piece.

It was, quite literally, the middle of nowhere.

Her plans of being noisy and hoping someone would rescue her disintegrated. He sauntered down the plane looking so relaxed that she felt like screaming in frustration.

She resisted the temptation, realising her best bet was

to lull him into a false sense of security by letting him think he was in charge, and that she was beaten.

He's not? You're not? she wondered.

'Right, I am glad you are being sensible.'

Carry on believing that, you rat, she thought, catching the piece of white garment he threw at her.

'Put it on.'

Without waiting to see if she did, obviously taking obedience as a given, he turned and walked back to the cockpit. When he returned a short time later his hair was concealed in a traditional white desert headdress, and Molly felt a quiver run down her spine. The covering emphasised the perfect bone structure and hard sculpted contours of his sternly beautiful face.

It also revealed the primitive quality that she found disturbingly compelling. The veneer of civilisation he cloaked himself in was paper-thin as he looked at her.

'Are you ready?'

Tair watched as she removed her hands from the armrests without saying a word. Fingers stiff, she unfastened the clasp of her belt and got to her feet.

Though she purposefully did not look at him, Molly was very conscious of his brooding presence towering over her. She lifted her lashes and when she saw his face again she lost her balance. As she took a staggering step back he reached out and grabbed her while saying something harsh-sounding in his own tongue.

A second later the breath left her lungs in a soft whoosh as she was brought into direct contact with the iron-hard surface of his chest.

'Are you all right?' he asked again.

Molly struggled to catch her breath and fought even

harder against the paralysis that caused her to lean into him, not because she had to, but because she wanted to.

Now that was scary!

One of his arms was wrapped around her ribs, but not so tightly as to confine her. It was her own starved senses that held her there as she drank in the male fragrance of his warm body.

Taking a deep breath, she managed to gain enough control to push away. His hands went to her shoulders and stayed there.

'Are you sure you're all right?' he asked again.

Molly nodded, feeling uncomfortably exposed as his blue eyes scanned her face. Glaring up at him, she breathed hard to drag air into her lungs.

'Let me tell you what will happen next.'

'I already know what will happen next,' she snapped, twisting away from him. The sound of his grunt of pain as her wild kick made contact with the most vulnerable part of his anatomy, delivered more by luck than skill, gave her a surge of satisfaction as, yelling at the top of her lungs, she flung herself towards the door.

She had not reached the opening before a hand looped around her waist. Her feet left the floor as she was pulled back against his hard physique. An adrenaline rush gave her strength and fear fuelled her desperation as she flailed out at him, her fists hammering into his chest. She was literally sobbing in frustration as he restrained her with insulting ease.

'Let me go, you… Help!'

'Nobody can hear you.' Through her pants of exertion his voice sounded calm. 'I don't want to hurt you, but that doesn't mean I won't.'

'My,' she sneered. 'Aren't you the big man?'

'Aren't you the little wild cat?' he countered, looking at

her with an expression that made her stomach flip. The fight drained out of her quite abruptly and if he hadn't been holding her she would have slid to the floor. 'Do not waste your energy.'

What energy? she thought, suddenly feeling as weak as a kitten and a harsh word away from humiliating tears.

'There is no one to hear you and nowhere to run. Do you understand?'

She nodded and he released her. Molly pushed a hank of hair from her face with her forearm—the last of her hair pins had been lost some time earlier—and fixed him with a steady unblinking regard.

'I hate you,' she announced shakily but with conviction, her golden eyes filled with loathing.

'I'm not exactly a fan of yours either. You kick like a mule. Remind me not to leave any sharp implements around.'

He picked up the white cotton garment from the floor. 'Now put it on.'

His lips tightened as she shook her head. 'It's just the sort of thing you like—baggy and shapeless. It will also protect you from the sun; it's another two hours before dusk.'

'Where are you taking me?'

'Somewhere where you can't do any harm,' he said, and then, because he could see the next question and didn't want to hear her voice again, added, 'My grandfather has an encampment a few kilometres from here.'

She sniffed and tossed her head, starting off a rippling motion in her loose hair before it settled straight and smooth down her back. 'So this abduction is a family business, is it? Your grandfather must be so proud of you.'

Tair watched her hair and thought about how it would feel brushing against his skin. Not that he intended finding out, but a man couldn't help but wonder.

'My grandfather won't be there.' His lips curved into an ironic smile as he imagined his grandfather's response to him turning up with a golden-eyed captive in tow. Explosive would hardly cover it!

His smile faded abruptly. His grandfather's reaction would not be any stronger than the desire that had exploded inside him when he had held Molly's soft and trembling body in his arms. He had wanted to both comfort her and taste her—neither of which were appropriate responses.

'He is attending a gathering…a race meeting.'

'Horse racing in the desert?'

'Camel.'

'You race camels?'

'It is tradition. The location varies but there is a large gathering every year.'

'And when you don't turn up?'

'I will.' He would regain a little perspective once there was a safe distance between them.

Molly couldn't hide her surprise—although shouldn't it be relief? 'So you're not staying with me.'

One corner of his mouth lifted in a taunting smile. 'Will you miss me?'

The hot colour flew to her cheeks. 'About as much as the flu.'

He laughed. 'Come on—your carriage awaits.'

Only it wasn't a carriage.

A few minutes later she stood looking at two camels, shaking her head. 'You have to be joking?'

He didn't respond, though he did crack a grin once or twice when she was attempting to get onto her camel with the assistance of one of the two men who had met them.

'This animal smells disgusting.'

'He probably thinks the same about you,' he retorted,

thinking not for the first time about the scent that clung to her hair.

She folded her arms and shook her head. 'I can't.'

'Show a bit of backbone. It's just like sitting in an armchair.'

'Show a bit of backbone?' she repeated, her voice rising an indignant octave. 'I'd like to see how much backbone you'd be showing if the roles were reversed. I've been kidnapped, verbally abused, starved and now you expect me to ride a damn camel. Well, enough is enough!' she said, sinking to the floor and proceeding to sit cross-legged.

The two men looked to Tair, who said something in Arabic that made them smile.

'What did you say to them about me?'

'I said that normally you have the sweet nature of a dove, but you're having a bad day.'

She threw him an acid look, then let out a shriek when one of the men picked her up, put her on the camel, then urged the animal forward.

'You're doing very well.'

'Save your words of encouragement. If I fall off and break my neck you'll have it on your conscience for ever.'

'You won't fall off—you're a natural.'

She grunted something indistinct and slung him a murderous glare. He grinned and urged his own mount ahead, leaving her precious little choice but to follow. She didn't know where they were or where they were going to. All around was an undulating vast expanse of nothingness.

Either the camels knew their way home or Tair was one of those people who possessed an inbuilt compass.

It was dusk when they reached the top of a rise and saw the encampment spread below them.

Molly caught her breath—it was amazing!

The clusters of tents were pitched around what must be an area that possessed a natural water supply, because as well as the palm trees swaying overhead she could hear the faint but distinctive sound of falling water above the buzz of people moving about their business. Fires had been lit, sending sparks into the velvet smoke-filled evening air.

Despite the fact she was hot, tired, uncomfortable and mad as hell, Molly was enchanted by the scene.

'It's beautiful.' Aware of Tair's eyes on her face, she added tetchily, 'I don't suppose anyone here is going to help me if I tell them you've kidnapped me?'

'Are you sure you want them to listen?'

Molly's cheeks scored with angry colour as she turned her head and nearly lost her balance in the process. 'Are you suggesting that I like being forced to endure your company and your insults just because you have a pretty face?'

She knew straight away that her words were a mistake and the speculative gleam that entered his eyes confirmed this.

'I wasn't thinking of my face particularly, I've never been called pretty before, but I'm naturally relieved that it meets with your approval, Miss Mouse.'

Molly gritted her teeth and refused to respond to the taunt.

'I was thinking that if I didn't know better...' His dark head, tilted a little to one side, subjected her face to a narrowed-eyed scrutiny until Molly could bear it no longer and snapped.

'If you didn't know better what?'

'If I didn't know better I'd say that you were enjoying your adventure.'

Her rebuttal to this crazy contention was instant and robust. 'And if you did say that I'd say you were insane.'

Tair didn't respond, but instead gave a shrug and tapped her mount sharply on the rump to get it moving.

What did he think she was? she wondered as she watched him ride ahead. Some sort of adrenaline junkie? Adventure indeed!

She loosed a scornful laugh at the notion. All the same there had been a few moments…

Moments of what, Molly—terror?

Dismissing the creeping doubts in her head, she clung on as her mount surged forwards, responding perhaps to the noise of greeting as Tair reached the camp.

It quickly became clear that they were expected. She watched from a distance as people gathered around Tair, their attitude welcoming but respectful.

She closed her eyes and held tight as her camel responded to a command from someone and lurched to the ground for her to dismount.

As Molly turned her head to thank the man who helped her extricate her stiff and aching body from the saddle her face dropped.

Unless it was his twin, it was the same man who had helped her into the saddle two hours earlier…two sweltering, gruelling and bottom-numbing hours earlier. Molly suspected that shortly she would be wishing she were still numb.

The next thing she saw was a four-wheel drive, solidifying her horrid suspicion. Tair was an utterly awful man. Picking up the overlong skirts of the white desert dress she wore, she stalked towards the distinctive tall figure of her persecutor.

'You did that on purpose, didn't you?' Voice quivering with outrage, she stabbed an accusing finger in Tair's direction. 'And don't,' she warned darkly, 'tell me you don't know what I'm talking about.'

She was vaguely conscious of the buzz of noise dying away, of people staring and parting like the sea as she took several more slightly unsteady steps towards Tair, who didn't even have the decency to show a scrap of remorse.

'They, those men…'

He folded his arms across his chest and inserted help-fully. 'Ahmed and Samir.'

Her teeth clenched. 'Ahmed and Samir travelled here in that car, and we could have too.'

He did not deny it and his provocative smile threw fuel on Molly's smouldering temper.

'But then you would have missed out on an experience that so few have firsthand.'

'For the very good reason that as a mode of transport those camels leave a lot to be desired.' She rubbed her bottom with feeling. 'They are in fact vile, smelly beasts, though not,' she added with another vicious jab in his di-rection, 'as vile as you!'

Her glance slid towards the dusty vehicle and her ex-pression grew wistful. 'I bet it's air-conditioned too. I probably have prickly heat.' She passed a hand across the overheated skin of her face and her fingers came away covered in grit and dust.

'I suppose this is your warped idea of getting back at me for my imaginary sins?' Thinking how she was taking the punishment without having enjoyed the pleasure.

The humour died from his face as his lips thinned into a contemptuous line. 'This is mild compared with what some of my ancestors' ideas of punishment would be for a woman like you.'

'You know nothing about women like me because when women like me see someone who shares your gene pool coming their way they cross the road. My God, when you topple off your high tower of comfortable smug superiority I really want to be there to see it.'

Right now she wasn't seeing anything much. The rash of red dots that had started dancing across her vision midway through her tirade of abuse had been replaced by a blackness that was closing in like a blanket.

She could see Tair, stern and contemptuous and so beautiful part of her wanted to weep; she could see his lips moving but she couldn't hear what he was saying. The only thing Molly could hear was a loud whooshing noise like a train in a tunnel.

The last she knew was that the floor was coming up to meet her very fast.

CHAPTER SEVEN

MOLLY opened her eyes and blinked in a dazed fashion. She was in a room with a high ceiling that appeared to be made of billowing silk. It was really very pretty.

She inhaled and her nostrils twitched. The air was filled with a faint spicy scent, an elusive mixture of incense and cinnamon. She turned her head towards the light breeze that made the glass lanterns hanging above her sway slightly, but could not see beyond the carved screen that stood there, filled with sconces that held flickering candles.

'You're awake.'

Oh, God!

She closed her eyes again and grunted. 'I wish I wasn't.' Suddenly it all came flooding back, the events of the last twelve hours.

She stared at her bare feet protruding from beneath a thin sheet that was covering her and didn't connect the groan she heard with herself. She wriggled her toes. Someone had taken off her shoes before placing her on what seemed to be a low divan.

'My head hurts.' Molly narrowed her eyes against the light from the overhead lanterns, which was being reflected in the surface of a large ornate mirror to her right. As was her face. She looked like a ghost, almost as pale as the compress laid across her forehead.

She removed it and let it fall to the ground from lax fingers.

The memory of how close she had been to hitting the hard ground head first before he'd caught her flashed vividly into Tair's mind, and his jaw tightened.

'That's because you're an idiot.'

An idiot, but also a woman.

A woman who had endured a day that would have physically and mentally taxed many men.

There had been a moment when he had held her seemingly lifeless body in his arms that he had thought… He swallowed as he pushed aside that memory.

He could rationalise his actions, but he knew that nothing she had done made him any less culpable for her collapse. He had been too full of self-righteous, crusading anger to take any account of her physical fragility when he had forced her to trek across the desert.

'Don't hold back, just tell it the way it is,' Molly drawled, raising herself on one elbow and squinting up at Tair, who had moved into her line of vision and was standing by her bed.

Her eyes had to go a long way up to reach his face.

Her stomach flipped. It was not the prince with the urbane charm and diplomatic manners and designer suit who stood there.

This man had a combustible edgy quality, as if, she mused, studying his strongly carved bronzed features, he was able to shed the thin veneer of civilisation in these surroundings and be himself.

'So this is my fault. Why am I not surprised?' she croaked… God, but her throat hurt, and why couldn't she stop staring like a kid pressing her nose against a sweet-shop window? 'I'm always amazed,' she said bitterly, 'at your ability to turn things around so that it's down to me that you're a total bastard with a vicious streak.'

Tair said something low and angry-sounding in his own language, then dragged a hand through his jet-black hair. 'I am aware that I am responsible.'

Molly grew wary as there was nothing to read in his stiff expression. He was admitting responsibility but not, as far as she could tell, any remorse.

'So you're going to let me go back home?'

'We will discuss that tomorrow.'

'You're just saying that to shut me up.'

'If I wanted to shut you up there are much more efficient ways I could do so!'

'I can imagine.'

Actually he doubted she could, but Tair was actively imagining ways in which her voice would be effectively stifled.

Even Miss Mouse might find it hard to talk when she was being kissed... He stared at her mouth and thought about how she would taste, the warmth of her lips and the sweet moisture of her mouth.

'Why are you staring at me like that?'

Tair gave himself a mental jolt and smoothly picked up the thread, saying, 'You want to discuss this? Fine—let's discuss how I repeatedly told you to take on fluids during the ride and you chose not to. You were dehydrated—that's why you passed out.'

Molly looked at him, wondering about the emotion she had briefly glimpsed on his face. But now he was looking at her through the screen of his dark lashes that were so long they brushed the slashing angle of his razor-edged cheekbones and she couldn't decide if she had imagined it or not.

'I never faint.'

There were big shadows under her eyes, she was the colour of paper and, having suffered the after-effects of dehydration himself, he knew she must be feeling like hell, but still she came out fighting.

He wondered that he had ever thought her mousy and timid.

'And I never look after stupid, half-dead women, but there is a first time for everything.'

She looked at the glass he held out to her and shook her head. 'I'm not thirsty.'

He moved impatiently, causing the ice to clink against the sides. 'Do I look like I care?'

She accepted the invitation to study his face. He didn't appear to care one bit, but he did look like someone capable of pouring the contents of the glass down her throat if she didn't co-operate.

He also looked everything a woman could wish for in her wildest dreams. Lean, dark and brooding with an edge of danger. Normally Molly's dreams were much more sedate but as she gazed at him her heartbeat did quicken perceptibly as the silence stretched.

'Fine!' With an ungracious sniff she snatched the glass from his hand and lifted it to her lips.

'All of it.'

Molly narrowed her eyes. 'I…'

He silenced her with a look and, sighing, she did as he requested. 'Satisfied?' she asked, flopping back on the pillows. Her head was pounding. So was her heart, but, she recognised, not necessarily from the same cause.

'Not really. I hate stupidity, so why did you tell me you had drunk on our journey when I asked? I told—'

'And I told you to go to hell but you didn't,' she inserted childishly. 'And I did drink.'

He arched a sardonic brow and produced a water bottle from somewhere. He tossed it in her direction and Molly caught it.

'You have good reflexes.' Lots of things about her were good—better than good, with the notable exception of her decision to pursue and sleep with her best friend's husband.

Are you mad because she chose to sleep with Tariq or because she didn't sleep with you?

Molly raised herself back up, tilted her head in acknowledgement of his comment, and shook the water bottle. 'See, I did drink.'

'It is over half full. A person who doesn't take the desert seriously is asking for trouble,' he said, listening to the voice in his head echo his last few words. A man who was thinking about doing what he was thinking of doing was asking for more than simple trouble.

'I didn't ask to be in the desert. I didn't have a choice, and I would have thought it would have suited your sadistic tendencies if I had suffered heatstroke.' She levelled a glare filled with resentment at his face and then let herself fall back down on the bed. She winced as the action sent an extra-strong stab of pain through her temples.

With a curse Tair was on his knees at her side in seconds. 'Are you all right?'

'Don't fuss!' she said crankily. 'You've said I'm just overheated. I still am,' she murmured, tugging at the light cover fretfully. She had folded it down as far as her waist before she realised that she was only wearing her bra and pants. With a yelp she pulled the sheets up to her chin again and turned to him, eyes dark with suspicion.

'Where are my clothes?'

He nodded without much interest to the neat pile on the chair behind him. 'As I said, you were hot and you needed cooling down.' At that moment Tair's own internal thermostat could do with some adjustment. Her skin was alabaster and she had looked smooth and soft all over.

'Who undressed me?' The idea of Tair removing her clothes, and his hands touching her skin, sent a ripple of horror through her body—at least she hoped it was horror!

'It would bother you if it was me?'

Oh, God, he had!

Move on, she told herself, don't give it another thought—he probably hasn't. She recognised this as excellent advice but found it impossible to follow. She wasn't even wearing matching bra and pants, she realised.

As if that would have made any difference to him!

'I'm sure you would have enjoyed it more if it had been Beatrice.' She closed her eyes, waved goodbye to what little pride she'd had left, and willed the floor to open up at her feet.

The floor didn't open but her eyes did at his response.

'You want me to give you a mark from one to ten, Beatrice being the perfect ten!'

'I do not!'

He raised a dark brow. 'It sounded that way to me.'

Molly compressed her lips. 'I'm well aware that Beatrice is beautiful and I'm not. I happen to have two sisters who are just as gorgeous as Bea and I do not compete. I realise you have women falling over themselves for your attention but I don't beg for approval from men I don't even like.'

As Tair studied her angry flushed face he doubted she had any idea of how revealing her comment had been, but it did explain the awful clothes. Like many an ugly duckling, she had no idea she'd turned into a swan, and he felt irritated with the family that hadn't bothered telling her.

What did it take to make her realise?

'For the record, enjoyment is not something I feel when I see a woman unconscious and know I am responsible for her being that way.'

The hard note of self-recrimination in his soft voice made Molly stare as he dragged a hand through his dark hair.

'Beatrice is a beautiful woman. I know this even though I have never seen her in her underclothes.'

Molly's eyes fell. She had noted he hadn't said he wouldn't like to, but then realistically what man wouldn't? If Beatrice weren't so nice it would have been fun to hate her.

'But you are also a beautiful woman and I've never seen you in your underclothes.' His lean features suddenly melted into a grin. 'Barring that very brief but promising flash a moment ago.'

'You're disgusting!' she choked. He thinks I'm beautiful…? 'So you didn't…'

'No, that was Sabra—she was the only one brave enough.'

'Brave?'

'You scared them. You scared me…'

She narrowed her eyes for a moment—she had been almost taking him seriously.

'You stood there and screamed abuse at me, and manners are very highly rated among my mother's people.'

She shot into a sitting position, carrying the sheet with her. 'I have manners!' She looked at his mouth, felt her stomach muscles quiver and thought how she had far too many out-of-control hormones as well.

Tair watched as she swung her legs over the side of the divan. Her actions had the uncoordinated grace of a newly born foal. He felt a wave of totally unfamiliar tenderness as he struggled not to go to her aid. 'Just sit there and calm down. Next time I might not be quick enough to catch you.'

'I'm not going to faint…you caught me?'

His hooded glance connected with her wide eyes. 'Just.'

Wasn't that typical? The one time she got to be held in the arms of an incredible man she was unconscious—not, she tried to tell herself, that as a modern and liberated woman she craved being swept off her feet in any sense of the word!

She looked at him thorough her lashes, feeling unaccountably shy. 'I suppose I should say thank you for your quick reflexes…and I would if it hadn't been your fault that I fainted.'

His grin softened the severity of his stern expression and deepened the creases around his eyes. 'For a moment there I thought you were going soft on me.'

She tried to smile but her lips felt stiff, so instead she lifted her chin. 'There are times when even you seem almost human.'

His eyes contacted briefly with her own and for no reason at all Molly's heart started beating very fast.

Principles, he reminded himself, were not elastic just because his libido had gone into overdrive. 'There are times when I almost forget you slept with my married cousin last night.'

As a mood breaker his comment was highly effective.

The soft look in her eyes turned to cold dignity as she drew herself up ramrod-straight. 'As you mention it so often I find that hard to believe, but as you have such a bad memory perhaps I should write on here…bad woman…' She wiped a finger across her forehead, then glanced with distaste at the grime covering it. 'I need to wash.'

'I'll send someone in to help you.'

He turned and strode away in a flurry of long robes as though he couldn't get out fast enough.

'Probably afraid you'll contaminate him,' she told her

reflection as she got to her feet. She ought to feel glad he had gone. The atmosphere had been getting a bit too...charged.

Intellectually she found him repellent, but the only problem was that it wasn't her intellect that was stimulated when she looked into his mesmerising eyes, or when he smiled, or even when he didn't smile. The fact was, she admitted with a sigh, the man was six feet four of rampant masculinity that would make any woman who wasn't dead from the waist down forget if she was actually not very highly sexed.

He was not a man she wanted to get involved with and, actually, the longer he carried on thinking she was poison, the better, because if he acted on the sexual attraction she sometimes felt was between them she wasn't sure if she was going to be able to respond on an intellectual level.

She was still exploring the room and trying to distract herself from thoughts of Tair and the strange fascination he exerted for her when a young girl, Sabra, appeared carrying food.

Molly, who was starving, sat on a pile of cushions at the low table the girl placed the tray on. The food, a spiced lamb dish with couscous and almonds, was melt-in-the-mouth delicious. When Molly told Sabra this in her not terribly good French, after she recognised that the girl didn't understand English, Sabra beamed with delight and immediately launched into a rapid speech in the same language.

Molly begged with the help of hand gestures for Sabra to slow down, but eventually understood that when she had finished eating she could bathe if she wished to.

Miming disgust when she touched her face, Molly assured Sabra that she definitely wished to!

CHAPTER EIGHT

'WHERE would you run to?'

Her hand on the heavy curtain at the door of the tent, Molly spun around, with her hair, still damp from her bath, swinging around her startled face.

Tair's head was bare and his dark hair, gleaming blue-black in the candlelight, was tousled and damp, as if he too had just bathed. The flowing robes he had worn earlier were gone to reveal a white tee shirt that clung disturbingly close to his hard-muscled torso, and moleskin riding breeches tucked into leather riding boots.

She let go of the curtain and it fell back into place with a swishing sound that seemed awfully final.

'I'm not running but, as you ask, any place would be better than here. I was actually looking for Sabra.'

'If you knew the desert you would not say that, *ma belle*,' he said drily.

'I'm not your "*belle*," or anything else of yours.'

He revealed his teeth in a wolfish smile and looked amused by her acid tone. 'There is no place to run, Molly. Accept it.'

His seductive voice was like rich, warm honey.

Molly struggled to maintain her attitude of angry

defiance while she fought not to recognise the part of her that didn't want to run.

'Why—because you say so?' She gave a contemptuous snort and felt her heart beating like a trapped bird in her chest as he took a step towards her.

His appearance was the essence of primitive, raw masculinity. Looking at him made her ache with longing.

'What did you want to ask Sabra? She has looked after you?'

'Yes, the food was marvellous.'

'The bathing facilities met with your approval?'

She nodded, the bathing facilities having been positively decadent. She had been reluctant to leave the deep scented water and her skin still glowed with the sweet-smelling oils that Sabra had shyly supplied for her use.

'I was going to ask Sabra about the sleeping arrangements. I'm assuming that I'm allowed some privacy.'

He had stopped a few feet away from her, close enough for her to be able to trace that thin white scar with her eyes. She wondered what it would feel like to trace it with her tongue, and then wished she hadn't as her face grew hot.

'The sleeping arrangements are entirely your choice.' His eyes slid from her face to the low divan piled with silken cushions. 'But it can get lonely at night.'

Molly swallowed and folded her arms across her chest in an instinctively protective gesture. 'I'm quite comfortable with my own company, thank you.'

'Don't worry—you won't have to protect your virtue. I have never felt the need to force a woman.'

The contempt in his voice stung. 'Just so long as you know I could and would.'

'My taste doesn't run to beige creatures.' Although anything less beige than the woman glaring at him with luminous eyes would, he admitted, have been difficult to imagine. His critical gaze ran over her crumpled skirt and blouse before he gave a faint grimace. 'Why are you wearing those things? I asked Sabra to give you some fresh clothes.'

Molly knew there were some women who got told by beautiful men they were gorgeous and she knew that she was not one of them. All the same his dismissive contempt stung.

'She did, but I prefer to wear my own clothes. And while we're on the subject of taste, mine doesn't run to…' Molly struggled to speak past the sudden constriction in her aching throat as she stared straight at his chest '…to men who kidnap me.'

'Think of it as a little adventure.'

Molly, who was thinking that the way her skin prickled with heat when she looked at him was insanity, gave a faint scornful snort… She was having a big problem with words.

'Try and be philosophical about this. Concentrate on the plus points.'

'Because there are so many?'

He laughed and Molly tried hard to maintain her attitude of defiance as her eyes clashed with his bold, glittering stare.

'When else would you have had the opportunity to study at such close…intimate quarters a foreign culture?' His voice had the seductive texture of warm silk. The sort of silk that would feel sensuous against your skin.

'If I want to know about foreign culture I'll read a book in the comfort of my armchair.'

It was one thing to be caught in a trap, it was another thing entirely to turn the key in the lock yourself, then give it to your jailer.

That would be crazy, and only crazy people would give into a sudden attraction that blazed for a short time, then left cold ashes of regret behind.

It wasn't a question of whether Tair would respect her in the morning if they spent the night together—he didn't respect her now—but it was a question of whether she would respect herself.

'There are some things you can't learn from a book.'

Their eyes connected and the blaze in his blitzed every sane thought from her head. As the stare lengthened the static hum in the air became a loud buzz in her ears. Every instinct of self-preservation she had screamed at her not to ask him what those things were—in her present state of mind and body she might like what she heard!

Get a grip, she advised herself as she lowered her gaze. Her skin felt so acutely sensitive that she was conscious of the feathery prickle of her lashes against her hot cheek as she struggled to control her uneven breaths.

'You're not one of those people who travel to foreign places and stay safely cocooned in sterile luxury behind the high resort walls?'

'In case it has slipped your memory, I'm not on holiday.'

Tair, who didn't deign to acknowledge her dry interjection, expanded on his theme, his low voice pitched barely above a sinfully seductive whisper that was doing all manner of damage to her nervous system.

'I think a person should seize the chance of new experiences whenever possible. If you don't,' he mused, 'who knows? You might live to regret it...?'

And he would, he knew, always regret it if he did not follow the instincts that a midnight ride through a starlit desert landscape had been unable to diminish.

He had been appalled to find himself actually looking for excuses for her behaviour...and reminding himself that she was all the things he despised in a woman and it had not lessened the fire that burned in his blood.

Their glances met but after a moment she lowered her eyes in apparent confusion.

'I do not expect the *ingénue* act. You do not need to play the part with me.'

Molly, wishing it weren't an act, forced herself to look at him. 'So all in all this is just a tremendous opportunity to expand my horizons?'

'A situation is what you make of it.'

'Silly me. I hadn't realised how lucky I am to be abducted against my will by a man who is a throwback to the good old days when a man was a man and a woman was a slave!'

'I don't require a slave.'

She stuck out her chin, stubbornly refusing to acknowledge the message in his gleaming eyes.

'I wasn't applying.' With a pretended cool she looked dismissively up the long, lean, muscle-packed length of vital body. Feeling her cool slip, she lowered her glance and gave a cynical snort. 'I don't suppose you need anything or anyone.' Tair took self-reliance to a new level.

'I wouldn't say that.'

A note she had not heard in his voice before brought her head up. Tired of skirting around the issue, she said what she had been thinking. 'Are you trying to seduce me?'

'Yes.'

The single raw word did more damage to her resolve than all the candlelit dinners and romantic gestures in the world—not that Tair would have offered her either.

The breath left her lungs in one long sibilant sigh as a pulse of longing slammed through Molly's body. Her eyes half closed, her breath coming fast, she leaned towards him, her body drawn as though by an invisible force. Every individual cell vibrated with the force of the desire that crashed over her like waves pounding on the shore as she lifted her face to his.

Tair stepped forward and lifted his hand to tangle his fingers into the sleek mesh of her hair and smooth back the silky strands that clung to her cheeks before framing her face between his big hands.

He was torn. He wanted to touch her with a need that threatened to consume him, but when he did he was conscious of a vulnerability inside him, an emptiness that he didn't want to acknowledge was there.

But he had to touch her.

As his thumbs moved over the curve of her cheeks he could feel her tremble with passion.

'What are you doing to me? Every time I look at your face, think of your mouth or the curve of your neck...' Unable to resist the desire to taste her any longer, he pressed his mouth to her throat.

Molly gave a fractured sigh as her head fell back. He ran his fingers slowly down the exposed column of pale skin, then, giving in to the silent invitation, he kissed his way slowly back up.

By the time he reached her mouth Molly couldn't breathe.

'Your skin tastes like flowers.'

Molly's heavy lids lifted as he tilted her face up to his. She stared greedily at him, memorising each primitive angle, every chiselled plane, and thought how she wished he would kiss her again soon because she was dying already.

It wasn't until he said, 'I couldn't have that on my conscience,' that she realised she had said it, not thought it.

'This is happening?'

'If you doubt it I'm doing something wrong.'

'I don't think that's possible.'

He laughed, but the laughter didn't last and there were

lines of strain etched in his face that Molly didn't see because the raw hunger in his eyes blinded her.

The warm well of excitement in her belly flared hot as he slowly angled her face first one way and then the other.

'You're beautiful.'

For once in her life Molly felt it, and anticipation made the pulses deep in her body throb as his face came close to hers. Tair whispered her name, his deep voice making her nerve endings tingle as he added throatily, 'So you want to be seduced?'

'I want you.'

'And I want you.'

'I thought I was beige…?' She groaned as his lips once again found her neck. Clinging to a thin strand of remaining sanity, she gasped. 'Oh, I really don't think this is a good idea.'

He nipped at the soft fullness of her lower lip and then traced the trembling outline of her mouth with the tip of his tongue. Her heavy lids lifted as he nudged the side of her nose with his, and his dark face swam into vision as she felt as much as heard his husky whisper.

'Sometimes bad is more fun than good.'

Holding her gaze with his hot blue eyes, he fitted his mouth to hers and kissed her slowly at first, then deeper, parting her lips and sliding his tongue into the warm moistness of her mouth.

'You taste so good,' he said against her mouth.

She slid her fingers into his thick lush hair and said, 'So do you,' in a fierce little voice before kissing him back hard.

She felt the vibration of a warm laugh in his chest, but soon he was kissing her some more with a hungry, bruising intensity and the force of her response made her tremble.

When his head lifted Tair was breathing hard, dragging air into his lungs through flared nostrils. She saw the tension in him now, felt it as he stood there like a man who was fighting against invisible bonds.

'If you look at me like that I'll…' His eyes darkened as he scanned her upturned features with a fierce predatory expression that made her insides dissolve like sugar in hot liquid. 'Have you any idea what your mouth has been doing to me?' he groaned.

She shook her head and lifted a hand to his cheek. Her lips parted, her expression rapt as she trailed a finger down the stubble-roughened curve of his cheek before tracing the line of the small white scar.

'How did you do that?' she whispered.

He said something indistinct, but even if he had shouted Molly wouldn't have been able to hear it; all she could hear was the throb of blood pulsing through her veins.

When he turned his head and touched his open mouth to the centre of her palm a fractured gasp escaped her aching throat. And when he took hold of her wrist and trailed kisses along the blue-veined inner aspect of her forearm the strength drained from her limbs.

An earthy moan of shocked pleasure left her lips as she felt his erection dig into the softness of her belly. 'You're…'

Tair smiled a fierce smile that made her skin prickle with dark heat. Her eyes squeezed closed as he bent his head, his fingers skimming under the neck of her blouse as he kissed her, increasing the erotic pressure.

Molly felt as though she were drowning in a swirling sea of sensation. She was painfully conscious of her body in a way that she never had been before, conscious of how her soft curves fitted into his hard angles.

She could smell the scent of soap on his skin mingled with the warm musky scent of his body and it sent a stab of lust through her. She leaned into him, holding on tight to his narrow waist because her legs would no longer support her. She could feel the taut muscles and the edge of his ribcage, and as their eyes met his were so hot and hungry that she felt dizzy with sheer wanting just looking at him.

'You are the most beautiful man, Tair, so beautiful. I can't stand up.'

'That works for me,' he growled, scooping her up into his arms and striding towards the low divan. He laid her down with a tenderness that was in stark contrast to the fierce need in his face.

'I still don't like you.'

He arranged his long lean length beside her and pushed the silky skein of hair back from her face.

'Do you suppose we could discuss this later?'

She nodded. 'I just thought I should be honest.'

'Your honesty is appreciated.'

'I do want you though.' She couldn't stop staring at his fingers as they slipped the buttons of her shirt undone. He had to be feeling her heart, it was thumping so hard against her ribcage.

'That was the message I was getting.'

She ran the tip of her tongue across her dry lips. 'You're trembling.' She could feel the shudders that were running through his taut frame.

'So are you.'

'There is something I have to say.'

'Not now.'

'About me and Tariq—he *really* is—'

'Definitely not now!' A nerve clenching in his cheek, he laid a finger against her lips and levered himself upright.

It took several deep breaths before the image in his head was extinguished and he could control the swell of mindless jealousy.

For a moment she thought he was going to walk away. The relief when he didn't was intense. Lying there, she watched as he pushed a few cushions out of the way and propped his broad shoulders against the carved headboard.

'Just shut up, come here and let me undress you, *ma belle*. I have been thinking about unwrapping you all day.'

CHAPTER NINE

MOLLY looked at the hand Tair stretched out towards her. She might not know much, but she knew a no-going-back moment when she saw one and this was it.

For a second she just stared at his hand, so much darker compared to her own, the fingers long and sensitive, a strong hand.

Her eyes lifted, and she thought how he was a strong man. A man with passion and conviction. One conviction unfortunately being that she was a home-wrecking tart, so it seemed safe to assume that his feelings for her had very little to do with respect.

This should have mattered, but by this point it didn't. She expelled the breath that had been trapped in her lungs in one shuddering sigh and stretched out her own hand to him.

Tair's fingers closed around hers, their eyes met in a moment of mutual understanding and then he pulled her towards him.

'That's right,' he approved as she put her knees either side of his thighs.

Her face was level with his when Molly, still kneeling with her skirt hitched above her knees, laid her hands either side of his face then in the same seamless action kissed him firmly on the mouth.

For a split second he didn't respond, but when he did it was as if a touch-paper had been ignited and the flame was contagious. When she met his tongue with her own and the kiss deepened her hips unconsciously moved with the same sensuous motion as her mouth.

Tair breathed words against her mouth in his own language, words she understood on a primal level. Words that made her skin crackle with heat and her quivering stomach muscles grow heavy with desire.

When Tair laid his hands on her shoulders Molly responded to the pressure, her skirt riding farther up, and she sat down, gasping sharply as the sensitive apex of her legs made contact with his hard thighs.

The raw desire in his face shook her to the core and made the excitement pulsing inside her expand. Her heart swelled with emotion… She wanted to give herself to him more than she wanted to take her next breath.

His cerulean eyes didn't leave hers for a second as he undid the last few buttons of her shirt and peeled it off her shoulders. A moment later the blouse was flung away.

A heartbeat later her bra followed.

She lifted her hands in an instinctive gesture, but with a growl he caught her wrists and held them firmly to her sides.

'I want to look at you. Don't hide yourself, Molly… never hide yourself from me.'

His eyes fell and she held her breath. It seemed impossible that someone who embodied every male physical attribute there was could be impressed by her unfeminine angles.

But amazingly he was.

'Dear, sweet…' His powerful chest lifted as a deep shuddering sigh moved through his body.

Molly felt the helpless response of her own sensitised flesh respond to his scrutiny. The tingling life that pulled the pink buds of her small trembling breasts to tight prominence was painful, but not in a bad way.

'You're so beautiful, so perfect...'

Tair drank in the sight of her, the delicate bones of her shoulders, the shape of her narrow ribcage and the soft twin mounds of her high, deliciously plump breasts. To watch them visibly respond to the feel of his eyes made him think about how sensitive they would be to his touch.

He closed a hand over one small firm mound of trembling flesh and then the next, his thumb moving across each tight nub, drawing a series of small throaty gasps from her parted lips.

'Like sweet, ripe little apples.'

His bent his head and ran his tongue across the tip of one quivering peak. Her back arched as she grabbed the back of his head to hold him there.

'Oh, God, Tair, you...'

With her eyes closed, her splayed fingers sank deep into the lush pelt of his hair, then tightened as his tongue began to explore and tease, evoking sensations inside her that she had not dreamt existed.

It was just about the most erotic image she had ever imagined, but the feelings it produced went farther. Right now, though, Molly would make no attempt to unravel the complex tangle of emotions that erupted when she looked at his mouth against her body.

When Tair lifted his head he was breathing hard and there were lines of dark colour etched along the contours of his high cheekbones.

Without a word Molly reached out and began to unfasten the buttons on his shirt.

He sat still, looking at the top of her bent head, fighting against the fire in his veins and the urge to rip apart the buttons of his shirt as her trembling fingers performed the task with what felt to him like agonising slowness.

His control lasted until she reached the last two buttons and then he could bear it no longer. With a groan he tore the shirt open sending the buttons flying across the room.

Molly sucked in a deep breath, her eyes darkening and her pupils expanding as she watched his muscles ripple beneath skin that gleamed like oiled satin.

Things tightened and stirred deep inside her and the heavy ache low down in her body intensified as her greedy gaze slid down his bronzed torso.

He had the perfect body. His shoulders were broad, his chest was covered in a light dusting of dark hair and his stomach was washboard-flat. There wasn't an ounce of surplus flesh on his body to blur the perfect muscle definition on display.

The stab of lustful heat that slid through her body made her gasp.

Tair swallowed, the muscles in his brown throat visibly contracting as he reached for the buckle on his belt and slid it from his narrow hips. 'Come, I need to feel your skin against mine.'

Molly, her eyes locked on his, placed a hand on the headboard either side of his head as she leaned forward. Tair placed one hand in the small of her back and the other behind her head. As their lips met in a deep, drowning kiss he jerked her up hard against him.

Molly's breasts were crushed against his chest and she moaned into his mouth as Tair's fingers tangled in her hair, and opened her mouth to deepen the kiss. She felt Tair's hands moving over her back, drawing her even closer to him.

But not close enough! Never close enough…to satisfy the knot of frustration inside her that tightened another painful notch. 'I want…'

When he pulled away the febrile glow in his eyes made her head spin. 'What do you want?'

'Everything. All of you.'

Without a word he slid down the bed and flipped her over onto her back. Molly's heart skipped as she saw the look in his eyes, the heat, and his hunger. She could feel them in her bones.

A moment later he pulled her beneath him and carried on kissing her with a frantic need that bruised her lips. She kissed him back, wanting it never to stop, loving the weight of his body on hers, loving the roughness of his jaw on her soft skin, loving the smell and taste of him.

There was nothing about him that didn't feel perfect and right.

She hadn't expected that feeling… The thought flitted through her brain and then his fingers were sliding under the waistband of her skirt, easing it down over her hips, and she couldn't think anything beyond please…and yes!

Tair levered himself off her, his intention to remove his boots and trousers distracted by the sight of her lying there so wanton and so willing, her tight nipples still wet from his ministrations.

'You are totally and absolutely…' He bent forward and kissed her stomach, letting his hands slide slowly down her slim hips. He marvelled at the texture of her skin and how the lightest touch made her tremble and shake.

She moaned his name, her back arching as his mouth slid lower leaving a wet trail on the soft curve of her belly. With a cry he forced himself from her.

'Remember where we were. I need to…' He pulled

off one boot and flashed her a look that made things inside her twist.

Even with his back to her Tair was aware of her big eyes watching his every move as he pulled off his second boot and then kicked aside his trousers and shorts. The knowledge that she was watching him increased the painful level of his arousal.

The line of his back and narrow hips, the length of his leg, the tautness of his male buttocks looked to Molly like a classical statue come to life. Then he turned and as her eyes slid down his body she forgot about statues and his classical grace.

The heat flooded her face as she struggled to lift her gaze, or, failing that, even blink or breathe.

Sucking in air through her nostrils, she shook her head and closed her eyes as all her lust and hunger fused into one intense ache of primitive yearning to have him inside her.

A deep, almost animal groan was ripped from his throat as he threw himself down beside her, rolling her onto her side until they lay face to face. Then he placed a hand in the small of her back and pulled her thigh across his hip.

'Have you noticed we fit really well?'

Molly, who on recent evidence was having doubts on this score, didn't say anything—she wasn't sure she could speak without crying… Was lust meant to feel this emotional? In all other ways it had outstripped her most optimistic expectations.

Tair nuzzled her throat before parting her lips with his tongue. Still kissing her, he took her hand and fed it onto his body, curling her fingers around his shaft.

He sucked in a deep breath as her fingers tightened and

when he slid his own hand between her legs she gasped. Then a moment later she sighed and pressed against his hand.

'This is for me?' he asked, sliding his fingers over her wetness and drawing sighs and cries from her as she rolled on her back and parted her thighs for him in silent invitation.

He kissed her and nuzzled her neck and watched as her back arched. A gasp deeper than any that had preceded it was wrenched from her parted lips as he slid a finger inside her.

Molly could feel his heartbeat as he lowered himself onto her, his hands either side of her face. She grabbed his shoulders, her fingers spread across his sweat-slick skin.

The nudge of the hot, silky-skinned tip of his erection against the apex of her parted thighs made Molly stiffen. Then Tair kissed and breathed words into her ear and she relaxed, though she was unable to stop tensing as he entered her.

'I can't!'

Above her Tair had gone very still.

'There is no *I* just *we…we* can, we will…just let it happen, *ma belle*, let me make it happen for you. Look at me, go with me…'

Molly responded to the coaxing of the velvet voice and opened her eyes as he slid another inch inside her.

'Oh, God, Tair, this is…'

'It will be,' he promised thickly. 'It will be…'

The breath left her lungs in a long sibilant sigh as he began to move.

Tair held her hips, murmuring her name thickly as he slid slowly deeper and deeper into her sweet slickness, then he repeated the process again and again, all the time conscious of the pressure he fought to control inside him building and burning.

As he felt Molly tighten around his length Tair's mind slipped into a dark primal gear where there was nothing in his world but the woman who cried his name as she moved beneath him and the need—the necessity—to reach a plateau where they could merge and be one.

Molly's entire being was focused on the incredible sensations she was experiencing, of Tair inside her, stretching and filling her. She felt things tighten in anticipation as the pleasure centres of her brain overloaded.

Tair watched her face, saw the rosy flush wash over her skin and her eyes widen in shock as the first soft flutters of climax hit her. Then he felt the vibration of the feral groan that came from deep inside her as her muscles began to spasm.

Tair let himself go, then allowed himself the final deep thrust into her as he was engulfed by a mind-shattering and spirit-lifting release.

For several minutes he lay on top of her until his heartbeat slowly returned to within shouting distance of normality.

When he rolled away she cuddled up to his side like a kitten and laid her head on his chest. It was one thing to take a conniving woman of experience to his bed, but it was, as they said, a whole different ball game to take a virgin!

'You didn't sleep with Tariq.' A bemused frown creased Tair's brow as he absently trailed his fingers down the curve of her spine. Molly arched her back under the pressure and almost purred.

'Don't be stupid!'

'He went into your bedroom. I saw him.'

His jaw clenched as he recalled how he had seen with his own eyes that Tariq was unable to take his eyes off her. The only way a man who wanted Molly could remain pure was if he removed himself to another continent!

'Men and women can do other things besides have sex in a bedroom.' Although not in Tair's bedroom, she thought.

'He was never your lover?' Tair's expression hardened to one of predatory possessiveness as he looked down at her silky head and thought how Tariq would now never be.

He would do everything within his power to make sure that Tariq never got near Molly again in his life.

'You've never slept with any man.' The wheels in Tair's mind seemed to be working tortuously slowly.

'No, I told you—Tariq and Khalid, they're my half-brothers.'

'Be seri—' She felt him stiffen. 'My God, he is…they are…Susan Al Kamal, the woman who divorced…she remarried?'

Molly nodded.

'You're Susan Al Kamal's daughter?'

Molly turned her face into his warm skin, breathing in the warm musky smell of him. 'And a bit of an embarrassment to the Al Kamals, the skeleton in the closet.'

He cursed softly in his own tongue and groaned.

'I did try and tell you.'

She heard him curse once more before he said, 'What have I done?'

'I thought you were the expert…' Her teasing tone faded as she added, 'Does it matter who my mother was?'

He caught her chin in his hand and brought her face up to his. 'Matter…you ask does it matter? I have taken your innocence.'

She watched, her sense of bewilderment increasing as he groaned and rolled onto his back. As he lay there with his eyes closed the tendons in his neck were tense as he dragged in air through his flared nostrils.

'I wasn't *innocent*, just *inexperienced*,' she said, allowing her eyes to roam over the sleek strong lines of his tautly muscled body before she turned on her side.

A hissing noise of exasperation escaped his lips as he opened his eyes and fixed her with a bright blue incredulous stare.

'You were a virgin.'

'You did nothing I didn't want you to, even if I didn't know that's what I wanted at the time.' He had intuitively known exactly how to please her, how to send her to heaven.

'Look at me.'

'I am.' It was possible she might never be able to stop!

'You must realise that this changes everything… Tariq is your half-brother, you were living under the protection of the royal house and I abducted you.'

'It doesn't have to change anything. I'll tell Tariq I came because I wanted to just the way you put it on the letter.'

Tair loosed an odd laugh. 'You think that would matter? You are not just *any* woman. If you were any woman I would take you as my mistress.' Until thirty seconds ago that had been his intention. 'But that of course is now out of the question.'

'Would I have had any say in the matter?' He acted as if she would have left her life at a word from him…a word he'd just made plain wasn't going to come her way now.

Tair, his face set into grim lines, did not even respond to her ironic comment. 'We must marry, of course.'

She searched his face, saw that he looked pale and his expression was darkly sombre. 'You're not serious…?'

'I have never been more serious.'

Molly shook her head, gathered the silk sheet around herself and swung her legs over the side of the bed. She was shaking. She had to break it to this man who was clearly living in a bygone century when family honour and a woman's reputation required preserving at all costs that things no longer worked this way. She tried to speak calmly.

'Don't be stupid. I can't marry you… You don't know me or love me or—'

His voice, terse and impatient, cut across her. 'This is not a question of love.'

Always a good thing to say when proposing.

She slung an incredulous look over her shoulder. He was lying there, one arm curved above his head, looking more incredible than any man had a right to look.

'It is,' he told her plainly, 'a question of honour.'

'Your honour, not mine. I'm living in the twenty-first century.'

Tariq shook his head and conceded, 'I know it's not something either of us planned to happen, but you'll get used to the idea.'

'Have you been listening to a word I've said?'

'Some women would not be insulted by the proposal.'

'I'm not some women.' The heat flared in her cheeks.

'My wife…'

She stuck out her chin. 'Don't be ludicrous.'

Her childish refusal to recognise the gravity of the situation frustrated him. 'Grow up, Molly. This is not what either of us would want, but in life there are consequences for our actions. You think *I* wanted this to happen?' he yelled, revealing suddenly that he wasn't as composed about this as he appeared.

'Thanks! Strange, but you didn't seem to be a man who was doing something against his will a few minutes ago!'

He looked irritated. 'That isn't what I meant! It has always been expected that I will marry to further the political and financial interest of our country…'

'A family tradition—how sweet,' she trilled. 'I wouldn't like to stand in the way of such romance,' she choked.

His lips tightened. 'That is obviously no longer possible.' His glance slid over her slim, stiff figure and a gleam ignited deep in his eyes. 'Still, there are plus points…' His hand suddenly shot out and curled around her arm.

'You know what I think?' She gave a grunt of anger as he pulled her back down onto the bed beside him.

'What do you think, Molly James?'

Tair watched her brush a gleaming strand of hair from her face as she glared up at him, breathing hard. He felt his recently satiated lust stir as he looked down into her angry golden eyes.

'I think that you slept with me because you thought you could make me forget any other man I'd ever been with…including, you thought, Tariq. Abducting me wasn't enough—you had to be doubly sure.'

Actually what she said made a lot of sense, supposing he was as cold and calculating as she apparently thought. The irony was that where Molly James was concerned he was incapable of thinking beyond touching her—clinical objectivity did not even register on his radar!

'You think I'm that good?'

The colour flew to her cheeks at the throaty taunt. 'Don't give me that,' she snapped. 'You know you are!' A woman who slept with Tair would forever be comparing future lovers with him and finding them sadly wanting.

The mocking light left his deepset sapphire eyes as he studied her face. 'It takes two…sometimes two people just mesh.' He took her chin gently in his hand and shook his head. 'It is rare, Molly.'

'Don't turn this into something it isn't. We had sex…I'm not marrying you because of some warped idea you have of honour and stuff. Tariq won't feel that way. He's modern…he's not a barbarian.'

'You think I am barbarian? You are reluctant to marry me because I don't have nice manners?'

A beautiful barbarian. 'I think this would have been a one-night stand if you hadn't cottoned on to the fact I was telling the truth when I said Tariq was my half-brother.'

'Is that what this is about? You think all I want is a one-night stand? You really think I'm going to leave in the morning? You think that in two days' time I was going to wave goodbye to you for ever?'

She swallowed. 'Weren't you?'

He shook his head and the blaze in his eyes held her as surely as his arms. 'I'm not going anywhere,' he promised, stroking the side of her face with his finger. 'Do you think that one night would be enough for me? I can't get enough of you, *ma belle*. Be honest, Molly—you don't want me to leave you now, do you?'

Molly told herself he was only saying these things because he wanted to make her agree to marrying him. 'I'm not marrying you.'

She sighed and turned her face into his palm. Just at the edge of her consciousness there lurked the knowledge that there was a limit to how honest she could allow herself to be!

But there was one thing she couldn't deny!

'I don't think I can get enough of you, Tair,' she admitted quietly.

She watched satisfaction, male and primitive, flare in his eyes and it was mingled with a tenderness that almost stopped her heart.

He bent towards her and her soft lips parted under the pressure of his mouth. Molly curled her arms around his neck as he kissed her deeply. His warm breath fanned over her cheek as their noses nudged and he speared his long fingers into her hair.

'I think you might have changed your mind about not being able to have enough of me by the morning, *ma belle*.'

'I might surprise you.'

'Now that is a claim I would like to put to the test.'

'This doesn't mean I'll marry you.'

His husky laugh was lost in her mouth.

CHAPTER TEN

'SO YOU'RE awake. I am disappointed. I was looking forward to waking you up.'

They had made love long into the night but when Molly had fallen asleep it had been deeply. She had not stirred when Tair had left their bed.

She didn't turn her head when he spoke, but held on tighter to the silk sheet she had wrapped sarong-wise about herself and allowed the hair she had anchored away from her face with her forearm to fall free to screen her face like a silken curtain.

'If you were looking forward to it so very much maybe you shouldn't have sneaked away while I was asleep.'

'I was not quiet, I made a great deal of noise, and if it makes you feel any better I had no desire to leave you, but there were certain matters that needed attending to.'

'I don't need to feel better. I feel totally fine.'

'What are you doing?'

She flashed him a scornful look but felt her stomach muscles quiver as she did— God, he looked incredible. She quickly diverted her eyes. 'What does it look like? What have you done with my clothes?'

'Relax. They will be returned to you when they are laundered.'

Molly straightened up. Was he kidding? How could she relax now? 'And what am I meant to do in the meantime?' she enquired. 'Or is this the way you like your women?' she asked, her eyes looking down to her own bare toes. 'Barefoot and tied to the kitchen sink?'

'This is not a kitchen.'

'Kitchen, bed—what's the difference? You know exactly what I mean.' She stopped and drew breath, thinking if he did know it was more than she did! She seemed to know nothing any more. Meeting him had turned her entire life upside down. 'And I,' she added hastily, 'am not a woman...that is, I am...a woman, obviously.'

It was certainly obvious that she was from where Tair was standing. He felt his desire stir as his glance dropped to the outline of her nipples pushing against the thin silk.

'Just not your woman...well, obviously...because, well, I'm my own woman...person...'

'You are very politically correct this morning, though not very accurate.'

Better late than never, Molly thought.

'You are my woman and you will be my wife.'

She ignored the little thrill of excitement inside her. 'My God, but you really are a male chauvinist! I thought you'd forgotten that daft idea by now.'

'But *your* male chauvinist, Molly Mouse.'

'How do you know I want you?'

'Because you were very convincing last night when you told me you did.' His husky laughter only intensified her blush. 'There are clothes there.'

'I can't wear any of those.'

She glanced to a pile of garments neatly stacked and gave a regretful sigh. The rich colours and sumptuous fabrics were beautiful, but not for her. 'Don't you have anything...?'

'In beige?' Tair suggested. He revealed his even white teeth in a sardonic grin and shook his head. 'Definitely not.'

'There is nothing wrong with beige,' she retorted with dignity. 'Some of my favourite outfits are beige.'

'Of that I have no doubt,' he said drily. 'But alas we have no beige or taupe or even mushroom. So it is this or nothing.'

'Were you born delivering ultimatums?'

Tair watched her eyes flash with militant fire. Aggressiveness was not a quality he admired in a woman, which made the stirrings of tenderness he felt when he watched her little chin lift all the more inexplicable. It could be that there were worse things in life than being married to Molly James.

'Were you born being pointlessly stubborn?' he retorted.

'I was born a clean slate, but I was brought up not to take orders from egotistical men.'

He gave an irritated click of his tongue. 'I am not attempting to subjugate you, just dress you.'

It was undressing that he was better suited to.

A hazy heat filmed her amber eyes as the memories of last night flooded back. She could still hear his harsh intake of breath as he had exposed her breasts. It seemed as if, once awoken, her sensation-saturated nerve endings might never return to normal.

'I can dress myself,' she protested.

He lifted a filmy diaphanous shawl from the selection of items, and let it slip slowly through his fingers. He arched a brow. 'Wear this or nothing?'

Lips pursed, she stared defiantly. 'Then it's nothing.'

He gave one of his inimical shrugs. 'Fair enough.'

'Right, good, then…'

'I have no problem with your decision, though the more

conservative-minded might be a little less open-minded about you walking around naked.'

'You know that's not what I meant,' she replied, infuriated with herself for blushing.

Tair's glance drifted over the smooth curve of her cheek and dropped to her mouth. 'A man is allowed his fantasies.' And he had never expected his to be fulfilled by a virgin who had a tongue that was as sharp as her skin was soft.

Molly knew that he was only being flippant, but the knowledge that she was part of his fantasies made her shiver in delight.

'The idea excites me.' The discovery brought a predatory gleam to his deep-set blue eyes.

'Well, it disgusts me!' she retorted. 'I would never walk around naked in front of any man!' That would require confidence or a killer body and she had neither.

'I would hope not. However, I think you will enjoy walking around naked in front of me.'

She opened her mouth, but the protest died on her tongue as she saw the blaze of hunger in his eyes.

'It's all about the chase with men.'

'I know you're not speaking from personal experience.'

'Because no man would chase me?'

A spasm of irritation crossed his lean face. 'Not in the beige outfit,' he agreed drily. His brow furrowed as he studied her face. 'I cannot understand why you constantly pull yourself down. You hide your beauty in the baggy clothes, you scrape back your beautiful hair, yet even in beige your innate sensuality still shines through.

'As for men and the chase—yes, there is some element of truth in that. We are programmed to chase, and sometimes the pursuit is more exciting than what is at the end of it, but with you...that is not so. You are the most exciting woman I have ever slept with and, in case you did not realise, the only virgin. Now I will leave you to dress.'

And he did just that, having reduced Molly to a state of open-mouthed shock.

The beaded hem of the silk gown swished sexily against her legs as she walked. The fabric had a sensual feel against her bare skin. She couldn't decide if it was her imagination, but she felt that the dress made her walk differently, with more of a sexy sway to her hips.

Maybe it was the silk that made her more conscious of her own femininity?

Molly was turning over the theory that the changes went deeper, that maybe it was less about the fabric brushing against her bare legs as she moved and more about her newly discovered sensuality, when she spotted the unmistakable tall, lean figure standing some distance away.

Molly immediately stopped theorising, she stopped thinking and even her breathing was a hit-and-miss affair. The ache of longing as she stared at him made her burn with emotions she was terrified to acknowledge.

He was beautiful.

'He's my lover.'

But not my husband.

Her hands clenched so hard that her nails left half-moon impressions in the soft flesh of her palms as she stared across at Tair.

He was talking to another man who was leading two horses that pawed the ground impatiently as Tair said something that made the other man laugh out loud.

Then suddenly, as if he sensed her eyes on him, Tair turned his head sharply. It was impossible from this distance for her to make out his expression and even if he had been closer his eyes were hidden behind a pair of designer shades.

He stood motionless and Molly's heart began to thud, the sound echoing in her ears as wave after wave of powerful, enervating lust and longing crashed over her.

There was activity in the compound, but Molly felt as if she were wrapped in a pocket of stillness. A stillness that was broken when one of the horses, spooked by a loud noise, began to dance restlessly. As the man Tair had been talking to struggled to calm the second horse, the spooked animal pulled free, rose up on his hind legs and began to paw the air.

Tair stepped forward, making no visible attempt to avoid the flailing hooves that were perilously close to his head.

Molly held her breath. Tair seemed to be speaking to the animal but it seemed to her that words were a pretty poor defence against razor-sharp hooves attached to several hundred pounds of equine muscle!

Why didn't he just walk away as any person with half a brain would?

'Oh, God!' she groaned, fear like an icy fist in her belly as the flashing hooves whistled past Tair's head and the snorting horse danced just out of reach.

For pity's sake, what was he trying to do to her?

Teeth clenched, breath coming in short, shallow gasps, she stood, her eyes glued to the scene. 'Stupid man!' she whispered.

Just because he looked like a god, did he think that quality extended to immortality?

An image of Tair lying pale and still on the floor, his life-blood seeping from the serrated edges of a wound, super-imposed itself over her vision. She shook her head to banish it. This was one of those moments when a vivid imagination was a definite curse!

Her heart was in her mouth as he advanced slowly, his hands held wide and all the time talking to the animal.

'You're going in the wrong direction, you crazy man.' Sensible people ran in the opposite direction when they encountered danger. He seemed to rush to meet it.

A silence fell over the encampment as Tair came close enough to pat the gleaming black flank of the wild-eyed animal. Molly couldn't believe what she was seeing when he laid his head close to the steaming horse's mane.

Molly's expression was now one of reluctant fascination. And she wasn't the only person held in thrall. People had stopped what they were doing to watch this masterly display. Tair, apparently oblivious to the hush, carried on speaking to the animal.

Molly shook her head. It was totally amazing when barely two minutes later the animal was nuzzling Tair's palm like a lamb. Tair responded with a laugh to some comment from the man holding the other horse and then glanced towards Molly.

A moment later he vaulted lightly onto the horse's bare back. The reins in one hand, he nudged the animal's flanks and the horse, responding to the pressure of the rider's thighs, broke into a canter.

Man and animal stopped a couple of feet from her. They made a pretty impressive picture, both beautiful and untamed.

Molly folded her arms across her chest and maintained an unimpressed expression that slipped when the horse pawed the ground. She stepped backwards nervously, pretending she hadn't seen Tair grin.

'He won't hurt you.'

No, but you will, she thought as he leaned down to pat the animal's neck and say something soft and soothing in his ear. You'll hurt me because I've let you into my heart.

Oh, God, she'd fallen in love with him.

Tair looked at her paper-pale face and the amusement die
from his face. 'You really are scared of horses, aren't you?'
He gave a self-recriminatory grimace and, casually looping
his leg over the animal's back, he slid down to the ground.

He lifted his hand and raised his voice to a young boy
standing a few feet away who immediately came running
over. Tair handed him the reins and, shooting a shy smile
in Molly's direction, the boy led the animal away.

'I suppose you think that display was smart?' Her chest
swelled with indignation as she added in a voice that
quavered with emotion, 'I suppose you think that you
looked good?' He always looked good. 'Well, just for the
record, and because I don't suppose anyone else will tell
you because it's probably against the law to tell someone
with blue blood they're a posy prat, but it wasn't smart, it
was s-stupid and irresponsible and it would serve you right
if you were lying on the floor.' She looked at the dusty floor
and imagined him there. 'With y-your neck broken, and
blood… I can't decide if you're an adrenaline junkie or just
a selfish show-off. Either way I…'

She stopped mid-rant just to draw breath and it dawned
on her with horror that she had been yelling at the top of
her lungs. With a gulp she pressed a hand to her mouth and
struggled to hold back the floods of tears that she knew
were only a blink away. She waited tensely for Tair to
respond in some way to her emotional outburst. Way too
emotional… If she didn't keep a tighter control he was
going to guess her true feelings for him and that would be
too mortifying to bear.

His eyes, concealed behind the mirrored surface of his
shades, made it impossible to read what he might be
thinking. A nerve clenching and unclenching in his lean

cheek as he stood there looking at her was about the only clue—though not much of one. Just when she thought he was not going to react at all he expelled a long sigh.

'I'm an adrenaline junkie,' he confessed.

She blinked as he pulled off the designer shades. The blaze of blue sent any control she'd managed to regain flying out the window.

'When you marry me you can tame me of the habit.'

'I don't want to tame you.' Why would any woman want to change the things that attracted her to a man in the first place?

Which might be a relevant realisation if you were actually going to marry the man, Molly.

'I'm sorry I scared you.'

Now able to read his expression, she was disturbed by it and her eyes fell from his. She shrugged. 'I don't like the sight of blood...any blood,' she added.

'Don't spoil it, Molly. I was feeling so special.'

She lifted her head, prepared to deliver a stinging retort to this mocking comment, only to find he was looking at her with nothing that resembled mockery.

He was looking at her with a kind of...*longing*...and she was so shocked that she said the first thing that popped into her head—which in her experience was nearly always a mistake and this time was no exception.

'You are special.' She glared accusingly at him, then, without intending to, took a step closer.

'You look stunning.'

She made a last-ditch attempt to resist the tug of his eyes. 'I look like I'm auditioning for a place in your harem, but don't get the wrong idea. I didn't dress like this for you.'

'Of course not,' he said, the amused placatory note in his voice bringing a resentful sparkle to her eyes. The resentment morphed to blushing confusion as he added throatily, 'But you'd get the place.'

'I wouldn't take it. I'm not joining the ranks of the thousands of stupid women who would stand on their heads to get your attention.'

'You really do not need to go to such lengths to get my attention, Molly. As my wife your place is assured.'

Struggling to maintain a façade of calm was not easy when her insides were melting and her brain refused to think about anything but his mouth. Eventually she managed to say, 'And I would like to be informed the moment my own clothes are—' She stopped dead as she found herself looking directly into his eyes. There was nothing covert about the message glowing in the azure depths.

Molly was instantly submerged by a wave of longing so strong that for a second her nervous system was totally paralysed.

'I can't take my eyes off you.'

'Oh, God!' she groaned, lifting a shaky hand to her trembling lips. 'Don't say things like that.'

'I thought you liked the truth?'

'So did I.' She lifted her shoulders and gave a distracted little grimace before revealing in a rush of honesty, 'But I don't know anything any more, Tair. I don't even know myself.' The woman she had seen in the mirror with the luminous eyes and secretive smile had not been her—it couldn't be. She didn't fall in love.

Tair could identify with her confusion.

In past relationships it had not been accidental that his partners had never asked where the relationship was going. He did not do emotional soul-searching and he did not get involved with women who were inclined that way.

Tair had never had a sexual relationship with anyone

who touched him on an emotional level and vulnerability was not a quality that he had ever sought in a woman.

So why did he respond the way he did to the perplexed pleat in Molly's smooth brow, the little wobble in her voice, and the bewildered look in her wide eyes? It was incomprehensible.

He felt a totally foreign urge to take her tenderly in his arms and find the words to soothe her.

Tair didn't fight the compulsion, but neither did he look too deeply within himself for its source as he stretched out his hand and let his thumb stroke her cheek. These were feelings he had never expected to find within or outside marriage.

The need to soothe became quickly submerged by a much more primitive, more compelling need as he felt the silky smoothness of her warm flesh and was reminded of how she felt beneath him—smooth and soft and hot. The hard kick of desire in his belly was physically painful as he framed her face between his hands.

'You're very beautiful.'

Mesmerised by the glow in his eyes, Molly leaned into him. 'It's the dress,' she whispered past the emotional constriction in her throat. She twitched the jewel-bright fabric with her hand and thought how much she wanted him. 'It isn't beige,' she said. And neither was Tair.

But her life *was* and it would be again, as soon she would be going back to it.

Her spirits took a downward lurch.

She turned her face a little, pressed her lips to his palm and told herself that she didn't really belong here in the desert, or in Tair's bed. There was no question of marriage…that would be insane. But while she was here it would be criminally stupid not to make the most of this little interlude.

An interlude that would always be precious to her, and one that she was definitely going to extract every last shred of pleasure from.

His dark head dipped towards hers and she closed her eyes, anticipating his kiss, feeling a serious anticlimax when his hands fell away from her face.

A moment later he swore.

She opened her eyes and saw he was staring out into the desert presumably seeing something that was way more interesting than kissing her. She resisted the strong impulse to remind him that she was the one he'd been kissing and shaded her eyes to follow the direction of his gaze.

At first Molly couldn't see anything, but then she caught the glint of sun reflecting off metal.

Slowly the silver ribbon in the distance and the cloud of dust above it got closer and defined itself as a convoy of vehicles.

CHAPTER ELEVEN

'YOU have visitors.'

Tair flicked Molly a look and put his hands on her shoulders. 'Yes.'

Molly took a shred of comfort from the contact and the fact he didn't sound any more pleased than she felt. She felt his long fingers tighten on her as the convoy stopped a few hundred yards away.

The sun shone off their tinted windows. At her side she was aware of Tair stiffening, and she glanced at him, a questioning look on her face just as the driver got out of the first vehicle.

Tair just shook his head, took his hands from her shoulders and said in a flat voice, 'Go inside, Molly.'

She ignored him.

'I said, go inside, Molly,' he repeated, his eyes trained on the driver scurrying around to open the passenger door.

'I heard you. I'm ignoring you.' Was her presence an embarrassment to him? The possibility hurt more than it should have.

'Please, Molly.'

'That was nicer,' she approved, still determinedly standing where she was.

She had read somewhere, and it had seemed sensible at the time, that you should establish some ground rules at the beginning of any relationship.

But this wasn't the start of a relationship or anything else. Molly turned her head as without warning her eyes filled with tears. It was one thing to acknowledge something on an intellectual level, but to be forced to do so emotionally was not nearly so easy to deal with.

At least he didn't know she loved him, though, strangely, the recognition of how much worse things could be did not make her feel better.

'Fine, Molly, message received, you don't do orders. But I really don't have time for this, so just do as you're told for once without an argument…'

He sounded so weary that she struggled to respond with the necessary level of belligerence the comment justified. The lines of strain bracketing his mouth worried her, which was stupid because if ever a man knew how to look after himself it was Tair.

'Have you any idea how sexist that sounds?'

He flashed her a look that said he didn't care, which about summed up his attitude to political correctness, but before she could respond to this silent provocation the driver, who had been joined by four tough-looking individuals clad in traditional white desert garb opened the passenger door and bowed his head.

Molly heard Tair swear softly under his breath as a man dressed in a similar fashion to the others emerged.

There the similarity ended.

Molly didn't need to see the other men bowing respectfully low to tell her this man was in charge; it was written all over him. The same, she realised, was true of Tair. His title was not the reason people showed him respect—he was simply the sort of man that people looked to when there were difficult decisions to be made. Tair was the man who made tough choices and took both the responsibility and the consequences that went with those decisions.

And who did Tair turn to for support? Was that one aspect of being the archetypal alpha male that was hidden away in the small print…?

This new alpha male didn't look as though he found the role a burden. He wasn't young, but it was difficult to gauge his age very precisely because, despite the lines in his leathery dark-skinned face, he stood erect and moved like a youthful man. She could feel the vitality he exuded from where she was standing.

He also exuded anger and towering disapproval.

The four muscular men took up positions at his side, their attitudes alert as they scanned for hidden enemies. The most disturbing factor from Molly's point of view was their sinister accessories, such as the rifles the men wore slung over their shoulders like fashion items. To her relief they showed no sign of pointing them at anyone and instead they bowed very low and respectfully to Tair, who nodded his head in response and said something in his native tongue.

They glanced towards the older man, who nodded almost imperceptibly as if confirming the order that Tair had given. He then walked towards them, before stopping a few feet away.

Tair moved in front of her a little.

It was tempting to tell herself the gesture was protective and that he was trying to shield her from the stern visitor's disapproval, but she knew it was much more likely he was embarrassed by her presence. Maybe this incident had achieved what she had failed to—he had finally realised that she did not fit into his life.

It shouldn't hurt, as she knew that despite his reluctant proposal Tair's feelings towards her went no deeper than sexual attraction, but it did anyway.

It hurt like a dull knife sliding between her ribs into her aching heart.

Pride made Molly lift her chin another defiant degree. She had nothing to be ashamed of. If you discounted stupidity, that was. She was stupid, not because she'd fallen in love, although that wasn't the smartest thing to do, but because she'd previously thought with a mixture of arrogance and ignorance that falling in love was something you had a choice about!

She stepped out of Tair's shadow, leaving her semi-concealment, and with her chin still raised said without looking at him, 'I'm sorry if you're ashamed of me, Tair, but I'm not about to hide away to spare your blushes in front of your friends.'

Tair muttered a savage imprecation and spun her around. One hand in the small of her narrow back, he curved the other around her chin and forced her face up to his.

When she had said blushes Molly had not actually believed him capable of that weakness, but the dark streaks of colour she could see running along the angle of his cheekbones suggested otherwise.

'Ashamed?' he bit out, apparently oblivious to the audience. 'The only thing I am ashamed of is having taken your innocence.'

She could hear the self-recrimination in his voice and in the space of a single heartbeat Molly went from rigid and defensive to melting and unguarded. The depth of her emotions shone in her amber eyes as she lifted a hand to his cheek. 'You didn't take...I gave.'

He inhaled sharply and groaned something in Arabic

before drawing her up on her tiptoes and covering her mouth in a kiss that went on and on.

The kiss was both fiercely possessive and exquisitely tender and there were tears of emotion standing in her eyes when he finally lifted his mouth from hers. They stayed close, lips not quite touching, motionless, eyes locked, breaths mingling. Tair's fingers trailed in her hair, his fingertips brushing the sensitive skin on the back of her nape, making her shiver.

It was Tair who broke the tableau. He drew a breath and said, 'Come.'

Molly stared for a moment at the hand extended to her, then reached out and allowed her fingers to be enfolded in his firm warm grip.

It took a few seconds for Molly to fight clear of the sensual thrall that enveloped her, and when she did her glance connected with the dark beady stare of the silent visitor. Her eyes opened wide as she was totally unnerved to realise she had forgotten he was there. She dredged a smile from somewhere and looked to Tair, her expression questioning.

'Molly, this is my grandfather, Sheikh Rashid bin-Rafiq.'

Molly's eyes widened, and she felt a slow flush of intense embarrassment wash over her skin as she became conscious that they had embraced in front of Tair's grandfather.

Great! As first impressions went this one took some beating. Presumably this conservative Arab sheikh, the product of a very different culture from her own, now had her mentally listed under the heading of shameless hussy. Maybe she should enjoy her notoriety and do something really shocking? It was an interesting idea, but her experience of shocking was severely limited.

'Grandfather, this is—'

'I know who she is, Tair.' The dark eyes flicked over

Molly before he turned his frowning attention to his grandson. 'It is your identity I am unsure of.' He looked at Tair and shook his head. 'I am most displeased.'

There was a spark of annoyance in Tair's eyes as he gave his grandfather an ironic bow. 'I'm sorry to have incurred your disapproval, Grandfather. I offer no excuses.'

The old man gave a snort. He glanced towards the stationary vehicles and in a lowered voice enquired, 'Have you lost your mind?'

Tair's lips curved into a sardonic smile. 'It is possible.'

The sheikh threw up his hands. 'I am out of patience with you.'

Clearly he was not the only one as almost before the words had left his mouth the door of the second vehicle was suddenly flung open and two men got out, the first in an explosive fashion, the second with a lot more reluctance.

The sheikh turned his head and said in a voice of irritation, 'Tariq, I thought we agreed—'

'I tried to hold him back,' Khalid cut in, huffing a bit as he quickened his pace to keep up with his brother who was striding towards them.

Twenty-four hours earlier Molly would have been ecstatic to see her brothers, but now her emotions were far less clear-cut.

The older man walked to intercept them. 'I thought we agreed you wait until Tair had a chance to tell me what is actually going on.'

'I can see what's going on!' Tariq retorted, slinging Tair a murderous glare. Tair just stood there looking unapologetic.

Molly squeezed her eyes closed. This was a nightmare!

'This isn't what it looks like,' she said, trying to pacify the situation.

Beside her Tair stiffened. 'Yes, it is.'

The quiet provocation drew a sharp hiss of anger from Tariq.

'I was talking to *them*, not you, Tair. And please do not start telling me to go indoors.' She turned to her brothers. 'This is all totally unnecessary.' Her last observation was addressed to all of the men and as far as she could tell made no impression on any of them.

'Let her go!' Tariq gritted, his eyes on Tair's fingers curled around her wrist.

'Tariq, calm down. What are you doing here anyway? I thought Beatrice was ill.'

'She's better.' Her brother's eyes searched her face. 'Are you all right?' The narrow-eyed glance he slid in Tair's direction made it pretty clear where he would lay the blame if she wasn't.

Very aware of Tair beside her, she tried to smile. It was clearly essential to diffuse this potentially explosive situation and as no one else showed any interest at all in playing peacemaker the role seemed to fall to her.

'I'm fine.' It seemed churlish to say that she didn't want to be rescued, so she struggled to adopt an expression approaching welcome as she moved to meet them halfway.

Her brothers stopped about a foot away and for a long moment nobody said a word. The aura of violence shimmering in the air as Tariq and Tair locked glances was almost tangible.

It was Tair who broke the silence.

The next few exchanges were in Arabic, with a few hair-raising French curses thrown in, but it wasn't exactly hard to get the general gist.

Khalid, who had not taken part in the interchange, was staring at Molly. 'Is that really you, Molly?' He shook his head. 'You look incredible.'

'Thanks, Khalid,' she said, then turned to Tair and Tariq. 'Look, you two, all this macho posturing is quite unnecessary. It's all just a silly misunderstanding…it's funny, really.'

Nobody laughed.

'I'm leaving, but not without Molly,' Tariq said.

Khalid cleared his throat and impressed Molly with his bravery by stepping between the two older men. 'Look, let's be sensible about this—nobody wants a fight.'

At that point Tariq landed a solid right to Tair's jaw. Tair, who was driven back several steps by the impetus, made no attempt to avoid it or retaliate. He just stood there looking so noble that Molly wanted to scream. Then she saw the blood and her stomach lurched.

Tariq, who looked disappointed by his cousin's response or, rather, lack of it, was too slow to stop Molly flying to Tair's side.

'Oh, my God, you're bleeding!' she cried in horror. 'Look what you've done, Tariq—how could you?' She sent her brother a fierce glare as she touched the blood seeping from the corner of Tair's mouth with her fingers.

'Come away from him, Molly,' Tariq warned.

Molly gritted her teeth. She was so sick of men and their orders.

'It is fine, Molly. Do not fuss, and it is nothing more than I deserve,' Tair said, appearing totally unappreciative of her frantic mediator act. 'It makes it no better, Tariq, but I did not know when I—'

'Abducted her,' Tariq finished for him.

There was a flush along Tair's cheekbones as he nodded and continued speaking, this time in his own tongue. From her brother's exclamations and the glances in her direction she assumed that Tariq was given a brief explanation.

When Tair stopped speaking Tariq turned to her.

'Why didn't you tell him, Molly?'

It was bad enough having Tair make this her fault, but she wasn't going to take that from her brother.

'Khalid is the one who told him I was Bea's friend to begin with, and you, Tariq, asked me to consider your father's feelings.'

Tariq turned to Tair. 'I still don't see how you could think I would have an affair, Tair?'

Beside his brother, Khalid cleared his throat. 'Before you get on your high horse, Tariq, you might recall that there was a time when *you* thought *I* was in love with Bea.'

Tair, speaking quietly, interrupted the brotherly interchange. 'She tried to tell me—' Tair's eyes glanced at her face '—and I didn't believe her. I'm sorry, Molly, and I beg your pardon for believing the things I did about your relationship with Tariq. My actions to you were inexcusable.'

'No argument here in that score.' Despite his words, Tariq looked visibly mollified by the unstinting apology.

Sheikh Rashid, who had watched the scene silently, now stepped forward.

'We will discuss this situation in more comfortable and private surroundings.'

It was not an invitation and all the men responded as such.

CHAPTER TWELVE

THE sheikh, who had arranged himself on a pile of silken cushions, impatiently waved away the refreshment and the people who offered it and waited for Molly and the three men to sit down.

Once he was satisfied that he had everyone's undivided attention he spoke. 'Of course you will marry her.'

It was not a question, just a simple statement of fact.

Tair inclined his head in acknowledgement. 'We have discussed it.'

Molly knew that in the future she would always associate the scent of incense that hung heavily in the air with insanity. Not that her future was likely to hold many incense-laden moments, which could not be a bad thing.

So why did her heart sink to somewhere below her knees at the thought of a return to her neatly ordered existence? Would it be that simple? she wondered uneasily. Getting on the plane would obviously be no problem, but would distance put an end to the fragmented steamy images that kept flickering across her vision at the most inappropriate of moments?

And would it stop the empty ache in her heart?

'I think we should settle on a date now.'

Out of respect for Tair's grandfather, Molly compressed her lips, locking the slightly hysterical laugh in her aching throat.

She watched her brothers exchange glances.

Khalid looked as if he wished he were somewhere else, a sentiment that Molly could readily identify with, and Tariq looked only a shade less grim than Tair.

'My uncle might feel awkward about their marriage,' Tariq remarked to nobody in particular. They were all acting as though she weren't there, a circumstance that Molly was finding increasingly aggravating.

The sheikh smiled grimly. 'Leave my son-in-law to me. I have some leverage in that direction.'

Tariq nodded. 'The wedding will therefore take place at the palace as soon as possible.'

Molly stared at the grave faces. This had to be an elaborate joke. Any minute now someone would laugh and shout, Got you!

Molly's eyes moved from one man to the next, her incredulity deepening—nobody was laughing yet. 'Have you all gone mad?'

They finally acknowledged her presence.

Tariq patted her hand in a soothing manner that made her want to scream. 'I understand that it isn't an ideal situation, Molly.'

Molly snatched her hand away and shrieked, 'Ideal!' She gave a hard laugh. 'It's insane is what it is! You lot look sane, but actually you're all stark raving mad! I thought you two at least were civilised,' she said to her brothers. 'Tair does not *want* to marry me.'

The pause before the sheikh spoke was ample time for Tair to say there was nothing more he would like in the world than to marry her. But of course he didn't and stupidly she felt totally bereft.

'It really does not matter what Tair wants,' Tariq explained soberly. 'He knows his duty.'

The sheikh looked sympathetic but his manner was unyielding as he added by way of explanation, 'My grandson has insulted, not just you, Molly, but your family. He will do the right thing, the only thing that is possible in this situation for a man of honour.'

Molly's hands balled into fists. 'I'm not being married off like a piece of damaged goods. People,' she exploded, 'do not get married just because they've had recreational sex!'

For the first time since this conversation had begun Tair's expression of stoic calm slipped and Molly was shocked by the blaze of white-hot anger in his incandescent eyes.

On some level Tair knew his rage was irrational, but that level was deeply buried under layer upon layer of gut-clenching fury. But for some reason hearing her reduce what they had shared to a sordid, shallow level felt like a betrayal, which he knew was ridiculous.

Almost as ridiculous as the fact that last night had been the most intense experience in his life.

'You will not speak in that manner,' he said, glaring at her.

The autocratic decree sent Molly's chin up a belligerent notch. 'I will speak in whatever manner I damned well please,' she growled back. 'And if it wasn't recreational, Tair,' she challenged, 'what was it? True love?' she taunted.

Tariq spoke before Tair responded to her jibe. 'Molly,' he reproached. 'You are being unreasonable.'

Her jaw dropped. Tariq of all people was siding with Tair—talk about male conspiracy.

'How is it everyone else can discuss my sex life but me?' she demanded shrilly.

'I'm sorry, Sheikh,' Tariq said, turning to the older man

who had gone rigid at her outburst. 'My sister doesn't understand.'

Eyes blazing, Molly turned on her brother. 'Don't you *dare* apologise for me.' Taking a deep breath, she struggled to regain her control as she turned to Tair's grandfather. 'I'm sorry, Sheikh, but I didn't mean to offend you.'

The sheikh read the genuine remorse in her eyes and nodded his head graciously. 'You appear to be a creature of strong passions, young lady.'

Molly gave another grimace of apology. 'I respect your customs and your beliefs,' she promised. 'I really do, but you have to see they're not mine.'

When he nodded his head she took it as encouragement.

'The thing is the only connection I have with this…' glancing around the exotic and utterly foreign surroundings '…is the fact my mother married a king, couldn't hack it and ran away. Genetically speaking I'm probably the worst woman in the world to marry a prince.'

'Young lady, you are forgetting the fact that your brother will be King of Zarhat and that you are under the cloak of his protection.'

'I don't need protection.' Molly struggled to get her point across even though she sensed she was losing the battle.

'It is not a question of what you need.'

'I'm not royal, I'm an ordinary teacher,' she said, a hint of the desperation she was feeling in her voice. 'I'm like thousands of others. I don't eat off gold plates, I eat microwave meals, I watch soaps, I cycle to work…'

The sheikh looked sympathetic but remained firm. 'My grandson abducted you and stole your innocence. Honour decrees…'

Molly covered her ears with her hands and closed her

eyes. She stayed that way until someone took hold of her wrists and brought her hands down.

Even before she opened her eyes she knew it was Tair. 'Go away!' she pleaded. When Tair was near her common sense went out the window. Things flew out of her mouth that were as much of a shock to her as anyone else, and they got her into trouble. Who was to say she wouldn't agree to marry him, just as she'd said yes to making love with him?

She needed to keep in very close contact with her common sense right now because a small part of her, the insanely optimistic part that had read too many romances, thought she could make him love her and wanted to say yes to this crazy proposal.

'Just calm down and listen!'

The request drew a low moan from her throat. 'I've listened long enough. You're all insane!' she cried, her glance encompassing all the men in the room. 'And look at you!' she said to Tair, thinking how she could look at him for ever and it would never be enough.

His air of studied cool was fooling nobody, least of all Molly. The signs of strain in his lean face were obvious.

'When I get married I don't want my bridegroom to look as if he's attending a wake. I don't want to be a man's penance. I want to be his love.' Tears stung her eyes as she sniffed and added bitterly, 'I simply can't believe you're suggesting a shotgun marriage and I'm not even pregnant!'

'Romance is all very well, Molly, but arranged marriages have been working for generations.'

'Like the arranged marriage you have with Bea, I suppose. I have heard a lot about honour, but not a lot about common sense. And, for the record, Tair did not abduct me.'

Tariq's brows meshed. 'What are you talking about, Molly?'

'He said that because he was trying to protect me.'

In the periphery of her vision Molly was conscious of Tair staring at her.

'I asked him to take me with him.'

'No, she didn't.'

Molly flung him a frustrated look. Couldn't he see she was trying to help him out here? She tried to send him a message with her eyes.

It was a message he either didn't hear or chose to ignore.

'I abducted her.'

The sheikh, looking impatient, waved a bejewelled hand. 'Well, whoever abducted who, the fact is she was an innocent—'

'No, I wasn't.' She felt their eyes on her and lifted her chin. She felt more comfortable with the lie than the subject.

Tair shook his head. 'She was a virgin.'

They all acted as though they were discussing nothing more intimate and private than the price of a barrel of oil.

Molly felt the colour rise up her neck until her face was burning. They didn't have an ounce of sensitivity between the lot of them!

'That's what I told you!' she choked.

The mask slipped and Tair's anger showed through. 'You told me nothing!'

'Would it have made any difference?'

'No.'

Their eyes locked, Molly's chest tightened and her eyes stung as a jumbled mass of contradictory emotions rose inside her as she got to her feet.

'I wasn't living under the protection of the royal family, and Tair didn't seduce me. That was my idea too. So you

see there is no crime of honour. Besides, this is academic.'
Molly adopted a cool manner that befitted the voice of
reason in this room of crazy people.

'You can plan as many weddings as you like, but it
doesn't alter the fact that you can't have a wedding without
a bride and I'm not marrying anyone.' Her façade fell away
as she turned her gaze on Tair and, in a voice that shook
with loathing, said, 'Especially you!'

'This is something that *will* happen.'

'There you go again, thinking something will happen
just because you say so. Well, maybe that's worked for you
before but not with me.

'When I get married it will be to someone who asks me
because I'm the most important person in the world to
them. Unrealistic, I know,' she added. 'But I'm willing to
hold out and if he never comes along—fine, I'll make do
with loads of recreational head-banging sex!'

Tair was aware of little but the dull roar in his ears, his
hands curled into fists at his sides. The thought of Molly
sharing as much as a kiss with anyone but him, let alone
the sex she spoke of, put a hot flame under his control.

She continued defiantly. 'I'm not settling for second-
best just to appease your warped sense of medieval
family honour. I'm sorry if you don't like it, but that's
the way it is.'

Outside the light was fading. It was a similar scene to the
one she had arrived to the previous evening. Molly could
hardly believe how much had happened to her since then.
The camp-fires around the encampment had been lit and
their smoke mingled with the cold night air. Molly walked
towards one, drawn by the glow.

She stood, watching the sparks dance.

A woman sitting close by left the family group she was with and came across to Molly. With a smile she offered her a plate filled with delicious-smelling spicy food.

Molly smiled but shook her head.

They left her alone, as if sensing that she needed the solitude. The incredible hospitality of the desert people was something that she would never forget.

That and other things.

'That was quite an exit.'

She ignored Tair's voice behind her and resisted the temptation to lean back into the solid warmth and strength she could feel inches away. You couldn't cosy up to a man when you'd virtually just said you'd prefer to extract your own wisdom teeth than marry him. Not if you wanted him to believe it.

'The desert is actually rather beautiful.'

'I thought it scared you.'

'It's growing on me. My mother hated it—it scared her.'

'It doesn't scare you?'

No, you do, she thought.

'Marry me, Molly.'

She closed her eyes and shook her head. 'Why?'

'Because, though modern society does not acknowledge it, there is such a thing as the right things and duty and service.'

And love and romance.

'Obviously such an offer is tempting…'

'Some women might think so.' Some women might not consider he was second-best.

'Then marry them.'

'Why are you being so unreasonable?'

She turned suddenly, appeal shining in her eyes as she caught hold of his hands within hers. 'Couldn't we go back to the way we were? I could be your mistress… It was what you wanted.'

An expression of baffled frustration mingled with outrage settled on his face as he looked at her. It might have been amusing under other circumstances.

'You want to be my mistress but not my wife? Is that what you're saying?'

'I suppose I am.'

'You must see that is no longer possible. That I would take a woman who is the sister of the future king to bed but not marry her would not be tolerated.'

She threw up her hands in seething frustration. 'I thought you were the royal rebel who slipped the leash of petty protocol whenever possible? How is it all right to marry someone you don't love but it is not all right to make love to the same person?'

'This is not what it's about.'

'So you're saying if I won't marry you…'

'It is marriage or nothing.'

Tears stood out in her eyes as she stared at him outlined against the desert night sky. 'My God, you and your damned ultimatums, Tair,' she said quietly. 'It has to be nothing.'

Without a word he turned and strode away into the darkness.

CHAPTER THIRTEEN

MOLLY'S little flat was in a village about five miles from the school where she taught. The village boasted a small shop-cum-post-office, a pub and a tea shop.

It had escaped the development that had changed many similar areas because of a generous landowner who had inserted a strict covenant when he'd left the park and woodland of his ancestral home to the local community, thus effectively preserving the area.

On a Saturday morning Molly was in the habit of taking a run in the park, but this was the third week she had forgone her run and settled for a walk and cup of tea and a scone in the teashop.

Molly was approaching the tree-lined avenue that led to the wrought-iron park gates, her thoughts very much concerned with the other alterations that she would shortly be forced to make to her lifestyle, when someone tapped her on the shoulder.

'Beatrice!' Molly exclaimed, her eyes opening to their fullest extent as she recognised the glamorous red-headed figure. 'What are you doing here? Is…?' She looked around, half expecting to see her brother, her feelings at the prospect mixed.

'No, don't worry, I'm quite alone—except for Sayed, of course.' As if hearing his name the figure who had been standing half concealed in the shadows stepped out. 'And Amid is parked around the corner.'

'Don't you find it weird? The bodyguard thing?'

'I did,' Beatrice admitted, 'but you get used to it.'

Molly doubted she ever could, but then a few months ago she would have been equally sceptical about the possibility she could fall in love with an Arab prince. She'd lived, learned and suffered.

Molly shut her eyes and tried to block the arguments that had been going around in her head ever since she had read that blue line on the test stick.

Essentially nothing had changed, she reminded herself for the millionth time.

Tair still didn't love her, and this time if she accepted the inevitable offer of self-sacrificial marriage there would be no get-out clause because Molly knew that, unlike her own mother, she could never leave her child to be brought up in another country.

But she was equally sure that Tair was the love of her life—her soul mate—and that she would never find what she had with him with anyone else.

It was not surprising that her internal debate never progressed beyond a bad headache.

She pinned on a belated smile of welcome and felt the start of another headache as she said, 'You look fantastic, Bea.'

It was the truth. As she hugged the glowing princess, whether illusion or not, Molly felt the warmth of the contented glow the new mother projected.

She was not surprised when Beatrice did not return the compliment. Molly knew she looked wretched. Her mirror told her that every time she consulted it.

Some mornings just dragging herself out of bed was an effort. So far her colleagues at work had accepted the story that she had contracted a nasty stomach bug while travelling during the summer break, but she knew the excuse had a shelf-life.

'Motherhood must suit you,' she added. Beatrice made a very good advertisement for the role.

'You didn't see me at the two o'clock, three o'clock and five o'clock feeds. I'm suffering from chronic sleep deprivation.'

'Well, you hide it well. How is the baby?'

Beatrice's beam of contentment went off the scale at the mention of the new arrival. 'He is gorgeous and already shows signs of being a child prodigy, much like his auntie.'

'I wouldn't wish that on anyone.' Being set apart from his or her peers was not something Molly would want for any child of hers. 'Not that I can see any child of yours and Tariq being considered a geek.'

Then, because she didn't want Beatrice to think she was canvassing the sympathy vote—whining was not to her way of thinking an appealing quality—she changed the subject.

'You still haven't said—what are you doing here? And where is your gorgeous baby?'

'I left him with Tariq in London. It's the first time so it feels really strange,' Beatrice admitted. 'But I wanted a little chat with you—alone, Molly.'

Molly's brow furrowed warily. 'Me…?'

'First, how is your father?'

Molly smiled. 'He's fine.'

She had arrived home to find that her father had already had his heart surgery. She had been pleased but puzzled about how things had happened so fast. Did waiting lists vanish overnight?

Her equally mystified sisters, who had met her at the airport, had also not been able to offer an explanation as to how their dad had leap-frogged his way to the top of the waiting list in such a spectacular fashion.

Some sort of government health initiative, I think someone said, was Rosie's response to Molly's enquiries.

Rosie hadn't been able to remember who this someone was and Sue's response to Molly's questions had been impatient.

'Why the interrogation? Who cares? It worked and Dad's better and that's all that matters. Now he doesn't have all those weeks worrying that every time he feels a twinge it's another attack. And wait until you see the hospital, Molly. It's incredible and the staff are lovely.'

When Molly went to visit her father she realised that her sister had not been exaggerating. The private clinic set in woody grounds was more luxurious than many five-star hotels.

The moment she saw the place she knew what must have happened and it turned out she was right.

The hospital, when taxed, admitted that her father was a private patient, but they had refused to reveal the name of the anonymous person who was footing the bill. Molly, however, had known immediately who it must be.

Now Molly took Beatrice's hand and squeezed it in silent gratitude. 'Thank you to you and Tariq for arranging the private treatment. I'm sure Dad would have been fine anyway, but the waiting and uncertainty was getting unbearable.'

She felt tears of emotion in her eyes that were triggered these days by any little thing, and blinked them back before saying huskily, 'I know that Tariq wanted to be anonymous, but could you let him know how I feel?'

Beatrice looked at her blankly for a moment and then said, 'You think Tariq arranged for your father's operation?'

'Well, didn't he?'

'He would have, if he thought of it, I'm sure, but he had a lot of other things on his mind around that time, like the baby coming four weeks early.'

Molly shook her head in bewilderment. 'But I don't understand—if it wasn't…then who…?'

Beatrice lifted her brows and the colour rushed to Molly's face as realisation hit like a stone.

'Tair…?' she asked in a small voice.

'Unless you know of any other candidates, I'd say he's a safe bet. Did he know about your dad being ill?'

'Yes.' Molly pressed a hand to her mouth. Bea was right—there was no other alternative. 'This is terrible.'

'Why?'

'I can't be indebted to him like this.'

'Why?'

'Because—' Molly broke off, shaking her head. 'I'll have to say thank you.'

'He won't want thanking.'

Molly felt her anger flare. 'I don't give a damn what he wants! I'm thanking him if I have to tie him down to listen.'

An interesting mental image accompanied this angry declaration, an image distracting enough to make it a full sixty seconds before she realised that Beatrice was staring at her, speculation written all over her face. Molly struggled to compose herself.

'I'm afraid I've had a gut full of bossy men.'

'God, those men!' Beatrice rolled her eyes in comical exasperation. 'When Tariq told me how they'd tried to force you into marrying Tair that way I couldn't believe it!' she exclaimed, shaking her head in disgust.

Molly turned her gaze to the toe of her shoe as though it were the most fascinating thing in the world. 'At least someone knows it would have been a total disaster.'

'I didn't say that.'

Molly's eyes lifted.

'I think you and Tair would make a great couple.' In response to the choking sound that emerged from Molly, the future queen of Zarhat lifted her brows and added with a twinkle in her eyes, 'I mean, there was a frisson between you from the moment you met. Talk about steamy…?'

Molly felt the guilty colour flood her face. 'I didn't… I don't even like him!'

Not like, maybe, but love, adore and feel empty without… Sometimes she felt ashamed of the weakness and her inability to summon up enthusiasm for anything else in life. God, she had turned into one of those people she had always despised!

'I frequently don't like Tariq even now,' Beatrice admitted. 'But I'm always crazy about him.'

'That's different.' Because Tariq loved Bea. Molly felt a surge of envy and was ashamed of it. If anyone deserved to be happy it was Beatrice.

'True,' Beatrice admitted. 'Actually, as things have turned out, you know, you were probably wise. But you already know that.'

I do? Molly gave a noncommittal grunt. 'I think so.'

Although late at night when she couldn't sleep it was sometimes less easy to be sure about her decision, especially since she'd realised that her night of desert passion had not been without consequences—long-lasting consequences.

She would have been tempted to offload the secret she had been unable to share with anyone on Beatrice had she not been concerned the news would filter through to Tariq.

Not that Beatrice would deliberately betray a confidence, but Molly knew Bea was totally unable to conceal even the most minor detail from her husband.

There were other people who needed to know before her brother, and it was the reaction of one of those people that was occupying her thoughts to the exclusion of just about everything else at the moment.

Beatrice nodded. 'Some people might think you had a narrow escape…'

Molly's brow furrowed as she knew now that she was missing something. No female who'd met him would call passing on the chance to become the wife of Tair Al Sharif a narrow escape. They might speculate about the mental health of the person who declined, but they wouldn't talk about narrow escape.

'Escape?'

'It sounds hard, but you've got to be practical, even if you are crazy mad in love with someone.' Molly stiffened and then relaxed her guard fractionally as Beatrice added seamlessly, 'Which you're obviously not, but what I'm saying is…' She stopped, clicking her tongue as she disentangled a fallen autumnal leaf from her bright hair, and Molly struggled to contain her impatience.

'Where was I?' Beatrice questioned once her hair was smooth and leaf-free. 'Oh, yes,' she said, picking up her thread just before Molly imploded. 'Even if a person were madly in love they'd think twice before they took on that sort of baggage.'

Molly swallowed her exasperation and wondered if Beatrice could be more vague if she tried. 'What sort of baggage, Bea?'

'Well, Tair's future is not exactly secure with everything that's going on.'

'What?' Apprehension lay like a cold stone in the pit of her stomach. She tried not to think the worst, although for that matter she didn't know what the worst could be.

'You haven't heard, then?' Beatrice asked, looking innocent as she studied Molly's white face.

Molly gritted her teeth. 'Heard what?' She was seriously tempted to shake the information out of Beatrice. It would be worth being rugby-tackled by the bodyguard to be put out of her misery!

'Well, just after you left, Tair's father had a brain hae-morrhage. They thought he would die, but he didn't. He's in what they call a persistent vegetative state. He could go tomorrow or stay like that for years, apparently.'

'So what does that mean for Tair?'

'He's King in all but name.'

'But you said it was insecure?'

Beatrice nodded. 'Apparently Tair didn't hang around. He has already made some pretty sweeping reforms and a lot of people who were on the gravy train in his father's time are not happy bunnies. A few of the more influential ones have been stirring it, starting rumours, suggesting that there are better people for the job than Tair.'

Molly's chest swelled with the strength of her indigna-tion. 'But there isn't!'

Beatrice made a soothing gesture in the direction of her bodyguard, who had instinctively stepped forward.

Molly took a deep breath and moderated her tone. 'They couldn't oust him, could they?'

Beatrice gave a careless shrug. 'Who knows?'

Molly had always liked Beatrice, but this callous display of indifference appalled her. 'But he does have people who believe in him and what he's trying to do?'

'Tair does have a lot of support,' Beatrice conceded, 'but

he doesn't have an heir, and the cousin that his enemies would like to see on the throne does. An heir and God knows how many spares.'

Molly's thoughts raced. 'So you think that Tair might marry to solidify his position?'

Beatrice shrugged again. 'He's certainly under a lot of pressure to do just that,' she admitted.

Molly gasped as a shaft of jealousy lanced through her with the viciousness of a knife blade. The thought of Tair married to a woman who would give him an heir and the requisite number of spares made her feel physically ill. The level of animosity she felt towards this unknown woman was shocking.

Molly could almost hear the sound of her shredded self-control finally snapping. 'No!' she yelled. 'He can't!' She saw Beatrice's expression and added quickly, 'Nobody should be forced into marriage for political reasons.'

'I know, but Tariq says Tair does have a very strong sense of duty. He thinks he'll put his country before his own happiness. But enough of politics,' she said, taking Molly's arm and adopting a coaxing smile as she led her through the open park gates. 'I came to invite you personally to my party.'

'Party?' Molly echoed, thinking she didn't give a damn about parties right now.

'A birthday party and, before you say a word, I promise there will be no kidnapping this time. Please come, Molly. It's a double celebration—my birthday and you'll be able to meet little Rayhan. He really is gorgeous,' the proud mother declared, her face softening as she spoke of her baby son. 'Please say you will. I know Tariq and Khalid want you to come. They still think you're mad with them.'

'I'm not…'

'I know you're not, but it won't do them any harm to go on thinking that for a little while. They could both do with a dose of humility. So you will come?'

'Will…will Tair be there?' Molly asked casually.

'Not if you don't want him to be.'

'No, I'm fine. Don't exclude him because of me.'

'Well, I have to say, Molly, I really admire your attitude.'

Molly, conscious of her ulterior motives, gave a slightly guilty shrug. 'Well, we're all grown-ups, after all.'

Beatrice laughed. 'I hope you're excluding the men from that statement. Now, come on, I need a cup of tea and I saw a sweet little teashop when we were driving into the village.'

CHAPTER FOURTEEN

'I MIGHT,' Molly conceded as she viewed herself in the full-length mirror, 'have put on a few pounds since I bought this dress.'

'In all the right places,' Khalid inserted with a mock leer as he avoided the blow his pretty blond wife Emma aimed at his ear.

Molly joined in the laughter, but she cast a last worried look at her reflection before she joined the other members of her extended family.

The retro-fifties look of the ballerina-length full skirt with its layers of frothy petticoat had appealed to her the moment she'd tried it on and at the time the lightly boned bodice of her strapless creation had seemed relatively modest.

That was before she had moved from a modest B to an in-your-face C cup seemingly overnight.

The others left the room and Molly lingered, doubting her ability to face the throngs of people that waited in the ballroom below.

'You look like a pole dancer,' she told her reflection before she took a deep breath and responded to the distant appeal from Khalid to get a move on.

As she walked into the room Molly's breath caught in

her throat. Architecturally, the room, a vast hall with its mosaic floor and vaulted ceiling inlaid with gold and lapis, was always magnificent. But the interior decorators had gone to town for the party and the place literally sparkled. Not just with the banks of snow-white sweet-smelling lilies and the glittering décor, but the people, especially the women, were equally dazzling.

The collection of scintillating jewels around the ladies' necks must be giving the security firm nightmares, Molly thought. They were certainly giving her confidence a severe battering.

People turned as they entered and, even though she knew they were not looking at her but the royal couples and the birthday girl in particular, Molly froze like a rabbit caught in the glare of headlights.

Then she heard Beatrice say in a sarcastic undertone to her husband, 'I love your unique take on a few close friends, darling,' and she relaxed a fraction. She felt better to realise that even the ultra-confident and elegant princess found walking into this daunting.

Tariq gave a shrug and admitted that things had got a little out of hand.

'A little…?' Beatrice snapped through a fixed smile.

'Later we will have a little party all of our own.'

'Our son might have other plans,' Beatrice retorted before she turned to Molly. 'Look, Molly, I've got to do the hostess stuff but Jean Paul will look after you, won't you, Jean?'

A young man that Molly had not noticed stepped forward. He gave a little bow and smiled. 'I'd be honoured.'

Beatrice and the family group moved away and Molly was left with the Frenchman. Clinging to her sense of purpose and hoping it would pass for poise, she lifted her chin and said, 'You're French.'

'I am, and you are English?'

Molly nodded.

'A real English rose. Would you like to dance?'

'Not really,' she said, her eyes scanning the crowd for one particular face. 'But if you do, I don't mind.'

Her companion looked amused. 'Would I be right in thinking that you do want to dance but not with me?'

Molly's eyes flew back to him, her expression contrite. 'I'm sorry, that was so rude... It's just I'm not very good at all this.'

'Don't worry, my manners are impeccable and I'm a diplomat, my father was a diplomat, my grandfather was a diplomat, so I am very, very good at all this.'

'And modest.'

He gave a rueful sigh. 'Alas, no, the modesty gene was never prominent in our family.'

Molly smiled and held out her hand. 'Shall we start again? I'm Molly.'

'Hello, Molly, I am Jean Paul.' Instead of shaking her hand he bowed low and brushed it lightly with his lips in a courtly fashion, though the expression in his eyes as he lifted his head was not so courtly. He straightened up with her hand still in his.

'Yes, you are very good at this.' He clearly expected her to be charmed and Molly, kind at heart, tried to oblige, but it wasn't easy. The man had the depth of a puddle. Slick and smooth really weren't her thing.

Two months earlier she hadn't known she had 'a thing', but now she knew it was blue eyes, a personality with more twists than a maze, a cruel tongue and a sinfully sensual mouth.

'But underneath the beautiful manners I am a dangerous man.'

Molly, who had met a dangerous man, tried hard not to laugh at the extravagant claim.

'Or at least I try to be—but do not worry. Tonight I am under strict orders from the lovely princess to behave. I got the impression you are looking for someone…?'

Molly didn't deny it. 'There is someone I need to speak with.'

'And that someone is male…pity,' the smooth Frenchman murmured with a soulful sigh when she didn't correct him. 'Perhaps I could help. I know everyone.'

Molly shook her head. 'It's not important,' she lied.

'Well, until you find who you are looking for, maybe you will allow me to entertain you.'

Molly shrugged. 'Why not?' she said, laying her hand on the arm that was offered to her and not protesting when a hand snaked around her waist.

'So how are you going to entertain me, Jean Paul?' She moved the hand that slipped to her bottom upwards and said firmly but without venom, 'Not like that.'

He gave a philosophical shrug. 'Oh, I don't just know everyone, I know their secrets too. '

Not mine, I hope, Molly thought, smiling. She could see that given time this young man's brand of brittle charm could wear pretty thin.

'I could tell you stories—'

'You mean you're a gossip.'

'I mean,' he corrected, looking unoffended by the accusation, 'that as a diplomat who wants to avoid putting his foot in it and causing offence it pays to know who is getting into bed with who. For instance,' he said, pointing towards a dark-haired beauty in a dress that, though modestly cut, revealed the voluptuous ripe curves of her body, 'not many people know it but that lady is destined to shortly become the wife of a very important man. One of the most important men in the region.'

'Really?' Molly said, pretending an interest. What was she going to do if Tair didn't come?

What was she going to do if he did?

The truth was Molly didn't have the faintest idea what she wanted to happen. Well, she did, but that was not an option because it required Tair to love her.

Every time she played the scene in her head it came out differently. It was, she kept telling herself, too pointless an exercise to speculate this way, but of course she continued to do so anyway.

The only thing left to do now was wing it. Play it by ear.

'So as the wife of Tair Al Sharif she will be a woman to stay on the right side of.'

Molly came to a dead halt, the blood draining from her face as his words penetrated her private dialogue. 'What did you say?'

'I said she—'

Molly interrupted. 'She's engaged to Tair?' Her eyes flew across the room to where the woman in question was holding court to a group of men who looked fascinated by every word she was saying.

She hadn't noticed when Jean Paul had originally pointed the brunette out, but Molly could now see that there was an unattractive hardness about her mouth.

The men around her did not appear too repelled by this deficiency and Molly knew she was searching for flaws in what was by anyone's standard a woman pretty close to perfection. Well, she was only human!

'Not officially, but according to my sources it's only a matter of time. You know the Crown prince, Molly?'

Molly saw the speculation in the Frenchman's eyes and produced a casual shrug from somewhere. 'We have met.'

'Not exactly an easy man, is he?'

Molly, who had called Tair a lot worse to his face, felt her hackles rise at the faintest hint of implied criticism in this observation. 'I think he takes his responsibilities very seriously.'

'Yes, well, he's certainly shook a lot of people up.'

Including me.

'Good evening, Molly.'

The breath left her lungs in one noisy gasp as she spun around, her skirts flaring around her legs like candyfloss.

'Tair…' She hadn't been prepared for what it would feel like to hear his voice again, but then maybe there were some things that couldn't be prepared for—and he was one of them.

The heat exploded in her belly and her legs began to tremble… Like her brothers, he was wearing full traditional dress and he looked incredible. Tall, lean, dangerous, vital and totally, unbelievably gorgeous… Her breath left her lungs in a series of soft fractured sighs as her eyes greedily drank in the details. There weren't enough superlatives to describe the way he looked.

The Frenchman's poise had been momentarily shaken when he'd seen the object of his speculation standing feet away, but he recovered quickly, producing his hand and a brilliant smile. 'Prince Tair.'

Tair, at his most regal or, as Molly privately phrased it, at his most incredibly rude, turned his head sharply, ignoring both the younger man's friendly overtures and the hand extended to him.

Molly found herself staring deep into his blazing blue unblinking stare, which did not improve her ability to think past the primitive impulse to throw herself at him.

Tair continued to blank the other man totally and kept his eyes trained on Molly's face with an intensity that was drawing a number of curious glances.

'This is Jean Paul.'

Tair inclined his head briefly towards the Frenchman.

'I know who he is.' His eyes still on Molly, Tair bared his teeth in a dismissive smile. 'If you were trying to make me jealous, Molly, you could have done better than *this*.'

The colour flew to her cheeks. 'I was not trying to make you jealous! My God, you're so arrogant, Tair!'

But would she want him any other way?

Turning a deaf ear to the intrusive question, Molly smiled warmly at Jean Paul and laid a hand on his arm. 'You think everything is about you, Tair. You owe poor Jean Paul an apology.'

She lifted her chin and allowed her narrowed-eyed, defiant glare to rest on Tair's lean dark face.

Jean Paul stammered, 'No...no, not at all, I did not know...know that you were both...'

To Molly's utter horror, instead of refuting the assumption or laughing it off Tair lifted his shoulders in an expressive shrug and observed, 'And now you do know.'

Molly rounded on him, her cheeks hot with mortified colour. 'There isn't anything to know.'

'There is no point being shy about this, *ma belle*. It is obvious.'

'The only thing that is obvious to me is that you are totally insane.' She lifted a finger to her own forehead and tapped it sharply. 'Not to mention thoughtless and...' Molly bit her lip, her eyes sliding briefly in the direction of the stunning brunette.

He elevated a dark brow. 'You were saying...?'

Molly averted her eyes and smiled at Jean Paul, who

was visibly struggling to cling to the shreds of his diplomatic cool, and ignored Tair. It wasn't as easy as it sounded when she was aware of him down to the cellular level, but she hoped the rigid back she presented him gave him the right message.

While her own feelings towards Tair's prospective bride were not exactly warm and mushy, she did think the woman deserved a little respect and consideration and Tair was not trying to be even slightly discreet. She was conscious that several conversations nearby had stilled while ears were strained to catch what he was saying.

'Prince Tair and I met briefly at a—'

'He doesn't believe a word you're saying, Molly.'

Molly swung back, her eyes blazing liquid gold. 'Will you shut up, Tair?'

She didn't shout at the top of her lungs, but her outburst did coincide with a general lull in the conversation and consequently her furious command—aided by great acoustics—was heard by the nearest hundred people or so.

Molly closed her eyes and groaned. God, Jean Paul was going to dine out on this story for the next ten years! She was not conscious of having voiced her thoughts out loud until Tair said with total confidence, 'Jean Paul is not going to be saying anything to anyone, are you?'

'What would I say? Nothing to say!' He held up his hands in a pacific gesture.

'I'm going to take Miss James off your hands.'

As if she were a piece of excess baggage!

The Frenchman made no attempt to stop Tair when he placed a firm hand in the small of Molly's back and steered her away, but then, Molly reflected bitterly, no one ever tried to stop him doing anything. If they had maybe he wouldn't be the arrogant, overbearing tyrant he was now!

She looked over her shoulder to where Jean Paul was standing staring after them.

'What possessed you?' she hissed at Tair, who carried on walking, ignoring several people who acknowledged him as they passed. 'I hope you realise that Jean Paul is putting the worst possible interpretation on that performance. The man is a gossip.' Presumably in his current situation Tair needed to take care what people said about him. Although he didn't seem to be going quite the right way about it.

'Tair, people are staring. Will you—?' She stopped, her loose hair tangling in the heavy fabric as Tair dragged her through a heavily brocaded velvet curtain and a pair of carved oak doors behind it.

He closed the heavy doors behind them, cutting off the noise from the party like a switch.

Molly, breathless, blinked as her eyes adjusted to the dimmer light of this small antechamber. She backed up until she felt her shoulder blades touch the carved screen behind her and tried to smooth down her hair with her hands.

'Tair…' She jumped as she heard him turn the lock with a decisive click.

CHAPTER FIFTEEN

MOLLY had wanted a private conversation, but not quite this private.

She pressed a hand to her throat where her fluttering pulse throbbed under the pale blue-veined skin.

Tair took a slow measured step towards her. Her oval face looked porcelain-pale and, in the light cast by the blue lantern overhead, slightly other-worldly. She looked perfect and there was nothing other-worldly about the white-hot hunger that roared like a furnace through his veins.

During the last couple of months duty and service had taken precedence, but it had been her face that had kept him going when things had been difficult, along with the knowledge that once he had sorted the mess that had been dumped in his lap he would be free to express the feelings in his heart. Feelings that Tair had not imagined he was capable of experiencing.

When Beatrice had invited him to the party his first inclination had been to refuse, until she had mentioned that they were hoping that Molly would be able to attend.

Suddenly his calendar had become conveniently accommodating.

'What are you doing?' she asked.

'I'm making sure we are not interrupted.'

'Open that door immediately.'

All she could think was how he smelt so good. The lonely weeks of telling herself that she was fine alone, that things would get better, had already been relegated to the level of childish fantasy.

'Why were you so rude to that poor man?'

'Was I rude? I'll apologise to the man some time if that will make you happy,' Tair offered generously. 'I missed you, Molly.'

The husky confession wiped all thought of his appalling manners from Molly's head.

'Did you miss me? Yes, you did, of course you did, and don't try and tell me otherwise,' he warned.

'I wasn't going to,' she admitted.

'I seduced you.'

Molly felt a surge of exasperation. 'You did not seduce me…well, you did, but only because I wanted to be seduced, and it was lovely.'

'Lovely…' He rolled the word on his tongue and nodded. 'Yes, it was, and you are…very lovely. But I wasn't going to apologise, Molly.'

'You weren't?'

He shook his dark head. 'I was going to say that I'm glad I seduced you.'

'Don't look at me like that,' she begged in a small voice.

He shrugged and took another step towards her. 'I like looking at you.' His eyes narrowed. 'Jean Paul is harmless but his hands were all over you.' His eyes slid down her body and his shoulders lifted as he took a deep breath. There was a self-mocking gleam in his eyes as he admitted, 'I did not like it.'

And would he like it when she told him?

Molly's own reaction had been total shock when, on that morning four weeks earlier, the blue line had appeared on the test paper.

Would Tair be equally stunned? Would he be angry, sad or as ecstatic as she had been after the initial numbness had worn off?

Tair was breathing hard.

'You look beautiful. I would not trust any man with you, even the Jean Paul Duponts of the world.'

The excitement swirling in her veins and the heat in his eyes conspired to make her reckless.

'Does any man include you?' she whispered, barely able to get the words out.

'Especially me, but you already know that.'

Molly tried to focus, but it was incredibly hard when he was looking at her that way. 'I don't know anything. I wasn't sure you'd be here tonight.'

'I wasn't going to be until Beatrice told me you would be.'

Molly's eyes widened as they searched his face. 'You wanted to see me?' It seemed a strange thing to say for someone who was about to marry another woman. Had Jean Paul got his facts right?

Don't go assuming anything…wait to get your facts straight, she cautioned herself.

Facts straight! As if she were capable of cool, objective thought this close to Tair.

'I wanted…' He stopped, his eyes falling from hers as he said something that sounded angry in his mother tongue. 'We parted…' He gave an impatient wave of his hand. 'There were things I should have said that I wanted to say… It must seem to you that you walked out of my life and I forgot you. This is not the case, Molly. Things happened that required my—'

'I know. Bea told me about your father. I'm sorry.' She took a deep breath. 'And I know as well what you did for my dad.'

She saw the caution slide into his eyes. 'Your father?'

His air of exaggerated innocence didn't fool her for a second. 'Just let me say thank you. It was a kind thing to do.'

'I have told you before, and my actions must have confirmed it to you, I do not do kind. The hospital care—it was nothing.' He dismissed the gesture with a shrug of his expressive shoulders.

'A pretty expensive nothing.'

Irritation at her persistence moved at the back of his eyes. 'It was something I could do, very little compared to what I wanted to do…'

The flash of searing emotion she saw when their glances locked made her heart stop dead in her chest.

Maybe she was just seeing what she wanted to. He was marrying someone else…but then why was he looking at her that way?

Her lashes flickered downwards. 'You didn't want to marry me, Tair. You thought you should because of some outdated notion of honour.'

'Honour is not outdated.'

'Some people think that marriage is,' she countered.

'Do you?'

'I've not given it a lot of thought,' she lied. 'I'm very grateful, Tair, for what you did for Dad.'

'I do not want your gratitude!' He saw her flinch and thought how he wanted her soul and her body. He wanted her love, not her gratitude.

'There is no need to yell.' It was not his raised voice that disturbed Molly, but the waves of emotion she could feel rolling off him.

But then if he was under the sort of pressure that Bea had suggested she supposed he would be pretty close to the edge.

He gave a snarling sound of frustration and looked at her with what seemed to Molly like utter loathing.

'I think there is every need to yell.'

'Well, don't blame the people at the clinic. They didn't tell me…when Bea said it wasn't Tariq I knew it must be you.' She lifted her chin. 'I'll pay you back, of course…'

'You will pay me back?' he echoed, looking at her mouth.

'It might take a while, of course…'

He pressed a finger to the groove between his dark brows and swore. 'I really can't decide if you try and insult me or if it just comes naturally to you?'

'The trouble with you is…' You don't love me.

'Why hold back now, Molly? You have never shied away from tearing my character to pieces before.'

'I was sorry to hear about your father.'

Tair shrugged and responded with a painful politeness. 'We have never been close,' he admitted. 'The doctors had warned him this could happen if he didn't reform his lifestyle.'

'But like you he doesn't take orders.'

A spasm of distaste contorted his features. 'I am nothing like my father.'

'Sorry…I didn't mean… I know you're nothing like your father,' she said with a rush. 'It must have been a difficult time for you, but you look well.' He had actually dropped a number of pounds and the weight loss on his already lean, muscle-packed frame had the effect of highlighting the chiselled angles of his proud face.

'You look…' A visible sigh shuddered through his frame. 'As always…I like looking at you.'

His blazing blue eyes had the same effect on her nervous system as being directly connected with the mains supply.

She lifted a self-conscious hand to the exposed upper slopes of her bosom. 'I hope you don't mind me being here.'

'This is your family. I am the guest here.'

'Tair…'

'I like the way you say my name…say it again.'

Molly stared transfixed and whispered softly, 'Tair.' Then she blinked and added brightly, 'I hear you might be getting married.'

He froze and studied her face.

'It is not out of the question,' he agreed.

Everything inside Molly just shut down, including her defences. She struggled to smile but only half got there before disintegrating inside.

'But it is not official yet.'

'It might never be if she saw you drag me out here like that. All I can say is it's not the way I would expect the man I was going to marry to act.'

He angled a dark brow and looked at her miserable face, suddenly appearing more relaxed than he had done since they'd walked into the room. 'And how would you expect the man you were going to marry to act, Molly?'

'I'm not going to marry anyone.'

'You might find someone when you least expect it. That does happen, so I believe…'

'Is that what happened to you? No…don't tell me,' she begged, covering her mouth with her trembling hand. 'I don't really want to know. But I'm very happy for you,' she lied. Being noble and selfless hurt like hell, and Molly could feel her more ignoble jealous self fighting to slip the leash. 'I saw her…Jean Paul pointed her out. She is very beautiful.' The sort who would run to fat in later years.

His lips thinned in distaste. 'Zara is not really to my taste—she is a little too obvious.' And she is not you.

'Then why are you marrying her?'

'I'm not.'

'But, Jean Paul said—'

'So of course it must be right,' he cut in sardonically.

She took a deep breath. 'Of course not…right, well, excellent.'

'Yes.'

'Right, well, excellent.'

'You said that.'

Molly felt something snap inside her. 'Well, I've been out of my mind with worry since Beatrice told me.'

'Since Beatrice told you what?'

'That you were perhaps in danger.'

He blinked. 'Really? I thought it was just my sanity I stood in danger of losing.'

'This isn't a joke, Tair!' she yelled, frustrated by his careless attitude. 'You've never taken security seriously and now…have you considered wearing body armour?'

Tair looked into her pale, earnest face for a long moment before asking, 'Just what has Beatrice been saying to you, Molly? Come sit down here.'

She shook her head. 'I don't want to sit down.'

'Why do you think I need…body armour?'

'Well, Beatrice didn't come right out and say that you were in *physical* danger, but it follows that these people are dangerous and they're playing for big stakes and they want you out of the picture any way they can.'

'You are talking about my critics in Zabrania?'

She nodded. 'Beatrice said they want to put a cousin of yours on the throne. That he has an heir and a spare and…I suppose that's why you're thinking of marriage…?'

'Heirs are the last thing on my mind at this precise moment, Molly,' he told her honestly.

'That's a pity, because the thing is, Tair…'

'The thing is?' he prompted.

She sucked in a deep breath and lifted her chin. This was never going to be easy. 'The thing is you've got one, or you will have in about seven months. I know this is shocking! Are you all right?' She angled a worried look at him.

He looked at her blankly. 'You're pregnant?' His hand fell away. 'Baby…?' His eyes fell to her stomach, then slowly rose to her face.

Molly was shocked by the grey tinge to his skin.

Tair was a man who rolled with the blows and came back for more. His resilience was an integral part of him. But the man standing there staring at her had the look of a man who had just received a mortal wound.

'*Dieu!*' he breathed, dragging a hand across his jaw. 'You are pregnant with our child?'

'I'm sorry.'

Tair blinked to banish the image of her holding a child in her arms from his head.

'Sorry…sorry?' His voice rose to an incredulous boom as he regarded her unhappy face with stark incredulity. '*You're* sorry? I am the one that put you in this position and left you *alone…*' His voice trailed off.

Molly had gone through the stunned stage herself and had some understanding of how he was feeling. 'It does take a while to sink in.'

His searching eyes moved over her before he asked thickly, 'You are well?'

'Fine,' she said, thinking that he didn't look it. 'I want this baby, Tair.'

'*Our baby…*' he said, still sounding as if the news had not quite fully registered.

'I know it might be difficult for you to think about it

logically right now, but although you might not be happy about it—'

'Did I say I'm not happy?'

'You didn't have to.'

'I suppose I don't have to say anything either because you will put words in my mouth. I am going to be a father…' He passed a hand across his eyes and shook his head.

'A baby needs a father.'

His fierce eyes flew to her face. 'Do you think I do not know this?'

'Let me finish, *please*, Tair,' she begged. 'A baby needs a father and your position might be more secure if you were married.'

Something moved behind his eyes. 'Molly, are you proposing to me?'

The colour rushed to her face, but she held his gaze. 'No…yes…I suppose I am,' she admitted. 'The things you said about arranged marriages, you know, actually make sense when you stop to think about it.'

She sounded as if she were selling double glazing!

'No, it doesn't.'

She felt the mortified colour rush to her face and wanted to die. 'Oh, well, it was just an idea.'

'Yes.'

She shook her head. 'Pardon?'

'I said yes, Molly, I will marry you.'

'This isn't a joke, Tair,' she reproached.

'I'm not joking. I've never been more serious in my life.'

'But you just said…'

'I just said that arranged marriages do not make sense. But you were not proposing an arranged marriage, were you, Molly? You love me.'

She held his steady gaze for a moment, then said with defiance, 'Yes, I do.'

Tair's shoulders slumped as weeks of tension fell from them.

His visible relief and the blaze of triumph in his blue eyes were lost to Molly who began to weep, tears sliding down her face.

The sound of her deep sobs made something twist in Tair's chest. 'My dear, fierce, beautiful Molly,' he said, pulling her into his arms. 'Is it so bad loving me?'

She lifted her tear-stained face from his chest, bit her trembling lip and wailed tragically, 'It's awful!'

Unable to resist any longer, Tair bent his head and kissed her hard. 'Is that a little less awful?'

Molly gulped and nodded. 'A bit,' she conceded. 'I'm a bit emotional right now…hormones and…'

His fingers tightened in her hair, pulling her head back so that he could look into her face. 'And you were afraid for me?'

No wonder he sounded so incredulous. He had a team of loyal men willing to lay down their lives for him—and she had acted as though she could make a difference.

'Well, I've seen how reckless you are…and…I know they've isolated you and spread rumours.' Molly breathed in the clean, male, marvellous scent of him and thought how she would never let anyone hurt him.

'And you felt it would improve the chances of my continued health if I married you and you gave me babies.'

She turned her face into his neck and snapped, 'Don't laugh at me, Tair.'

'Believe me, I'm not laughing, *ma belle*.'

'Beatrice said…'

A flash of annoyance crossed Tair's lean face as he laid

a finger across her lips. 'It seems to me that Beatrice has said far too much. She has caused you so much anguish.'

'I'm glad she told me. I have a right to know—'

'I'm not in danger, Molly.'

Her narrowed eyes lifted to his face. 'Beatrice wouldn't lie.'

'Not directly,' he conceded. 'But she has bent the truth to the point of snapping. I did upset some influential people when I took control.' He smiled down into her anxious face. 'And they would, I do not doubt, have been more than happy if I vanished, but they have never been in a position to make that happen.'

Molly felt a flicker of cautious relief. 'They haven't?'

'They are in a minority and over the years when they milked the system they made many enemies, some powerful. Those enemies are now my allies. My critics have no popular support among either the people or the ruling classes.'

'So you're not in danger?' she sniffed, still not totally convinced.

'No. The only threat to my authority, the only person who has ever rebelled against me, is you, Miss Mouse.'

The relief now was so intense that Molly felt dizzy with it. 'Oh, God, I've been so *so* worried.' She could smile about it now that he was safe. 'But why would Beatrice say those things if…?'

His lips stretched in a sardonic smile. 'I think Beatrice might have been trying to play cupid.'

Molly began to shake her head in automatic dismissal of such a ludicrous theory and then stopped, a look of shocked comprehension crossing her face. 'My God, she was, you're right, and I didn't tell her about the baby so she's going to think it worked.'

Tair muttered something under his breath and grabbed her by the shoulders, turning her to face him. 'Can you still think that I'm marrying you because of the baby?' he asked incredulously. 'Not even you are that stupid!'

'I'm not stupid…' Her heartbeat quickened as she read the extraordinary message in his eyes. 'But you…can't *want* to marry me.'

He kissed her hard. 'Do not put words in my mouth. I am quite capable of speaking for myself. Thinking about marrying you, Molly, is the only thing that has kept me going during the past weeks.' He reached out to touch a finger to the single tear that had escaped her overflowing eyes and admitted, 'That you are pregnant with our child is admittedly a plus point.'

'You're *glad* about the baby?'

He looked insulted that she could think otherwise. 'I am over the moon about this baby!' He curved a big hand over her stomach. 'And I want this baby because it is ours…yours and mine…and we made it with our love, and I want to marry you because my life is empty without you in it. I love you, Molly Mouse. I love your golden eyes, I love your sharp tongue…I love the entire beautiful, irresistible package. *Dieu!*' he groaned, gathering her in his arms. 'I have been half a man without you these weeks.'

The tenderness in his long, lingering kiss brought more tears to Molly's eyes.

'I can't believe this is happening. I have loved you almost from the first, Tair.'

'Yet when I asked you to marry me you refused me because I was second-best, and that hurt.' The mocking gleam in his eyes was directed at his own stupid pride.

'I refused, Tair, because I didn't want you to marry me out of duty.'

'I know,' he said, taking her small hand in both of his and lifting it to his lips. A delicious shudder rippled through Molly's body as he turned it and kissed her palm.

'I wanted you to marry me out of love,' she said in a throaty whisper.

'And I was too stubborn to admit even to myself that I was in love…' Transferring his attention to the blue-veined inner aspect of her delicate wrist, he continued. 'You have no idea how often I have regretted it in the weeks since.'

'Not as often as I've regretted refusing to be your wife,' she retorted. 'I have been so lonely without you.'

'Good!'

'That is not a very nice thing to say,' she reproached.

'I have told you, Molly, I am not a very nice man.'

'You are the only man I want.'

Heat flared like blue flames in his eyes. 'Or have ever had… You have no idea what it did to me to know that I was your first lover.' His eyes darkened at the memory. 'I should have regretted it but I didn't,' he admitted huskily.

'Neither did I.'

'Tariq is one of my closest friends, but when I thought of him with you I…' Tair shook his head, still shocked by the memory of his primitive reaction.

Molly ran a loving finger down the curve of his cheek. 'I wasn't too happy to see them either,' she murmured. 'I wanted you to myself and I wanted a chance to tell you that I was actually the sister nobody really wanted to acknowledge.' She had understood the situation, but it had hurt.

Tair bent his head to hers. 'Their loss!' he said fiercely as he pulled her into his arms.

With a sigh Molly looped her arms around his neck as he swept her off her feet and kissed her with a ruthless hunger she could feel in her bones.

They were still kissing when there was a loud knock on the door.

'Ignore it,' Tair said thickly.

It was advice that Molly was only too happy to go along with.

The second and third knock she could ignore, but it was more difficult when Khalid's voice called their names through the door. 'Tair… Molly!'

'He knows we're in here, Tair. You have to answer.'

'I don't see why.'

'Because he's not going away.' The bangs were getting louder.

'Tair…?'

He looked at her and heaved a frustrated sigh. 'All right, then.'

Khalid, who seemed oblivious to the lack of warmth in Tair's manner when he unlocked the door, explained that Beatrice needed them in the ballroom. It was an emergency, he explained in response to Molly's concerned questions.

He remained quite vague about what form the emergency took as he led them back into the crowds.

Five minutes later Tair's patience was wearing thin.

He gave a discontented scowl as he looked around the glittering room. 'What emergency? Bea's not here and I don't see why we have to stay.'

Molly gave him a warning glance. 'It would be rude,' she scolded. 'And she wouldn't say there was an emergency if there wasn't.'

Tair bent down, his breath brushing the sensitive skin of her earlobe as he whispered, 'I'm in pain.'

Molly felt a lustful kick in her stomach. 'Behave,' she

pleaded without an awful lot of conviction before adding, 'Me too.'

A hush fell over the hall, but Molly, who was still gazing into Tair's eyes, did not notice at first.

'Friends.' The king's voice, aided by excellent acoustics, carried to every corner of the room.

Molly's startled glance flickered to the regal figure who stood in the centre of the hall. She looked at Tair, who shrugged and shook his head.

Molly's attention strayed every few seconds to the man beside her. Her heart was so full of love she felt as though she might explode and she listened with half an ear as the white-haired king wished his daughter-in-law a happy birthday and welcomed his new grandson.

'And lastly,' said the king, 'there is another person I must welcome to our family. My sons' sister, Miss Molly James.'

Molly froze in shock as the crowds opened up between her and the king, a clear corridor down which her brothers began to walk.

It was Tair who pushed her towards them.

Flanked by her smiling brothers, her ears ringing to the sound of clapping hands, Molly walked towards the king. The emotional occlusion in her aching throat thickened as he took her by the shoulders and formally kissed her on both cheeks.

The clapping had begun to die away when she turned and saw Tair walking towards them. His blue eyes held hers as he joined them.

He bowed formally to the king and murmured, 'Honoured, Uncle.' Turning, he took Molly's hand in his before allowing his glance to move over the faces of the avidly curious onlookers.

'What are you doing?' Molly muttered.

'I would like to formally request the hand of Miss Molly James in marriage, Uncle.'

'Is that so, Prince Tair?' The king raised a sardonic brow. 'I have no objections, though I do feel that Molly might do better, nephew.'

'Molly James.' Holding her eyes, Tair dropped down on one knee. 'I have asked you once and you refused me, but I ask you again. Will you do me the great honour of accepting me as your husband?'

Molly, acutely aware of every eye in the room on her and hating the attention, mumbled with a lot less regal confidence than either man, 'Yes, I will.'

Tair grinned in response to her agitated whisper for him to get up and rose with fluid grace before kissing her hand and turning to the room. He announced her with pride that brought tears to her eyes. 'My princess.'

Under the cover of clapping and cheering Molly squeaked, 'If you do that to me again I will never forgive you.'

Tair, looking unrepentant, bent his head to her ear. 'You are mine and I wanted everyone to know it.'

Molly saw the fire of pride and love shining in his eyes and the joy inside her rose up like a warm wave.

She was the luckiest woman on earth!

Without a word she took his face between her hands and kissed him hard on the mouth.

When she released him Tair gave a silent whistle. 'For a woman who doesn't like people staring, Molly Mouse… that was…?'

Molly grinned. 'I want everyone to know you're mine too, Prince Tair.'

'I think,' Tair said, his solemn expression belied by the warmth and laughter dancing in his eyes, 'that someone in the corner over there might not have got the message.'

'In that case…' Laughing, she allowed herself to be swept up into an embrace that left nobody in the room in any doubt about who belonged to whom.

They belonged to each other.

*Royal Affairs – luxurious and
bound by duty yet still captive to desire!*

**Royal Affairs: Desert
Princes & Defiant Virgins**

Available 3rd June 2011

**Royal Affairs:
Princesses & Protectors**

Available 1st July 2011

**Royal Affairs:
Mistresses & Marriages**

Available 5th August 2011

**Royal Affairs: Revenge
Secrets & Seduction**

Available
2nd September 2011

MILLS & BOON®

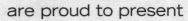

are proud to present

June 2011
Ordinary Girl in a Tiara
by Jessica Hart
from Mills & Boon® Riva™

Caro Cartwright's had enough of romance – she's after a quiet life. Until an old school friend begs her to stage a gossip-worthy royal diversion! Reluctantly, Caro prepares to masquerade as a European prince's latest squeeze...

Available 3rd June 2011

July 2011
Lady Drusilla's Road to Ruin
by Christine Merrill
from Mills & Boon® Historical

Considered a spinster, Lady Drusilla Rudney has only one role in life: to chaperon her sister. So when her flighty sibling elopes, Dru employs the help of a fellow travelling companion, ex-army captain John Hendricks, who looks harmless enough...

Available 1st July 2011

Tell us what you think!

millsandboon.co.uk/community
facebook.com/romancehq
twitter.com/millsandboonuk

Polo, players & passion

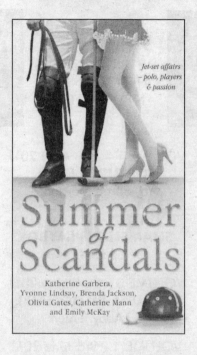

Jet-set affairs – polo, players & passion

Summer of Scandals

Katherine Garbera,
Yvonne Lindsay, Brenda Jackson,
Olivia Gates, Catherine Mann
and Emily McKay

*The polo season—the rich mingle,
passions run hot and
scandals surface…*

25/MB345

BAD BL⬯⬯D

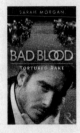

A POWERFUL
DYNASTY,
WHERE SECRETS
AND SCANDAL
NEVER SLEEP!

VOLUME 1 – 15th April 2011
TORTURED RAKE
by Sarah Morgan

VOLUME 2 – 6th May 2011
SHAMELESS PLAYBOY
by Caitlin Crews

VOLUME 3 – 20th May 2011
RESTLESS BILLIONAIRE
by Abby Green

VOLUME 4 – 3rd June 2011
FEARLESS MAVERICK
by Robyn Grady

8 VOLUMES IN ALL TO COLLECT!

MILLS
BOON

www.millsandboon.co.uk

BAD BLOOD

A POWERFUL
DYNASTY,
WHERE SECRETS
AND SCANDAL
NEVER SLEEP!

VOLUME 5 – 17th June 2011
HEARTLESS REBEL
by Lynn Raye Harris

VOLUME 6 – 1st July 2011
ILLEGITIMATE TYCOON
by Janette Kenny

VOLUME 7 – 15th July 2011
FORGOTTEN DAUGHTER
by Jennie Lucas

VOLUME 8 – 5th August 2011
LONE WOLFE
by Kate Hewitt

8 VOLUMES IN ALL TO COLLECT!

www.millsandboon.co.uk

SIZZLING HOLIDAY FLING...OR THE REAL THING?

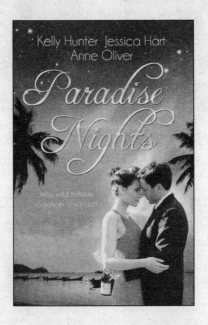

Who said holiday romances didn't last?
As the sun sets the seduction begins...
Who can resist the baddest of boys?

Intense passion and glamour from our bestselling stars of international romance

Available 20th May 2011   Available 17th June 2011

Available 15th July 2011   Available 19th August 2011